W9-BYZ-780

Heartfelt Praise for *A Sundog Moment*

First Place, Virginia Press Women
Communications Award for Fiction

"Sharon Baldacci's stunning debut novel is the story of Elizabeth Whittaker, a carefree homemaker whose world is turned upside down by earth-shattering news that changes the course of her life and marriage forever. Beautifully told with humor and warmth, you will root for her every step of the way on her journey of despair, acceptance, and ultimately the triumph of her faith. You will love this story!"

—Adriana Trigiani, author of the Big Stone Gap trilogy
and *Lucia, Lucia*

"Readers, especially those whose lives have been touched by MS, should find solace and support in Baldacci's touching novel."

—*Publishers Weekly*

"A SUNDOG MOMENT is engaging, original, and inspirational. This beautifully written first novel proves that brother David isn't the only Baldacci who inherited the writing genes."

—Richard Paul Evans, *New York Times* bestselling author of
The Christmas Box and *A Perfect Day*

"[A] carefully crafted first novel from Baldacci."

—*BookPage*

A Sundog Moment

A NOVEL OF HOPE

Sharon Baldacci

CENTER
STREET

NEW YORK BOSTON NASHVILLE

If you purchase this book without a cover you should be aware that this book may have been stolen property and reported as "unsold and destroyed" to the publisher. In such case neither the author nor the publisher has received any payment for this "stripped book."

This book is a work of fiction. Names, characters, places, and incidents are the product of the author's imagination or are used fictitiously. Any resemblance to actual events, locales, or persons, living or dead, is coincidental.

Copyright © 2004 by Sharon Baldacci
Reading Group Guide copyright © 2006 by Time Warner Book Group
All rights reserved.

Center Street

Time Warner Book Group
1271 Avenue of the Americas, New York, NY 10020
Visit our Web site at www.twbookmark.com.

The Center Street name and logo are registered trademarks of Warner Books.

Printed in the United States of America

Originally published in hardcover by Warner Books
First Trade Edition: February 2006
10 9 8 7 6 5 4 3 2 1

The Library of Congress has cataloged the hardcover edition as follows:
Baldacci, Sharon.
   A sundog moment / Sharon Baldacci.
     p. cm.
    ISBN 0-446-53366-1
    1. Multiple sclerosis—Patients—Fiction.   2. Pain—Treatment—Fiction.   3. Self-help
groups—Fiction.   4. Drug traffic—Fiction.   5. Women—Fiction.   I. Title.
PS3602.A595S86   2004
813' .6—dc22

                             2003025804

ISBN: 1-931722-64-1 (pbk.)

Acknowledgments

Unending thanks to my parents, Rudy and Joyce, for their love and encouragement; to brother Rudy and also brother David and his wife, Michelle, all your love and support is so very appreciated; to my in-laws, John and Betty, for your help in so many ways and for believing in this story.

Special thanks to Sara Sullivan Robson, my friend since first grade, who kept telling me this was a great story even when literary agents disagreed; to Adriana Trigiani for that gentle push that got me here; to Maureen Egen, who set the wheels in motion by asking a simple question; to Rolf Zettersten for wanting to publish it; to Karen Owen, the first professional writer to say it was a good story when it still needed a lot of work; to Attorney Jane (Jinkie) Wrightson, my legal adviser; to April Kranda, Helen Weddle, Howard and Lynn York, Hoyt and Joan Wheeland, Phyllis TeStrake, Anna and Pat Brennan, and Pat Dalzell for your kind encouragement; to Ann Muncy for your observations that ended up making it a better story; and to Terry Elam, for writing out all those addresses for me at the post office, and to Sheriff Stanley Clark—your suggestions helped so much.

A very special thank-you to Susan Stallings, the friend who had the dream and told me about it over coffee one morning, and to the parents, Therese and Terry Bowen, thank you so much for letting me share the tragedy of your son's death and the triumph of what happened afterward—the godchild written about in these pages is the story of your son, Gregory Bowen. A true sundog moment!

To the founding members of the Northern Neck Neuro-Muscular Support Group: Pat, Sylvia, Brenda, and Eleanor—here's hoping we all will get better with each passing year.

To Arlene Walker, the daughter of a waterman, who pointed out the sun dogs one afternoon, and explained what they meant; to Jane Henson and Maureen Roberts, who read all the incarnations of this story and liked them all; to Meade Kilduff, my contemporary and kindred spirit; to Father Jeffrey Cerar and his wife, Lynne, what a journey! To the gang at EFM, where I shared my sun dogs and discovered a metaphor for faith, and to all the family at St. Stephen's Episcopal Church in Heathsville, Virginia. May our growth and questing continue.

A Sundog Moment

Chapter One

The dance floor was crowded with tuxedos and sparkling evening gowns, creating a breathing, living organism of excitement; it was New Year's Eve at the large corporate building that housed Whittaker Industries, and the collective ensemble glittered like a bevy of Christmas gifts waiting to be handed out.

Leaning against the rail of a balcony overlooking the party was a stunningly beautiful woman, Elizabeth Whittaker, who wore a seductive black evening gown. A hint of a smile adorned her face as she felt the enthusiasm and energy generated from the people down below. A man in a tuxedo inched close behind her.

"Dance with me," he commanded, putting a hand on her arm. She moved slightly away, her eyebrows rising disdainfully. "I'll have you know, I'm a married woman."

His smile deepened. "Believe me, I love married women," he assured her, "especially—"

Her interruption was curt. "I'm sure you do. I'm sure you have several silly married women just dangling, thinking you have eyes only for them."

"No"—he held up a hand—"I was only going to say that I especially love . . ." He looked hard at her.

She waited, watching him before she finally prompted impatiently, "And what do you especially love?"

"Not what, who," he corrected. Her eyes narrowed as she drummed her fingers against the top of the rail. Finally, she sighed. "And whom do you especially love?"

"The woman I'm married to," he murmured, seeing a reluctant smile start to glimmer in her eyes. He leaned closer, but she twisted

away so she could look straight at him for a long moment. Then, just as quickly, she pulled his head down to whisper directly into his ear.

"Scoundrel!" The voice was throaty and sensual and made his knees weak. Then her lips fastened on his for a kiss so loving and deep it made him slightly dizzy.

Below them, a small orchestra lifted instruments in a fluid motion on the conductor's cue and began playing; within moments the room was filled with a dazzling array of movements flowing with the timeless rhythm of the waltz.

"Dance with me?" She smiled, dazzling him all over again.

"Whatever you want, you've got it," he said helplessly. Hand in hand, they ran lightly down the stairs.

Once they swept into the crowd, it wasn't long before everyone began voluntarily moving back to watch the grace and grandeur of this special couple, a man and a woman who had adoring eyes only for each other.

Their movements intimately in tune, Michael and Elizabeth Whittaker were so enchanted by the beauty of the music and each other, they had no idea they were the only ones left on the floor. They were the center of attention, but had no clue until the dance ended and spontaneous applause erupted. Startled, they looked around, bewildered.

He merely laughed with pleasure, while Elizabeth's hand flew to her face. Still holding hands with his wife, Michael ducked into one of the hallways to escape, wanting some privacy. Elizabeth's face was pink; she had totally forgotten she was in a public place. How could she still feel like a newlywed after being married to this man for so many years? Michael's face beamed.

He was consumed with the pleasure of knowing he was exactly where he wanted to be with precisely the right person. Life was good, so very, very good. Still laughing, he led the way into his empty office.

The door was soon firmly shut and locked.

Elizabeth, now relaxing, smiled back at Michael, knowing there was no place in this world she would rather be than here, with her very foolish husband. Her color deepened at the way he was looking at her. He loved it that after so many years of marriage she was still vulnerable enough to blush.

"I love you, Mrs. Whittaker," he said softly, holding her closer and closer. She held up a hand against his chest.

"And I think . . . ," she whispered, looking at him and then dropping her eyes to his mouth.

"You think?" he asked, doing the same.

"Yes, I think I might be able to . . ." She breathed deeply as he pulled her closer.

"You might be able to . . . ," he prompted, kissing her forehead.

"To say . . . ," she whispered, her voice low, her breathing shallow.

"Say . . ." He leaned closer, breathing in her fragrance.

"The same thing," she finally breathed, closing her eyes, ready to lose herself in him. He suddenly stopped moving, which was enough to cause her eyes to fly open and see dark eyes brimming with laughter.

"You love Mrs. Whittaker, too?"

She blinked and threw back her head in laughter, then they held on to each other as they both dissolved into giggles.

"You wretch; you are a wretch," she gasped, "and I intend to go home—" Her last word was cut off in a definitive kiss that went on and on . . . then there was no more conversation. Their bodies swiftly folded into each other, enjoying a familiar and exciting duet of touching and kissing . . .

The small rattle of a hospital door jerked Michael awake, the dream that was a memory shattered like glass breaking. Quickly he looked toward the bed. No movement. *Good. God knows she needs to rest.*

He quietly met the doctor right inside the room. Michael motioned toward the hall and they didn't speak until the door was firmly closed behind them.

"Well?" The question was stark, asked roughly by a man sandwiched between a myriad of dreadful possibilities. Michael already knew a stroke, the first suspected cause, had mercifully been ruled out. He could barely breathe waiting for the news.

Records in hand, the doctor walked over and sat down on a nearby padded bench. He hit with the good news first. "It's not a brain tumor as we feared, Michael."

"Thank God." Limp with relief, he sagged against the wall, his eyes closing briefly. Nothing, he was sure, could be worse than that suspicion.

"Then what is it? Do you know?"

Dr. Gordon Jones didn't like giving bad news to his patients; it was that much harder when it was a friend. He said nothing, merely held out a piece of paper. Michael looked at it and his mouth went dry and his heart was suddenly beating so hard his chest hurt. The noise in his head was deafening.

Gordon was speaking, but Michael just looked at him, dazed. "What?"

"Multiple sclerosis, as you may know, is chronic and incurable, but there are some new therapies that might buy us some time. My recommendation is to get her started on one as soon as possible. And Michael, there is every reason to be hopeful. Research is getting closer and closer. I don't want you, or her, to forget that. There is every reason to remain very optimistic."

Gordon wondered if his friend even heard him as he saw the stunned look, the wash of countless emotions sweep over Michael's face. He was sorry. But there was nothing he could do. "Do you want me to tell her? Or would you rather—"

Michael shook his head immediately. "God, I don't want to. But I'll try . . . tomorrow. After I see how she is. Do you . . . think she'll be better?"

Gordon shrugged. "Possibly. Hopefully. I'll be here early to check on her."

Michael nodded. "I'll be here." He looked hard at the doctor. "You are quite sure?" His voice was colorless.

"Completely sure. I've been consulting with the best neurologist in the city. He concurs. The MRI shows more than one lesion. Lesions or scarring is the result of the inflammation," he explained, "and that's causing the symptoms. The loss of coordination, the spasticity. That will, hopefully, be temporary. However, there may be some residual impairments. Or not. We'll just have to wait and see."

They stood and Gordon gave Michael a reassuring handshake. "Don't forget, there is a great deal of promising research going on." With these hopeful words hanging in the air, he left.

Michael walked into the silence of a deserted parking lot, shadows from the streetlights making it an eerie and unfamiliar place. He got into his car carefully, his movements as weighted and as heavy as his spirit.

When he arrived home the house was dark and looked as lonely as he felt. He entered through the back door, flipping on lights as he moved from room to room. He retrieved yet another newspaper from the front porch and tossed it on top of all the others that had been left unread over the past days. Last month it had seemed imperative to keep pace with current events nationally and internationally. Now the only event he was concerned about was sheltered in a small hospital room with uncertainties shrouding it.

⌒

Eventually the night began bowing out to morning and Elizabeth woke early, with no memories of the dreams that raced and snatched through the night, leaving only a dim trace of confused and scattered emotions.

Slowly, tentatively, her blue eyes opened to a shadowed room, a few faint brushes of gray etched on the drawn shades.

Tight, anxious breath escaped in a singular sigh of relief. Gone was the awful spinning, like an out-of-control top, and now that the world was no longer twirling it was soundless, the quiet so rich she felt she could snuggle down into it. This was not the case days ago, or was it weeks? Time had little meaning then. A second had taken on the weight of hours as she waited and prayed and hoped and bargained for life to shrink back to normal.

That infamous moment when she had got up in the middle of the night and stepped out of bed into a frenetic world of swirling motion with earsplitting calamity was too real a nightmare. She no longer had command over her own body, nothing worked, it was too horrible . . .

But now, in its place was the world she knew, had known all her life, one of checks and glorious balances, of gravity and reality that could not do what was unintended. The relief was enormous. How long had it taken for this to be resurrected? Had it happened a month ago? Two days ago? She was clueless.

Elizabeth stretched timidly, rewarded as a smile began to erase the worry from her face. Everything worked! Her legs were just where they were supposed to be. She could feel them and almost laughed out loud at the pleasure of it all.

She looked toward the clock; it was very early. She should be sleeping. Then her eyes caught the play of light from the early morning sun on the wall and she was mesmerized. How could something that was nothing have such energy? She wondered what music made it dance so lively.

When she noticed the clock again she was astonished that thirty minutes had passed. Suddenly the early morning reached for her, pulling grateful eyes slowly shut, and she drifted off to sleep a little longer. Her last conscious thought was heartfelt prayer: *Thank You, God!*

Hours later, with her eyes still closed, Elizabeth could feel Michael's presence. A smile started lifting her heart, and when he leaned near enough to kiss her forehead, blue eyes opened slowly, cautiously.

"Michael," she breathed, embracing the smile he gave her and giving one in return; she was so happy to see him.

His heart jumped. "Elizabeth darling, how are you today? Better?" His eyes were encouraging but the voice was tentative.

"I can hardly believe how much better I am today; it's a miracle."

He had missed the sound of her voice, he suddenly realized. It had been several tense days, and she had been too dizzy, too sick to do more than slur a few words together, or to whisper, her voice ragged and strange. Now it was a sound that moved him nearly to tears.

Her voice was a husky alto and danced with the cadence of cultured Virginia at its southern best, like a pretty woman wrapped in fur—and nothing else. He cleared his throat. "Nothing could make me happier, Beth."

Impulsively she held out her arms. "Watch." Both arms straight out from her sides, she held his gaze, then shut her eyes and slowly brought both hands with knowledge to touch the tip of her nose. She felt his exultation even before he hugged her.

"Elizabeth, my God, that is wonderful. It's incredible." Yesterday she couldn't do this simple thing. That she could today was too wonderful to put into words.

Moments later the door swung open and Dr. Gordon Jones walked in, shuffling papers. He was a tall, solid man who was often unkempt.

Either his hair was in need of a trim or his shirt was skewed because buttons done in a perpetual hurry were mismatched; there was too little precious time to waste on nonessentials. His appearance was deceiving because he was a first-rate doctor. And the kind of friend who'd meet you anywhere at a moment's notice if you needed him.

Elizabeth clutched her husband's hand a little tighter as Gordon came closer. The doctor sat down in the small rolling chair, dropped the charts on the side of the bed, and smiled. "How are you feeling this morning?"

"Incredibly better. Whatever is in that liquid you have dripping through my veins? Why, it must be magic!" Her smile became a little smaller as she asked the next reluctant question. "Gordon, what happened to me?" She gripped Michael's hand even tighter.

Gordon's eyes glanced toward Michael, eyebrows raised. He noted the slight shake and cleared his throat and donned his professional cloak. "Elizabeth, the good news is that it's not a brain tumor—"

Her shocked exclamation cut him off. "No one told me that was ever considered. Michael, did you know?" Astonished, she looked at Michael and saw his face redden.

"I didn't want to worry you, Elizabeth, until we knew for sure. Remember, you weren't in any shape to . . . discuss this." He squeezed her hand, his face anxious.

Elizabeth's attention riveted on the doctor. "So . . . now do we know—for sure? Do you know, Michael?" Again this was directed at her husband, but he kept his eyes averted while he frowned.

"Gordon told me last night, Elizabeth. You were asleep and I wasn't about to wake you. I was going to tell you this morning, but, well, there wasn't time. Gordon can explain it better than I. And then you can get mad at him; you know, the bearer of bad news and all." He was so nervous he hardly knew what he was saying. His hoped-for levity fell flat as a burst water balloon; he suddenly felt clammy, every bit of him dreading what was to come. Then he heard Elizabeth's voice, felt her hand leave his.

"I would never get angry at you, Michael, for telling me the truth." The words were quiet, but he heard the reproach and was momentarily surprised. What had he done wrong?

"Gordon, if it's not a brain tumor, what is it?"

With a neutral voice he gave her the clinical details.

"Multiple sclerosis, probably the milder form, which is relapsing/remitting. You've responded well to the treatment . . ." He continued talking, giving her an overview and then a detailed clinical description of the disease. Most of it she couldn't understand.

As she tried to listen intently to everything he said, one word bolted from the rest and she repeated it in disbelief.

"Incurable?" In others' lives, she knew there were some things medicine couldn't cure, but now that it was personal, she couldn't believe it.

"Yes. However, there is every reason to be optimistic. Research is coming up with more and more information. It's merely a matter of time before we have a cure. Or at the least better treatment. There are already some therapies currently available that may slow down the progression. So again, there is every reason to hope."

The next question was asked with the confident expectation of someone who has been healthy all her life. It demanded a suitable answer. "What can I do to keep this from ever happening again?"

She watched him shake his head. "I don't know how to answer that definitively, Elizabeth. You may never have another attack, or exacerbation, again. We don't know what triggers an episode, though there are theories. As far as what to do, continue maintaining a good, healthy lifestyle with moderate exercise, and keep stress to a minimum."

Incredulous, she could find no words to say, but it was Michael's voice that spoke for her. "Come on, Gordon, surely there has to be something!" Michael interjected. "Someone, somewhere in the world must be doing something—" He stopped as the doctor slowly shook his head. "Money is not a problem; I can mortgage the business or sell it if the insurance won't pay. There has to be something more . . . anything?" Michael insisted.

Gordon held up a hand, keeping his face devoid of emotion. At this moment he wasn't a friend, he was the doctor. "There is nothing that has been scientifically proven. There are therapies people have used in other parts of the world that do not have the backing of any qualitative double-blind studies that any scientist in our country would accept. And as for throwing money at this disease, there are plenty of people out there who would be delighted to take your cash, Michael, but you would do just as well to flush it down the toilet. Same difference. Believe me. I wouldn't tell you this if it weren't true."

They listened as Gordon went on to say hopeful things about research, but the only thing they heard was the sadness in his voice.

Finally, Elizabeth couldn't bear to hear anymore. She wanted to get away from this place; she wanted to put it behind her, and the sooner that happened, the better.

"Gordon," she interrupted, "when can I go home?"

"Another six days or so. You have to be weaned off these drugs slowly, they are very potent. Once we do that, you'll be discharged. In the meantime, I've called the local MS chapter and asked them to send some literature to you. I also want you to see the neurologist I've consulted about your case. In about a month, he'll be able to check for any residual neurological weaknesses and also monitor you over time. Any questions?"

There were none. Dr. Jones left with a perfunctory smile and a last bit of encouragement. With the shutting of the door there was an echo of another door slamming shut, the one defining a prior life set apart from this uncertain present. Today would forever be tagged with the identity of before and after diagnosis. Elizabeth almost heard it, but when she caught sight of Michael's stunned face, her only thoughts were to make it better. To fix it and put a smile back on his face.

She glanced at the window and bit her lip. The normalcy that was framed by the small window beckoned. She realized the sun was still shining, the sky still blue and cloudless, and suddenly this constancy was enough to steady her. She instinctively knew they simply could not make sense out of this now; there was simply too much coming at both of them from all sides. Too much, too fast. She looked to her husband and realized that "reality" was her love for this man and his for her.

Their life together was much too real to be held hostage by the confusion in this room. Instinctively, she pushed it as far away from them both as she could, and by doing that felt her spirits lift.

It occurred to her she had not looked into a mirror in God knew how long. It was almost an electric shock that her outward appearance had been left to the hands of strangers.

She wanted her clothes and her makeup, and she wanted them

now. She knew if she looked good, she would feel good. Hope swelled as she thought that it could very well be that simple. She gave Michael a smile that was like catching the sun. He blinked.

"Michael, go home and get my makeup—everything I left on the vanity in our bathroom. And please get some decent clothes. I'm sick to death of hospital gowns."

Irrationally, his own spirits brightened at the sight of his brave wife and an answering smile met hers. She looked as beautiful as the day they had married. But more than that, the sparkle was back in her eyes.

"What are you grinning at, Mr. Whittaker?" She took his hand and squeezed it.

"Oh, just thinking about going home and having to take the trash out," he teased, hearing the sarcasm dripping from her voice as she said, "Oh you . . . you . . . hopeless romantic."

His relieved arms wrapped around her. "In truth, I was thinking how nice it is to have you back. I've been damn worried. I still am, frankly." Her hand touched his mouth to still those words and then she began to stroke his face.

"You worry too much. Stop it immediately," she commanded, and then her face became serious. "I'm going to be just fine. Perfect. I promise." She tweaked his nose just before she pulled him closer.

They were interrupted by the door swinging open and there stood her mother, Virginia Mae Bartlette, wearing a fluid mauve dress with rows of double buttons down the front and a darker gauzy scarf tied around the neck. Her white hair was styled to perfection, and there were matching dark mauve hoops in her ears. A determined smile was pasted on her face.

The couple on the bed jerked apart like teenagers caught necking on the couch. "Mother?" Elizabeth didn't sound too pleased.

"Virginia Mae, you said you weren't going to stop by today." Michael frowned and tightened his grip on Elizabeth's hand. He did not want her upset.

"I know, I know; I changed my mind. A mother's prerogative." Virginia Mae sniffed. "I decided my place at a time like this should be with my daughter." With stoic demeanor and squared shoulders, she walked over to the bed and looked down at Elizabeth.

The composure lasted for a few brief moments before it began, inevitably, to crumble. The lips began to quiver and eyes started to glisten and then tears began to fall. She threw her hands over her face and dropped like a stone to the side of the bed. "Shoot! I wasn't going to cry."

Elizabeth looked helplessly at Michael, who dutifully went over to put a comforting arm around his mother-in-law. Michael had known the instant she entered the room it was a sure bet that exactly this would happen.

How many times had he done this over the years, even before old Mr. Bartlette passed away? Even though it was what she always expected, Virginia Mae did not take bad news well at all. Despite being a woman whose life had been comfortable, nothing was ever as right as it should be, and for that she was always personally affronted. It was a dichotomy that grated on everyone who knew her at one time or another.

"It's all right, Mother. I'm doing so much better. Please don't worry so," Elizabeth begged, hoping to quell those tears. Michael remained there, gently patting his mother-in-law's back, tight-lipped as he watched while his wife consoled her mother.

When the tears stopped and she had blown her nose, Virginia Mae looked at her daughter. "I know you're just putting on a brave front for me. You always do, just like your father. Mercy, Elizabeth, I miss him so." The sadness settled on the older woman's face like a veil, revealing at the same time a vulnerability Virginia Mae tried hard not to display.

"I know, Mother. I'm sorry. I wish I could make it better." She hugged her mother close, sharing this grayness. Michael, mouth stretched into a thin line, watched his wife doing what he had so often seen her do—comforting, consoling, and then brightening her mother with a loving word or anecdote. He waited a little impatiently for all this to take place, highly irritated at seeing his wife, who was the sick one here, having to expend energy shoring up her healthy but unhappy mother.

Virginia Mae, more composed now, took Elizabeth's hand in hers. Gazing straight into her daughter's eyes, she suggested something she had obviously thought a great deal about.

"Ever since Michael called me last night, I've been racking my brain trying to figure out how to help. What could I do for you?"

Virginia Mae shut her eyes, sighed, and then gazed lovingly at her daughter's face. "Then I knew what had to be done. I knew you wouldn't want to be inundated with inquiries from all the people who know you. It would be tiresome and exhausting and, frankly, it's nobody's business. I don't think anyone needs to know about this; don't you think that's for the best?"

Surprised, Elizabeth wondered what her mother was really trying to say. Elizabeth wasn't in the habit of keeping things from friends but, on the other hand, it would be very nice not to have to talk about this. Good Lord, she had to get used to it herself. This could be a good idea. But even as she slowly nodded her agreement, Elizabeth suddenly realized that the underlying reason was a little more personal.

With a diagnosis like this, Virginia Mae's daughter would no longer be perfect . . .

Michael understood completely and was furious. "Virginia Mae, there's nothing to be ashamed of. My God, we're talking—" Michael began to protest but was immediately cut off.

"How dare you! I am not ashamed of my daughter; how on earth could you possibly think such a thing? I am merely trying to circumvent nosey, unwanted questions from people who have no business knowing a darn thing about us. That's all." She glared at him before settling concerned eyes on her daughter. "Elizabeth understands," she said. "You do, don't you, darling?"

Elizabeth could honestly agree that the fewer questions from others, the better. It would be preferable, at least for now. "I do, Mother, but has anyone told Father Joe? I think he should know. Surely that would be all right?" Virginia Mae looked at Michael, who in turn answered.

"No, I've been so busy with juggling work, coming here, and keeping Kellan informed, I haven't had the time." Actually it had never occurred to him to call their priest.

"I feel like someone's been praying for me, I am so much better."

Virginia Mae immediately spoke. "Well, of course I've been praying for you, nonstop, Elizabeth. I've been begging God to give me the strength to help you."

Michael concurred peripherally. "We've all been very worried, Elizabeth."

Was that the same as having a prayer lifted up for her specifically?

Elizabeth wondered, but let that thought slip away. Her mother had now taken hold of one of her hands again, stroking it and then talking, a little fretfully this time.

"Carol is back in town, I think for good. Her mother has done everything but actually tell me the divorce has finally gone through. I spoke with her three days ago, and I was so upset. I told her you were in the hospital, that we didn't know what was wrong, but I think, knowing my sister Julia, that Carol is going to come visiting very soon. Of course, it's up to you what you tell her. But I would advise anything you do tell her be in confidence." Although her voice was implacable, Virginia Mae hastily added, "But, of course, it's up to you."

Ever positioned between these two women who had been an integral part of all his adult life, Michael was trying hard not to say anything. He could see how this old woman manipulated his wife, but Elizabeth had never been able to recognize this. She was too busy standing up for her mother, smoothing the way, making things all right.

Without surprise, he watched as his wife, a determined glint in her weary eye, cajoled a smile from Virginia Mae.

Trying not to tap his foot impatiently, Michael watched until it finally looked as if Virginia Mae was smiling enough to make her daughter happy.

He stood up and announced it was time for everyone to leave and let Elizabeth get some rest. "Come, Virginia Mae, I'll take you home. No? You have your car? Fine, I'll walk you to it." He leaned over and brushed Elizabeth's face with a light kiss. "I'll be back later," he promised, but she couldn't help noticing the worried shadows on his face.

Chapter Two

Waiting through the long days at the hospital, Elizabeth felt as cloistered as a nun. Since no one knew about her illness, no friends came visiting. Not even her priest.

During those empty hours alone, she devoured every book Michael brought her, every magazine her mother left, had done a cross-stitch sampler, countless crossword puzzles, and wrote in a notebook daily. She tried hard to push away the impatience for healing. The fact that it bored her to death had to be carefully played against the fact that she was so much better. It was vitally important to be grateful. She appreciated Michael's visits after work; Elizabeth was determined to be cheerful for him, but it wasn't a stretch, it was her nature. She also tried, for his sake, to be flippant about the mild side effects of the massive introduction of steroids. Like the puffiness in her face she had been horrified to see in the mirror the first time she was allowed to go to the bathroom by herself. The nurses and doctors repeating over and over that this was only temporary had softened the shock. She didn't like seeing what seemed like large amounts of blonde hair staying in her brush, but kept reminding herself she wasn't losing all of it. It was all temporary. By the time she was weaned from the drugs, she'd be back to normal.

Another habit gained was to give herself pep talks to manage the rush of fears that often started fluttering up and down like neurotic butterflies. During one of these jittery moments, the solid memory of her paternal grandmother, Mimi, came rushing back like an anchor. Mimi had an ongoing conversation with God up until the day she died, and as a child, Elizabeth had imitated her, having serious discussions with God about everything. She didn't remember too many answers, but that didn't seem to matter.

As Elizabeth grew older, these conversations seemed childish and had been discarded as life became busy and other things became more important. Alone now, this habit of talking and thanking God was renewed. To a large measure, touching the past added a level of comfort to her present.

Elizabeth realized she didn't like change. She much preferred life to remain predictable. It might be boring to some, but Elizabeth loved the life she and Michael had created. It was exciting enough, its boundaries well known and defined. And thank God, her old life was coming back.

She also held on tightly to her prayers, especially in the middle of the night when the world slept and she was haunted by the memories of what had brought her here, whispering in the darkness.

◡◠

Release was now a stretch of hours away and she sat on its edge, with only one more night to go. Full of plans, she had been chatting happily with Michael until a few moments ago. Now, propped up against the sterile white pillows and already dressed for bed, she was waiting for him to come back with hot tea from the hospital cafeteria on the first floor. She was writing lists about what she wanted to do as soon as she got home. She had just jotted down yet another idea when the door was flung open.

Fifteen minutes before the end of visiting hours, Carol Stephens stood dramatically in the doorway, dressed in glamorous evening clothes and a regal attitude.

"Carol!" Elizabeth squealed.

"Now," Carol said in a drawl, "I left early from a tedious dinner to come and visit my oh-so-sick cousin, and what do I find?" Sequins sparkled as she strode toward the bed, her arms swinging in dramatic sweeps as she continued. "My oh-so-sick cousin propped up in bed looking as healthy as the proverbial horse. That she is also gorgeous will remain unsaid."

As soon as Carol sat down on the edge of the bed, all pretenses fell and they wrapped arms around each other, laughing and giggling like kids.

Carol at last sat back, took one of Elizabeth's hands and asked in a husky whisper, "Are you hiding a sick person in here someplace? And where's your guard dog, anyway?"

She jumped at Michael's voice, dry as sand. "Hello, Carol."

There was a heartbeat of silence.

"Do you know visiting hours are almost over?" His voice was as disapproving as ever. Carol had a way of exploding into their lives at inopportune moments, and he didn't like it and he didn't like her. That feeling was mutual.

He gave a cup of tea to Elizabeth and held out the other one. "Would you like this? I can go back down and get more," he offered tonelessly.

Carol smiled sweetly. "No, I don't want a cup of tea, but why don't you go back down there and wait awhile so Elizabeth and I can talk?

Then you can come back and remind me once again when visiting hours are over. I do remember how obsessive you are about time."

His nod was marginally polite. "Fine. I'll be back."

As soon as he'd left, the two women turned eagerly toward each other. "How are you, Carol; how long has it been?"

"Too long," Carol assured her, "and that's going to change, but first tell me why I'm visiting you *here*? What on earth is wrong? And tell me quick, before your guard comes back and chases me out."

Elizabeth chuckled. "Carol, behave! Michael's not that bad. You're just jealous."

Carol surprised her; her face dropped all pretenses and became serious. Her cousin was slowly nodding. "You're right. I am."

Elizabeth was caught off guard. Uncertain, she looked hard into her cousin's face and then Carol reached out and snapped her fingers right under her nose. "Gotcha!"

It was like old times as they went off into gales of laughter. After things quieted down, Elizabeth wanted to know about Carol. "Is it over? Are you finally a free woman, or are you headed back to Tinseltown? Are you home for good? I've missed you, you weasel."

Carol's smile was one of utter disdain, although her eyes were dancing. "Don't call me weasel, you vermin," she hissed and then became serious. "Yes, the divorce is final, and he is paying for it handsomely. But that's enough about me, I insist. What about you? Mother made such a fuss that I had to come see you, and since I was informed only tonight that you would be going home tomorrow, I got to cut short a dismal dinner party Mother made me attend with her. For that I thank you, but I don't think you planned to be here to get me out of a boring evening, so why, precisely, are you here?"

Elizabeth had no qualms about uttering the unfamiliar words that described her illness to her cousin. They were family, and their closeness couldn't be diminished by distance. What she was unprepared for was Carol's reaction.

The attractive face, the features highlighted with color, suddenly paled and started to crumple. Elizabeth sat back, shocked.

"Carol," she said sharply, "don't! Oh, come on, you can't be crying; don't be like this. I'm fine."

Before answering, Carol took some deep breaths, but it did nothing to settle the sick feeling wrenching her stomach. During her ten-year sojourn in Hollywood, scripting stories and working with talent and egos, Carol had watched more than one friend succumb to disease, illness, even AIDS. Not to mention the self-inflicted destruction that abounded in Hollywood. That, along with the end of her marriage, had left scars she wouldn't admit to; the mere mention of anything that held the hint of a promise of being bad for someone she loved chilled her. Carol licked numb lips, hating these feelings.

"Elizabeth," she started, and then stopped. "This is really, really serious stuff." She looked hard at her cousin. "Isn't it?"

Elizabeth immediately shook her head, her smile firm. "Nope. It's not, and don't look like that. I don't need that from you. And you know it."

"How? I can't read your mind, and how can you say this isn't serious? Do you know anything about it?" Carol couldn't push away the bad feelings sweeping over her. She knew Elizabeth was going to be upset with her, but my God, how could she deny that this was devastating, horrible . . .

Carol frowned and crossed her arms. "You know, I'm sitting here feeling devastated for you, but all of a sudden I realize you look absolutely wonderful. You look so awfully healthy while I feel so awful, it would make more sense for me to be in that bed! Are you sure the doctor's right?"

Elizabeth shrugged, a mischievous smile lighting up her face. "I don't think so."

Carol's frown deepened. "Who's your doctor? Don't tell me good old Michael didn't get you the best specialist in town, because I won't believe you. Who is it?"

"Gordon Jones. But he's been consulting with a Dr. William O'Day, who is the big-wheel specialist, so I guess they think they know what they're doing."

"Gordon Jones?" Carol threw back her head and whooped. "That shrimpy nerd who was in junior high with us? You've got to be kidding! He became a doctor? I can't believe it." She shook her head, chuckling. "God, he was as wide as he was tall. Did he ever grow? Or is he still a short, fat geek?"

A deep voice sounded directly behind her. "Not exactly."

Carol froze, her cheeks coloring furiously. "Elizabeth, please tell me that was your husband trying unsuccessfully to be funny."

Elizabeth's smile widened, and then she started laughing. "Sorry, no can do. Gordon, come in and meet my cousin Carol Stephens. I'm sure you remember her from the old days?"

Reluctantly, Carol slowly turned around and looked up. And then up some more into an amused face that looked vaguely familiar.

"Uh, you didn't hear what, uh, my cousin and I . . ." Carol's voice trailed off as she watched the smile deepen. An obviously trim and very tall man in a white lab coat held out his hand.

"Every word." Gordon nodded cheerfully. "How are you, Carol?"

She cleared her throat, aware of Elizabeth laughing disgustingly hard in the background. She took his hand and gave him a correct social smile. "Fine, Gordon, and you?"

"Couldn't be better. Sorry about the divorce; I know it must have been hard." No smile now, just a look of concern.

"Ah, thank you, but how did you know?" Her frown was small. "No press releases have gone out."

"My mother plays bridge with yours and Elizabeth's. They like to tell each other every little thing about their children. You know gossip travels fast in those circles, and it's usually quite accurate."

"Oh." Carol couldn't think of anything to say, and it was Gordon who finally released her hand, nodded, and turned to Elizabeth. "Everything is looking very good, Elizabeth. I'll be back tomorrow morning and we'll let you go home by early afternoon."

"Thank God! That will be great, Gordon, thank you." Elizabeth watched as Gordon paused by the door, turned, and suggested to Carol they get together and catch up over lunch soon.

"Sure. Give me a call." She nodded as she spoke, looking vague and disinterested. She had no intention of going out with any man, for a very long time. Maybe not ever.

He closed the door and Carol turned back to her cousin. "That was Gordon Jones?"

"Yep." Her cousin couldn't resist teasing her. "You should have seen your face!" Elizabeth laughed so hard even Carol smiled. When Elizabeth was finally over her giggling fit, Carol suggested they get together very soon; Elizabeth had a better idea.

"Why don't we put together a foursome? Michael, you and Gordon, and me. Now, wouldn't that be nice?" she asked, her face bright with expectation.

"No, it wouldn't." Carol frowned. "I don't intend to be part of a foursome, or anything remotely imitating a couple, for a long, long time. Even longer than that. Don't even contemplate that thought."

Startled, Elizabeth sat back. "Why?" She knew that Carol must have misunderstood. "Just because we go out to dinner doesn't mean—"

She was cut off as Carol held up a firm hand. "No. You and I can go out to raise some hell, but no men."

Elizabeth's face was as concerned as Carol's was empty.

"Carol, what happened in California? Ray adored you, and you, well, you both seemed to be so deeply in love, so happy. I know the times we visited you out there, and when you came here, it seemed everything was wonderful. You were so perfect." She faltered as her cousin again held up a hand.

"There's nothing left to say. So . . ." Carol took a deep long breath, let the air out slowly, and changed the subject. "So let's talk about . . . Kellan. Am I going to see my godchild soon, or is she having too great a time at Mr. Jefferson's university?"

There was a moment of awkward silence before Elizabeth smiled wanly, accepting the change of subject for now.

"She's supposed to come home tomorrow night, but I'm not sure how long she's going to be around. She's finished with semester midterms, and I think she had something planned with friends for the small break. I'll tell her that her fairy godmother is here asking about her."

"You do that, and tell her I want a date for dinner and shopping, my treat."

Elizabeth shook her head. "You'll spoil that child."

"Some child, she's taller than me," Carol scoffed. "Besides, it's what godmothers get to do," Carol said with a cocky smile.

Elizabeth touched Carol's arm. "And you and I have a date for dinner soon, *my* treat."

Carol shrugged. "Well, when you get out of here, you and I are going to raise some serious mischief in this town. That'll make both of us feel better. I'll rent a limo and we'll go barhopping, or someplace dangerous. Okay?"

Before Elizabeth could say anything more, Michael was back, announcing the end of visiting hours. He promptly took Carol's arm and escorted her to the door, even as she yelled, "Elizabeth, I'll call you, and don't forget what I said." Michael shut the door behind her.

"And don't forget I'll be back here in the morning," he promised, his kiss long and gentle before he finally left.

⌒

Sitting just inside the small hospital room she jokingly called her jail cell, Elizabeth waited impatiently for Gordon and Michael. The hospital had confined her world long enough.

She looked like a fashion model. Dressed in a cropped autumn jacket in herringbone tweed with matching pants, she was just strapping on beige high-heeled shoes when her doctor walked in. As soon as he saw her feet he frowned.

"Elizabeth." Gordon Jones was very much the doctor; his face and voice stern. "Until you see Dr. O'Day, I want you to be very careful about those kinds of shoes. Low heels would be much better. Tennis shoes with a good arch support are excellent." He picked up her charts off the back of the door, not expecting her reaction.

"Gordon, you've got to be kidding!" Her voice was incredulous and she looked at him like he had lost his mind. "I don't think I own a pair of flats, thank you very much, but I do have a closet full of these kinds of shoes that I will continue to wear. And don't worry, I'm just fine." But her lofty sureness was ruined when she stood and took a step forward, only to feel the floor rushing toward her. This happened just as Michael walked in and, with a muttered curse, caught her.

"What the—are you all right?" His face was white as he helped her back to the chair.

Her face was red and angry, but she summarily waved away his concern. "I'm fine. I just slipped on something. Actually"—and she leveled a look of disapproval at Gordon—"it felt like a nail snagged my shoe." Elizabeth leaned forward to stare accusingly at the floor, certain something was there that ought not to be. Didn't they ever sweep these floors?

It was only after Michael actually got down on his hands and knees to scrutinize the area and found nothing that she stopped fussing.

"Well, what on earth could it have been?" she said, irritation wrinkling her brow.

"I told you those shoes aren't a good idea, Elizabeth," Gordon said mildly, thinking the sooner she saw the neurologist the better he would feel.

Michael's frown deepened. "Then why are you wearing them, Elizabeth?" Concern clipped his voice with anger.

Her sidelong glance was stubborn. "Because I want to."

"Gordon just said that's not a good idea. And you nearly fell." He studied her rebellious face and took control. "We'll stop by a shoe store on the way home. We can get you whatever you need then." To make sure she understood the point, he bent down, took the shoes off her feet, and threw them in the trash can.

"Michael!" She was outraged.

He ignored her and spoke to the doctor. "Can we go now?" Gordon nodded and Michael put a strong hand on Elizabeth's arm and helped her up.

"She can use a wheelchair to get to the lobby," Gordon said. As if on cue, a nurse arrived at the door to help seat a fussing Elizabeth. "I didn't even use a wheelchair when I had Kellan," she said. "And Michael, go back and get me my shoes. Now. I'm not leaving them here."

After a brief staring contest, he guided her into the wheelchair and only then did as she asked, dumping the shoes in her lap.

Neither spoke until they were in the car driving away. Michael stared at the road as he asked, "Where do you want to stop?"

Elizabeth closed her eyes and leaned against the cushion. "I don't want to stop anywhere. I want to go home, Michael. I'm tired."

He nodded, wanting the same thing but not wanting her to think the matter of the shoes was forgotten. "All right, fine, but no more heels. You can wear tennis shoes to go out and get some other shoes. We can do that tomorrow." That would be soon enough.

She kept her eyes shut, quietly searching for the happy anticipation about going home, because it was now nowhere to be found. Silence hummed as they drove home; her eyes opened only when she felt the car turning into the front circular drive, instead of going straight to the back of the house as they usually did. "Wait here."

"Why, Michael? Why are you stopping here?" She frowned as she watched him move around the car to her door. She grabbed the shoes out of the backseat and started to put them on. He didn't give her time.

In one fluid motion, Michael reached in and picked her up. "Can't have you walking in bare feet, can we?" He smiled down at her before walking up the steps to the front door. He heard her wonderful laugh and then her arms were embracing his neck.

"I feel like a bride," she murmured into his ear.

He put her down at the front door and gave her a long, welcoming kiss. "Keep that thought for tonight," he said, even as the door opened and her mother held out welcoming arms.

"Elizabeth! Come in, come in; my goodness, where are your shoes? I packed them for her, didn't I, Michael?" Flustered, Virginia Mae didn't wait for an answer. She drew Elizabeth inside even as Michael went back out to park the car and bring in the suitcase.

Elizabeth smiled, smelling the fresh cut flowers that graced the sideboard in the foyer. Her mother knew how much she loved the house to be filled with flowers. Seeing Elizabeth's pleased face, Virginia Mae wrapped her in a loving embrace and held on too tightly and for too long. And fussed about the flowers. "You would not believe how long it took me to find these flowers. Everywhere I looked, no one had fresh. Oh, they said they were fresh, but by the time I saw them, they were drooping, within moments of dropping all their petals. And the fragrance! Nothing, unless you like the smell of a dying rose."

"Mother." Finally, Elizabeth disengaged herself. "Thank you. The flowers are a lovely touch, and I appreciate all your effort. It's good to be home. Let's go into the living room. I am a tad bit tired."

Michael, who had returned, brought slippers for her feet. "Maybe you should go rest, Elizabeth."

Perversely, she didn't want to do it simply because he suggested it. "No, I'm fine. I'd like to sit and chat with Mother for a little while. Is Kellan going to be here soon?"

He glanced at the mantel clock as he guided her to the couch. "She said she'd be here after her last class. About five o'clock. Before dinner."

"Good. I've missed her. You talked to her just last night?"

He nodded and abruptly leaned down to give her a kiss. "I've got to get back to work. I'll be back here before Virginia Mae leaves. And don't fix dinner. We'll call for takeout."

After he left, her mother went to make them some tea.

Elizabeth looked with approval around the spacious room, which she had redecorated just last year. The ceiling and trim were crisp white, walls deep hunter green. Huge paintings decorated the walls; a few of her own creations were also hung there.

She savored the quiet, the peacefulness emanating from this room, from this house. What a welcome change. It was wonderful to be here and yet . . . It was odd, but she felt she didn't belong. It was a strange thought, unbalancing. She leaned against the soft cushions of the sofa and closed her eyes in defense, but still there was a slight off-center feeling to the world and she couldn't figure out why.

She awoke with a jolt an hour later and listened to her mother's plaintive voice. "Well, finally. I'm afraid the tea, what's left of it, is cold."

The disapproving thread in that familiar voice was so normal, so usual, it was a relief to hear it. It was so good to be home. Things were becoming normal. "Sorry. I must have been more tired than I thought."

Her mother's lips compressed into a familiar thin line. "You should have listened to Michael and gone right to bed." Her mother always thought she should do precisely what Michael told her to do, and Elizabeth found even that reassuring.

By the time Michael got home, she had changed into jeans and a comfortable shirt. Elizabeth was still wearing the slippers. Virginia Mae readied to leave as Michael came into the kitchen and gave his wife a hug and a kiss. "Are you feeling better?" This had become standard over the last three weeks, his face anxious. "Any more falls?"

"None," she assured him, even as her mother echoed, "Falls? Elizabeth, did you fall and no one told me?" Disapproval moved a notch higher.

"No, Mother, I didn't really fall. I just . . . stumbled. There is not the slightest need to be upset," she assured her, knowing it was best not to go into details with Virginia Mae. She ignored the mild irritation that Michael had to mention it in front of her mother. "I'm sorry you can't stay to see Kellan."

Virginia Mae sighed, her lips thinned with regret. "So am I, but tonight is dinner with Gladys Nelson, and we've planned this for so long, I can't cancel. But tell my granddaughter I will see her for breakfast tomorrow. Bright and early." Virginia Mae kissed her daughter and left in a cloud of perfume and purpose.

Elizabeth watched from the open front doorway, waiting to wave good-bye because her mother would expect it. She wandered into the bedroom and watched her husband change. "How'd work go today?"

"Fine. We've added another hospital chain. I have to fly to California next week to take contracts. Want to go?"

Michael nearly two decades ago had the foresight to get into the manufacturing and marketing of artificial hips and knees. He had built the company into a leader of the industry by operating better and smarter than anyone else. Recently, the company had expanded into heart-monitoring devices that could instantly distinguish a heart attack from a range of other symptoms. By diagnosing an attack quicker and more accurately, proper treatment could be started almost immediately, thereby saving time and lives. He had been determined to keep the cost affordable. Business had never been better.

She shrugged. "Maybe." She sat down on the side of the bed and idly traced the embroidered flowers on the spread. The colors were subtle and delicate. She remembered buying it from the Amish in Pennsylvania several years ago. When she saw it she knew it would feel like having an indoor garden on their bed. That was how she created her house; it was filled with special things she had bought carefully and thoughtfully over the years. They wrapped her life in memory, color, and time.

"What are you thinking?" He had come to stand next to her, lightly touching her shoulder, and she looked up. He had pulled on a polo shirt the color of corn, and it contrasted nicely with the dark jeans.

"How nice it is to be home," she said, and then tilted her head back and gave him a jaunty grin. "Hospitals stink." He chuckled as she continued, her nose wrinkling. "They smell like all the ammonia and antibacterial detergents, like the inside of a toilet bowl. Awful."

Michael laughed again. "I don't think I've ever heard you say that before. What about when you visit the babies? Isn't that the same smell?"

She shook her head emphatically. "Nope. The babies smell wonderful. You can't wash away baby smells, despite all the industrial cleaners they use. Babies are always . . . sweet and fresh, like a new moment. There is nothing like holding a little one, letting them know they matter. Babies are the best." A smile lit her up from the inside. "I can hardly wait to get back to them, I've missed them so much. Now, that's something that will make me rest and behave myself—to be able to hold and feed as many babies as I can."

Her volunteer work at the hospital, hugging and touching babies who needed a little extra loving, was immensely fulfilling.

Michael, for his part, did not find her expectations pleasing at all. He decided to call the doctor tomorrow before Elizabeth made the trek to the state hospital to cuddle children who needed her.

He touched her shoulder. She looked up and saw his face. "I've been worried about you, Beth."

She was standing, her smile and words strong. "Don't worry. You heard Gordon. Nothing else will happen."

"Might happen," he corrected.

"Won't happen. Let's forget it, okay? That's what I want to do; that's what I want us both to do."

The front door banged open. "Hello. I'm home. Where is everybody?"

Kellan Lane Whittaker met her parents in the hallway, hugging and laughing and talking a mile a minute. Elizabeth blinked back some foolish tears trying to slip out and wondered how she'd been able to survive two months without seeing her daughter. Before she could stop herself, one word flew out: "Transfer."

The noise stopped. "What?" Kellan pulled back.

"Well . . . I said"—Elizabeth took a big breath—"transfer. Why can't you go to college here and live at home? I've missed you."

Kellan laughed hard and hugged her mother tighter. "How sweet. I've missed you, too. But I can't transfer. I've got a scholarship, remember?"

Elizabeth didn't care. "Oh, pooh. We'll pay." Even as she said it, she knew her daughter and knew she wouldn't be coming back.

"Yeah. Right. But hey, how are you? You've had me worried." Kellan began asking for information, wanting to know all about her mother's recent hospital stay, every last detail. They walked arm in arm into the kitchen, Michael following.

His daughter, clad in jeans tucked into low black boots and topped with a red sweater, was a commanding presence. A few inches taller than her mother, her trim, lean-muscled form was the result of running, horseback riding, and playing a wicked game of tennis.

Kellan sat down at the kitchen table opposite Elizabeth. Her wavy blonde hair rippled away from a face that bore a striking resemblance to her mother's.

Although Elizabeth's preference was to hear about what Kellan had been doing at school, Kellan was focused fully on her mother. Earnest and concerned, with a sharpshooter's knack for asking questions that hit the mark, she was making Elizabeth uneasy. After all, she had just told her husband to forget this entire incident. Kellan's questions included the hospital stay and medication, and, more precisely, what the doctors said.

Sipping tea to gain time, Elizabeth personally thought by giving this so much discussion, it was making her recent problem too important, too . . . real. But she did her best because Kellan wasn't going to accept anything less.

"A brain tumor!" Astonished, Kellan shot her father an accusing look. "You never told me that!"

"He never told me that either," Elizabeth said and watched Michael hold up his hands, surrendering to his women.

"There was no reason to tell you anything until we knew for sure."

Questions kept coming from an insatiable Kellan, until she stumbled over the same word her parents were struggling with.

"Incurable? Does that mean you're going to get worse?" Kellan's face went pale.

It was the last thing Elizabeth wanted to hear, and when she answered, her voice was stern, even though the answer was meant to be reassuring. "There's nothing to get worse because I'm fine; the medicine did the trick and nothing else is going to happen. This was a . . . fluke. I'm not worried. And you shouldn't be either," Elizabeth said firmly. "Now. I'd like to officially change the subject. Tell me about school."

Kellan spoke briefly about her various classes and then, a little tentatively, asked about alternative medicine. "Have you thought about investigating other treatments, like holistic therapies? I heard about some up at school, after Dad finally called to let me know what they found. Did you know that NIH even has a center now, just for that?"

"We'd be willing to listen," her father said in a neutral voice. Elizabeth nodded.

Kellan smiled and squeezed her mother's hand. "Let's order Chinese, you want to? I'm starved."

"Sure." Michael pulled out one of the kitchen drawers and tossed some menus on the table. "Tell me what you want and I'll call it in."

Kellan scanned the items. "Something with an attitude. Szechuan, medium, if you please."

She smiled wickedly as her mother groaned. "I'll be smelling hot peppers and garlic all night."

"And you love it as much as I do," Kellan pointed out smugly, making her mother laugh.

Within the hour, dinner had been served and while they were eating, Elizabeth turned to Kellan. "Tell me, how long do we have you? Would you like to go shopping tomorrow after breakfast? Your grandmother's coming early to see you. Oh, and Carol is looking for a date of lunch and shopping, her treat."

Kellan shrugged, her face and voice regretful. "I have to leave way early tomorrow. I told Dad," she said, "that I couldn't stay long at all. A bunch of us are going hiking up in the mountains of Madison County. John Duncan's family has a huge orchard and cattle farm up there, adjacent to one of the parks. We'll be on those hills roughing it through Monday. We had planned to leave tonight. I was going to cancel everything to stay here, but Dad said you were so much better. I did want to see you before I left. They're waiting for me. I'll be gone before you get up."

"Oh." Surprise and disappointment wiped away her smile as Elizabeth looked at her husband. "Michael, you should have told my mother before she left. She's going to be even more disappointed than I am." And Elizabeth knew she would hear not only how disappointed her mother was but also how somehow this was her fault.

God, she hated to disappoint her mother. Reading his wife's face accurately, Michael said, "I'm sorry, Beth, I completely forgot."

"Having one of those senior moments, eh, Dad?" Kellan asked with a grin that widened when her father slapped the air near her and said, "Brat."

The levity was short-lived; he saw the furrowed brow on his wife's face. "I really did forget. I'll call Virginia Mae for you later. Don't worry about anything." He reached and covered her hand.

"I'm not worried," Elizabeth lied, relief sweeping the anxiety from her eyes. Virginia Mae's emotional illogic was legend; her feelings bounced back and forth like a ball in erratic motion, making conversations just as dizzying since little was based on fact. Instead, her mother used whatever feeling was central at the moment, either as a shield or a weapon. Situations that changed without a lot of advance notice were grounds for a tirade. Poor old thing, Elizabeth thought, knowing how lonely her mother was now. Then she turned her full attention back to her daughter.

"I'll miss you, beanpole. Who's going hiking with you?"

With enthusiasm, Kellan told her, and also what they planned to do. "We'll end up at Graves Mountain Lodge by Sunday night. You know their meals are to die for, so that's going to be our reward for roughing it."

"What if you run into a bear or some other wild animal?" Elizabeth's worries started flaring.

"John's bringing a hunting rifle, not to worry. We're going to try to do some fishing and plant gathering, stuff like that. Our goal is to survive on whatever we can scrounge off the land. At least as much as we can."

"You're not going to take food with you at all?" Michael asked, his skepticism obvious.

Kellan's eyes rolled. "Do you think we're idiots? Of course we'll have some food with us, just in case. We want adventure, not starvation."

It was late when they finally called it a night. A chorus of good nights ended the evening, and then Michael led Elizabeth to their master bedroom in the back of the house.

She yawned several times as she and Michael got ready for bed. It was wonderful to be home, but wearing. Part of her wanted to drift off to sleep but she finished brushing her teeth, walked back into the room, and was met by Michael. His arms were around her, his lips teasing and hovering over hers, and she knew the night was far from over. She shivered in anticipation. Before proceeding any further, he pulled back and looked carefully into her eyes. "Are you feeling okay?"

She reached up and touched his mouth and then reached for him, murmuring words of love and endearment as she pulled him closer.

By the time they reached the bed, their clothes were off and they were entangled as only familiar lovers can be. The recent absence made each shared caress, each ragged and quivering breath . . . more.

Perhaps that was why they lingered over each touch, savored each kiss like fine wine. It was all enjoyed more completely, more fully while the journey to fulfillment was gentler, hotter, more deliberate, yet more delicate than it had ever been.

It took several minutes for their breathing and heartbeats to slow. As they curled up against each other, Elizabeth should have drifted into an easy gentle sleep, as Michael was already doing.

She shut her eyes but couldn't shut off her thoughts. Instead of curling up and sleeping, everything was fluttering with intense exhaustion. A switch had been turned on; thoughts and pictures raced about at breakneck speed and would not stop.

She tried to move into a more restful position. And then tried another. Several moments passed before she realized that, incredibly, she was too tired to go to sleep.

After another several minutes of trying not to disturb Michael she finally gave up, got up, and walked out of the room. She would make some hot tea and read something boring. The silence of the house was deafening and every simple, normal sound she made was so much louder because of it.

The fragrant tea—marketed as a sleeping aid—was useless. She drained the cup, put it in the sink and leaned against the counter, so exhausted she felt sick. Never in memory had sleep been so elusive. She couldn't understand it.

Walking into the living room, she squinted through the bookshelves, thinking she could read herself to sleep. Something she had read before, something slow-paced, known.

Finally, she chose *Silas Marner*. She reclined on the emerald couch, propped up slightly by a pillow, and let her eyes drift wearily over the small letters. It was slow reading. The closer she got to the bottom of the page, the lower her eyelids sank until, finally, they closed. The stillness was wrapped around her tightly until she was snared by sleep. Breathing deeply, she slept hard. Still, within the deepest recesses of her mind, she dreamed her eyes snapped open, and she was completely alert.

The book slipped to the floor as she sat up. Blinking, she looked around. There was no sense of time; she felt as if she could have been asleep for days, but it was still dark. She sat up, her hands covering a huge yawn.

A quiver of anxiety made her stand up. Overwhelmed by restlessness, there was a need to move, her legs needed motion. The kitchen was dark when she heard a car pull out, and at the back door she saw a pair of red taillights burn brightly before disappearing. Kellan had indeed gotten an early start.

Elizabeth turned and headed toward the dining room at the front of the house. The outside street lamps lent enough light to see. Her hand trailed along the table and she glanced around at the shadows of the room, knowing everything by heart.

It was what she didn't see that stopped her like a slap. Her heart started to race as she realized the large mahogany china cabinet they had inherited from Michael's great-grandmother was gone!

Shivers kept time with her shallow gasps as she examined the massive, metal door that now dominated the large wall, startled to see it was ajar. Confused, she thought hard about what to do. Where was Michael? Shouldn't she call for him? Even as she opened her mouth her legs started moving, and then she forgot about everything as she pushed the door wide open.

Who had the audacity to steal her beautiful antique and then put this ugly thing here? Did they think she wouldn't notice? It was a mystery, and suddenly she was angrier than she had ever been in her entire life. She wanted her dining room back to its original shape, and she wanted it done now! Feeling powerful, Elizabeth boldly strode through the door, intent on discovering how this had happened and getting it fixed.

She stopped abruptly as she heard the metal hinges creak and groan and then the entire metal door slammed shut behind her.

She could hear nothing but the clamor of her heart as she turned back and fumbled for the door handle.

She was in total darkness.

Raking fingernails against the sides of the door, there was nothing but a smooth surface—no door handle. Nothing!

She licked dry lips and felt her legs weaken. Where was she? How had this happened? What could she do?

Michael! Where was Michael? She would scream for him and he would come and save her; yes, that was what she would do. This heartened her until she tried to open her mouth and realized she had no voice.

Paralyzed, she stood there for a breathless moment and then with a resolution borne of the finality of not having a choice, she turned slowly to face what was ahead. The darkness was palpable, she felt tangled in it. She had never known such blackness; it was numbing and cold, stripping breath from her lungs. She had to do something. She took a step and then another one.

She did this for several minutes, until all her thoughts were centered on finding some sort of light, some kind of end to this place. Suddenly consumed by anxiety, she halfway turned to start back. She wanted, needed, to go back.

Was that a flicker? Or were her eyes tricking her? Just as she thought she saw a flash of movement, she took one more step—and felt nothing but air. She fell, and kept falling, turning head over heels, twisting and turning like a dead leaf dropping from a living tree. There was no end to the falling . . .

Chapter Three

Sleep drifted away slowly from Michael, like the dying embers of a campfire. Noting it was still dark outside, Michael lazily stretched out an arm to embrace his wife. Connecting to nothing was enough to jolt his eyes open. Blinking, he turned on the table lamp and saw the light spill into an empty room. Not stopping for a robe or slippers, he left to find her. The kitchen was empty. He looked outside and saw Kellan's car was gone. Well, she said she was going to leave before they got up.

He wiped away some of the sleep, wondering where Elizabeth was and, more to the point, why she wasn't in bed with him.

He wandered next into the dining room, puzzled but not yet concerned. Logically, she had to be somewhere in the house. There would be a reasonable explanation.

He crossed the hall, entered the living room, and was gripped by fear that was so consuming he couldn't move, couldn't breathe. *Elizabeth!*

His wife was on the floor in front of the couch, slumped over on her side, and his first frantic thought was that she was dead. Dear God, where had he been when this horrible thing happened? He was sweating, hyperventilating. He cursed himself, the grayness of despair so real and menacing he felt his knees begin to wobble and start to collapse. He had to crawl to her. Relief almost made him cry out at the sight of her chest moving, then as he felt her warmth. She was alive!

His grateful sigh immediately slid into a devastating thought. She must be ill again. Got up, fell, and hit her head; she was unconscious.

An ambulance! He needed an ambulance. He tried to get up, reach toward the phone, but fear made his movements spastic, and all the while his wife was hurt.

He had never been this vulnerable and at that moment, deep within him, a cold wind of betrayal slipped inside, as subtle as a shadow at night. *This was not supposed to happen to us! How could she let this horrible thing come into our lives?* It was a soundless melody that would start to color how he looked at everything, at his life, at his Elizabeth.

He started fumbling to pick up the phone again; he had to help his wife.

Her eyes suddenly opened. "Michael?"

"Shhh," he soothed, touching her face. "Don't move. Something may be hurt. Hush, I'll call the rescue squad; just don't move, everything will be all right." He moved to get up and she stopped him cold by trying to sit up.

He was furious she wouldn't listen. "Dammit, Elizabeth! Don't move. You could be hurt, something may be broken; just be still."

"Michael, stop." Elizabeth sat up, vaguely aware he was angry but not understanding why. "How did I get here?" She looked around, confused.

Short of bodily forcing her to lie back down, he couldn't stop her from moving, and she *was* acting normally. "That's what I'd like to know. Elizabeth, why are you in here? I almost had a heart attack when I discovered you weren't in bed."

"I'm sorry," she said contritely, and then it all came back in a rush as she looked at him. Then she saw the book that had dropped beside her.

"I couldn't sleep. I didn't want to wake you, so I came in here and started reading something. I suppose I fell asleep. I must have fallen off the couch. Look, here's the book."

Suddenly the adrenaline rush dissolved and Michael was exhausted. He rubbed the back of his neck. "God, I'm tired."

Instantly, he felt her hand rubbing gently against his, her voice a whisper. "I'm sorry. Let's go back to bed."

He helped her up and stood looking down at her. "Elizabeth, do you promise you're all right?"

There was that winning smile, and he hugged her hard, wishing, hoping, things really would be all right again.

It was late morning when she woke. Michael was already awake but had been reluctant to interrupt her sleep. While he sat there in the chair next to the bed, he watched her, enjoying a rush of memories that now were tinged with worry. Was last night a fluke? Would he, God forbid, wake up again in the middle of the night to find her slumped to the floor? The uncertainties were dancing all over his rational thoughts and left him edgy.

Resting on her side, Elizabeth's face was smooth, her lips gently curling. He hoped she was dreaming of him. Their lovemaking had been so good, so satisfying, he wondered why sleep had been such a problem for her last night. He finally realized he was clenching his hands as well as his jaw, and consciously forced himself to relax.

Her eyes opened to see him reading, looking relaxed and content, and she smiled. She loved seeing him like that, loved having him at home with her. She moved slightly and their eyes met.

"Well. Sleeping Beauty awakes." His smile was tentative, eyes filled with the moments of the previous night.

She sat up, stretched, and then winced. "Ow. I must have hit the floor a little harder than I thought. And thank you for letting me sleep in. What time is it?" She glanced at the clock and her eyes widened. "Goodness! It's almost noon. I can't believe I slept that long." A thought edged to the forefront. "Oh. Did you talk to Mother?"

He nodded. "Got hold of her early this morning. She's disappointed, but I told her Kellan said she would call her when she got back from camping and let her know when she can visit. How's that?"

"Good. Thanks." It was a heaviness she hadn't realized was there until it slipped off. Her mother was the only one who could make her nervous like this. Actually, it was simply because she hated to see Virginia Mae disappointed. In a way she couldn't explain, she felt a duty to keep her mother happy and content. She never noticed how stressful that responsibility could be because it was not a conscious choice; it was what she needed to do. She felt the same way about her daughter and husband and, to some extent, her cousin and friends.

Elizabeth got out of bed and began to fall as one foot slipped away. Michael moved like a shot, grabbing her arms in a crushing hold. "Are you okay?"

"I don't know," she murmured, frowning.

He helped her sit on the side of the bed. "Elizabeth, were you dizzy again, is that it?"

"No, no, I'm not. My foot, it just . . . slipped out. Actually, I don't really know what happened. Here, let me get up again." And she did and took some steps forward without any problem. But when she turned back to Michael, the left foot didn't move with her and she started falling. His arms, seconds away, again caught her and helped her sit back down.

"Isn't that odd?" She frowned, pulling her foot up, looking at it as if it didn't belong to her. She was trying hard to ignore the rapid beating of her heart.

"Odd? Elizabeth, isn't that the same one you had trouble with yesterday morning?" It wasn't his intention, but his voice sounded accusing. She bristled.

"No," she said curtly. She thought for a few moments more and then got up slowly. Carefully, she walked with exaggerated attention to what she was doing and succeeded in moving to the bathroom door. "See? I'll be fine." She smiled brightly and was startled by his scowl.

"You're not." How could she say such nonsense and smile? "You should see yourself. Something is terribly wrong. Stay here and don't move. I'm calling Gordon." He insisted she sit down on the chair he had vacated. He glanced at the clock on the wall. "I don't remember the number to his cell phone, I've got to look it up. I won't be long."

She watched him leave the room and felt some tension go with him. *God*, she silently asked, *why is this happening?*

What would Mimi have to say about all this? White hair pulled away from a worn, pleasant face, her grandmother always had good things to eat and words that would make her smile. Mimi's constant stream of dialogue to the Almighty had been practical, quick, short, and to the point. "Dear Lord, where did I put that needle and thread?" or "Father, thank You for not letting me make a bigger fool of myself than I did."

At this moment, though, Elizabeth was wondering about getting some answers. She was also trying not to be impatient because Michael was making such a fuss about all this, when she knew it was going to be absolutely all right. It had to be.

Something else caught her eye. The dust balls hanging from the corner near the bathroom door. Since Elizabeth had become ill, her part-time housekeeper, Sudie Babcock, had been coming once a week instead of three times. It showed.

She would call and make sure Sudie came on Monday. Elizabeth detested a dirty home as much as she hated a cluttered one. She felt personally offended if everything wasn't in its particular place. She turned to look as her husband stalked back into the room, as unhappy as when he'd left.

"It's going to be five weeks before you can see the specialist. Gordon said he couldn't get the appointment any sooner than that. He also said there's probably some residual damage; you might need an ankle brace, he's not certain. But one thing's for sure, no high heels!"

Damage? Her next immediate thought was succinct. *No way!*

He picked her up and carried her to the bathroom. "Do you want me to help you in the shower?" The aid was offered so grimly, she didn't need to think twice. "No, I'll be careful. Just go."

"All right. I'll be right here reading." He motioned to the love seat. She watched him turn to leave.

The shower went without incident. That was a small triumph, and she congratulated herself on succeeding by concentrating on what she was doing. Thoughtfully, she slowly let the relaxing water run over her, knowing everything was going to be fine. Slowing down didn't have to be a bad thing. Everyone should slow down. Maybe that was the key. Maybe that was the answer, she mused, as she thanked God for it, just in case.

By the end of the afternoon she had new tennis shoes, as well as walking shoes in black and brown, and black leather Mary Janes for dresses. They were bought at Michael's insistence, but secretly Elizabeth was determined never to wear them.

She went to bed that night tired and after a long, healing sleep, all traces of weakness disappeared. Elizabeth was delighted to find she could walk without any difficulty, without thought. It was the ease of it, she thought, luxuriating in the taste of the word. *Ease*. Without thought, without concentration, to just be able to move.

She was thrilled, but not surprised. Michael didn't share her optimism. As he went to call the doctor yet again, Elizabeth shook her head.

"Gordon's going to change his cell number and not tell you what it is! You've called that poor man more in the last two days than you have in the last two years." Her laughter didn't appear to ease Michael's anxiety one bit.

The brief talk with Gordon had only confirmed his suspicions. "He said remissions are very common with this disease. And remissions can happen at any time. That's why they call it relapsing/remitting."

Despite his explanation being delivered with such a dour expression, she let it slide over her like water off a duck. She merely smiled. "Would you like some coffee?"

He pushed back his chair. "I'll get it," he said, but she was already setting a steaming mug in front of him.

"Drink all of it and eat your cherry pastry," she instructed him. "I sincerely hope it improves your disposition." The gaiety of her smile did not soften his mood, and he remained silent, worried lines drawing his face down.

✐

A week slipped by before Elizabeth sat at the small Queen Anne desk in the library for the first time since all this had started. She pulled out the latest journal, flipped to the last entry, and grimaced when she saw the date. She had never missed so many days—weeks—before.

She finally shrugged and tore the pages from the notebook she had written in at the hospital and slipped them inside. She had been keeping daily journals since she was eighteen. It not only helped chronicle her life, but it also made sense of her present.

Taking the time to write down thoughts about what was going on and how she was feeling about events in her life let her carefully and thoughtfully sort out tangles that occurred. She also loved the feel of a pen in her hand, and there was deep satisfaction in forming letters that were as perfect as only a true artist could make them. This belonged completely to her.

How to begin? There was still a swirl of disbelief that mocked everything she had been told. Her eyes roamed over the volumes of books that lined the shelves. People's lives decorated these walls—their thoughts, their stories. Some amusing, some wrenching, some uplifting, some not. All she wanted to do was make sense of her recent past.

She bent over and started.

It's odd, the changes and upheavals that set us all on edge, only to be placed right back where we started. It's all confusing, but I'm glad, I'm grateful. I have been well my entire life. Now, after the merest blip, they tell me everything's changed. I hear the words that Gordon has to say, and certainly those of my husband, but . . . I have to wonder— what has actually changed?

Not much. I can still do whatever I want to do. Those first little missteps I had right after I left the hospital have evaporated into the past, and as far as I'm concerned, permanently. Well, all right, I will concede I don't have all my energy back, but how could I, after what I've been through? And there are my husband and my doctor, thinking all these horrible thoughts; my mother is worrying herself sick, and even my daughter! Poor Kellan. She called last night because of a story a friend told her. I swear, when there's bad news it's like getting a bunch of mothers together at a baby shower and their stories must be compulsively aired in vivid detail to the mother-to-be. Stories of hellish labors, deliveries that almost assured death . . . always the worst things to bring up at bad moments. I wonder if Eve did that with Adam?

Probably. I think it's human nature and I know if I thought long enough, I'd be able to come up with my own transgressions. But back to Kellan . . . She asked me a hypothetical question that I was at a loss to answer. She said she understood, but I have to wonder if she did, because I'm having a hard time dealing with it myself.

Kellan had just met a student whose mother had this same illness for twenty-five years. Within the last year, when the mother got to the point she could no longer swallow, the woman had refused to be fed intravenously, thereby ending her life. "Mom, without even thinking twice, I blurted out that the woman just gave up! This girl said no, no, that wasn't the case; her mother was just too tired to fight anymore." Kellan was horrified and asked me point-blank, "You would never do that, would you?"

Am I supposed to know? I told her emphatically I had no intention of ever getting to that point, so don't waste a single brain cell worrying about something that would never happen. I then proceeded to spout off all the good and bright reasons to be hopeful à la Gordon and the specialist, about how a cure was right around the corner, etc., etc., then Kellan stopped me dead. It seems that's just what that mother had been told for twenty-five years.

After I regained my breath, I reassured my only child that there was nothing to worry about, then we chatted about inconsequential things, about happy thoughts and future plans. I hung up the phone after doing a superb Pollyanna act, then sank into my own thoughts of what-ifs and what-might-bes, all pounding around inside my head.

That lasted longer than I care to admit. Finally, I hauled myself up and gave myself a stern pep talk about all the good things I've been repeating over and over since that moment in the hospital when I regained my life. I forced myself to evaluate things clearly.

So all right, I admit I don't have the energy I did. But just as important, neither do I have those horrible moments that lasted only a handful of seconds, comparatively. Yet my mother still looks at me as if she intends to burst into tears at any moment. She keeps telling me how brave I am, until I want to toss those words out of the English language. What does it mean? I'm not a bit different—she is.

Elizabeth closed her eyes and shook her head. Her innate sense of fairness couldn't be ignored.

Poor Mother. I'm sure she's trying her best to cope. I wish she would realize there is nothing to cope with. I AM FINE. If I died today in a car wreck, I hope they'd put that on my tombstone: SHE WAS FINE.

The only one who treats me as she always has is Carol. But I think that's because she's very self-absorbed right now, pushing away the divorce (she still won't talk about it), and drinking more alcohol than I've ever seen her consume. Granted, I haven't been around her very much over these last years, but I still think it's excessive. She remains even more slender than she was before, so I know she's not eating like she should, and is constantly exercising on all the equipment she has littered around the house.

I have to say one thing for her, though, she hasn't lost her wit. She has gleefully turned into a male-basher and makes no apology for it. Maybe it's part of healing; if you make fun of the hurt, it can't slap back so hard.

Michael is another story. Things have changed subtly but enough for me to notice. He watches intently, pretending that he doesn't, but I can tell. It's as if he's waiting for the inevitable moment when he has to jump up and take over. If I fumble with the silverware setting the table, he is there to take the pieces out of my hands and finish. I have to wonder, Why isn't he proactive? Why doesn't he do it for me while I'm doing something else?

It's that waiting, like he's holding his breath for another moment that will unbalance us. "For Pete's sake," I want to scream, "lighten up!"

A new thought bolted through Elizabeth's mind and she sat very still as she slowly considered it.

I wonder if it's their collective fear that is draining me, pulling at me so constantly, enough to keep me tired? Suddenly, I see the strain of having to be as normal as possible, even though the hilarity is that I am just

like I've always been. Huh! Whenever Michael is around, there can be
no mistakes because he will jump to his own conclusions. When my
mother is around, I have to be as normal as possible (whatever that is)
because she is ready to be devastated for me instantly.

Do they think they are helping? Good grief, I'm getting exhausted
just thinking about how they are wearing me out! Well. This can't go
on. What I have to do is disregard them, and just do the best I can. If I
ignore their constant hovering and especially their expectations, then I
will be fine . . . Gee, I wonder how they'll handle that?

With that last gibe, Elizabeth closed her journal with a loud slap
and smiled. She had made some discoveries she hadn't realized by
sorting through her feelings. That always made her feel in charge.
She picked up the large journal, carried it to an armoire at the back
of the room, and locked it in with dozens of others. She always kept
her written thoughts locked up. It made her feel secure, even
though no one in the family had ever pried or even asked her about
what she wrote.

Feeling refreshed and focused, she walked into the kitchen, set the
table *before* Michael got home from work, and began fixing dinner.

During the next several days, Elizabeth returned to the known
patterns of her life. While she tried not to remember too much
about those days in the hospital, she continued praying in snatches
as her grandmother used to do. Mostly it was thanking God for this,
letting Him know she was grateful for something as mundane as being able to enjoy sitting on the deck overlooking her backyard, sipping coffee or tea. She was very alert to the movement of her legs
and hands. The pleasure of simply moving in harmony was as immense as it was indescribable.

～～

Elizabeth's happiness was so palpable that finally even Michael was
able to relax. He loved his wife, wanted her to be happy and well
and, more than anything, wanted their lives to flow past those horrible moments . . . so he tried to focus on her smiles, on her easy
movements and more than anything the laughter that bubbled up
from her heart, spontaneous as summer breezes.

Chapter Four

The church grounds were dotted with people heading to the building for weekly worship. It was the first time Elizabeth had attended church since leaving the hospital and she was intensely glad to be back to normal, to be coming to this place again.

Carol met them in the courtyard that fronted the church. The structure was ancient as American buildings go, parts dating back to the early 1700s. Of course it was colonial, but with the angles and grandeur of England outlining its dimensions.

The cousins looked at each other and smiled.

Shared memories flooded over the two women; they had practically grown up at this church. The private school they had attended, supported by the Episcopal diocese, inevitably focused part of its teaching within and about this holy place. The rest of the time, their dutiful parents had brought them here to learn and socialize and become productive citizens of society. At least the parents hoped that was what they were accomplishing. Carol could feel the past rolling over her in nostalgic waves and could almost see the innocence of their youth waving from a distance.

"God, to think we used to practically live in this place! Maybe if I'd kept up with this part of my life in California, things wouldn't have gotten so . . . crazy." Carol shook her head, a wry smile tugging her lips.

"Do you think so?" Elizabeth asked, wondering—again—just what had gone wrong, exactly, in California. It seemed to her that she and Carol were overdue for some serious talking. That would have to be remedied. And soon.

"That's what Father Wells thinks," Carol said, squinting up at the cross on the steeple, her voice casual.

"Oh, you've met him?" Elizabeth was surprised. "When was that?"

"When I first got back for good, after I knew the divorce was final. I needed some . . . spiritual comforting." Carol's sober glance fell on one of the many stained-glass windows decorating the brick walls and she suddenly laughed. "Elizabeth, remember when we got in trouble for throwing spitballs at the Crosby twins during confirmation class?"

Elizabeth glanced at a disinterested Michael, and then grinned. "Behave, or I won't take you out in public again."

Michael remained silent, not really listening, instead nodding pleasantly to acquaintances as they walked closer to the entrance of the old Episcopal church. Michael and Elizabeth were married in this church; Kellan was baptized and later confirmed here. It was a building that held a host of memories for all of them.

Footsteps came closer behind them and then stopped.

"Hello, folks."

They turned in unison and saw Dr. Gordon Jones smiling at them, hands in the pockets of khakis, a dark brown sports jacket over a clean white shirt, with a tie that actually looked nice. "Beautiful day, isn't it?" His smile included all of them before settling on Carol.

Elizabeth was surprised at his sudden appearance. "What are you doing here? I thought you only got one Sunday off a month."

His nod was amiable. "That's right. The third one."

Three pairs of eyebrows rose as Carol pointed out before an anxious Elizabeth could, "I hate to be the one to tell you this, Gordon, but this is the *second* Sunday of the month."

"Damn!" He hit his forehead with an open palm. "Where am I supposed to be then?" He waited to see their concern, and then he relaxed, smiled, and pushed his glasses up. "Kevin Bliley asked me to switch with him. He needs that weekend because his twins are being baptized. Gotcha, huh?"

Carol rolled her eyes. "And it's always a pleasure to see you, too."

"Right, you can say that again." Elizabeth punched his arm. Michael, with a bored smile, listened to them and glanced at his watch. "We'd better get a move on, folks. The bells are going to start ringing any minute."

"Oh, yes, Michael does have a thing about time, doesn't he? Are you getting more obsessive about punctuality or is it just me?" Carol inquired with sarcasm, her smile bright and brittle. He ignored her and took Elizabeth's hand.

"Come on." Michael pulled his wife along, leaving the other two to follow. Within moments they were just yards away from the huge arched double-door entry of the church.

Elizabeth half turned back to Carol to point out some of the colorful fall plantings by the walkway when she stumbled. It was a small misstep, one she could have easily remedied.

But everyone reacted.

Michael felt her dip sideways and tried to pull her back the other way but only succeeded in further unbalancing her. Gordon, who had been walking behind with Carol, made a grab for her other arm and missed. It was Carol, who was directly behind her, who reached out just as Elizabeth started falling backward.

With too many hands fumbling to help, gravity finally prevailed and Elizabeth fell back hard, directly on top of Carol, knocking them both to the sidewalk with a loud thump.

"Elizabeth!" Michael had to steady himself before he could help her. "Dammit, I told you not to wear those shoes!" Incredibly, his wife was laughing, which did nothing to improve his temper. He didn't recognize the embarrassment or nervousness that echoed in her hilarity; he was too concerned for her.

Gordon also knelt down to help untangle the mess. "Carol, are you okay? You sure got the brunt of that one." With the help of both men, the two women were up within moments, brushing off the leaves that clung to them.

Carol removed her arm from Gordon's hand and smoothed out her black skirt. Straightening caused a slight grimace, and she heard a bone crunch somewhere in the vicinity of her backside. With a steadying hand there, she took a deep breath and sent a mock glare Elizabeth's way. "The only thing that's hurt is my dignity and my butt," she said, rubbing the latter. They glanced at each other and began giggling like the schoolgirls they had been years ago.

Gordon and Michael made eye contact. Gordon, amused, just shrugged. But Michael was more irritated, not only by what happened to his wife, but also by their giggling response. Immediately, his thoughts flew back to all the information he had been reading, all the symptoms, and the endless possibilities . . . and they thought it was funny?

The grip he placed on his wife's arm was unrelenting. "Elizabeth, this is the last time you will ever wear shoes with heels. You are not going to give me a near heart attack every time we go out."

"Michael," she chided patiently, "it's an old cobblestone sidewalk.

It's always been uneven. I just stumbled, and if everyone had not been in such a hurry to help, I would have been fine." Although she was a little shaken, there was no way on this earth she would admit to the sudden weakness in that leg. It was fine now, that was all that mattered. *Thank You, God. I'm fine, I'm going to be fine . . .*

"Yeah," Carol chimed in from behind them. "And if she hadn't fallen on *me*, I'd be fine, too."

Gordon fell in step next to her. "Let me know if you find you're in any discomfort. I can get you some heavy-duty Tylenol for pain," he offered. "Just say the word."

"I'm fine," Carol snapped, and immediately bit her lip. He was just trying to help. Her glance was apologetic. "Thanks. I'll . . . let you know."

They entered the sanctuary and found their pew; there was no more discussion about anything.

Chapter Five

Now faith is the substance of hope, the evidence of things not seen . . ." Father Joseph Wells read the Scripture again. Elizabeth had quickly come to love the new rector. He had come to St. Matthews Episcopal Church two years ago. Almost from the beginning, his presence and his words had begun to breathe new life into the old building. His light blue eyes held the warmth of years of heeding a calling that had stretched his soul and mind in countless ways. He was, Elizabeth often thought, *real*. And his sermons were practical, almost personal, getting to the heart of the message that touched people in new ways. Maybe that's why so many people were coming to hear him preach, reaching out to learn the same things in a different way that touched hearts.

Today's sermon was obviously about faith, and Elizabeth sat up attentively.

Since she had started praying again, a yearning had started pulsing within her, a restlessness she couldn't explain. Elizabeth had always been perfectly content with the romantic ideals of her religion, but since she had started an ongoing dialogue with God, she knew something was missing.

"On a visit to the Chesapeake Bay a few months ago, a friend took me out fishing, someone who is a member of this church, as a matter of fact. He asked me not to reveal his name. I told him I would try to remember, but I couldn't promise it wouldn't slip out. Sorry to say, I have these inadvertent senior moments that keep crowding closer together and in the course of telling this, I may blurt out a name, so I apologize in advance if that happens.

"It was a great day for fishing; they were biting vigorously, at least in the morning. We were so busy for the first, oh, say, hour or so, we had no time for conversation. But after that—nothing. The fish must have realized what we were up to, because they left us high and dry holding on to some mighty fresh wriggling bait."

His smile was reflected in his eyes.

"I enjoyed catching the fish, but I enjoyed the conversation that ensued even more. Since my fishing partner wishes to remain nameless, I can be frank and tell you how much fun he made of my being a city slicker and how long he laughed at my, uh, lack of knowledge about the sporting life. I made him promise not to tell any fish stories about the ones that got away from me. He *is* supposed to let me acknowledge how large they were and how I very nearly had them! In honesty, on that particular day, I caught eight I could keep and two that had to be thrown back.

"When the fish stopped biting, there was nothing to do but talk. And how my friend can talk!

"Well, a little ways into our idle chatter, he asked if I had noticed the sun dogs." Father Wells's gaze swept over the large, arched room full of familiar and new faces. "Does anyone know what a sun dog is? Come on, a show of hands, if you please. Be honest." A sprinkling of uplifted hands joined the ripple of laughter.

"Well, let me tell you, I had to ask him to say it twice, I thought I had misunderstood him. When I finally figured out he was talking about dogs, I looked toward land and asked, 'Where are they? Are they at your house? In the car?' I couldn't remember seeing any animals at his place." More laughter.

Father Wells shook his head. "'Nope,' was the answer. I must tell you, by this time Hoyt Johnson was laughing so hard he was rolling, and I thought we were going to end up swimming to shore. Oh, sorry, Hoyt. I forgot you wanted to keep out of this, but Lord only knows how you could ever be anonymous." Another loud spate of laughter erupted because those who were acquainted with the gregarious Hoyt Johnson knew that was futile. The rector gazed down with an uplifted hand toward the man in question. "Please forgive me. But you're an integral part of this story." He chuckled. "Well, I won't leave you in suspense. My friend, who is no longer nameless, pointed to the sky and said, 'Look. Look up there, next to the sun. Hold your hand up to block out the sun if you have to, and look to the right. See, there, a little farther down. There's two more. See?'

"I looked where he was pointing, but I had no idea what he wanted me to see. A sun dog in the sky sounded pretty strange. At first I thought he was making a joke, but no—he was pointing and looking up and he was being serious.

"'Hoyt,' I finally asked, 'what am I supposed to see?' He looked at me like I must have something wrong with my hearing. 'The rainbows,' he said very patiently. He started talking more slowly and louder, perhaps thinking I might understand better. And his voice was incredulous that I would ask what I was supposed to be seeing when they were right there in the sky, sitting there plain as the nose on my face.

"He explained what a sun dog was. 'See, those are thin cirrus clouds. When those clouds are twenty-three degrees from the sun at the same elevation, sunlight will hit the ice in the clouds and make little rainbows. Any waterman knows that a sun dog in the sky means the weather's going to change within forty-eight hours. Kind of like a warning. And a promise. Enjoy the day because change is on the way.'"

Father Wells paused, eyes twinkling. "Obviously, I'm not a waterman. I had never heard the story of sun dogs before, but I was charmed. When we motored up to the Johnson dock, our wives came down to greet us. I immediately wanted to share my new knowledge and impress my partner in crime—er, make that life. My wife, as some of you may know, also grew up in the city, so I knew she had never heard of sun dogs. 'Estelle,' I asked, relishing my new knowledge, 'did you see the sun dogs?'

"She looked at me with that look of superiority wives sometimes get and said, 'Yes, I did. Very pretty.'

"I was merely going to nod and keep quiet, but Hoyt walked up behind me and announced, 'Joseph had never heard about our sun dogs, but he has now. So he'll be able to look for them and predict the weather.'

"My wife gave me a knowing look and turned to Hoyt. 'No, he won't.'

"'Sure he will,' Hoyt insisted, but he was obviously puzzled. I can't say as I blame him. My wife has kept me puzzled for years. But in this case, she knew what she was talking about. Estelle, with the sureness of our thirty-five years together, again shook her head and said with authority, 'No, he won't.'

"Hoyt was quick to take up for me yet again, when my wife interrupted to finally explain something few people know, because it's simply not important. She said, 'Joseph didn't see the sun dogs today, and he won't see them next time. He's color-blind, has been for what, fifteen years now, dear?'

"We grinned at each other and I nodded. It was about that long ago when I had severe and unexpected eye inflammations that unfortunately damaged my ability to see color. I see perfectly, but life is like a black-and-white television set. In the lingo of current business practices, you might say my eyes got downgraded." He grinned, enjoying the familial intimacy of shared laughter.

"But that didn't stop me that day. Everywhere I went and saw people I knew as well as plenty I didn't, I would ask if they had seen the sun dogs. Since I was in waterman country, the majority of them already knew, but I had a wonderful time anyway, talking about what the weather might do. And there were a few, from the city I guess, whom I was able to share new knowledge with. I had a wonderful time.

"As I often do, I let Estelle read my sermon—to get her reaction, to see if there's anything I've left unclear. Also, whenever she is a part of the sermon, I generally like to let her know about it in advance. I've found that is generally better for maintaining a harmonious relationship." He waited for the chuckles to end.

"She read it, looked at me, and had two things to say. The first was 'Why?'

"'Why what?' I asked. She wanted to know why I was so delighted to tell people about something I couldn't see. And the next thing was, she felt it was unfair the way I glossed over the part about losing the ability to see color, portraying it as unimportant." His expression sobered.

"Well." His face grayed slightly with darkness only he knew, and he looked, seemingly, at every person in the church. "In all honesty, when it happened I was devastated. It was a rare time when I was in between parishes. I had been prayerfully seeking God's direction as to what I should do, where I should go to serve Him most effectively. One day my vision started blurring slightly, and after only a day I went to the doctors, who in turn were puzzled. Let me tell you, that is a scary situation when your own doctors don't have a clue! They set up testing for the very next day to try to figure out just what was going on. But as I slept, my world became as colorless as night.

"The shock was enormous, but nothing compared to how I felt when I discovered the doctors could do nothing to bring back the color in my life." Father Wells shrugged. "'Sorry,' they said. 'We'll monitor you from time to time to see if anything else may be going on, but just be thankful you can still see. Life isn't so bad.'

"Well." Father Wells looked stern, his normal smile turned upside down, and Elizabeth could feel the bleakness, the desperation in that memory.

"I wasn't thankful. Fury, rage, and any other emotion you care to imagine ripped through me. It was definitely not all right, and all I could do was tell this, scream this, to God over and over and over again."

His eyes were downcast as he confessed, "It didn't take very long to become the kind of person I don't care to be around. And I was like that for far longer than I care to admit. I only thought about my loss, how awful and terrible and unfair it was."

Gazing into the sympathetic and attentive eyes of his congregation, Father Wells's face slowly brightened, like the sun parting through shadowed clouds. Elizabeth was holding her breath.

"Finally, a dear friend, Father Albert Simmons from the diocese, came and took me firmly in hand three months after my world became colorless. He made me go with him to a rehabilitation center for the blind. Believe me when I tell you that this was the last place on earth I wanted to be, but it turned into one of the most profound moments of my life. Here were people who had started out as sighted individuals and now were having to learn to live in complete and total darkness.

"There was a young man there; he was barely thirty then, and his name was Cal. Albert most particularly wanted me to meet him. Cal had been extremely successful in commodities trading, a highly technological gambler who had become a millionaire several times over through his own efforts. As Cal told his story, he made it clear what he did in his life had never been enough. He craved more and more of the tension and stress of the competition, the adrenaline rush of almost losing, then making a fortune over and over again. But in time, even that ceased to be enough to satisfy whatever was lacking in his life.

"The money enabled him to live a frantic lifestyle earmarked by excesses. It was this extreme way of living that finally culminated in a horrendous car accident. Now his old life was over. He had to learn to start living a new life. The accident cost him his sight.

"When Cal held his hand out for me to shake, I will never forget his bright, energetic smile as he looked at me without seeing.

"There was no return smile on my face. I was livid. I was outraged that God would let this young man lose his sight, and I felt he should have been even more horrified and angry than I was. But he wasn't.

"I asked him, with my own indignation making my words tremble, 'How can you smile like that, after what has happened?' I was rude and blunt. Why wasn't he raging and yelling and screeching at the top of his lungs at how wrong this was, at this terrible, terrible loss? This man had far more reason and right than I to be furious."

Father Wells shook his head, his wonderment at what had happened next already lightening his demeanor.

"He sort of laughed under his breath, shrugged, and said it wasn't so bad. When I pressed him, he looked straight at me as if he could actually see me and started explaining.

"It was because of what happened, he told me with utter certainty in his voice, that he not only could fully understand his old life but also appreciate his new one. 'I was surrounded by people who only wanted a piece of me for the sole purpose of furthering their own ambitions,' he said. Within himself there had always been this incredible need to push forward and up, his unrelenting ambition for total success on his terms or nothing. And despite the fact he achieved so much, it still wasn't enough. That's why he continued working hard and playing so destructively. To fill a need he couldn't name. He was so focused on the next moment, the next goal, the next adventure, he bypassed the moment he was in.

"'When I woke after the accident, and realized the loss, what had happened . . . after the doctors told me and left the room, what I remember most vividly was the quiet,' Cal said. 'The room was empty, my so-called friends didn't exist, and my family was en route. For the first time in longer than I can remember, darkness and stillness engulfed me and I was able to see, really see what I had been doing. *God*, I thought, *how am I going to live like this?* Mind you, I wasn't asking God a question, it was simply a figure of speech.

"'But suddenly I wasn't alone. An embrace, like the warmth of a hug, engulfed me. It was incredible! You can't imagine how I wish I had the words to explain it to you more precisely. But for the first time in my memory, I wasn't racked by insecurities, wasn't overwhelmed by this insane desire to achieve. Regardless of what I accomplished, it was simply never enough. Not for me. At that moment, for the first time there was no speculation about what I should do next because, again, for the first time in my life I knew I was right where I was supposed to be. Where I belonged, where God wanted me.'

"Cal never lost that feeling, not from the moment he first woke up. And he's never been happier. That's what he meant when he first told me, 'It's not too bad.' He could say that with certainty because God is with him, and that makes it all completely right."

The smile on the rector's face brightened the church. "And he was correct. It *is* all right. I'm where I'm supposed to be. And just because I can't see sun dogs doesn't make them any less real. I can see them in my mind. I can see the colors in my imagination, and I have to tell you, that is an extraordinary gift. It makes me want to share even more, to let everyone know that God has everything under control. I love the story about the sun dogs; each time anyone sees a sun dog, they see a promise and a warning for change. Extraordinary.

"As I was preparing for my sermon today, these Scriptures spoke to me in new ways, and I marveled how my little story of the sun dogs intertwined so neatly with the concept of faith. Again, from Hebrews it is written, 'Faith is the substance of hope, the evidence of things not seen.'

"I can't see sun dogs, but I am excited about them. I still want to share that story—when someone happens to let me know there are sun dogs in the sky.

"I'm still charmed by the idea that God would let His children see His marks in the sky as a message to enjoy the day and the beautiful colors in the sky, but prepare for inclement weather because change is on the way.

"Are we prepared for changes in our lives? Sometimes it's only through those changes that God can get our attention. Only through those dark moments can we be still long enough to listen and learn. Sometimes change can lead us into the kind of faith God wants all of us to have. After rereading this passage in Hebrews, it suddenly occurred to me that my little story is something that illustrates faith in a way I never could.

"When I got to really thinking about it, I realized this was one of the many epiphanies that have happened in my life, when God has put together circumstances to reveal Himself to me. Sun dogs! I know they exist; I'm excited they exist, and I want everyone to know about them! That I can't see them is beside the point.

"Each of us, I hope and pray, will discover our own sun dog, a moment so filled with clarity and truth that it will compel us to faith. When the threads of circumstances we have no control over conspire to come together to make a moment larger than itself. They are out there, if we look for them with our eyes and hearts open. God is faithful and we are only asked—simply—to reciprocate. I pray each of you will find your own moments of faith—your own sundog moments. Amen."

⌒

They stood to recite the ancient Nicene Creed from the Book of Common Prayer; Elizabeth's face was softened by the glow she felt from listening to the sermon, and she couldn't wait to go out and search the skies. Father Wells always had a telling story, a personal anecdote to emphasize a bit of Scripture, to somehow make God real. She thought it was wonderful. Throughout the rest of the service, the Communion and the ending prayers, the story kept replaying in her mind and she thought, *He's made faith so much more accessible.*

Following the choir's recession, Elizabeth followed the others outside, conscious of Michael's firm grip on her arm.

People stood in line to speak to Father Wells, and while she waited her turn Elizabeth scanned the skies. Clear and eggshell blue. When the rector caught sight of Elizabeth, he flung open his arms. "Elizabeth! I've missed you. I hope your vacation was wonderful," he said, giving her a brisk hug. Her smile faltered a bit as she realized again that he had not been told.

"Father Joe, what a wonderful story," she said. "I just loved it."

"I had no idea you were color-blind," Carol said, her voice deep with sympathy. "It must be horrible. But you're always so nicely dressed. How on earth do you manage?"

His eyes twinkled as he gestured to his wife, who was standing and laughing with some other couples farther down the sidewalk. "My lady over there. You see, that's one of the ways she makes me toe the line. If I don't, she's threatened to make *me* look like a mismatched rainbow."

Their laughter drew Estelle Wells closer. She had been standing well within earshot of what her husband had just said. She shook a finger at him and chided, "Telling lies about me again? God'll get you for that, Joseph, shame on you." Her grin matched her husband's as she slid a hand through his.

"Now, dear, it seems to me you *have* uttered that threat against me a time or two."

"Gee, I don't recall," Estelle deadpanned, eyes crinkling as she looked up at him. "I do have one admonishment for you right now, though." She tried to eye him sternly but couldn't keep her mouth from quivering. "Stop gossiping!" She gracefully moved on to speak to others lingering on the grounds of the church.

"I guess she put me in my place," Joseph Wells murmured to no one in particular as he watched her walk off, his eyes amused.

"Gordon, why don't you drive Carol over, and Michael and I will meet you at Brenner's?" Elizabeth suggested casually as they neared the parking lot.

No one had a chance to say anything before Carol took control of the moment.

"I've got a better idea," Carol announced firmly, wearing a tiny smile as flat as her voice. "I'll drive Elizabeth over because she and I need to have some serious girl talk." She quickly moved to where Elizabeth was standing and firmly took her arm. "Don't worry, Michael, I won't let her fall on anything but me."

Then, without listening for an answer, she led an astonished Elizabeth toward her black sports car. "Get in, dear," Carol ordered as the smile disappeared. Elizabeth did as she was told, confused. As soon as Carol got in, Elizabeth turned. "What on earth is the matter?"

Instead of answering, Carol gunned the car out onto the road and quickly shifted into high gear as she sped away.

When she spoke at last Carol's voice was tired but angry. "I told you before, I don't want to be part of a foursome. Ever. Did you forget?" Her voice was like ice.

Stung, Elizabeth gaped. "This isn't a foursome! It's a . . . a chance meeting among friends. I didn't know Gordon was coming today. You, Michael, and I were going to brunch, remember? I suppose I should have just said, 'So long, see you later, we're going out to eat, but we're not inviting you because my cousin doesn't want to be around you or anyone else who happens to be male.' Is that what I should have done? Come to think of it, I suppose I should tell Michael to go home and leave us alone, too. Is that what you want?"

Carol punched the gas as the car darted onto the interstate. "You always were a rotten liar." Carol ignored the logic of what Elizabeth said.

The silence grew until it became too loud to ignore. Elizabeth suddenly was drained, that brief burst of anger having evaporated the energy that had been humming inside her since the service.

"Fine. Whatever you say. I'm sorry you misunderstood. And I promise I won't do anything like that to you. But I didn't this time. For the record, this wasn't planned. I really, really didn't know he was coming." She waited until Carol pulled up to the valet parking before she asked tentatively, "You are going to at least eat with us, aren't you?"

Carol drummed her fingers on the steering wheel as she waited impatiently for the attendant to come around the car to get the keys. She shook her head. "I'm not staying." Then, to the attendant, "My friend needs to be escorted to the restaurant, she has a walking impairment. Friends will be meeting her soon." She handed him the twenty-dollar bill she had just dug out of her purse. "See that she gets there safely."

"Absolutely," the young man said, hurrying around to the passenger side.

"Carol." Elizabeth couldn't believe it. But before she could say more, she was already being helped out of the car. She belatedly bit her lip as she watched the little car fly away.

"Ma'am?" The attendant held out his arm. Exasperated, she knew there was no choice but to be escorted into the building. She would have to wait for the others. Impatiently, she wondered how she was going to fix this.

⌒

Within her elegant house in the city, Carol stayed in constant motion. It had been that way ever since she'd left Elizabeth at the restaurant. She refused to think any more about it, which was her way of coping with most things these days. She just didn't want to think, because thinking might lead to feeling.

Since that moment when her schmuck of an ex-husband betrayed her, she had ceased to think beyond the moment she was in. Feelings were not allowed because they were just too dangerous. Action had replaced thought; first, the divorce—getting everything she wanted, and then coming back home to her roots. Everything else was coasting.

One more abdominal crunch, then another and another . . . then she jumped up and reset the treadmill for another mile. She alternated. When she got too tired, she'd stop awhile and read some pleasantly boring nonfiction self-help book that inspired no passion.

She easily avoided the computer terminal set up for God knew what reason. She had no intention of writing again; that would involve thought that would provoke . . . other things. She purposely kept herself too busy for any serious thoughts to snag her soul. She paused at different moments to pour another glass of wine.

Through the late afternoon, as the sun started its slow descent westward, Carol kept to this routine, until the front doorbell buzzed loudly. And then again. And again.

Annoyed, she looked through the glass surrounds of the front door and her face darkened visibly.

"I don't want any visitors," she said tersely, only slightly opening the door, staring at Dr. Gordon Jones carrying two large Styrofoam boxes.

"I'm here on a mission of mercy," he informed her with the friendliest of smiles. "You didn't want to eat with us, but that's okay. You still have to eat and from what I can see, you haven't been doing much of that. Now, I'm just the delivery boy. Let me drop these off, and I'll be on my way."

She looked at him and was prepared to send him on his way with the boxes in hand, but a whiff of something delicious stopped her— *Was that eggs with garlic?*

Her stomach growled loudly, suddenly making her remember she had not eaten anything today beyond morning toast. There hadn't been much eaten yesterday either, come to think of it. Delicious scents were making her mouth water.

But she was suspicious. "Do you promise you'll just drop them off and leave?"

"Scout's honor." He nodded. She thought she smelled hot buttered toast; was that roasted potatoes? In a decisive gesture, she flung open the door.

"You probably were never a Scout," she muttered, letting him pass, following closely behind him, the tantalizing smells of food beckoning.

Gordon walked in through the foyer and took a left, heading through the yellow dining room, guessing correctly the kitchen was toward the back.

Carol frowned, wondering why she hadn't stopped him at the door and simply taken the boxes.

A few more steps and he set the food down on the kitchen table. His glance took in the natural tones of granite counters, the matching island, and the well-equipped kitchen. "Nice." He smiled, approving.

He turned as she walked toward him. "Now, I didn't bring coffee," he said with apology. "Would you like me to brew some?" His manners and his polite gesture weren't expected.

The shake of her head was decisive. "No, but thanks, this is more than enough. And after all, you have to be on your way . . . remember? Scout's honor?" She watched in disbelief when he began opening cabinet doors to find a plate, which he set out on the table, next to the boxes. Another foray into the drawers and he placed the fork, knife, and spoon next to the plate.

"Do you have any juice? I'll pour," he offered and then added with a wry smile, "You were right, I was never a Scout."

"Scout or not, it's time for you to leave, Gordon." She started toward him and watched him put up his hands.

"Fine. Just give me a minute. I've got two things to say to you." He watched as she stopped in front of him and folded her arms, irritation highly visible in that stance. He noted the irritated face that reflected the body language.

"Well?"

He drew in a long breath and let it out. "I did not. Elizabeth did not. You misconstrued."

She never blinked. "I misconstrued?"

He leaned against the counter and she wondered how he could seem so at ease, knowing he wasn't wanted.

"There was no setup. She didn't know I was going to be there. *I* didn't know I was going to be there until last night when I got the call from my friend asking if we could switch."

Her eyes narrowed as she examined his face and saw no deceit, but that was irrelevant. She knew some of the best actors in the world and how they could lie. Her ex-husband was one of them. "How do I know you aren't just a good liar?" she asked, trying to push Elizabeth's startled face out of her mind.

"You'd have to get to know me better"—he smiled—"but you've just gotten a divorce. You're not ready for a relationship. And neither am I, frankly. So, if you want to get to know me, it will have to be strictly as friends, absolutely nothing more." He continued looking at her, his hands now resting easily on the counter behind him.

"You just had a divorce, too?" Surely Elizabeth would have mentioned it—or maybe she would have if given the chance, Carol thought a little guiltily. She suddenly realized that although his name had been mentioned throughout her lifetime as someone she had once known, she didn't know the first thing about him now.

He answered her question by shaking his head. The statement was quiet. "No. Allison died fourteen months ago. Cancer."

Carol felt the air being knocked out of her with that one horrible word. One hand caught the top of a ladder-back chair as the other pressed hard against her heart, and she felt so sorry, but that was okay. It was a neutral emotion that didn't drag her spiraling downward because it was directed at someone else.

Her voice was direct and sincere. "I'm so sorry, Gordon, I had no idea! I . . . you must think I'm an idiot. I don't know what to say. I'm so sorry . . ."

"Nah, don't be. I'm sorry enough for both of us. And I don't think you're an idiot. I think you're hurting, perhaps in a different way, but pain is pain. Don't worry about me, I'm okay." She wondered again at his calmness. His words really touched her.

"You're . . . okay?" Again there was that steadiness that intrigued. Was it possible to get through such misery and survive?

His answer was slow and thoughtful. "It's okay. I've gotten over the shock of no longer having her. Sort of." There was the lopsided grin. "Allison and I, well, we had a few years, really good years, despite fighting the disease. That part's all right. I do miss her. I don't think that will ever change."

His voice was direct, without shading. It was as he said it was and no more. No actor or liar could do that.

"Here, sit down. I'll make us both some coffee. While it's brewing will you forgive me for eating this wonderful food you brought, or will you share some . . . no?"

"Thank you, no. Coffee would be wonderful." He sat down.

She made precisely two cups, thinking their conversation would last that long and no more. The wall clock had ticked off fifteen minutes when Carol was finished eating and most of the coffee was gone. There had not been much conversation. Carol touched her lips with a napkin. "You said there were two things you wanted to say to me?" she reminded him.

He sat a little straighter and cleared his throat. Carol watched, fascinated as the doctor changed into the teacher beginning a lecture.

"A doctor in practice for any length of time sees this one thing over and over. When a person suffers a deep emotional shock, and I know this sounds sexist but this happens to women far more than to men . . . the one sure thing we can expect is the likelihood of a major illness or health problem within six months or so. It might be cancer or some other serious health catastrophe. I can't tell you the number of times over the years I've seen this. One of my patients becomes a widow, then bam! Six to ten months later all hell breaks loose with her body." His look was meaningful.

Clearly she was missing the point. "I wasn't widowed." She shrugged.

He cleared his throat. "The point is that it's pretty easy so see you're carrying around a truckload of anger. That and the stress of a divorce, especially one that's had so much publicity—it's not healthy. I know I'm not your doctor, but your mother has been telling my mother about you for years. You're a legend in my family, so I, uh, simply want you to take care of yourself." He produced a card from his pocket. "This is a psychologist I would recommend. She is, I think, a gifted doctor. She really helped me when I needed help to sort things out emotionally."

Carol looked at him intently. "You mean needed help to get over your wife's death?"

He nodded and then there was that crooked smile again. "That, and help to get past the idea of trying to join her."

Carol's fingers tapped the card thoughtfully. If her impression of him was correct, he had the most uncomplicated face she had ever seen. She made a snap decision.

"I'll put on some more coffee."

~

Later that night, Elizabeth rested against the white-laced pillows, watching Michael get ready for bed.

"Do you think Carol is going to be all right?" she asked.

He shrugged. "What do you mean? She's the same as she's always been. Only a whole lot richer."

"No, that's not what I mean. I couldn't believe she wouldn't even eat with us today. I don't know where this is coming from; she's so suspicious. I mean, we all could have had a nice time, chatting about things. Talking about that wonderful sermon Father Wells gave today."

Michael walked into their bathroom without saying a word. She sighed. Carol was of no interest to him, she knew, but still . . . She glanced at the clock. It was after ten, but she was tempted to call her just to see what she was doing. They used to call each other any time of the day or night; they had been so close.

Elizabeth jumped as the phone rang.

"Hello?"

Carol's breathless voice rushed over the line like a strong breeze. "Elizabeth, sorry I'm calling so late but Gordon just left. I wanted to apologize for being so snotty today. I had my reasons, but, oh well, I wanted to thank you for sending him over with the food. It was wonderful! I had no idea I was so famished until he showed up on my doorstep with that heavenly Greek omelet and the bread. It was the best I've had anywhere . . . or maybe everything tasted so great because I was hungry. Oh well, what? You didn't send him over with any food? Well, even better. No, never mind, I'll call you later this week and we'll get together. Bye."

Michael walked back into the bedroom and saw her surprise. "Who was that calling so late?"

"Carol."

"Oh." He slid into bed.

"Gordon went to see her, took her some food I guess from the restaurant and . . . he just left. He was there for hours. What do you make of that?"

"Nothing. He's a nice guy. Nice guys do nice things for people, deserving or not," Michael said, turning off the lights. "Come here." He kissed her. "I'm much more interested in doing nice things for you," he murmured, letting his hands slide over her, and she responded in kind.

All thoughts of Carol and Gordon evaporated as the heat began building between them. Their lovemaking was slow and measured and as fulfilling as ever; it took a conscious effort, but Elizabeth ignored the bruises that had started to darken on her leg from the fall earlier that day, concentrating only on giving and receiving pleasure. Consequently, both of them slept very well that night.

Chapter Six

Adrienne and Ian Moore sat in the hospital room, not quite understanding how they had got there. Just like Michael and Elizabeth, they were trying to understand something that had just swept their old life away like yesterday's news. The changes facing them were more intense and immediate. And completely out of their control.

Ian and Adrienne held hands and listened, trying to understand what the doctors—these experts in a field that had little information—were saying.

The diagnosis? Spinal muscular atrophy. On the list that belongs to the muscular dystrophies, one of forty different neuromuscular diseases made famous by the annual Jerry Lewis Labor Day Telethon. Adrienne was now one of Jerry's kids.

Dazed at the label, she couldn't focus. How on earth could this be happening to her? There had been no loud explosions, no gritty smoke, and yet the world as she knew it had just been destroyed.

The quiet intensified, as if gravity had expanded itself to push on their shoulders. The doctors made their announcements efficiently and would have answered any questions if the couple had been able to think. Within a very few moments, the men in white lab coats left. Not one of them had looked him or his wife in the eye, Ian noticed. Their clinical explanation, he thought, was basically worthless, because nothing could explain *this*.

SMA was an inherited genetic disorder they had never heard of. The doctors explained that if both her parents were carriers of this defective gene, then she would have a one in four chance of developing it between the ages of eighteen and fifty. She was fifty-five.

She had never known her birth parents because she had been adopted. It was assumed she was from hardy stock because Adrienne had enjoyed wonderful health all her life. Indeed, she was the picture of what doing all the right things will bring you. Tall and sturdy, exercise was as much a part of her as breathing. There had been no notice, no whisper of a clue that something like this could happen.

Adrienne's personality would never allow her to be anonymous. She was gregarious, spontaneous, and extremely direct. For years she had been a lobbyist for noble causes, racing up and down the halls and offices of Congress, bartering, battering, cajoling, and trading to get legislation through that would benefit women, children, and mothers.

That she had effected change made her highly respected, which mattered more than the relatively modest salary she earned. Unlike the other powerhouse lobbyists with Goliath bankrolls behind them from tobacco, alcohol, and pharmaceuticals, her salary was strictly funded through nonprofit organizations that were high on cause and low on cash.

The booming economy still left the lower, unskilled labor market far behind while making everything cost more, a dichotomy that continued to fuel her passion for justice. It was infuriating that the chasm kept widening, always stretching out of the reach of honest, hardworking citizens who had no voice in government other than a single vote.

Adrienne had been married before to a lawyer. Graduating with degrees within weeks of each other, they were married, embarking on careers at the same time. They were driven workaholics, which was an easy reason why years slipped by before they noticed their lives had been racing in two different directions. The relationship had ceased existing over that time. Twelve years ago it had been a midlife crisis—his—that had freed her.

Adrienne was mildly sorry about the divorce, but once single again, she made up her mind to try some new things. She signed up for a college evening class with a literature professor named Dr. Ian Moore.

His amused baritone voice made her laugh, and she very much enjoyed discussing the works of American poets, past and present. Dr. Moore immediately noticed her because of her quick mind and what she brought to the class in the way of insightful questions and comments. She wasn't there to fulfill a requirement; she was there because she wanted to be. He found her as refreshing as a brisk shower on a hot summer day.

It was inevitable they would meet for coffee. She had been amazed when he told her he had never married. "No one ever interested me as much as the stories that have already been written," he explained with disarming frankness, "until now."

His ways were courtly, that of a gentleman seeking to endear himself to his lady. Somehow they created something bigger than themselves. Adrienne had never dreamed such a relationship was possible. Ian had read of lives being interwoven so magically with love and was incredibly grateful it had finally happened to him.

Because work schedules were chaotic, this couple found their time together precious. He might have a night lecture when she was at home, or he might have a free afternoon while she had to work late. After a year, they married. "Soul mates, united for eternity," was Ian's toast at the wedding reception.

During those early days, work remained within the frantic world of the interstates and highways snaking around the college and the District. They stayed married and devoted inside the confines of the Beltway, an area surrounding the most powerful government on earth, a geographical area that held mores and values distinctly and narcissistically its own. It was not an atmosphere conducive to exclusive monogamy and commitment. There was too much power, too much wealth, far too many egos, and the basic rhythm was one of constant change.

Spinal muscular atrophy. Rare. It was rare for children to develop it and even more rare for adults. But it happened. They had listened to the diagnosis intently as the doctors told them everything they knew, which was precious little. The voices had droned on without emotion, clinical in detail, but devoid of humanity or hope. For adults, the onset was usually slow. It was the motor neurons, in charge of voluntary movement, that would eventually atrophy, disintegrate. No, there was no medication, although they should look into clinical trials taking place. But research was racing toward more and new information. Treatment, if not a cure, would be a matter of time, they assured the silent couple.

"How long a matter of time?" a hoarse Ian asked.

The doctors shook collective heads. "We can't say," one said, "but it's also a matter of money for research, as well as time."

Left alone, the couple did not speak. Moments passed as scattered thoughts fell silently like discarded dreams. Finally, Ian, breathing heavily and licking dry lips, faintly quipped, "Well, love, I always knew you were an original. I just had no idea how unique." The smile never got past his lips, and he realized he was trembling from the effort it took to remain calm. He heard her draw in a quick breath, followed by a slight chuckle rolled into a sob.

Then they were holding each other, crying hard, and easing their hurt by sharing it. Tears mingled until there was nothing left. They still held each other as a calmness settled over then.

"You look like hell," Adrienne murmured, snatching up a tissue and blowing her nose.

Ian grinned, his eyes still red, but steadier. He took the Kleenex that was offered. "Then we are a pair, Dree. We are a pair."

He looked around the tightly efficient room and suddenly felt claustrophobic. His hand grazed her arm. "Let's blow this joint. Want to go down to the coffee shop?"

"Sounds divine." He helped her out of bed, as best he could, and settled her awkwardly in the wheelchair. "Bring the crutches. I'll use them once we get there," she told him. She settled herself into the chair, rearranged her robe, and then put her hand on his resting on the back of the chair. "No speeding. Promise?" Her smile was wavering, and he tried to keep his own from trembling.

He cleared his throat. "I'll try to hold it down to the limit, ma'am," he promised and then gripping the handles; the wheels started moving slowly.

She insisted on using the crutches to get inside the crowded shop. Ian bit his lip, forcing himself not to help her, knowing that was the last thing his strong, independent wife wanted. Or needed. A harsh sigh of relief was the only sound he made when they sat down. "Let me go to the counter. What would you like?"

She looked at him, feeling very worn from this little bit of exertion. "You can do it this time. Next time I'll be the one to get our coffee," she said, a stoic certainty in her voice and face.

"Of course." He shrugged. "One of the things I've always liked about you is the way you insist on waiting on me, eager to fulfill my every whim."

He grinned, hearing her giggle. It was as ludicrous a statement as he'd ever made.

In moments, he placed on the table Styrofoam cups of hot black coffee for both. Adrienne warmed her hands over it before she took a sip. She looked her husband in the eye. "I'm going to get better. I'll beat this thing."

"Of course you will." He nodded.

Her confidence faltered. "What if I can't?"

He stretched out a strong hand to cover hers. "Then you don't. And we will adjust. They said . . . this disease, it's slow when it happens to adults. You—we—will be just fine." It was left unsaid that if it were slow, why was she having so much trouble walking? They were handling all they could right now.

Her mouth crinkled, and even though there were tears behind the smile, she asked, "How do you always know just the right thing to say?"

He considered this seriously and then gave her a conspiratorial wink. "I'm an English teacher. After reading all the best literature in the world, I hope I'd be able to come up with some humble words of my own."

Her foolish, foolish man. She laughed and said with a catch in her voice, "That's not what I meant."

"I know." He smiled back at her, wishing he could snap his fingers and give her back everything she had lost. And might still lose. Then again, he wished he could snap his fingers for a million dollars, too. Ah, if wishes were horses . . .

He cleared his throat to rid himself of such trite thoughts. "I can only say I hope I'll always say the right things to you, for you," he said sincerely, adding with dry humor, "because if I don't, I have no doubt you'll use those crutches on me."

The people sitting at other tables and in booths suddenly turned to watch the man in a sweater and tan pants laughing with a woman slapping the table, knocking over her crutches with a thunderous clang. That made the couple laugh even louder, and then when the man bent low to pick up the crutches he banged heads with the woman, who was also trying to help. The slapstick humor, spontaneous and innocent, ignited the whole restaurant into laughter, and then applause. Several people jumped up to set things right, still laughing and creating an easy atmosphere that had not existed before.

Chapter Seven

"Elizabeth, would you like to go out with me Friday night?"

Carol sounded a little too bright. It was four o'clock in the afternoon, and Elizabeth wondered if she'd been imbibing already. Her cousin was often more mellow than she should be, at least on the days Elizabeth called her or they got together. There was always an open bottle of wine or something stronger around Carol's house or in the refrigerator. Sometimes several opened bottles.

"What do you want to do?" Elizabeth asked cautiously, glancing at the calendar on her wall. That night was clear.

"It's time to give this town a kick. Remember that night I came to see you in the hospital? That's been over a month ago, and we agreed to go out and raise some hell. I'll treat everything—the ride, the food and the booze, all of it. Just say you'll be my date."

Elizabeth laughed. "That sounds like a mighty ambitious night for a divorcée and a married woman. Where, exactly, are these bars you're planning to take over?" Elizabeth's voice lightened. It could be fun. Her only complaint was being tired, but she could rest up for this, of course she could.

"Hey!" Carol ignored the question, having had an excellent idea. "What about Kellan? Do you think she'd like to come along?"

Elizabeth was indignant. "You want to take my daughter out bar-hopping? You've got to be kidding. This is her mother you're talking to, remember?"

Carol's sigh was exaggerated. "Uh-huh. And what were *you* doing at her age?" She already knew but wondered if Elizabeth could remember that far back.

"What has that to do with anything? What time Friday?" She walked over to pencil in the date as Michael walked in. "Fine. I'll be ready. Cocktail clothes?"

"Glamorous, glittery, and so sexy you'll give your old man a heart attack," Carol instructed.

"Gotcha." Elizabeth laughed and hung up. She looked at Michael, who was fixing himself tea to drink. "I've got a date for tomorrow night."

"Oh, yeah?" He smiled back, liking how relaxed she looked in blue jeans and tennis shoes. "Do I know him?"

She grinned. "He prefers to remain anonymous. But my date will pick me up tomorrow."

Michael acted impressed as he smiled back at her, catching her enthusiasm. He decided to be mysterious as well, since he knew all about this plan. And knowing allowed him to let her go with a smile and a hug. It wasn't something he had to worry about.

In a way he couldn't understand, Gordon and Carol had become friends. He always seemed to be over at her house for some reason or another. The lightbulbs in the ceiling fans needed replacing, and since Gordon could change them without a stepladder, he was in great demand. Michael knew Gordon had invited Carol to some medical social gatherings. He was glad they had found each other, but he couldn't understand what the attraction was.

He had never thought much of Carol, even though he had known her as long as he'd known his wife. In those days, Carol had always been hanging around, always interrupting, Michael felt. Since friends always surrounded Carol, he had never noticed that despite the circle in which she always seemed to be the center, she was basically a loner. She didn't relate to people on anything but a superficial level. Elizabeth, on the other hand, had never met a stranger. People would spill their guts, their most intimate secrets, to Elizabeth within a dramatically short time of meeting her. It was one of many qualities about her cousin that Carol envied.

But Michael never saw that. He just saw the cousin who needed Elizabeth more than she was needed. The fact Elizabeth remained staunchly her cousin's best friend and loyal supporter was just a burden that had to be endured.

Neither Michael nor Carol realized the simple truth about each other: They were both jealous because they each loved Elizabeth.

Whatever the reason Gordon found to be around Carol, Michael was just glad the situation this Friday had worked itself out. He wouldn't have to worry.

Elizabeth stood inside her closet, fingering dresses suitable for a night on the town. Something glittery, her cousin said. Elizabeth smiled. She could accommodate. The closet was arranged not only to maximize space but also for coordination. Slacks and suits hung with appropriate accessories and shoes aligned underneath. Casual clothes, dress clothes, then formalwear and cocktail dresses. Coats were hung at the other end, again with other appropriate outerwear. Elizabeth's style was classic. She loved finding the right outfit and then making it her own by adding unusual jewelry or scarves tied dramatically.

She was a confident shopper. When she wore an outfit it was right from top to bottom, inside out. Whatever she chose for tonight would already have matching shoes and bag, and since it was cool out, an evening wrap.

At the designated time, Elizabeth was more than ready—she was ripe for adventure. Clad in a black, tea-length silk dress, she wore the matching high stiletto shoes without a second thought. Michael looked at her feet with a frown but chose not to say anything. She wouldn't have listened because there was no way to wear anything but very high heels with this dress. The shoes had glitter to match the sparkles on the sweetheart neckline.

The front doorbell chimed and Michael went with her to answer the door. There on the front steps was a uniformed driver, hat in hand.

Gleaming in the curving driveway was a white stretch limousine. "Looks like your date decided to get fancy," Michael remarked with a grin, giving his giddy wife a hug. She left a red kiss on his cheek, whispering, "Don't wait up!"

He watched the chauffeur escort his wife, his grin tightening. "Like hell I won't," he murmured under his breath.

"These things are wonderful, but they are hard to get in and out of," Elizabeth exclaimed as she climbed into the car. Finally seated, she turned to see not one, but two companions.

"Gordon!" Elizabeth was stunned. She looked at Carol, who was laughing so hard she was shaking. "I thought you said no men."

Overcome by hilarity, Carol could barely catch her breath. "He's . . . he's not a man, he's here as m-my doctor, for quality control." She slapped her hands against her legs and then Elizabeth saw the uncorked champagne. "Starting without me, eh?"

Carol finally stopped laughing long enough to explain. "Gordon invited himself tonight, so he's not a man, he's coming for you, too.

He insisted on coming for our protection, but I don't believe it. I think he's coming to be our old man and keep us out of trouble." Again a squirt of laughter, causing more champagne to spill as she tried to refill her glass.

"She's only had two so far," Gordon said as he took the bottle away and poured a small amount into Carol's glass and offered one to Elizabeth, who shook her head.

"Really, she's only had two?" Elizabeth frowned.

Gordon shrugged. "That I've seen. I don't know how much she had before I got to her house."

"She didn't pick you up?" That was a surprise.

"I wanted to have my own car, just in case." He wouldn't say anything more.

⌒

Cary Town, a long cluster of blocks and blocks of upscale dining, specialty shops, and clothing stores, catered to every age, shape, and size, male and female and in between. On the weekend it also flowed with nightlife. The Byrd Theatre anchored one of several corners, its grand architecture a nostalgic icon from the early days of cinema. It now catered to a sophisticated film viewer, offering rarely seen classics and richly made foreign films. Although it was a highly respectable and safe part of the city, streets slicing through it led to other shadowed, at times ominous, areas.

The car rolled farther east, continuing to stop at a variety of establishments. Carol would look out the window and see something she liked, demand the driver to stop, and they would follow her in. At each stop, Carol insisted on buying everyone at the bar the house specialty, consume it herself as Gordon and Elizabeth slowly sipped, and then she would lead them like the pied piper back to the car.

The car inched farther along until they got to the Shockoe Slip, a popular area of bars and restaurants that beckoned professionals working in the downtown district to come, relax, and find company. The Slip, so named for the Shacquaohocan Creek that once flowed through the area, was a jewel that fed the city's economy.

They had actually stayed at the Tobacco Warehouse bar for almost an hour because Carol had become friendly with the pianist, who was delighted to allow her the chance to finger out some hot jazz on his piano. Surprisingly, she played with competence, even passion, with no hint of the influence of the many drinks that now flowed through her bloodstream.

They had moved yet deeper down into the Shockoe Bottom, where the upscale butted heads with a less-discriminating crowd looking for a good time. There had been a recent murder outside a Bottom's bar.

Elizabeth had not had much to drink by Carol's standards, but too much by her own. At the last place, vodka had been served and, thinking it was wine, she drank more than she should have. And didn't like it.

Elizabeth had never been much of a drinker. She had followed friends to bars in college, not because she desired an evening of shared drunkenness, but to watch. She had never understood the allure of a room filled with strangers, determined to contrive an intimacy made hazy—and thereby acceptable—by alcohol.

She wasn't drunk, she assured Gordon as they stumbled back into the car, even while Carol emitted gales of loud, meaningless laughter. When Carol insisted they stop a half block down the street, Gordon kept a hard grip on each of them, guiding them toward a bar/restaurant with a doorman in whose pocket Carol stashed a hundred-dollar bill.

Inside to the right of the main restaurant was a rich mahogany counter that was centered on the sidewall; on the back wall was a live band. The music was beating a contagious rhythm that vibrated the marble floor, which was covered with people doing a variety of dances, some moving with the beat, others to a rhythm in their heads.

At least the clientele was made up of mostly suits, Elizabeth thought with relief. Along with loosened ties was a heightened sense of frivolity, brightened, no doubt, by its being the end of the workweek; presumably tomorrow they could sleep it off.

The women seemed tastefully dressed, not much skin showing, which had not been the case at the last place Carol had insisted entering. That had been a strip club, so darkened with smoke and dim lights one could hardly see more than rotating shadows with a flash of what could possibly be a censored body part.

As she had also done at some of the others, Carol promptly ordered drinks for the whole crowd, flashing a credit card like a weapon.

"In honor of my cousin," she crooned to the whole crowd, whose applause was greedy and spontaneous.

After offering free drinks with the easy largesse of a queen, Carol melted onto the dance floor, the red sequins undulating with each ripple of her athletic body. "Whoah, what a babe!" someone yelled, and Carol was soon surrounded by partners. It seemed to Gordon, sitting at a table on the periphery with an exhausted Elizabeth, she was dancing with all of them, from one set of arms into another.

"I'm getting old," Elizabeth murmured, sipping the dry white wine she'd ordered, stifling a yawn. She suddenly wished Michael were sitting next to her. She wouldn't mind dancing a little, but only with him. He would never let her fall, she thought, and sat up as she wondered where on earth *that* had come from.

She grabbed Gordon's hand. "Dance!" She was pulling him up out of his seat. They tried to move with the beat of the music, and almost succeeded until Carol draped herself in between them, pulling a tall man with blond hair, cut to emphasize high cheekbones and a high opinion.

"Hey, guys, meet my new friend; his name is—uh, whatdyasayit-was?" Carol slurred the sentence into one word.

"Eric." He smiled down at her, an intimate arm hooking her toward him.

"Well, Eeeeric," she crooned, caressing his face and then mussing up his hair, ignoring the sudden frown, "let's sit down and have a drink, something cold and icy because I'm all hot and bothered."

"You sure are," Eric agreed, eyes bright with admiration. He held her hand as they all followed her back to the table and sat down, motioning to the hovering waiter. "F-fresh drinks, aaaall-arrround." Then she hiccuped, slapping a hand over her mouth, giggling. " 'Scuseme."

Now truly exhausted, Elizabeth felt the tap of a headache starting to drum with insistence between her eyes. She also knew she didn't want anything more to drink. When the waiter came back, she declined and insisted on only "Coffee, plain."

"Irish?"

"No. Black and straight up." Elizabeth was concerned about this new man Carol had just picked up, wondering just what her cousin had in mind. The possibilities made her uneasy, and she wondered what to do.

Carol was smiling and touching Eric Stanley, who looked like he was equally as enamored. Elizabeth didn't think Carol would notice or care if she and Gordon left. Probably would prefer it—and that only made her more concerned.

Carol slammed both her hands on the table, jostling the new drinks that had just been placed in front of them. Elizabeth's coffee sloshed onto the table. "Know what? I kn-know what! I-I know what we can do next," she exclaimed, her smile encompassing the world at that table, before fastening her eyes on her new friend. "We all cannn go back to my-my h-house and play games!"

"I'd love to play games with you," Eric assured her, taking up her hand and kissing it on top and then turning it over and giving it another lingering moist one.

Carol shrieked, snatching her hand away. "'at tickles."

Elizabeth stood up suddenly and grabbled Carol's other hand. "Come on, I need to freshen up."

"Oh." Carol giggled. "I think I need to, too," she said and hiccuped. "You boyss wait for us, hearrr? Don't go." The men stood automatically as the women left, Elizabeth holding on to Carol with a hard grasp, trying not to stumble with her.

"So, Gordon, what do you do?" Eric asked, eyes darting around the restaurant, a hand drumming as he lounged back in the wooden chair, trying to make it more comfortable.

"I'm a doctor."

Eric's eyes flashed respect as he held up his drink and saluted. "Super. And this is your lucky day, 'cause I guarantee I can do great things with your portfolio. I'm a stockbroker and a damn good one."

Gordon smiled and leaned closer. "Give me your card." He waited for the man to fumble one out of his wallet. Gordon pretended to stare at it for a serious moment and then leaned forward. "Thanks. Look, you seem like a good guy and I'll give you a call next week, but . . . I feel I have to tell you this. I *am* Carol's doctor and I won't betray doctor-patient confidentiality, but . . ." He waited for Eric's eyes to dart back to his and saw the face sober.

"But?"

Gordon sighed heavily and saw the women coming back, Carol

weaving and dragging Elizabeth along with her. "But I would *strongly* advise against the exchange of bodily fluids."

With eyebrows raised, Gordon waited for Eric to absorb the message. The man wasn't stupid and he wasn't too drunk. He was up like a shot. "Sorry, I just saw my wife walk in. Later." And was gone, fortunately in the opposite direction of Carol and Elizabeth, who reached the table just in time to see Eric's departing back.

"Where'ss he going?" Carol sputtered.

Gordon took her hand. "He got a call from his wife."

"Oh." She absorbed this slowly and then it finally registered. "Bastard! Fine, forget'im. Now, wheredoya want to go next?"

"We have to go back to the limo first," Gordon explained firmly, helping her stand up and making sure Elizabeth was all right.

"Okeydokey," Carol agreed happily, following along. They were inside the car before Gordon explained the evening was over.

"There's only one place we can go now," Gordon explained, his voice reasonable but absolute.

She yawned. "Where?"

"Home."

Elizabeth leaned back against the cushions. Thank God.

"But whyyy?" Carol wailed. They had barely made a dent in this evening, and now Gordon was saying it was over? Was that fair?

"Because the driver has to go home," Gordon explained. "Don't you remember? It's past his bedtime; it was in the contract."

She frowned, concentrating as she tried to remember about contracts. Contracts and home?

She started giggling. "Ahhh, yeah, bedtime. Otherwise, he turns into a punkin, riiight?" She waited for Gordon to nod and then with a satisfied smile fell back in the seat. The motion of the car seemed to lull her into some quiet thoughts and she said no more.

~

Michael let Elizabeth sleep late and was in the kitchen finishing the last bit of brewed coffee when she wandered in, still in a robe and slippers.

She sat down at the table and looked over at the empty coffeepot. "Make me some more?"

He got up and discovered the coffee can was empty. "Instant okay?" He didn't wait for her to answer but put a mug of water in the microwave. "Do you have a hangover?"

"No. I didn't have that much to drink. I bet Carol does, though. You should have seen her; everywhere we went she bought drinks for everybody." Elizabeth shook her head. "I've never seen her like that before. Oh, and guess who went with us?"

"Gordon." Michael set the instant coffee in front of her.

She frowned, partly at the smell of coffee as well as his answer. "How did you know?"

"Surely you didn't think I'd let you go with Carol alone?"

Her frown deepened. Not knowing what to say, she took a small sip, making a face. Bitter. She wondered if he had paid any attention to how much he'd spooned into the cup.

"He called me before, told me he'd insisted to Carol she needed her doctor to go along with both of you in case of any medical emergency, so I knew it would be all right; he'd take care of you, too." His smugness irritated her as much as his not leaving her any decent coffee. Did he think he lived here alone?

"Michael, if I want to go out for a night on the town with Carol by myself, I will. I hardly need your permission or anyone else's."

"Elizabeth." He held up his hands and then grinned. "You're a 'drown-up.' You can do whatever you like." The word was pronounced to rhyme with grown-up. The sudden memory triggered laughter she couldn't suppress.

How many years had it been, Elizabeth wondered. Kellan had not been talking long, so it had to be well over seventeen years ago. The little girl had trouble with the hard "g" sound. One day she had gotten furious at her father for not letting her do something.

"Well," the child had huffed, angrily crossing her arms and glaring. "Well, I can't wait till I'm a drown-up, and then I can do whatever I want!"

"As long as you don't forget that this 'drown-up' is going to do as she pleases," Elizabeth said archly, and then chuckled. "Oh, I miss Kellan. I wish she hadn't taken that Saturday class this semester! It's been ages since we've seen her."

"So why don't we call this afternoon and see if she has plans for lunch tomorrow?"

"Wonderful," she exclaimed, glancing at the wall clock; her class wouldn't be over for another hour.

As they chatted, Elizabeth dumped out the rest of the coffee and made herself some more, being very careful of the measurements. She munched on some cold toast as they waited out the time. They reached Kellan on the first try and made arrangements for the following day.

Later, while Michael was running an errand for Elizabeth, she went to her writing desk. She wanted to get these thoughts down while they were still fresh.

Michael. He had sidelined the conversation about her going out with Carol with humor, but she kept replaying the tone of his voice as he'd said, "Surely you didn't think I'd let you go with Carol alone?"

It had been patronizing and she couldn't shake it off. Finally, she picked up the pen.

I know Michael is protective of me because he loves me. I don't have a problem with that, but he sounded . . . controlling. No, not that exactly, but definitely patronizing. I've been thinking and thinking, and it is slowly dawning that this is something I have done. I have let him make decisions for me because I have always trusted him, but . . .

I'm a grown woman, the mother of his child, and I have enough common sense to make my own decisions. He knows that, so this is puzzling. Is it only because it was Carol? I know he's never thought much of her, but still, she is my cousin, and I love her.

He has done this other times, and I suppose since I have allowed it, the blame is really mine. This is something I must be conscious of and not let happen again.

Yes, I'll be on my guard.

Snapping the book shut, she felt better. She had no idea her decision to start taking up for herself might not be understood. How could she, when it made perfect sense to her?

⌒

The smell of coffee reached deep inside Carol's sleeping mind and with each breath brought her closer to the surface. When her eyes finally opened she was surprised to find herself in bed.

She blinked a few times to keep the world from revolving and then became aware of a pounding in her head. Her eyelids felt like lead weights.

"Carol?"

She visibly started and looked up. "Would you like a cup of coffee?"

Gordon stood there in an extra-large bathrobe, extending a cup. "Or would you rather have something to eat?" With a gesture he drew her attention to the table in the alcove, set prettily with dishes, and wonderful smells wafted over toward them. Orange juice was already poured. She tried to sit up and groaned, her hand pressing against the hammer pounding inside her head trying to get out.

He immediately set the cup down. "Here. Don't move. I've got some pain medicine. Maybe you should take that first."

Obediently, she swallowed two horse pills and then slumped back against the pillows. It wasn't long before she was ready to try again to get up. This time the procedure was slower, done with more caution.

As she got out of bed, she dimly realized she had on a nightgown. She grabbed the robe he offered and put it on.

She didn't have much to say and he let her eat in silence. Gordon filled her cup of coffee and she finally sat back, closed her eyes, and asked with a growing trepidation, "What happened last night?"

Gordon hesitated for a moment. "You mean before or after we consummated our friendship?"

Her eyes flew open, dismay flooding her face, and she groaned again. "Oh, God. You're kidding! Aren't you?" Her eyes darted around, her hand fumbling at the neckline of her flimsy nightgown, the robe untied, suddenly taking into account his bare legs under that navy robe. She put a shaking hand over her eyes.

"Carol?"

She wouldn't look at him, so he pulled her hand away and said again, "Carol?" and waited for her to slowly look up. In that brief spate of time he recalled everything that had happened after Elizabeth had been delivered home.

For his part, he'd only intended to come into the house with Carol and make sure she was all right and then go home to his own bed. Once inside she'd become violently sick. They had barely made it to the downstairs bathroom, and even then she had missed the toilet as the heaving jerked her body backward. She had ended up a mess and so had he. He wet several hand towels to clean her face and wipe off some of his clothing.

By the time they got upstairs, she had started flinging her clothes off, wrathfully muttering about the smell. He thought briefly about getting her in the shower, but the uncoordinated movements made him decide against it. Instead he found a nightgown, draped it over her head, and shuffled her arms through. By this time he was feeling dirty and sweaty himself and wondered why the hell he was there at all. Then he answered his own question.

Because she reminds you of yourself. You were just like this for hellish months after Allison's death . . .

He tucked Carol in, intending on leaving when she grabbed his hand. Eyes closed, with a remarkably coherent voice, she asked, "Stay. Don't leave me. Please?" Despair was the backdrop for the loneliness he heard. More than anything else he heard the pain.

The grip on his hand wouldn't let go. Gordon sighed. "All right. Let me get these dirty clothes off first."

He threw his soiled pants in the laundry basket and slid under the covers with her, curling up close to her as he had done with his wife in another lifetime. The irony wasn't lost on him. Here he was in bed with a pretty, desirable woman, and all he could think of was his wife. Gordon's last conscious thought was a whisper to his wife. *Allison, I miss you so much . . . so very much . . .*

Now, in the clear light of day, he wondered why he had used the word *consummate.* He wasn't surprised at her reaction because he felt the same way. The last thing he wanted to do was get emotionally or physically involved with anyone.

"What I mean," he said carefully, "is that I held you while you threw up all those awful things you insisted on guzzling last night. It's what friends do for each other." He watched a confused mixture of emotions fill her face. Finally, a small, relieved smile began to flicker and her face relaxed.

"Of course," he added with his own smile, "these sorts of things usually happen only during the end of puberty, the last hurrah before adulthood. But I guess everyone is allowed one midlife crisis. But only one."

Carol squeezed his hand. "Was I awful last night?"

"Terrible," he assured her, and she snatched her hand back.

"You invited yourself, remember? You didn't have to come," she pointed out, sulky as a child.

"Yes, I had to go along. It was the only way Elizabeth could go, who, as a matter of fact, behaved like an adult."

Carol rolled her eyes and winced. "Elizabeth's a saint. She's perfect, always has been. I thought you knew that. I'm just the opposite."

"The only thing I know is you're hurting."

Startled, she remained very still and kept her eyes averted. He sat next to her, touching her hand.

Gordon waited until her eyes finally met his. "I know you haven't gone to see the therapist I recommended. I also know you can't keep hurting yourself because your marriage broke up. It wasn't your fault. You have to know that and accept it. And stop beating yourself up over it." Perhaps it was his gentleness that undid her or maybe because she was exhausted from running so hard from the pain.

She tried to keep her face from crumpling but couldn't and then he was holding her, letting her cry and cry and cry. It was long overdue, he thought as he held her and rubbed her back and let her get out all the bad feelings, the grief that had been killing her. This also, he thought, is what friends do for each other.

Finally, there was nothing left, no more tears. Carol, truly exhausted, excused herself to shower and change.

When she met him later in the kitchen, he also had changed into the spare set of clothes he kept in his car for emergencies. She walked in feeling fresher, wet hair slicked back, and he handed her a cup of tea. "Antioxidants. Good for you."

"Thanks." Seated at the wooden kitchen table, the silence between them was easy. She glanced at him now and then, glad he was still there.

Weeks ago they had mutually decided to use each other. By being seen together as a couple when they weren't, it kept friends from wanting to set them up, and it certainly pleased their respective parents. One less stress from that department.

"Carol, I hope you won't feel I'm intruding," he started to say, ignoring her impatient snort, "but I can't help but feel I'm looking at myself when I see what you're doing. In a way, you're doing better than I did after Allison died. I took off three solid months, went down to the beach in North Carolina, and drank oceans of liquor. If I could have injected it, I would have . . . but guzzling it was much more socially acceptable."

"You?" She didn't believe it. In the small amount of time she had gotten to know him, he seemed much too settled, much too *normal* to do something like that.

"Oh, yeah!" He looked down at the cup, hoping he was far enough from the past to be able to share a little of it.

"Why?"

"The same reason you're doing it. It's great for numbing the soul, isn't it?" He glanced up, seeing her surprise. "Are you going to try to tell me that being half-lit is your normal approach to life?" She bit her lip and shook her head. She hadn't thought about it; alcohol was filling a need so she kept pouring it in. Being numb was certainly preferable to feelings.

"What made you stop drinking then?" she wondered. "Was it this therapist you're forcing me to go see?"

It was his turn to shake his head. "I'm not forcing you, and although she helped afterward, that wasn't the reason I stopped." His eyes turned dark at some bad episodes only he could see. She waited and after several moments he began speaking.

"While I was at the beach, literally trying to drown myself into oblivion, I couldn't stand not having a glass of liquor in my hand, and this one night I ran out. I suppose I miscalculated my supply, or else I was too wasted to notice. But I knew I couldn't get through the night without some major inventory. Sleeping off a drunk was the only way I slept, the only way I knew to be able to sleep without dreaming. Sure, I could have given myself sleeping pills, but I wanted the pain of a hangover, then wanted to do it all over again. I wanted to stay . . . anesthetized.

"This night I got in the car, pulled out of the driveway of the house I was renting, and managed to keep it on the gravel road, but—there was a kid on a bike and I was almost on top of him before I knew it."

"Gordon, no. Oh, no!" Carol was horrified. "You didn't hit him, did you?"

"No. But I didn't know that at the time. I had no idea he had run into the ditch to avoid me. I thought I had hit him. Instead of stopping . . ." He closed his eyes at the pain of that moment. "I was a coward, and I just kept driving. When I got out to the highway, I pulled over and waited for the cops to come. Although the shock had sobered me, my central nervous system was still shot, my thoughts still broken as I tried to sort out what had just happened. But I knew that surely the kid's parents must have seen the whole thing, must have called the authorities. I knew I'd be arrested. That didn't matter; my only thought was *I am so sorry. God, I am so sorry, Allison, so sorry. That poor kid, he didn't deserve this. God. Please."*

Beads of sweat covered his brow, the feelings washing over him as if it had just happened. Carol didn't want him to share this with her, but she couldn't turn away.

Finally, she had to ask. "What happened?"

"I drove slowly to my house with the high beams on, trying to see. I finally made it back without seeing any trace of him. I was too full of adrenaline and self-loathing to sleep. I got through the night by pacing and telling myself I—a doctor committed to healing, helping people—had not only let my wife down, but I had just killed a poor kid and my life was over. I was ready the next morning to walk into the ocean as far and as deep as I could go. And never come back."

He took a deep breath, let it out slowly; incredibly, there was a smile starting to tug at his lips. "I walked out on the beach, knowing it was all over, and then"—he shook his head in wonder—"there was that kid right down the beach! I was so happy he was there and alive; I hadn't hit him! It was the biggest moment in my life. The relief was enormous, my legs gave out and I fell down on my knees. 'Thank God,' I kept repeating to myself. I couldn't believe the kid was alive!

"He ran straight up to me. And just as quickly the relief I'd felt disappeared, because I knew he was going to start accusing me of trying to kill him last night. In that moment I knew I was a fool for thinking I would get off that easy."

His smile was wry and amused. "That was the furthest thing from his mind. Just as I had lived the night in terror, so had he. This kid pleaded with me not to tell his parents what happened; he wasn't supposed to ride his bike after dark, he had no reflectors or lights, and if I told he was going to be in big trouble." His laugh echoed the irony. "Can you believe it?"

Carol blinked away moisture gathering in her eyes and sniffed.

"No, I can't believe it. Because it's so unbelievable. You were so lucky," she said, relief flooding through her.

"No," Gordon said quietly, "it wasn't luck. Father Joe says there's no such thing. It's all grace." Gordon looked at her with certainty, and the calm that permeated everything about him was back. "God's grace."

Chapter Eight

Elizabeth got out of her car. Shivers coursed over her neck and shoulders, and she knew it wasn't from the cool day. She was dressed warmly, even down to the small-heeled boots. Was it apprehension? Elizabeth wasn't one to meet with her priest, although she certainly helped out in the church. This day, she had taken the initiative and called for an appointment.

Since hearing the sundog sermon, a question had taken hold and wouldn't let go. She walked slowly into the adjoining parish house, down the hall to his office. He was expecting her. She was a little breathless the closer the walk brought her to her destination. Shivering again, she became impatient with herself. This was ridiculous. She simply wanted what Father Joseph had, and since she believed in what he believed, it shouldn't be that hard, right?

"Elizabeth!" The smile alone was worth the visit. She settled comfortably into the chair he offered.

"Coffee? Tea? What can I get? Nothing? Fine. Now, tell me. How are you? When you called to tell me your news I lifted you in prayer immediately. You know you would have been on the prayer list had I known, but I understand why you've decided to keep quiet."

His eyes reminded her of her father's, Elizabeth thought, oddly reassured. "I'm fine, thanks. It was a bit nasty there for a while, but you can look at me and see I'm completely back to normal."

And it was true. Although she often gave in to Michael's fear about her shoes and most often wore only very moderate heels, her walking was perfect. She had no problems because there weren't any. "And I thank God for it every day," she said fervently.

"As do I." His smile was sincere. "What can I do for you today?"

Suddenly shy, Elizabeth glanced away for a moment and then looked directly at him. "I loved the sermon about the sun dogs. In fact, I have enjoyed all your sermons."

She saw his surprised pleasure and then a flush of color flooding his face as he nodded and turned away briefly to pour a cup of coffee he wouldn't drink.

"I want to know," she began. How to ask? She cleared her throat. "I believe the same way you do; I mean, the church has always been a big part of my life. I was raised in it, support it, work for it . . . but I don't have the stories you have. You make it all seem so personal, so integral a part of your life. I suppose I'm . . . wondering . . . why I don't have those kinds of stories."

Joseph Wells moved the cup out of the way and rested his elbows on the desk to look fully at Elizabeth.

"We all have our own stories to tell, our moments with God that belong to us. One might say because my job is being a priest, I'm surrounded by circumstances that fall easily into storytelling. The real reason, I'm sorry to say, is simply because I'm needy."

He sat back.

"Needy?" Elizabeth frowned.

"Needy," he assured her. "My whole life has been spent serving God, and I believe in every word of the Bible, prayer book, every hymn I've ever sung, yet there are moments of doubt; there are moments when my sureness stumbles. That's why I am always looking for God in everyday things, in normal boring moments, in the usualness of life. And because of this need to assail the doubts, because I'm looking, I see what's always there. And because of that I can stand up every Sunday and share my moments of faith. Those moments I believe God keeps giving me because, again, He knows I'm needy."

His humbleness was endearing, but Elizabeth had to bite back a suspicion he was doing it for effect. Talk about doubts. A faint smile hovered. "Does that mean, since I don't have your kind of stories to tell, that I'm *not* so needy?"

Father Joe chuckled and shook his head. "No."

"But I want to have those moments of faith. Like the sun dogs. So, I suppose my real question is, How do I find them?"

This man had the kindest eyes, she thought as he reached for her hand and held it. In a heartbeat of a moment there was such a somberness about him, she was almost reluctant to hear what he was going to say.

"When you need something, you look for it, don't you." He waited for her nod. "If you are looking for God, you will find Him, and by seeking Him you will find faith, too. But what most people don't realize is that there is a great responsibility that goes with this. It's never easy, and at times it may even hurt to be molded and blended into His magnificent image. But the rewards, the joy of knowing you are precisely right where you belong, are unimaginable. Keep looking, Elizabeth. And you will find your stories, your moments of faith; about that, I have no doubt."

Elizabeth zeroed in on one word. "Hurt? Do you mean God will make bad things happen to me?" That was alarming, but no, he was shaking his head.

"No, God doesn't *make* bad things happen; that is part of our imperfect world. But how we deal with the aftermath of those treacherous moments that belong to the world and its devious ways is how we discern, learn, and find God. A question I try to ask myself, on wonderful occasions as well as awful ones, is, Where is God in all this? Looking, searching for the meaning underneath or on top of all the moments in our lives, that is where we find God, and it is only through the very humanness of His Son, Jesus Christ, I believe, that we are enabled to do that."

Elizabeth listened intently and tried to assimilate all he said. Emotionally, it felt like there was so much, but at face value did it really make sense? She wasn't sure. All she did know was this man seemed as certain as granite of his convictions.

She shared the silence with him as thoughts flowed into new ones without a destination. Even if she wasn't brave, couldn't God help? Even if she wasn't sure she wanted a closeness that could hurt, wouldn't He be able to take care of that? After all, her life had been a gentle one, with lots of love . . . What really could change, after all?

Father Joe was silent for a moment longer, thinking. When he spoke his demeanor and tone of voice were subtly yet distinctively different.

"For some reason, I am reminded of the story of Jacob. He was a man who had stolen his brother's birthright and ran away from his crime. He had to work twice as long to marry the woman he loved because he in turn was defrauded. And he continued to work and have children with the two sisters he married . . . But there was a point in his life when he had need to see his brother whom he had wronged, perhaps to mend that relationship, to ask forgiveness. He traveled a long distance to see his brother for the first time in years, but before he got there he went on ahead of his family, spent the night in prayer by himself, and asked God for a blessing. During the course of that night, he wrestled with an angel that turned out to be God; Jacob wouldn't give up and fought all night, knowing how precious and vital that blessing was. That night was one of the few times when the boundaries between heaven and earth were bridged. Jacob won his blessing but was lame for the rest of his life. His blessing came with a cost, but it was more than worth it."

Dismayed, Elizabeth searched his face. "Does this mean I'm going to become lame? I'm not asking for a blessing exactly . . ." Her voice trailed off as Father Joe looked at her intently. For a moment, she had the oddest feeling he wasn't seeing her; he was seeing something beyond her.

When he spoke it was with an absoluteness she found frightening. "God wants to bless you and let you feel His heart. You are His, Elizabeth, and He knows your heart is searching, and He already has found you. Keep looking, and you will find everything your heart and soul needs." He blinked and suddenly he was the same, ordinary priest she had known for the last two years.

"Could we pray?" he asked, his eyes bright on hers. She nodded, unsure yet wanting . . . something more. They held hands, heads bowed.

"Our Father, Ruler of the universe and Commander of all that is good and pure, we come humbly to You with a request for this child of Yours, Elizabeth, so recently touched by illness. She wants to know You more deeply, feel Your extraordinary presence in every moment of her life. We ask You to hold her in Your arms and be with her, because she is Yours, Almighty God, now and forever. In the name of the Father, the precious Son, and Holy Spirit, amen."

A brief hug and a smile and she departed. Outside, Elizabeth discovered that somehow her eyes had been polished; everything seemed brighter, clearer . . . focused. Scanning the deep blue sky of this windy day, she wondered if anything new would happen, and where she was supposed to be looking. Reluctant but hopeful, she got in her car and left.

~

She woke up and knew immediately; her old energy was back, humming and crackling through her. Elizabeth welcomed it like an old friend. *Thank You, God, I'm back to where I want to be. Thank You; oh, thank You.*

Michael had left for work a half hour ago. The day was all hers, and she knew exactly what she was going to do with it.

Her babies! She wanted to cradle them in her arms, feed them, smile and stretch her heart around them.

A few years ago, she had not been looking for anything to add to her life, but that changed when she read in the church bulletin one Sunday morning about the need for hugs. A local hospital was beginning a Cuddles and Hugs program for premature and sick babies whose parents couldn't be with them often enough. Parents signed up their new babies for the program, which also included babies who had been abandoned and were waiting to be placed in foster care.

Elizabeth was one of the first to volunteer. The fact that she was able to help a premature baby gain needed weight and help it go home was more satisfying than anything she had ever done.

Her heart broke while tending the few babies who had actually been abandoned. She would sing and smile and love them until they were—she hoped—placed with a good and nurturing foster family. Occasionally, a mother was simply too ill to care for her baby and while she was recovering, Elizabeth's arms were filled.

She thought of this as her special ministry, though she never spoke the words out loud. Her prayers for these babies were pleas of hope that the God she talked with, that her grandmother held in such high regard, the God who was so intriguing and mysterious, would somehow make things better for these babies. It was such a little thing, and it always made her heart feel a little gladder.

On the floor housing the maternity ward, she saw and smiled at the nurses she recognized, her expression softening as she heard muted cries from outside the glass. She was humming to herself as she entered the nurses' lounge to dress in scrubs and gloves. She wore surgical masks only on the rare occasions she had a cold, but more often because the infant in her arms was sick. That part made her sorry. She would rather touch them skin to skin, but regulations and safety were the rule here.

She was nearly finished and ready to go in search of a baby when a pediatric nurse, Ann Holiday, discovered her. "Elizabeth! Hello. Have you seen Ellen? No? Well, she's in her office. I think you really need to see her . . ."

Elizabeth was so glad to be back she halfway thought Ellen Steelman would want an explanation of where she had been all this time. Or perhaps to welcome her back. Nothing prepared her for what actually was on the supervising nurse's mind.

⌒

"He . . . what?" Elizabeth, unbelieving, half rose from the chair. Surprise dropped her back into the seat. Ellen's small office closed around her as she tried to gather scattered thoughts. She was glad she was sitting down because she didn't think her legs would hold her. If someone had suddenly punched her hard in the gut, she couldn't be more winded. Or hurt.

Ellen Steelman was actually *smiling*!

"Michael and your doctors have only your very best interests at heart, Elizabeth. We all do! And think of this as not only for your protection but for the babies', too," Ellen said, her eyes sympathetic but her voice firm. "You have an autoimmune disease—a very serious and potentially crippling illness."

Ellen paused, wanting those words to sink in deeply to the woman sitting in front of her. Elizabeth was dazed, completely taken by surprise, but she had to understand what was at stake here. There was also anger brewing inside Ellen, because she had never intended to do this. Michael said he would take care of everything, and here sat his wife, completely blindsided.

"There is no cure, there are no substantive treatments. Of course, there are some new therapies, but I've heard differing opinions from friends who take them. What is vitally important is that you not disturb your immune system. If you do that, it might kick into overdrive and cause another exacerbation. That's why you should avoid putting yourself in a position where you might be exposed to germs.

"It is also because your disease is incurable that we have to consider the babies. One theory, and I know it's only a theory, says a person can be genetically predisposed to this disease. Later in life something triggers it, causes the immune system to turn on itself. Who knows whether or not you're carrying that trigger inside of you now? We have no idea how that might affect the babies later in life. We just don't know."

Ellen paused again, waiting for some response from Elizabeth. She got none.

"I can see you're disappointed. You have been a wonderful mama for these children, but we have to think of what's best . . . for everyone."

Ellen pushed her chair back and walked over to where Elizabeth was still sitting. Ellen reached out and gave Elizabeth a hearty hug. "You look absolutely wonderful; I can't tell you how glad I am that you are doing so much better." Ellen kept on talking, even as she helped her up and began walking them both out of the office and toward the elevator. "I am happy the drugs seemed to work for you. Last year a good friend of mine had a horrible attack. They didn't know what was wrong with her; they diagnosed all sorts of horrible things but finally concluded it was MS. Poor thing, she's still in a nursing home, getting physical therapy, but it looks like she'll be able to come back home soon." They were finally in front of the elevators and Ellen pushed the down button.

"Keep in touch, please? Maybe we can find you a place elsewhere in the hospital. A safe place." Ellen waved good-bye, her smile genuine and dismissive.

The elevator doors shut and two floors had already gone by when Elizabeth realized she had never said one word. Not one word. It wouldn't have mattered, though, she suddenly knew, because no one was listening anyway.

By the time she got home, the anger began burning inside and when Michael walked into the house, it was all-consuming.

She waited until he tried to give her a hug before she pushed him away and demanded to know why he had done this awful thing to her. She didn't notice the flowers in his hands; she didn't see anything but the rage inside her.

Chapter Nine

How could he do that without even asking you?" Carol was livid.

They were sitting in Elizabeth's kitchen and Carol was boiling, ready to get in the car and travel to Michael's office and punch him. Their tea sat forgotten, cooling on the linen place mats.

The incident with the babies had happened the week before, but it was only now that Elizabeth had been able to talk about it. It had allowed her time to reflect on all the reasons that Michael had given her. For the first time, she had glimpsed his deep, wrenching fears for her.

After listening to Carol rant and say things she had already considered, Elizabeth gently pointed out, "You have to understand, his heart was in the right place."

"Yeah, right in the seat of his pants," Carol snorted, ignoring Elizabeth's shocked giggle.

"Carol!"

"I just can't understand how you can be so calm about this."

"I wasn't, not at first."

"So what changed?" Carol demanded.

"I told you he was shocked I had gone there without telling him. Believe me, I was upset. I had never been so angry with him, but he walked in, his face so white I thought he was going to pass out. 'Elizabeth,' he said, 'I can't tell you how sorry I am. Forgive me, I had no idea you were going to go down there. I wanted to discuss it, to tell you why the doctors and the nursery felt it wasn't best for you to do this now . . . I'm so, so sorry.' He couldn't say he was sorry enough. Carol, we have had so few arguments; why, we always, nearly always, agree on everything. I was mad; I said some things that probably would have been better left unsaid. He let me rant and rave, get it out of my system, and then he wrapped his arms around me and kept telling me over and over how sorry he was."

She paused, finally sipping some tea. "He had his reasons, validated by the doctors—not only Gordon, but the specialist I told you about. Finally, Michael, he . . . he almost broke down when he told me how worried he is. Oh, Carol, he almost started crying. Do you know, in all the years we've known each other, I've never seen him cry?" Elizabeth said this in such wonderment, Carol almost snorted again.

"What has ever happened to make him cry? Anything?" Carol asked it impatiently, already knowing the answer.

"Well . . . not much really." Elizabeth thought for a moment. "I mean, when his parents died, first his father and then his mother, they had been so sick, it was more of a relief. A blessing.

"Then when my father died, Dad had been suffering, too, just not as long, so . . . Now that you ask, I suppose nothing really bad *has* happened to us."

Carol set the white teacup down on the table with precision, looked up, and said, "Until now."

Elizabeth didn't like hearing that and shifted her attention from Carol to the window. She saw white flakes cascading and swirling, a gusting wind making them dance.

"I didn't know they were calling for flurries," she said, surprised.

Carol barely looked. "I knew something was up. I saw a sun dog day before yesterday."

"Why didn't you tell me? I've been looking for them ever since Father Joe told that story."

Carol was puzzled by how upset Elizabeth was. "I didn't see you that day."

"Well, promise me next time you'll call, okay?"

Puzzled, Carol shrugged. "Okay."

"Did they look like he said they would?"

"Yep. Liquid color, pastels, really. And yes, next time I'll call you. If I remember," Carol qualified. "I really will try."

Gingerly, Elizabeth changed the subject.

"Carol, we've talked enough about me and my minuscule problems. I want to talk about you. What happened in California?" She had kept her voice neutral, but when she looked at Carol she saw that face closing like a door slamming.

"Carol." Her hand touched her cousin's arm. "I'm not prying; I'm simply worried. It's been wonderful to have you here, back at home, but . . . there's this edge to you I don't understand. Aren't you happy about the divorce? Or is that too simplistic?"

Carol's shoulders suddenly sagged, as if the anger were the only thing propping her up. "No, I'm not happy about much of anything. Don't get me wrong, the divorce is final. I care for him, but I also never want to see him again." The emptiness of her voice was reflected on Carol's face. "I don't want to talk about it anymore."

Impulsively, Elizabeth got up and wrapped her cousin in a hard hug. "Fine. But I'm here whenever you need me. Can you stay for dinner with us?"

Carol shook her head. "No. Mother has issued a command for my performance—ah—presence tonight. And she is most certainly having guests." A small sigh slipped out as she pushed back a stray hair. "I'm her local attraction; you know, the daughter who used to hobnob with movie stars. She loves for me to regale her friends with these fascinating and completely worthless tidbits from my life in Tinseltown."

Elizabeth chuckled and kept an arm around Carol's shoulders as they walked out of the room. In a voice of false scolding, she said, "It's your own fault you couldn't stay put right here in Richmond like the rest of us. You're the one who dared to go so far away . . . and then make a success of your life. So sad . . ." Their shared amusement was brief. Carol turned at the door, resting a hand on the brass knob.

"As long as we ignore the fact," Carol drawled, "that when I sold my first screenplay for more money than I'd ever seen in my life, I went out and bought the requisite mansion, sports car, and other frippery things attached to such success. Unfortunately, as you know, I never got great marks in math. All of these things added up to more, much more, than I had. Selling one screenplay gave the money a finite life span. Oh, no, we won't talk about how Carol had to file for bankruptcy."

She grinned at her cousin's shocked face.

"Carol, I had no idea. Why didn't you tell us? We could have helped . . ."

"Are you kidding? I never even told my mother, and you better not either. No, she likes for me to tell only the glamour stories. Then she finishes it off with the punch line."

Carol was too funny; Elizabeth couldn't help but laugh. "What punch line?"

"Carol came home because of the illicit and tawdry immorality of that sinful city, because of the infidelities and the horrendous liberal idiots—and especially because of that heathen she is no longer married to; thank You, God." Head thrown back, a hand held dramatically limp at her brow, Carol theatrically mimicked her mother but Elizabeth heard only one thing.

"He was running around on you, then? Having affairs with pretty little bimbos?"

"No. That I could have handled . . ." And then she was running down the steps to her car and was gone.

Chapter Ten

Adrienne Moore sat motionless in the family room, gazing out the large window toward the river and clear sky. It was late afternoon, and the water was dark and rolling with a restlessness she felt. She heard Ian walk in.

This new house they had built and waited nine months to occupy was a mess. Boxes of their former lives filled each room, contents written on the outside for easy unpacking, but there were so many of them—everywhere she looked, as far as the eye could see. It was overwhelming.

"Ian." She watched as he brought another box of books to be placed on the built-in shelves surrounding the fireplace. He smiled. "Yes?"

She took a mournful breath. "Have we made a mistake?"

He carefully put the box down, walked over to her, and squatted down so they would be at eye level, placing a large hand over hers.

"This is a trick question, right?" His eyes swept over the boxes and the clutter as he shook his head and thought of the last several weeks and all the changes that had taken place.

"Not really. But do you think we were too hasty?"

He sat down next to her, his voice patient and conciliatory as if to humor her. "All right, Adrienne, if you want to regress, I'll see if we can buy our house back. I kind of doubt it, though, since the family who brought their six kids and two dogs have been settled in for, what, six months." A deep, long-suffering sigh was expelled. "But I'll try." His puppy dog eyes drooped even as he tried to hide the twinkle lurking in those depths. He was so pathetic, it made Adrienne giggle.

"Oh, stop, you poor beleaguered soul." She wrapped her arms around his neck and kissed his cheek. "I'm sorry," she whispered. "I get a little scared sometimes."

"I know, I know," he murmured, holding her, comforting her, wanting her to know everything would be just fine. Even though they both knew better.

"I keep wondering, Did I try hard enough? Surely I could have gone back, I could have made it work . . . if only I had tried harder?" Her eyes searched his face.

He thought of all the heartache she'd encountered on the Hill, people too busy pitying her to listen, people flying by her to get to their own destinations, not thinking twice about leaving her behind, about how she had felt seeing herself reflected in their eyes, their uneasiness . . .

"You did more than enough. They didn't and don't deserve you." She took small comfort in this, but still couldn't shake the doubts.

"You know, in the paper today, I read that a new congressman is being sworn in. He's a quadriplegic . . . Maybe that will set a new tone; maybe if I went back and tried again . . ." Her voice trailed off at the quick shake of his head.

His voice was firm. "We are retired. There is no going back in our lives, only going forward. And don't think we won't have plenty of adventures here, my girl. You just wait and see. My only apprehension is—" And at this point his eyes dropped and he was silent.

Immediately concerned, Adrienne asked, "What? What on earth could make you apprehensive here? You told me just yesterday we were in God's country, remember?"

"My one big fear is that living with me twenty-four hours a day, seven days a week, you will get fed up and send me packing." He had mustered just enough sincerity to make her throw back her head and laugh.

"You dog!" Adrienne hooked her arms around his neck and they both rocked with shared laughter. Suddenly, the daunting task of opening all these boxes and unpacking a new life didn't seem so awful.

"Come, help me get these books on the shelves. And later I want to go and take a look at that splendid Gothic church down the way. We could go there Sunday?"

She considered, her face tilted. "The one on the main road?" He nodded and she frowned. "There's no handicapped ramp there."

"There's one in the back. I saw it as I was rounding the bend in the road."

"In the back? How inviting," she said with sarcasm.

"Now, now, Adrienne," he chided gently, wanting to interest her in a possible new project. "At least they're trying. Don't you think you could help expand their consciousness to see why a ramp in the back of the church is not . . . very welcoming?"

He saw her face flush, her shoulders straighten. "You bet I could! Sure. Let's go on Sunday. What do you want me to do now?" She knew what he was doing; it didn't take much to play along but, oddly enough, she did feel energized. And it helped to push away the insecurities that always seemed to be hovering in the background, as annoying and taunting as a gnat.

He pointed to the boxes of books and she began sorting through them and filling up shelves.

⌣

The small old man pushed the door open to the sanctuary and welcomed the smell of incense and aging wood; this had been his spiritual home for more than fifty years.

He needed the guidance of a higher authority every day, but especially on this one. Dr. Milton M. Meade was facing one of the hardest tasks a doctor has to face—telling a patient bad news.

Lord knew, this had happened many times since he had begun practicing medicine in this river village a half century ago. He made it his practice to rise early, eat a small breakfast, and come here to pray before he opened the doors of his office. When there were far fewer years to tote around, he had served in all the church offices diligently. Some would say too diligently; hadn't this old doctor been the reason more than one rector had left?

Oh, well, it didn't matter now. He had reached that place in his life, mellowed by years of being too right and too wrong, realizing the simple importance of doing what he did best . . . and letting the rest slide where it may.

Age had taken much from his body in these last years, putting boundaries on his practice. Now in his seventies, this had forced him to become semiretired. Hard to believe that only ten years before he had still made house calls. It was at that time, with a lot less trepidation than he had ever thought possible, he had also turned over the running of the church to younger people. That said, these solitary moments inside his sanctuary were the most important part of his day. It was here he felt the presence of his wife, dead now three years. What felt more real to him were all those years they had worshiped in this very pew, holding hands. God, where had that time gone? It had rushed right by him like the waters that rushed by this county before flowing into the bay that emptied into the Atlantic, never to be seen again. All those years gone, in the snap of fingers.

On his knees, eyes closed, his heart heavy, he put his petition to the Lord and asked for guidance in how to tell a young person whose time was stretching out in front of him what that future would probably hold.

Lord, have mercy. Most merciful God, give my mind the words to say what needs to be said, with the wisdom that only You can provide . . .

∼

The doctor was finishing up his morning hours in a brick one-story office as weathered as he was. He had built it behind his home the year he started practicing medicine, when most of the things in his medicine bag were herbs and tinctures to make patients feel better.

In his long career, he easily recalled the immense importance of antibiotics, of the inching toward the future of medical miracles and now the explosive growth of biochemical engineering and genetics. What he had seen in his lifetime was incredible. And with a memory that age couldn't touch, Dr. Meade held all those threads at his fingertips. But everything he knew wouldn't help him this day. He walked out into the small waiting room and found what he expected, the strong, handsome young man who was the boy he had kept healthy for all of his twenty-eight years.

Dr. Meade couldn't look Gregory Jamison in the eyes. Instead he waved him through the door with a quick greeting. "Come on in, Gregory. Good to see you, son." Dr. Meade led the way past the main examining room with its long tables, shelves, and counters that had seen thousands of tests conducted.

Since he had cut back his time, Dr. Meade did no testing there. He sent vials away to licensed laboratories. This is what he had done for Gregory Jamison three months ago. He had sent out the blood to be tested under the name of John Doe for privacy.

Dr. Meade had tried to talk him out of it. Presymptomatic testing for amyotrophic lateral sclerosis was of no useful benefit, since there was no treatment available—as of yet. There was no sense in it, he insisted, but found deaf ears. He pointed out in a lengthy diatribe to the boy that the test would only confirm if he had the defective gene, meaning his chances of developing it were fifty-fifty or less. Even if he did get it, he might die of something else because no one could predict when it would happen. There were just too many variables, but Gregory wouldn't listen.

⌒

Gregory had hoped for the best until he saw Dr. Meade; alarm bells buzzed and his throat tightened.

The bottom line was, he had to know. Not only for himself, but also for his fiancée, Melanie. Just her name caused a smile to crease his face, even while waiting for the disaster to be confirmed.

"Well, Dr. Meade. You said the results are back. So. What do they say?"

The question hung like an insurmountable fence until Dr. Meade removed his glasses, sighed heavily, and simply said, "I'm sorry, son. God knows, I'm so very sorry."

Gregory Jamison didn't crumple, didn't dissolve into a wash of tears, but sat there in the chair and understood within himself that he had known it all along.

"God." He could barely think. "Dammit." He had just uttered the most profound and sincere prayer that had ever passed his lips.

"You have to realize, Gregory, this may very well not even be a problem until you're seventy or so. Think of that! You've got your best years ahead of you. And all the while, research is finally getting within spitting distance of doing something. Are you listening to me?" Dr. Meade had seen the eyes darken, seen the young man look aimlessly out the back window toward the rose garden.

"How many years have you been cultivating that garden?" Gregory's voice was toneless.

Dr. Meade thought a moment, aware of the regret and stillness in this young man's question. "Forty years, give or take a few. Why?"

Gregory blew out a deflated sigh. "Your roses are older than I am." His smile was brief before he looked directly at the doctor. "You can't tell me with any certainty that what happened to my uncle won't happen to me. Can you?"

Dr. Meade wasn't letting him get away with that. "Statistically speaking, I most assuredly can! And don't forget what I said about research. And there's another thing. Just think, my boy, you can relish every minute you've got and take comfort in the fact that you have time. Time! Your uncle, God rest his soul, didn't know what hit him. If he had, don't you think he would have lived his life a little differently?"

"Would it have mattered?" Gregory didn't think so. He wondered if his uncle had lived and played so hard because he knew his life was going to end so quickly.

The doctor shrugged. "I would think so, but no, I don't know for sure. The point is to stay as healthy as you can. You work out; you take care of yourself. Your mother, whenever she sees me here or at the grocery store, tells me how fantastic that business of yours is doing, the one you and your friends started. You've got a lot of things going for you. Don't give up!" The doctor was firm.

Gregory's nod was a faint, tiny movement. "Right. I'm not going to give up."

He was incapable of keeping the most important question facing him silent.

"What do I tell Melanie?" Startled that he actually heard himself say those words out loud, his white face colored.

"Does it matter?" Dr. Meade asked sharply, sternly implying that it should not.

Gregory, slumped back in the chair, looked at the ceiling and then passed a trembling hand over his brow, raking back the hair that had fallen into his eyes. "Oh, yeah. Yeah, it really, really matters."

Melanie, with dark hair, luminous eyes that engulfed him, lips that entranced him. Melanie, who played hard and loved hard, who had stolen his heart the first time he'd caught sight of her.

As soon as Gregory knew there was a blood test he could take to find out if ALS was in his future, he agonized for several months over whether to take it. The agony of not knowing, he finally decided, couldn't be worse than knowing.

He looked out at the roses through the window. Forty years? Would he have that long before it was over? Would he have even half that long?

Melanie loved him too much to wait for their wedding vows, something he was perfectly willing to go along with. She loved him so much, wanted him so much, and since he fully intended to spend the rest of his life making her happy, he didn't think it mattered. But now? Dear God, if she wasn't willing to wait for something as wonderful and sacred as their vows, how on earth would she ever be able to wait for him . . . to die?

She couldn't. And he wouldn't let her. It was his burden.

He shuddered as he watched his future shattering and falling around him, invisible boulders that no one could salvage.

Chapter Eleven

The next year held no surprises for the Whittaker family, lulling everyone into the deceit of complacency. Collective lives rolled fluidly into busy futures. They were content.

Gordon didn't see Elizabeth anymore as a patient and at odd times throughout the year would think of her and wonder how she was doing. He saw her and Michael occasionally at church or a social function, and she looked wonderful. As he did for all his patients and friends, he hoped for the best.

He did see Carol often but not regularly. She made several trips with her mother, which pleased Julia to no end. She also made a few quiet trips to New York; there was talk of possibly creating a network series. She wouldn't say much about it, but often when her car was parked in front of her house and he was driving home, he could see a third-floor light on and knew she was in her office, writing. Gordon was glad she continued to see the therapist. He also knew she wasn't happy, that she had problems to work out. Gordon kept his attention focused on his practice and patients so completely, he didn't have to face the fact that he, too, was unhappy.

⌒

Michael was anticipating the upcoming holidays with the eagerness of a kid. Completely different from a year ago, Christmas would still be quiet, a family affair, but this New Year's was going to be different. It would include plenty of friends, lots of food and champagne. A real celebration because Michael knew he had much to be thankful for.

Elizabeth's health was perfect; he began to believe it had been indeed what Elizabeth insisted: an aberration, a moment out of time that was past and gone.

Long before they sent out formal invitations, they agreed it shouldn't be too big. The problem was, they had too many close friends. A guest list of no more than six or seven couples quickly swelled to twenty.

"Let's have it catered; you don't want to be in the middle of all that work," he suggested.

Elizabeth would have none of it. "Nope. I know exactly what I'm going to do. Don't worry." There would be lots of heavy hors d'oeuvres, plenty of wine, desserts, and champagne for midnight. "It'll be a piece of cake. So to speak." Her sputter of laughter, as always, was contagious.

"Are you sure?" Michael tried to be serious, but she almost bristled at the doubt she heard.

"I'm positive. It'll be wonderful, and you will be so proud of me," she declared, chin up.

What else could he do but reach for her and whisper how he was always proud of her and then hug and kiss and love her? And then there was always the loving back that melted him like butter

⌒

Several days after the big party, Michael leaned back in the large executive chair in his office, feeling deflated. The top of his desk was clear, there was nothing left for him to do, but he didn't move. He was staring blankly into space, reliving New Year's Eve.

He had offered to help her with the cooking, offered to buy additional frozen gourmet items so she wouldn't have to do so much, but other than discuss the menu and let him purchase the champagne, she refused everything else.

Michael also tried to get Elizabeth to at least let the housekeeper help with the preparation. All Elizabeth would agree on was to hire people to serve.

Michael's jaw tightened; he wondered how things could have changed without any warning. Elizabeth was always the detail person, holding all the strings in one hand that tied their parties together perfectly from start to finish.

She had thrown herself into cooking, arranging all the flowers, and making sure everything was perfect. And everything was perfect, but he hadn't known that the physical cost to her was too great—she was exhausted before the party even started. That was something he didn't know until the day after, when she finally admitted how awful she had felt. From the very first guest arriving until the moment the last one left, she had been the smiling, glowing hostess offering the bounty of her home, the epitome of graciousness. He never had an inkling.

She looked breathtakingly beautiful; everyone had been charmed by her smiles. He heard over and over again how impressive his wife was—his brave, valiant wife, who glowed with good health. Somehow, it had become common knowledge she had been ill and what the diagnosis was. If he had heard once, he'd heard a million times about how young and vibrantly healthy she looked—he got quite a lot of hazing about robbing the cradle. That was fine. He loved it that Elizabeth was not only beautiful, but she glowed with vitality. She was still everything he wanted; she was everything he needed. But something changed that night.

Shortly after midnight when the last of their guests departed, his wife disappeared. After he locked the door, he also discovered the servers were nowhere to be found.

He walked into a kitchen that was chaos. Sinks were filled with empty trays, plates, and cups and glasses, not to mention silverware. Garbage that had been bagged had not been taken outside, there was still food left in the dining room on the long sideboards and open bottles of champagne in ice buckets.

Dismayed, he looked at what had been left for someone else to do. With all the parties they had ever given, he couldn't remember a time when something like this had happened. Wondering what was going on, he went to find her.

Surprise rendered him motionless at the bedroom door; she was curled up in the middle of the bed, sound asleep.

This had never happened. Always after a party they'd sit and relax, talking and relating bits and pieces the other might have missed. His eyebrows rose at the dress carelessly dropped on the floor, shoes—high heels—kicked off a few feet away. This was not like his fastidious Elizabeth. Something was wrong, but he could see nothing good would come from waking her. Obviously, she needed sleep.

Sighing, he closed the door and quietly went back into the kitchen, rolling up his sleeves.

It was after two o'clock in the morning when he finished wiping down the last granite countertop. Very quietly, he got ready for bed and slipped soundlessly under the covers.

She didn't move.

~~

Elizabeth's memory of the evening differed greatly from Michael's.

An hour before the doorbell began ringing, she was at the dressing table, puzzled. She couldn't remember the last time she had ever been so tired. And she had done nothing to cause this fatigue. The day had been exhilarating—putting finishing touches on the food, the tables, making certain everything was perfect.

Now all she wanted to do was crawl into bed and close her eyes. It made no sense, none. It has to get better, she assured herself, adding a little shadow to her eyes, then applying red lipstick carefully. Of course I'll be fine. *Thank You, God, for letting me be just fine. This will be a wonderful night . . .*

Moments before guests were due to arrive, she sat on a foyer chair, waiting, wondering how she was ever going to get through this evening. Michael came from the kitchen, gave her a great big hug and whispered, "Everything smells wonderful! You've outdone yourself." She managed a weak smile, and then the doorbell chimed and he turned his attention there.

"Come in, come in. We're so glad you could come." Michael was the smiling and handsome host and Elizabeth, now standing beside him, kept a serene smile on her face, floating on the fringes of the social graces instilled in her a lifetime ago.

That's how the whole evening unfolded, with her being gracious and Michael being the life of the party. Going through her paces like a trained racehorse, Elizabeth smiled with her mouth and at times with her eyes.

She never stayed in one place long enough to engage in a lengthy conversation. That would require thought, which would require energy that had been left behind somewhere.

In the dining room, at the long tables brimming with excellent food, it was easy to limit conversation by having something in your mouth. It was also easy to encourage others to do all the talking. A frank question, a complimentary sentence, and all she had to do was nibble and nod and look interested. It was a relief.

Thank God, Carol was there with Gordon. Her cousin would understand. She would realize how incredulous, how unbelievable it was that people kept saying this one stupid comment, gushing about how healthy she looked, over and over again.

It was a lie that was driving Elizabeth crazy: Couldn't these people see what was as plain as the nose on their face? She, Elizabeth Whittaker, was exhausted.

After the comments began piling up like compost, she was ready to scream, but of course she was far too well mannered for such a display of honesty.

She hooked arms with Carol, who was sipping a glass of red wine, showing off for a small audience. Elizabeth confiscated her easily by saying, "Excuse us."

"What do you need, Elizabeth?" Carol put the nearly full glass of cabernet on a marble-topped table in the hall. "This is a great party. You've done the old man proud; he should be pleased." The small talk was annoying, and Elizabeth pulled her closer and began whispering.

"If I hear one more time about how wonderfully healthy I look, I'm going to puke!"

Carol started to laugh, then had a fit of coughing, trying to curtail any amusement, when she saw Elizabeth's glare. She finally calmed down and cleared her throat.

"But you do!" Elizabeth rolled her eyes at Carol's surprise.

"I'm so tired I feel sick. I have never been so exhausted in my entire life. How on earth could they say such a thing?"

Carol, trying to say the right thing, of course said it precisely wrong. "Aren't you glad it's not the other way around?"

Elizabeth closed her eyes briefly. She looked at Carol through dimmed eyes. "You mean . . . ?"

"What if you looked the way you felt?"

Elizabeth just couldn't have cared less. She felt like she was holding on by her fingertips to the window ledge of a very high building. At any moment she would slip off the edge and disappear.

Watching closely, Carol straightened with real concern. Elizabeth was very, very pale. "Do you want me to get Michael? Or Gordon? I'm sorry, Elizabeth, what can I do?"

Elizabeth was absolutely sure she didn't want them to know. That was something she knew she couldn't handle on top of everything else. Their worry would just be too heavy.

She forced herself to push away from the wall and paste a smile back on. "Please, forget I said anything, I'm sorry, too, for whining." She managed a small shrug. "So I'm a little tired, big deal. That's what I get for doing too much. Tell you what, could you get me a cup of tea? Something hot might perk me up a bit."

Elizabeth slowly followed her into the small hallway adjoining the dining room and nearly slipped. It was doing it again!

It had started a few hours ago, while she was rising from her chair after eating a few bites Michael had gotten for her. Odd little stabs of pain exploded at the back of her neck, rushed down her back like a jolt of electricity, and jumped out of her left foot.

The sensation kept repeating itself like a merry-go-round. She suddenly realized it kept happening each time she turned her head a certain way. The rush, the pain, the explosion, and then nothing. It was annoying.

What Elizabeth didn't know then, she would find out several weeks later. On this night she did the only thing she could. She ignored it and was very careful about the way she moved her head.

The moment the last guests left and the front doors were closed, Elizabeth turned and went to the bedroom. She was beyond numb. She was so tired she felt physically ill. She was too tired to even think beyond the moments of getting her clothes off, putting on a gown, and then sliding into bed. Her eyes were barely closed before she was asleep.

The next morning she was still tired, but nothing compared to the way she had felt the previous night.

She had wrongly assumed, however, that the servers had cleaned the kitchen; it simply never occurred to her she had not included that as part of the job. She had other things to think about.

⌒

"Mr. Whittaker, your mother-in-law has been waiting for you," his secretary said in a low, warning voice as soon as he got back from lunch. Alarmed because Virginia Mae never came here, his heart started beating faster as he walked quickly to his office.

"Virginia Mae, is everything all right? Has something happened to Elizabeth?" She was sitting there on the black leather love seat, a scathingly disapproving look on her face. He rushed in and went quickly to sit in the seat opposite her. "What is it?"

She clasped heavily jeweled hands together. "My daughter has lost her mind, and she's making me lose mine." She spoke these words slowly and succinctly, high irritation underlining each one.

Michael was almost ragged with relief. Obviously, nothing awful had happened to his wife, but she sure as hell had riled her mother. He took a deep breath and tried not to smile. "Okay, what's going on?"

"I've spent the morning out shopping with her. Every ten steps she lost her balance and began to fall, then caught herself on something or someone, laughed like it was the best joke in the world and then walked another ten or twelve steps and repeated the whole process. I am a nervous wreck. I was desperately afraid she was finally going to fall and break something." She stared at him with cold fury. "There is only one thing I want to know: What do you intend to do about it?"

She expected an instant answer and was unwavering in her belief that Michael should fix it. It was his duty, his responsibility to keep his wife from self-destructing.

He closed his eyes briefly; he would have sworn under his breath if he'd thought that would help. He looked directly at his agitated mother-in-law. "What would you have me do?"

Virginia Mae glared. "How do I know? She's your wife."

"Virginia Mae, you are really upset, aren't you?"

She ignored that. "You have to do something; she shouldn't be allowed out in public when she is tripping over nonexistent things. She's going to hurt herself."

He had not seen evidence lately of anything like what Virginia Mae was talking about. And he didn't feel inclined to have a deep discussion with her about this. He repeated, "What do you want me to do?"

Virginia Mae threw up her hands, utterly disgusted. "If I knew the answer to that, do you think I'd be here? She's your wife; she always listens to you. Tell her to—" She stopped, blinked her eyes several times, and took several deep breaths before whispering, "Start using something. I don't know, she needs, well, I don't know what she needs, but you've got to find out what's going on. And fix it."

It had been a difficult morning with her daughter. Elizabeth was in a mood to flitter here and yonder, window-shopping and not paying the least attention to how she looked. In Virginia Mae's eyes, her daughter looked like a drunk weaving up and down the wide corridors of the mall; it was embarrassing.

Yet Elizabeth kept insisting everything was fine, just as vehemently as her mother kept pointing out it was not.

Michael stood up and walked her to the door. "I'll talk to her tonight, okay? But I haven't noticed anything like that at the house."

"Then go shopping with her," Virginia Mae snapped.

⌒

Kellan was not having a very good day. When all this disease mess with her mother had started, her friends were really supportive. They were constantly bringing her optimistic news clippings, or telling her of friends who knew other people with the illness who were doing great, all following certain but different regimens.

Then those friends enlisted the help of other friends, and she still thought it was dear of them to care. When had enough become too much? She looked at her desk in dismay then at the e-mail messages winking at her, many redundant. Obviously, some buddies had discovered the same Web sites and wanted to make sure she had seen them: Cures for MS! Alternative treatments guaranteed . . . What the Doctors Don't Want You to Know!!! and on and on.

She had started keeping a file of all the printed materials that had been given to her, mailed to her, or left at the small house she rented with her roommates. It was bulging now, and the school year was only beginning its second semester.

She shook her head, wondering if anyone had actually read these before sending them her way. If they had, would they have picked up on the fact that several of these so-called sure cures contradicted themselves?

No-fat, low-fat, high-fat—each diet was proclaimed to be the absolute best for people like her mother. But you had to follow a specific diet regimen that could be individualized for you by paying just $29.95, plus shipping.

How naive would a person have to be to buy into this crap? Kellan wondered.

And what about those testimonials! All from people who had only initials for names. And then there were the prayer chains that had been constantly coming her way on the Internet: Read this and send it to ten of your friends and then back to the person who sent it, and you will be assured of having your prayers answered. Always at the end was a vague warning against not doing as instructed. Electronic chain letters! She could not believe it. Since when did God start reading e-mail?

She quickly read through a professional-looking booklet that touted the healing promises of a patch developed by a medical professional with MS. This medicine could be obtained only through an apothecary shop and then only with a doctor's prescription, even though no one knew what was in it. Actually, Kellan read this one with interest. It helped with fatigue and though her mother didn't speak of it, Kellan had heard about how tired her mother was— from her grandmother, her father, Carol . . .

A small bud of hope started opening as she read intently. Then she read the smaller print on the very back.

Possible side effects: *Stroke? Heart attack? Death?* They had to be kidding! Did they expect people to hand out money for the hint of a promise of healing that was tied directly to such horrible possibilities?

If you were desperate enough . . . A memory pushed through all the clutter. It was about that girl she'd met, the one whose mother had MS for twenty-five years, the one who had refused the feeding tubes, deliberately ending her life.

Kellan's reaction had been instant: The woman had given up. How could anyone choose death over life?

Looking over the piles of papers littering her desk and the blinking lights on her computer, she suddenly realized with startling clarity that the woman had not given up.

She had simply let go.

With sudden decisiveness, Kellan pulled the wastebasket over and swiped clean her desktop, throwing out the bulging file as well. She was letting go, too.

~

Michael walked through the back door into the kitchen that evening and was stopped by an aroma that started his mouth watering. It was a roast, with fresh spices, new potatoes, carrots . . . He breathed deeply. The table was set with china and crystal, linen napkins, and there was a favorite merlot breathing on the table.

Elizabeth entered just then, wearing something that floated. Before he could say a word, her smile made his heart skip. Flashes of memories popped up—it had been a long time since she had surprised him like this. All memory of Virginia Mae's visit that day vanished.

She took his briefcase and gave him a kiss. "Go freshen up and then come have a glass of wine before we eat. Dinner is everything you like."

It was indeed. He finished the last bit of food and sat back in contentment. "You've outdone yourself. What made you decide on all this?"

She shrugged lightly. "Just because."

His smile met hers and he enjoyed the intense attraction that had only grown stronger since the first time they laid eyes on each other. "What did you do today?"

She rolled her eyes and sighed. "Went shopping with Mother. She's getting so paranoid. Every time I turned around, there she was, grabbing my arm or acting like she was going to catch me. It was very annoying."

She picked up a piece of bread and nibbled it delicately. "So I came back here, rested for a bit, and a cooking spell came over me and—voilà!" She gestured toward the table. "So do you like?" Her eyes and voice made the simple question an erotic exercise.

Michael let his eyes roam over the table and then to his wife, looking her over in great, intimate detail.

"I like, no, I love," he said, his voice husky, and this time when their eyes met, the feelings that swept over them began heating.

They stood up at the same time, napkins cascading to the floor. It was crazy, she thought as her hands drifted up to cradle his dear head, pulling him close, loving the feel of his hands on her body, touching and exploring and giving. After all these years of loving each other, the passion never dimmed; it just flamed hotter . . . better.

By the time they got to the bedroom, clothes littered the hallway. They stood naked next to the bed. He held her away just to look at her, the sight he'd seen hundreds of times in hundreds of ways still new. With a groan made husky with desire, he pulled her back into his arms. They slowly tumbled onto the bed, kissing and exploring each other with all the intensity of newlyweds.

Much later, her head nestled in the crook of his arm, Michael finally mentioned his unexpected visitor. "Your mother came to the office today."

Elizabeth leaned on one elbow and looked at him in surprise. "You're kidding! What did she want?"

He cleared his throat, feeling warm at the touch of her hand on his face. Then he grabbed it. "You're making me lose my concentration." A kiss was in order and it was long, hard, and made both of them a little breathless. Then she nestled down next to him again.

"So? What did she want?"

"She was worried—about you . . . said you were stumbling and laughing and making her lose her mind. Those were her words, but not exactly in that order."

"Hmm." Elizabeth thought of this morning and didn't remember it like that. "What I recall is that I *was* tired, but since you wore me out last night, I thought I should keep those details to myself and not explain it to her." She poked a finger in his side hard and made him laugh.

"I didn't think I'd tired you out *that* much," he teased. Then he tickled her back.

"Stop!" She laughed breathlessly, grabbing his hand and holding it.

"You promise you were just tired? There wasn't anything else going on?"

"Would I lie to you?" she murmured, suddenly sliding on top of him and kissing his neck. He breathed deeply, surprised to feel himself responding again.

"You're making me lose my concentration again," he murmured, and then suddenly he pulled her close and rolled over, determined to make her lose all concentration. *This is what love will do to you*, he thought briefly, before he lost himself completely. He no longer knew where he ended and she began because they were one in the truest, most honorable sense of the word.

⤴

What started on New Year's Eve kept shifting and changing until it was something Elizabeth could no longer ignore. She had indeed started stumbling, even with the tennis shoes Michael insisted she wear. Something . . . odd was happening, but Elizabeth couldn't explain it because she didn't have the words. Michael had asked over and over again what was going on, and she couldn't tell him.

"Do you think it's the MS?" Worry, not anger, made his voice tight and stern, a frown of concern darkening his face; she couldn't discern the difference.

She bristled. "No! It's nothing like what happened before. No. Maybe I pulled something."

⤴

She had made the appointment to see Gordon, finally, after small things started adding up and her comfort level was dropping lower and lower. Now she was in discomfort (*pain* sounded like much too harsh a word), but it was constant and it was wearing. Elizabeth never thought about seeing the specialist; it never occurred to her that this had anything to do with the MS.

"It's on the lower part, on both legs." Elizabeth pointed to the places that had begun to throb several days ago. She wore very loose pants, no socks, and tennis shoes to visit him in his medical office adjacent to the hospital.

She was upset and baffled. "It's driving me crazy, Gordon. I have no idea what could be wrong. It feels like it's scorched, but see, it looks perfectly normal."

"What does this feel like?" He felt her wince as he ran his hand over the portion of seemingly healthy skin.

"It hurts. Well, I don't know how to describe it; I've never had a feeling, a pain like this before. Like a toothache." She frowned. "No, that's not any good."

"Does it feel as if your leg has been asleep, those pins and needles that shimmer all over as the nerves start to wake up?"

Her eyes widened. "Yes, sort of. But it hurts so much more." She looked at him, wondering. "What made you think of that?"

Before he could answer, she suddenly winced and clapped a hand to the back of her neck as her left foot shook.

"What happened?" Gordon's face was as professionally blank as a white sheet of paper. He was now very concerned.

"Something that's been happening off and on. By the time I think I should come and tell you about it, it goes away. It's very, very strange. It hurts for just a moment and then it's over."

Gordon sat back, his face grim. "Let me guess. At times when you turn your head a certain way, or even if you don't, something like an electric jolt sweeps down your spinal column and out your foot."

Elizabeth's mouth fell open. "How on earth?"

He smiled without any pleasure at her amazement. "It's called Lhermitte's sign, so named for the French doctor who diagnosed this as being a symptom of your disease."

Now this was really too much, Elizabeth decided furiously. "You've got to be kidding! How could it be? It's nothing like the problems I had last year." She knew he was wrong, absolutely, but then a thought stopped her cold: *How had he known?*

He remained silent and reached into one of the cabinets and took out a reflex hammer. Holding her left foot up, he raked the sole in different places, looking for corresponding movement in her toes. He didn't see everything he was looking for. Holding it at a right angle, he instructed her to bend the left foot away from him.

It barely moved. He looked at her and saw the fear and wished there was something more he could do. Small doses of steroids could alleviate the pain, but he couldn't do much to alleviate the fear.

Chapter Twelve

Virginia Mae was quivering, her heart hammering, nerves overloading. On one hand, she was finally doing something positive for her daughter. On the other, she felt duplicitous, which was stupid because what she was doing would only help her Elizabeth. It was something that had to be done. And now was the perfect time.

She knew for a fact her daughter would be gone all morning long to be fitted with that ankle thing, a brace to help her walk. It would take hours.

So Michael had said.

Desperate for something to do, Virginia Mae had jumped on the idea while she was talking to her son-in-law. "What on earth is Elizabeth going to do with all the shoes she can't wear anymore?"

Michael had responded in a rhetorical way with a suggestion, but Virginia Mae immediately grabbed it: This was something she could do for her poor dear daughter.

Now it was getting close to the middle of the day, and she was getting very nervous. She kept looking at the time. At first Carol, who had been enlisted to help, was too busy packing up shoes to notice, but the older woman kept fluttering around and glancing at her wristwatch as if she had a nervous tic. Finally, Carol started feeling suspicious; she hoped she was wrong.

"Aunt Mae." Carol stood up and arched her stiff back. She waited until their eyes connected. "She knows we're doing this, right?"

Caught off guard, redness spread out over the old woman's face like a guilty stain.

"Oh, of course, of course; now come on, let's hurry and get this mess cleaned up." Virginia Mae's hands were now shaking so badly the shoes crashed out of the box she was trying to stack on top of several others leaning against a dolly.

"Oh, damn," she blurted out. Her hands flew to her face and she apologized profusely. "I'm sorry, Carol, what must you think of me? Please excuse me, it's just . . . this has been a most trying day, most difficult." Virginia Mae sat down wearily on the side of the bed, shoulders drooping.

Carol started to have a very bad feeling. "Why has it been such an awful day?"

Her aunt answered vaguely. "It just has been, that's all. Come. Let's get this over with before poor Elizabeth comes back."

Instead of moving, Carol folded her arms across her chest. "Why do we have to get this done *before* she gets back?"

"Because we just do, that's all. Now, don't just stand there, help me. Please!" Desperation colored the last word so vividly Carol guessed at the reason.

"She didn't ask you to do this, did she? Elizabeth doesn't know anything about this at all." Carol walked closer to where her aunt stood. "Does she?"

Virginia Mae passed a weary hand over her face. "No. She doesn't. But don't you think she has enough on her plate without having the added burden of getting rid of all this stuff? Don't you think I know what my daughter wants?"

Carol's eyes narrowed. "Did you decide to do this . . . or did Michael suggest it?" She watched as her aunt stood erect, pulling together a haughty appearance that had always intimidated Carol as a child.

The bluff that didn't work anymore.

"I am perfectly capable of thinking and making up my own mind, thank you." Then all bravado fled as Virginia Mae closed her eyes, shaking her head. When those old blue eyes opened again they were teary. "Would you want to come home to a closet full of shoes you can no longer ever hope to wear? Elizabeth is getting her ankle brace today, Carol. She has to wear only flat shoes that tie or have a sturdy ankle strap. Now tell me, what should I do? Nothing? I can't. I'm going crazy not being able to do anything for her." A sob caught in her throat and she turned her face away, struggling for composure.

Wearily, Carol touched her arm. "Of course you want to help. We all do." Her mouth tightened, her frustration evident. "I think you should have asked her. I mean, this is all her stuff. You know how particular she is with her clothes and—"

They both froze as they heard the back door open.

Carol's first instinct was to run, but there was no time. Within seconds, Elizabeth was in the doorway.

Her cousin and mother looked as startled as Elizabeth was at seeing them in her bedroom. Her pale face suddenly became whiter. "Mother? Carol? What are you doing here?" She looked from one to the other and then saw the shoeboxes.

Elizabeth sat down on the bed, clutching the cane they had given her along with the brace.

Pulling herself together, Virginia Mae tried to arrange her features in a reasonably happy, yet concerned expression. "My dear," she said softly, "I know how hard this has been for you, these awful changes. It just breaks my heart! I've been racking my brain trying to figure out what I could do to help you. I finally decided if I could get these shoes packed and given away so you wouldn't have to do it, surely that would alleviate some of this stress." Her hands clasped over her heart, Virginia Mae waited for her daughter's thanks.

Feeling like a traitor, Carol spoke hesitantly. "Elizabeth, your mother asked for my help. I thought you knew, that you had approved all this . . ." Carol watched as Elizabeth's face got paler.

"Did Michael suggest this?" This was directed at her mother, and when Elizabeth saw those pair of eyes guiltily look away, she had her answer. She suddenly stood up, grabbed the cane, and without another word walked out. The last thing they heard was the violent slam of the door.

Before Elizabeth started the car, she hit the steering wheel hard; it was the only immediate way to vent this terrible, terrible anger. Rigid self-control kept the speed in check until she got out on the highway leading to the river. Once she turned onto those empty ribbons of asphalt, she set the cruise control; it was the middle of the day, and there was no traffic and no lights for the next forty minutes.

She was free to let the anger boil over at them, at the situation, at the *unfairness* of it all. She wanted to scream; she wanted to hit something. Consumed for several miles by venomous thoughts aimed at all of them, but mostly her mother, a sudden quick thought struck her so hard she wanted to cry.

I can't use those shoes anymore. None of them.

They were right. Her mother, unfortunately, was right. All those shoes had to be packed up. Eventually.

She didn't have to struggle very hard to regain some righteous anger: Why couldn't they have waited until she made that decision for herself? Why couldn't they have waited?

Better yet, why couldn't they let her get used to this new place before making her deal with yet another change? Of course. It had been Michael's idea, with her mother as an accomplice.

She closed her eyes briefly and forced herself to let it go. It didn't matter. They didn't matter. All that mattered was she would get through this. On her terms.

She had already crossed over Downings Bridge, which linked the northern peninsula to the rest of the state. It was a place Indians once described as the River of Swans to the north and the Quick Rising River to the south, meaning the Potomac and Rappahannock Rivers. For city dwellers in Richmond and Washington, D.C., it was a favorite place to spend hot Virginia summers. To many Richmonders, having a cottage at the "rivah" was as necessary as sunscreen. She had begun to relax as soon as she crossed over the Rappahannock River into Richmond County.

It was late afternoon of a horrible day, and Elizabeth had not eaten since morning. While she thought about different places to stop, each near the house she and Michael owned, she also decided she was going to spend the night there. The way she felt now, it would be a whole lot better place to be than home—with him. His arrogance was indefensible.

She decided to stop and eat at a place called Café Latte. She hoped the owners wouldn't be there. Although long pants hid the new brace, the cane was not something she could hide.

She got out of the car slowly, standing to let the breeze of a mild March day cool her face. She clutched the cane and walked slowly toward the entrance.

The large white clapboard building had a wide porch with two ramps spanning each side. It was far easier to go up a ramp than to walk around the front and use the steps. Most everyone used them, but that was small consolation for Elizabeth at this moment in time.

As she got closer to the entrance, she couldn't help but notice a tall woman using crutches walking up the ramp on the other side. They arrived within several feet of each other.

"Hey, there." The woman waited until she caught Elizabeth's eyes. "Race you?" She cocked a crutch toward the entrance, a smile spilling into laughter.

Elizabeth's face was frozen as she looked at the woman laughing at the joke that was on both of them. And it *was* funny. Elizabeth could feel a smile creeping onto her stiff mouth, but the remnants of the day wouldn't disappear.

A man came up next to the woman with the crutches and put a gentle hand on her shoulder. "Doing all right, Adrienne? Need any help?"

That gentleness did it. Elizabeth, overloaded with too wide a range of emotions, did the only thing she could possibly do.

She burst into tears.

~

When Michael got home, Virginia Mae and Carol were finishing up the boxing. They had little to say.

Michael couldn't say enough. "You let her walk out? You just let her leave?" He couldn't believe it. "Where did she go?"

"She was angry, Michael." Carol's reply was terse. "How could you do this to her? Why in God's name do you think you have the authority to decide everything for her? She was devastated, and it's all your fault." She practically pushed her accusing finger in his face.

He was furious with both of them for doing this to his wife. He glanced at Virginia Mae, who wouldn't meet his eyes. If they had done what they were supposed to do, none of this would be happening. Why couldn't they get it right?

With effort he kept his voice even. "I don't care whose fault it is. What I do care about is where Elizabeth has gone. You're sure she hasn't called? Why didn't you call me? She's been gone, what, four hours?"

"Longer." Carol gave him a nasty smile. "But a person has to be missing for twenty-four hours before the police will do anything like search for them. So what are you, the man who has all the answers, going to do about it? Huh?" She saw his color rise and felt delight that she'd hit a nerve. He was insufferable.

"I know exactly what I'm going to do," he said. "I'm throwing you out." Her arm was enclosed in a steel grip as he propelled her out of the room.

She stopped cold and glared. "I'll be glad to get out of here, but you take your hand off me *right now!*"

His hand dropped immediately but he opened the front door for her and slammed it shut behind her.

"Michael?" Virginia Mae's voice was distraught, her words dangling as if tied by a light thread. He turned toward her, seeing her outlined by the hall light, an old woman with uncertainty slowing her movements. "I thought we were doing the right thing. Didn't you?" Her voice faltered as her eyes filled with tears. She didn't know her own daughter anymore. She never expected her to react like this.

"Do you—do you think she's all right?" Her hand shot up to stifle a sob, and Michael immediately put his arms around her, trying to dredge up assurances he didn't feel.

Chapter Thirteen

Just because I was having a great day, I shouldn't have assumed you were, too. I should never have said that to you," Adrienne Moore apologized again.

They were seated inside the dining room, waiting for their food. Ian Moore had insisted Elizabeth be their guest. "If only to make up for my wife's sad sense of humor," he said, and Adrienne had agreed.

The tears had dried, but Elizabeth's face was cloudy. Normally, she would have been terribly embarrassed about falling apart in front of strangers. Yet she wasn't. The day's events had scraped her heart raw. She was open and vulnerable and this couple actually *understood*. She felt an intimacy with them that her own family couldn't begin to offer. After she had explained what had transpired that morning, she had received staunch sympathy from Adrienne, while Ian gently asked a few questions.

"Are you angry that they did it for you, or are you angry that they did it without telling you?" Ian buttered the hot, herbed bread that had just been brought to the table.

Adrienne nodded with approval. "Good question. He used to be a college professor," she informed Elizabeth brightly, as if that explained it.

The answer to that question required moments to sort through a tumult of feelings.

"Both, I think," she said slowly, warming her cold hands around the hot teacup.

"And why not?" Adrienne exclaimed. "It was a rotten thing to do all the way around."

Ian motioned with his fork. "Adrienne, eat. Let this poor lady examine her own thoughts. She doesn't need to hear your conclusions."

She gave him an irrepressible smile, stuck a big chunk of crab quiche in her mouth, and munched very dramatically.

Ian nodded at Elizabeth. "I can see the whole thing has been a shock. But from their point of view, they were merely trying to help. Is that how they've helped in the past?"

Her babies! She shivered, new thoughts spilling over like a dam bursting. "He has! He's taken the control away. How could he think that helps?" She looked at Ian, the question so novel she was still wrapping her mind around it.

"By 'he,' I take it you mean Michael?" He waited for her nod.

Adrienne started to say something again, and Ian held up a hand. He knew his wife; she would jump headfirst into this stranger's problems, see only one side, and have it solved to her satisfaction before dessert. But her satisfaction didn't count. Only Elizabeth's did.

"Hasn't he always done that? You said he has nurtured a successful business, you two have rarely disagreed about anything, that he is upset about your health—certainly he must feel at a loss over what to do. Let me ask you—what would you have him do?"

Elizabeth stared down at the crumbs on her plate, mildly surprised she had been able to eat. His question was huge and she tried to climb over it, around it, or under it, but finally could only say softly, "I don't know."

"Well," Ian said, taking the bill that the waitress had laid on the table into his hand. "Think about it. Ponder it. You don't have to have answers now. Let these questions nest a bit, sleep on them, and see what comes to you tomorrow. Time always seems to help me sort out my thoughts." He got up to pay the bill and squeezed Adrienne's shoulder as he left. "Behave."

"What does he mean, behave?" Elizabeth wondered.

"He knows I talk too much and I'll make up your mind for you." Adrienne laughed. "Or so he thinks. Tell me about the shoes. Even as tall as I am, I loved wearing heels, the higher the better."

"You're lucky you're tall," Elizabeth said. "Even though I'm supposedly of average height, I've always had to look up at people or over and . . . I hate feeling short."

"That's how you feel?"

"How else would I feel?" Elizabeth shrugged, irritated.

"Oh, I don't know." Adrienne looked out the window, reflective. "I hate using these crutches, but at least I can. And I know how you feel about the shoes, but when I get weepy-eyed over something, over the things I can no longer do or can't control, I try to put things in perspective."

"Put what in perspective?" Ian sat down and looked at them.

Her face was full of mischief. "Oh, I was just thinking how we should take Elizabeth to see"—she turned to her new friend—"the woman with no feet."

◡◠

"Elizabeth, where are you? Are you okay?" Michael was hoarse. For the past hour he had been alone, and his imagination had conjured up in vivid detail every frightening possibility that could happen to his wife.

"I'm fine." Her voice sounded weary, and his hand clutched the phone even tighter.

"You sound exhausted. Where are you? I'll come and get you." There was that authority back in his voice, full throttle. Elizabeth passed a hand over her eyes, more tired of everything, everyone, and in particular, him.

"No. Don't." Anger put a spark of authority into her own voice. "I'm at the cottage. I'm going to spend the night here. I wanted to let you know where I was."

"Elizabeth, you've been gone for hours! Why the cottage? Look, they told me you were upset. I'm sorry, I thought this would be helpful; you know that, don't you?" He ran a hand through his already disheveled hair. "It's just that Virginia Mae thought—"

"She told me it was your idea." He heard the ice in her voice and sighed.

"I don't remember it that way, but it doesn't matter. We just wanted to help." He wanted to say more, but Elizabeth wasn't up to listening.

"Michael, I don't want to talk about it now. I'll be home sometime tomorrow." She hung up and turned toward the back family room, standing inside the addition they had built five years ago.

She could see the Potomac River and shivered. Questions were swirling around her with mocking impudence because her heart knew there were no answers.

She also trembled as she thought of Father Wells. He had said trying to follow God's heart carried a responsibility. She didn't want that anymore. Not if it meant all this. What she wanted more than anything was for her life to be the way it used to be.

She wandered through the house, passing through the memories it sheltered, the laughter, the bright moments that had wrapped her life in a happy bubble.

Coming back to the family room, she didn't turn the lights on; instead she looked out over the darkness, seeing the line between night and the rolling body of water that never slept.

Memories were washing over her and she could feel the past floating, just out of reach. Suddenly, a memory, unbidden and unwanted, vividly appeared. It was of a New Year's Eve party at the company headquarters. They had danced and laughed, and then escaped into his office for privacy, to celebrate the new year alone. There was no place she wanted to be but in his arms; he was the half that made her whole—but now? It was just a memory, things had changed, she told herself, and then the tears started. There was no going back . . .

Finally, there was nothing left; she was beyond tears. Elizabeth slumped against the sofa and wondered how she would ever endure.

～

"Did they really take you to see the woman with no feet?" Carol was fascinated.

Elizabeth shook her head. She was at Carol's house because she had not wanted to walk into her empty home. Michael had called her early this morning to let her know when he would be home and not to do anything about dinner, he was taking care of everything. Elizabeth wanted to talk a little about yesterday.

"No. It was the implication," Elizabeth said, "but it sure put things into focus."

"Did she really look at you and say 'Race you' when you got to the door?"

With a faint smile, Elizabeth nodded. "She cocked one crutch at the door as she said it." Carol fell back against the chair, roaring with laughter.

"What a hoot! I haven't even met her, but I like this woman." Carol cackled. "A Washington lobbyist and a college English professor? Here I thought 'rivah' country was made up of only 'rivahnecks.'"

"You'd be surprised," Elizabeth said.

There was a comfortable pause between them. Finally, Carol spoke. "Thank you for not blaming me. I had no idea . . ."

Elizabeth shrugged. "It doesn't matter."

Carol could tell she was very tired, and who could blame her? "Maybe you should go home and rest, or you could go upstairs and lie down in one of the bedrooms? Then you can tell me if you've come up with an answer to those questions that Ian guy asked."

Elizabeth responded with a tiny shake of her head. There was no more conversation until finally Elizabeth checked her watch, stood up, and said a brief good-bye.

Back at home, Elizabeth entered her kitchen, surprised to find that the table was already set. Fresh roses perfumed the air, candles provided the only light. Michael met her and then lifted her hand to his mouth and lightly kissed it. Earnest eyes sought hers, his apology simple. "I'm sorry. I'm so sorry, Beth. Please forgive me."

The dinner he provided that night came from one of their favorite restaurants. Crab bisque, blackened salmon with a fine, fresh salad on the side, and crusty rolls with sweet butter. White wine to sip along with the sparkling water freshened with slices of lemon. There was fresh fruit for dessert.

Elizabeth sat down across from him and saw his face was anxious. After he had asked her forgiveness, the hug he gave her was long, as if he could press away the recent bad moments. "I missed you last night," he said, looking down at her with a troubled face, kissing her cheek. "Here, sit down; let me do everything."

And he did. He had created a beautiful picture with enticing food. He had thought of everything that was tangible to please her.

He kept a flow of conversation going about inconsequential things, smiling at her and touching her arm as he went back and forth from the counter or the oven, doing his best to make her understand how important she was to him.

He was thoughtful and made a conscious effort not to notice the brace or the cane. It was that small thing, more than anything else, that caused her finally to relax and begin to enjoy herself. For the rest of the evening they let their feelings for each other overcome the hurts. They laughed over nothing and loved despite everything. That there was no resolution over what he had done created a mutually unspoken decision not to talk about it.

They fell into this because neither one knew the right words to say. So they enjoyed the moment and each other and let the rest drift away with the scent of the flowers.

Chapter Fourteen

Father Joe!" Elizabeth embraced the priest. "Thank you for coming." He stood inside the foyer, his cleric's white collar and black shirt a nice foil for the dark brown sports jacket he wore. Elizabeth couldn't help but notice that the navy shoes didn't match. "How's Estelle?" she asked.

"Visiting her sister for a few days, so I've been on my own." He followed her into the living room, saddened by the cane and at seeing her walk so stiff and slow. Elizabeth was grateful he didn't try to take her arm and help.

He already knew about the shoes, the leg brace, and the cane. He had been given the details of what had taken place by Virginia Mae, who had been to see him twice already. Virginia Mae was desperately worried about her daughter. And worried sick that Elizabeth would stay mad at her forever. There were times when Father Wells felt she wanted absolution. Just give her a penance to do, or even better yet, a dispensation, so she could get on with her life. She wasn't Catholic, he pointed out during their last conversation, and her church didn't work that way. Virginia Mae had fussed strongly about that, putting the blame squarely on Martin Luther and his Reformation. No, Father Wells had corrected her again, the Reformation wasn't his, it was God's.

They sat and he turned to her. "I'm glad you called. I have also heard from your mother about what happened. She's very upset. I know it's a mess but, Elizabeth, remember: They did everything because they love you." His eyes were focused on hers, warm and caring, and she vaguely wondered why Michael couldn't look at her like that.

"I know, but . . ." She waved a hand feebly. "Frankly, I wonder what their real motivation was—to make themselves feel better or to help me? Because it didn't. They never asked, and I feel they went behind my back. Like they betrayed me."

He nodded. "It's hard, I know. You are, all of you, in a new place, and no one knows how to act. That's understandable. But I also understand that regardless of the way they made you feel, it is still your responsibility to forgive them."

She frowned. She didn't feel forgiving. "How do I make them understand that as awful as these changes have been for them, it's even harder on me? And all they seem to do is make it worse."

"I'm praying for all of you, but perhaps you need to pray together," he suggested, but immediately she dismissed it. She didn't think so. Michael was certainly a good man and did whatever was needed at the church and for people, but pray together?

"From the time I was in the hospital over a year ago, I haven't stopped praying, but . . . I'm not getting any answers. It's like the phone in heaven is off the hook." She sounded frayed.

"I know that's maybe how it seems, but He always answers. Oftentimes it may not be what we want, but there is always an answer."

She sighed. There was so much more. "The bigger question is, Why is this happening to me in the first place? I keep remembering when you and I talked about the sun dogs and faith. You mentioned Jacob wanting a blessing so much he was willing to fight God for it. And he was left lame for the rest of his life. Father Joe, I don't want this—I don't want to have to use this brace or cane for the rest of my life. I feel . . . caught." Tears suddenly stung her eyes.

This was always so hard, he knew—unwanted, unpleasant changes that couldn't be controlled. It all hurt. "Of course you don't want any of this," he assured her. "None of us want the awful things, but they do happen. And by the way, don't ever let anyone tell you this is your fault, that you did something wrong and you're being punished for it." He saw her surprise. "Oh, yes, there are plenty of Job's friends still around, ready and eager to convince you God is punishing you. Nonsense. Nonsense! Bad things happen to wonderful people. The difference between a believer and a nonbeliever is that God is faithful and will never leave you. You, Elizabeth Whittaker, have the company of heaven with you at all times. Believe it, because it is true." His voice was pulpit loud, as if sound would strengthen the content. It didn't.

Her face froze. "You sound like you're preaching."

Surprised, he stopped, then chuckled. "It gets my blood flowing, and I just can't help it. Occupational hazard, I suppose." He reached down and took some papers from his briefcase. "I won't preach anymore, but I did bring you some things to read, some words I hope will be helpful."

She settled back against the couch, her chin propped up in her hand, watching him ruffle through the sheets of paper. "Always, when bad moments happen to faithful people, I'm reminded of what Dietrich Bonhoeffer wrote when he was imprisoned by the Nazis. He later died in a concentration camp. His words speak to me about your desire for faith, as well as the situation you now find yourself in." He cleared his throat. "He wrote that it is only by living completely in this world that one learns to have faith. To me that means fully immersing yourself in everything—the good and the bad. Find God in all of it by living unreservedly in life's duties, problems, successes and failures, experiences and perplexities. In this way, we throw ourselves completely into the arms of God. That, I think, is faith . . . That is how one becomes a human being and a Christian."

He held out the small book to her. "His other writings might speak to you, also. And I have one other thing for you."

"What is it?" The wrenching fact Bonhoeffer was imprisoned in a concentration camp made her own problems shrivel by comparison.

She suddenly remembered the woman with no feet, and a faint smile hovered in her eyes.

"Lynne Sears Howard was one of my daughter's best friends growing up. She was over at our house so much she became like a second daughter. Last week, my daughter sent me this. Lynne wrote it. They still remain in touch, though they live far apart. It turns out Lynne has been dealing with the same illness you have. Although she is about ten years younger, she has had it far longer. This is a very moving essay she wrote about life, her faith, and this disease. I would like very much to share this with you."

He held it out and she reached for it eagerly. Would things be clearer, she wondered, wanting so much for the confusion to be smoothed away and everything to be made crystal clear.

"Can I read this while you're here, or would you rather I do it later?" she asked, not wanting to be rude.

"Read it now, Elizabeth. I'll wait right here, make some notes on my sermon, and afterward we can talk." He smiled. "I think you will find some comfort in her words. She has been right where you are."

It was titled "Life on the Edge." An unusual title, Elizabeth thought.

The children are visiting their grandmother, and I sit here in the silence of a rare, solitary afternoon pondering the randomness of life. Sun filters through white shades and softens the edges of some of the hardest memories that stain the past.

Gingerly, peering over just a few at a time, I still feel traces of emotions shiver down my spine, and I am so grateful, so relieved to be merely looking back. Whatever the future holds can take care of itself. The present is the only thing that can actually touch me now.

Still, as I gaze over my life, it's not what I expected. This tapestry isn't the disjointed patchwork of frayed and broken threads I supposed it would be.

Instead, its form and depth show logic and meaning, with an almost mystical continuity.

I know with certainty there was nothing I did to achieve this. I was simply a bystander, watching, waiting, utterly defenseless. My life has unfolded this way because I was forced down a path I never wanted to travel. Daily I am reminded how little command I have over my destiny. And yet some-thing, somehow, is directing. I know it is nothing I did.

When I was younger, control and career were the two things most important to me and, like most who don't have years of experience to refute it, I was invincible.

I was in charge, and I intended to have a brilliant career.

Even during college days while studying for a journalism degree, the details of my future were hazy, like trying to squint past the sun. But it just didn't matter. I was consumed with ambition and half-formed plans. As long as I raced forward, the dream and I would collide and happiness would be waiting.

It didn't work.

Looking back in safety from this midway point, I wonder at my naïveté. Reality has stamped the years with such irony its flavor makes me flinch as much as it makes me laugh. It is so bit-tersweet its twang overwhelms at times, like fingernails scraping across a blackboard.

Simultaneously, laughter is ever present and gurgles up with the force of a geyser because I know, I know I taste joy in depths far richer than I could ever have discovered on my own.

If my vague plans had been fulfilled, there would have been neither room nor time for children. The saddest part is, I never would have known enough to miss them.

All my haughty proclamations that started with "I will never . . ." have been raised up as demons that tweak me over and over then run off in riotous laughter.

I was never going to be tied down in marriage.

This is my second-plus decade of being wedded to a man whose name I have never shared, yet whose presence intensi-fies the good moments in unforgettable and countless ways. He remains steadfast despite the many, many bad moments, the wrenching tears, and ultimately the changes.

Elizabeth stopped, seized by an emotion so virulent she couldn't breathe. Without expression, she turned carefully to Father Joseph, who was engrossed in his own reading. She hesitated, unsure of what to do. She felt horrible and while she couldn't understand it, she knew she needed to be alone. Elizabeth cleared her throat. "Do you mind if I read this later and call you? All of a sudden I'm feeling very, very tired. I think I need to rest."

Immediately, he stood up. "Of course, I'm sorry I tired you. Read it today, next week, whenever the mood strikes you. And call me anytime. We'll talk, okay?"

She nodded and began to stand up. "No, don't get up, Elizabeth. I'll see myself out. You just go on and rest," he insisted. "I'll talk with you very soon." He made the sign of the cross and said with sincerity, "May God bless you as only He can do. Amen."

Within moments she was alone, but instead of going to her bedroom she went into the kitchen, fixed a cup of tea, and reread the last sentences.

This is my second-plus decade of being wedded to a man whose name I have never shared, yet whose presence intensifies the good moments in unforgettable and countless ways. He remains steadfast despite the many, many bad moments, the wrenching tears, and ultimately the changes.

Envy drowned her, its taste so bitter it took away all breath. A husband who remains steadfast! How? How had they accomplished that? And his presence intensified the good moments? Her stomach clenched. And they cried together?

Elizabeth had cried alone last night. She had come to the end of the day overwhelmed by what she could not do. At the library where she volunteered, she had stumbled more than once, and everyone near had jumped to help—but she didn't need it, didn't want it, and felt horrible to be the recipient of not only helping arms and hands but also—pity.

Michael was out of town, and within the safety and silence of her bedroom she had thrown the brace against the wall, angered at how much she needed it. After the awful day she had discovered too late that she couldn't wear it with slippers. She had dissolved into tears and cried hard for a long, long time . . . alone.

She couldn't imagine crying in Michael's arms. Instinctively, she knew he could never allow it; he'd be too busy trying to talk her out of it. Suddenly, crying in her husband's arms seemed far too intimate.

Thinking of that new couple she had just met, Adrienne and Ian Moore, she recalled a snippet of their conversation at the restaurant.

"What did you do when you first heard the diagnosis?" Elizabeth asked, curious.

Adrienne and Ian had looked at each other. "Cried our eyes out," Adrienne said. Ian nodded, now, incredibly, smiling at the memory. "And after we finished getting each other's shoulders wet, Adrienne promptly told me—"

"You look like hell. Well, Ian, you did." She turned to Elizabeth. "You should have seen him. His hair was sticking up on end, his face was blotched, and his nose was running." She chuckled. "But to me, really, at that moment he looked like my white knight in shining armor, a rock in a sea of disaster. Of course, I would never tell him such a thing, it might cause him to get puffed up, you see." She grinned, hearing his accompanying snort.

These two had a closeness that seemed much like the one Lynne Sears Howard had with her husband. What was the secret? Elizabeth was desperate to know it.

After another cup of tea, she had managed to compose herself enough to start reading again.

> I was never going to get sick; a chronic illness caught me nineteen years ago and never let go.
>
> I was never going to have children; my sons were both born the same October day four years apart.
>
> I never wanted anyone to support me because I was going to succeed, by my standards, and in the world I intended to conquer.
>
> Now if I make it through a day or perhaps a week without too many bruises or falls, without too much exhaustion, I have lived the true definition of the word *success*.

Elizabeth shuddered. Was this what her life would be like? It was still too new to think in terms of living this way forever . . . but could it be possible? Surely her future wouldn't darken . . . would it? Her eyes dropped to the next line.

> This bizarre, unpredictable illness has left invisible scars that have only in the last handful of years become noticeable.

The limp. The balance that weaves and wavers like an autumn leaf caught in the wind. The visual impairments and sensory deficits. So much of it silent to others, yet so deafening and abrasive to me.

Because of the illness I learned selfishness; because of my children I am learning to be selfless.

The many physical catastrophes that have no known explanation have allowed me to learn the pricelessness of living in this moment. I don't—can't—take anything for granted. Memories are created and then hoarded to a safe place because I know too well how quickly they can start to dissolve and fade into a mere glimmer of what used to be.

Elizabeth grimaced. God, she knew about that; never in a million years would she have ever thought she'd be in this place. And in these shoes, she thought without humor, staring at her feet encased in top-of-the-line tennis shoes that she would always find ugly.

She picked up the thread of this story again.

It is through the losses I have learned substance. Because of the hurts a rocky faith has solidified. I don't like the slotted niches of theology, so I simply describe myself as a *Christian*, but it's not enough.

The word sounds old and worn, used too easily by those who have no idea of the power hovering just beyond their reach. I almost use it reluctantly because I have so little in common with those who fix their boundaries that divide and define their rules as truth.

It is also too small a word for its meaning, but because of it, the faith I have discovered (or perhaps it discovered me) is sure and remains dynamic and growing. Far from being static, it hums with the energy of a new day.

And I have been warmed by many emerging lights that have crossed my path during these years of trying to reconcile the insanity of illness with the hope of restoration.

These are the bright memories of people I began seeking soon after the doctors, who at first could offer no diagnosis, started hinting at what my future might hold.

I didn't believe them.

Yet it was hard to ignore completely the physical changes that were already taking place, although only noticeable to me.

I was a newspaper reporter who became fascinated by people who were facing extraordinary circumstances through no fault of their own, yet somehow were not only surviving, but thriving. I wrote many of their stories, hoping to figure out the why as well as the secrets as I fumbled toward my own uncertain future.

Elizabeth paused again, thinking of her own life. She had gotten a degree in painting, but her only real career had been Kellan. And now her daughter was, for the most part, gone, stretching her own wings and learning about what she wanted to do with the rest of her life. Michael had never wanted her to work full-time. In those early days after Kellan was born, when his business required flexibility, he enjoyed having his family with him when he had to fly all over the country. She enjoyed it, had loved it, actually, but now she wondered in hindsight, How much had she really given up? She pulled the pages toward her again.

It has been the knowledge of their strength and quiet courage that has sustained me more than once when fears and darkness started descending, when the danger was in not only becoming physically crippled but emotionally crippled as well.

But what they couldn't prepare me for were the people who have all the answers and others who have all the cures. Invariably, they are the ones without the tragedies or the illnesses.

I have yet to meet anyone whose health surges and wanes like waves on the ocean's shoreline who hasn't encountered these attitudes.

One judgment, based in part on fragments of a holy book, is that the fault is completely and all mine.

Sure.

Another is to deny everything until it goes away. That way, their God can be praised for a miraculous healing, and they can pat themselves on the back for being the conduit. What they ask for are lies. (Isn't that supposed to be wrong somewhere in that holy book?)

My legs are obviously not listening. Neither are my eyes. The hands continue to feel like they're wrapped in gloves. The weight of fatigue suffocates as intensely as ever. But again, the fault is strictly mine.

Right.

There are other varieties, including the cures that are mine for the taking if only I would listen. How many times have I commiserated with others who are as incredulous as I over the outrageous things other people will say to us with certainty in their voices and haughty reproof of our inaction.

Sometimes I struggle over whether to laugh or cry, but I also realize how grateful I am; all these people have caused me to search and discern what is real and what I believe. The truth isn't about religion, it is simply about God; that's not necessarily the same thing.

I'm also sad for them, those who claim to believe as I do and yet pick and choose words from a holy book to fit their precepts, simply ignoring the rest. They don't have a clue.

It's too simple. By struggling to find the way to real peace, you begin to understand the fallacies and presuppositions can only wither away when placed under the light of plain truth. But to know its fullness takes courage. My children and husband are among the many reasons I survive, but it's more than just existing. Regardless of how I feel now, my deep-down, gut-level bottom line is one of immense joy. All the darker emotions that flutter across, like anger and depression, merely skim this surface. All of this has happened despite—or because of—the changes in my life.

Throughout these years I have been confused, comforted, broken and made better, stretched and reborn, by a God—a Spirit I used to think would be so easy to tame. Now that I'm listening through a broken heart, I hear what has always been playing.

Each time, from that dark abyss of illness I keep falling into (a place well known to anyone whose health is always on the edge), I try to reach for that greater prize: understanding myself and those around me through eyes filled with a love that has no conditions, no boundaries . . .

I may not like where I've been, and there are recollections that remain safely locked away except on strong, good days, but the joy of hope, the hope that is faith, wraps tangible arms around my life, extends to the ones I love, and even more so than this illness, won't ever let go.

I'm still reaching.

There it was again: faith. Elizabeth sat back, and her thoughts tripped and somersaulted as she tried to sort through and make sense of them. She looked out the window to a clear, uncomplicated sky and saw nothing.

Certainly this was a very moving essay; Lynne Howard was a talented writer, yet the content made her want to—what? She wanted to do much more than understand, she wanted to absorb it . . . but how? It was like reaching for the past as memories kept dimming.

Did Lynne know how lucky she was? Did she have any idea? She and Michael had formed a silent truce since the shoe incident, but she could feel his deep concern. She knew he was edgier around her, as if coiled, ready to spring into action if she needed help. He was anticipating the worst and she hated it. He never said anything, but she knew how his mind worked.

Michael, on the other hand, tried hard not to let his concern show and thought he was being successful. They were easing along like two polite strangers, although they were still intimate. There was a wall, protective or otherwise, neither of them was willing or able to scale. Elizabeth jumped as she heard the back door open and Michael came in, suitcase in hand, a smile growing when he saw her.

She hadn't thought it was that late but now saw the oven clock and realized it was much, much later. In some ways, she thought, it was too late.

⌁

In typical fashion, Virginia Mae had waited a whole week after Elizabeth returned from the river before barging in early one morning. She had thrown herself dramatically into her daughter's arms.

"I'm sorry; I'm so sorry, Elizabeth. I was only trying to help. Please, you have to forgive me." Her tone was insistent, determined, and Elizabeth, ready to acquiesce, suddenly saw the truth.

Clearly, this had nothing to do with what *she* wanted, it had everything to do with what her mother wanted.

Elizabeth sighed, patting her mother on the back. "Of course I forgive you." There was little conviction in her voice, but it was the words that mattered, not the sincerity, she noted, as Virginia Mae straightened and dabbed her eyes and nose with a handkerchief. She clutched Elizabeth's hand with her free one and marched them both into the kitchen.

"I'll make coffee while you go and get dressed. I have all morning free, and I want very much to spend it with my daughter."

Elizabeth sadly thought of her desire to return to bed; she had planned to sleep in this morning but realized it wasn't an option. Not when Virginia Mae had already decided her morning for her.

Clad in jeans, tennis shoes, and a sweater, she wandered back into the kitchen, breathing in the percolating coffee. She saw that her mother had set the table nicely and had brought cake. "It's cheese Danish, from that little shop on Grove Avenue you like so much." Virginia Mae finished cutting a piece for each of them and then licked her finger. "Delicious."

Elizabeth admired her mother's rose silk dress, high heels, and pearls and wondered if her mother had gotten so dressed up just to demand forgiveness. She commented on how nice she looked.

"Oh, Julia and I are having lunch at the Jefferson with the executive committee of the state women's club."

That would do it, Elizabeth thought.

After her mother left, Elizabeth picked up the dishes and put them in the sink. She heard the mail slide through the door slot and went to get it.

She had gotten a response! She had written Lynn Sears Howard after reading the essay and was thankful for the quick response. After reading the letter, Elizabeth immediately went to her journal.

Lynne Sears Howard wrote today. Her letter is as well written as her essay. Why do words fall into place so easily for some, while others like me fumble and stumble before fleshing out a thought that still doesn't sing?

She tells me not to be too hard on my husband, that the adjustments hit each person differently. "There is no right or wrong way to react. As long as you keep your hearts open to discussion, things will keep balancing. And that's what it is, a balancing act," *Lynne wrote.*

"I will tell you, my husband was furious with me when I declined the doctor's advice. All my sight had left during one horrible night that will remain infamous till the day I die . . . I already knew the more I used the steroid treatments, the less they would work. Why? My specialists can't tell me, so I have to wonder if taking them changes something in our bodies so healing can't take place each time.

"I have questions; they don't have answers—yet. Anyhow, my husband, Conrad, was livid, and I understood his fury came from his intense worry about me.

"I didn't realize it at the time, but intuitively I had lost control over so much, I wasn't going to lose control over my choice of treatment!

"Within ten days my sight started to come back, and by the end of six months my eyes were perfect. I knew I had done the right thing for me and, eventually, my husband agreed. After Conrad read everything I already knew, and after my vision began returning, he apologized. But he made me promise this would never happen to me again.

"I can make such a promise because no one knows what will happen. So I'm free to decide for myself. And there is no one who can tell me differently. Follow your own instincts, Elizabeth! Learn everything you need to make the best decisions for yourself and then listen to your body.

"Father Wells has told me how special you are. I'm praying for you."

Elizabeth closed the journal after placing the letter inside. Throughout the day she thought about portions of it. So Lynne and her husband had not always agreed? That made Elizabeth feel slightly better about Michael. Perhaps realizing change was inevitable—not expecting it, but not being blindsided when it happened, maybe that was the key, that was the way she and Michael could both deal with it.

It might have worked had she ever thought to discuss it with him.

Chapter Fifteen

Coffee hour following church was as inevitable as day following night. The staunch parishioners were always there, steady as the brick foundation anchoring the church, along with newer members, young and old.

Elizabeth stood near the wall. This was the second Sunday she had attended with cane in hand, the only outward sign that something was wrong—or different. The necessity of the brace had caused her for the first time ever to start wearing pants to church. What else could she do? There were no decent dress shoes available to accommodate the hated brace. She smiled and nodded to people she knew, thankful no one came up to talk; it was just like last Sunday. Elizabeth was still very self-conscious about the cane, so it didn't bother her that no one came up to speak. She did find herself wishing Carol was here today, but Carol's mother had declared it was time to visit friends in Florida.

She kept taking small sips of her coffee and tried not to blush; would she ever get over feeling this conspicuous?

Michael was talking to Gordon and some other contemporaries but kept a surreptitious eye on his wife, who looked beautiful, he thought. He was also glad he'd talked her into letting him invest in that sturdy, ergonomically correct cane. Of course, she had insisted that the handle also had to look good.

He stared as a man he'd never seen before walked over to Elizabeth and started talking. Tall and well built, the stranger had white close-cropped hair that would indicate military. Michael wondered who he was.

"I couldn't help noticing your beautiful cane. I wanted to come over and ask, what did you do to your leg?" The question was posed in a very charming, confident tone. Elizabeth looked at him blankly.

"What did I do?" she repeated, the question not making any sense. He nodded expectantly, and it was his turn to look surprised when she said in an incredulous voice, "Nothing." The simple, God's honest truth was she had done nothing to need to use a cane, and that was the real bite.

He was startled for a moment, but then something clicked. His eyes cleared and his mouth lifted up as he realized his mistake. "Oh, I see. I'm sorry. You're making a fashion statement. Well done."

He nodded amiably and left Elizabeth standing perfectly still, too shocked to speak. Fashion statement? He thought she was making a fashion statement? How dare he!

By the time Michael walked over, she was almost trembling from this new injustice. How dare that man accuse her of using a cane for no useful purpose. All somebody had to do was look at her to see she needed it. How could he say such a thing to her?

Michael listened to her whispered rage and then fed that anger by pointing out in a reasonable voice, "But you told him you didn't do anything, what else was he supposed to think?"

She glared at him and he held up his hands. "Hey, look, point him out to me. I'll go beat him up, okay?"

Her reluctant smile broke into a giggle. She shushed him. "Don't be silly. But it was ridiculous for him to assume such a stupid thing. All you have to do is look at me to see I need it."

Michael surprised her. "That's where you're wrong," he said. "You *don't* look like you need it. With this little stick, you move more gracefully than any of the other women here today." His smile was full of admiration, something she hadn't seen or noticed in a long time.

"Really?" She had no idea he felt that way.

"Really. Absolutely. Positively. Now, do you still want me to go after that guy?" His grin embraced and lifted her.

"Well, not this Sunday," she said, taking his arm.

The atmosphere at home that afternoon was a little easier, a little friendlier. They talked and laughed, and Elizabeth actually felt relaxed by the time the day was over. She made note of it in her journal the next day because it had been such a long time since that had happened.

❧

"Have you thought about herbs?" Carol wanted to know.

They were inside the Whittaker family room. Elizabeth was resting on the couch, her legs tucked up beneath her; Carol was on the opposite settee, rummaging through a large tote bag she had brought with her this morning. Wearing jeans and a sweatshirt, she looked like a college kid.

"Herbs?" Elizabeth repeated without interest.

"Yeah, herbs. Look, I got this book from the store. It has diseases broken down in the index and tells which herbs can help with each disease." She handed the large and colorful book to Elizabeth, who dutifully reached for it and then nearly dropped it, it was so heavy.

"They say it can really help. Why, some people have been almost totally cured. It says it all in there." Carol, pleased with her findings, looked expectantly at Elizabeth.

" 'They' say it helps?" Elizabeth put a little extra emphasis on the word *they*.

"Yes. It's very interesting. Oh, and I also got you a book about a low-fat diet. It's definitely supposed to help people like you."

"Marvelous!" Elizabeth murmured. "But I've always eaten low-fat; you know that."

"Yes, but this is very, very low-fat. See, it has specific recipes and everything. They say it has really helped people with your disease. Some people have had this thing thirty years and more and they've remained very stable. They haven't gotten, you know, worse."

" 'They' again," Elizabeth repeated and sat up a little straighter, as if to give herself a little boost of energy. "You know, I have to say, I have never met the euphemistic 'they' you keep talking about. I suppose it's a wonderful, useful word that encompasses so much . . . but says so little." She looked at Carol's confused face and smiled.

"Oh, I'll look at everything, I will. Do you know I've been reading about bee venom therapy, too? And instead of 'they,' there are actual people who are willing to put their names out as being helped by this. What do you think of that?"

She saw Carol's eyes roll. "I think you could kill yourself with that. Have you ever heard of anaphylactic shock?"

Elizabeth shrugged. "Other people manage to work it out."

Carol couldn't imagine. Since the shoe episode, Elizabeth's attitude toward life had become hard to figure. There were shutters that hadn't been there before. Her cousin had always been easy to read; you knew where you stood with Elizabeth because she would tell you. No surprises. Carol wasn't sure if Elizabeth was serious about this bee thing or just throwing that out to deflect what she was trying to do, which was only to help.

"Don't tell me you're going to start beekeeping here?" Carol teased, but she was uneasy. Was Elizabeth serious? She wondered if she should tell Michael but immediately discarded that thought. She didn't need to tell that man squat about his wife. She wasn't going to betray her cousin.

But bee venom?

Elizabeth moved into a more comfortable position and looked intently at Carol. "Why was a stretch limo in front of your house for hours yesterday?"

She watched as differing emotions washed over Carol's face before she frowned.

"It was Ray."

The surprise was enormous. "You're kidding! I heard the car was out front all afternoon."

Carol made a face. "Since he didn't have the courtesy to tell me he was coming, I wasn't home. Gordon and I went to the medical association luncheon together."

"So Gordon got to meet Ray? I bet that was interesting." Elizabeth couldn't imagine.

"Not really." Carol was vague.

Elizabeth waited, but when Carol remained silent she finally asked, "What did he want?"

Carol bit her lip and looked away. "He wanted me back. He came to tell me he loved me and that what happened before was a case of temporary insanity on his part."

"You mean his affairs?"

"Affair," Carol said quietly. "He only had one."

"Oh."

Carol, silent and lost in her own thoughts, seemed to come to a decision.

"Elizabeth, the reason I left him was because he betrayed me. I came home early—after almost two months of traveling for research. I came home earlier than I planned, or he expected, because I missed him." Carol closed her eyes, as if that could deflect some of the pain that still lingered.

"I found him in our bed—"

Her voice caught, and Elizabeth tried to finish for her in a sad voice, "With another woman."

Carol shook her head. "With another man."

The words hung naked in the air. Elizabeth looked at her in disbelief. "You're kidding! He's gay?"

Carol shook her head.

She was out of her league, perplexed. "I don't understand."

"As he told me," Carol repeated, "he was lonely and horny. He also said he lost his mind because he was *merely* infatuated with this man. His psychiatrist had helped him discover this was *merely* a midlife crisis and I shouldn't have taken it so seriously, meaning a divorce was neither necessary nor appropriate. Oh yes, he wants me back. Now that he is no longer insane, he knows he loves only me."

"And he can just go to hell," Elizabeth said, furious. "How dare he do this to you! Carol, I'm so sorry." She looked at her cousin. "What did you say to him?"

"I pretty much told him what you said, only my words weren't so pretty."

"Good."

Carol smiled briefly. "You've got to swear you won't tell a word of this to anyone. And that includes Michael."

Elizabeth ran one finger across her mouth. "My lips are sealed."

A little smile settled over Carol's features. "I certainly hope so. You know, this feels good. You're the only person I've spoken to about this, besides Father Joseph."

"What did he say?"

Carol was vague. "A lot of reassuring things. He's a remarkable person, a very practical man of faith who makes it all seem so accessible. But I have to say, Gordon has helped a great deal, too. He's been through so very much himself. Did I tell you he recommended a therapist?"

Elizabeth shook her head. So that's why Carol seemed a little easier. And thank God there had been no more barhopping dates.

"She's the one he used . . . to deal with his wife's death. Gordon's a good guy."

She was glad Carol had finally trusted her enough to share this awful secret. A sudden question popped into her mind.

"When you . . . found them together, what did you do? Throw

something at him, scream, demand an explanation?" Elizabeth didn't have the imagination to figure out what she'd do.

"It was pretty self-explanatory," Carol pointed out drily. "I left. The first thing I did was go to my doctor and get checked out for any STDs, AIDS; you know, all the capital-letter stuff." Her laugh was harsh. "I'm in the clear, thank God, but I have no idea about Ray."

"Yes, thank God he didn't give you anything." Elizabeth was suddenly shocked by how little she really knew of life. "It suddenly occurs to me I've led a very sheltered and naive life."

Carol's response was succinct. "Be thankful for it."

Chapter Sixteen

Come in." Adrienne's smile was as big as the day, waiting as Elizabeth walked up the ramp to their house.

"You aren't using your crutches?" Elizabeth was immediately sorry those words slipped out, but she had never seen Adrienne use a motorized wheelchair. What did that mean? Did this mean Adrienne had gotten worse in the weeks since she'd met her?

"She's paying for overdoing yesterday, big-time," Ian announced, putting a hand on Elizabeth's arm and escorting her inside their home.

She looked around with approval at the large open room with high ceilings and exposed beams and loved all the windows, which allowed the daylight to stream in. "What a marvelous place."

There were small walls dividing large rooms, keeping doorways wide and easily accommodating Adrienne's motorized wheelchair. "What did you do yesterday?" Elizabeth wanted to know, sitting down on one of several love seats in the family room, a large room in the back of the house that boasted three walls of windows overlooking a portion of Elizabeth's river.

Adrienne shrugged and looked at Ian. "Do I have to tell?" Her voice was plaintive, a child caught with her hand in the cookie jar.

"Of course not," Elizabeth quickly assured her, even as Ian admonished, "Don't baby her. She's dying to tell you what she did and how she wouldn't listen to anyone with a shred of common sense."

He was gruff even as he was trying not to smile. Actually, he wasn't entirely pleased with his wife's behavior. If she just wasn't so much fun when she was getting herself into trouble, he might be able to play the heavy and insist she not do stupid things. Then again, one of the things he loved about her was that defiance; a mixed blessing, at the very least, he constantly reminded himself.

"Well," Adrienne began, placing fingertips together, gathering her thoughts. "It was for an excellent cause. I walked the gym track at the high school five times at midday and raised five hundred dollars for the church building fund."

"Five hundred dollars?" Elizabeth was impressed. "Instead of using the wheelchair you used the crutches?"

"Yes, and now I can't even lift my arms past my shoulders, and Ian's been grumpy with me ever since. I'm glad you came. Maybe you can get him to stop fussing and lighten up."

"I don't know, Adrienne, you probably didn't do yourself any favors," Elizabeth said, and then stopped herself as Ian started wagging a finger at her, only half amused.

"Speaking of which, has Mrs. Whittaker decided yet what she wants *her* husband to do? You see, I haven't forgotten our last conversation. I recall the good man had your very best interests at heart, as I do Adrienne's, and you, ma'am, were less than appreciative. Just like my wife. We husbands are clueless; we just can't win."

Under his amused scrutiny, Elizabeth colored.

Adrienne, however, waved him off. "You get off that high horse immediately, Ian Moore! It's not the same at all, and you know it. Don't pay him any attention; he's trying to compare apples and mangoes. It simply won't work. Elizabeth is my friend, and of course she's concerned for me. But she would have been out there yesterday cheering me on, I have no doubt."

She started to turn away somewhat dramatically to dismiss him, but then thought of something. "Why don't you bring in the tea you so graciously made this morning, and we'll let bygones be bygones," she added sweetly.

His response was to walk out of the room, shaking his head and pretending to mutter darkly under his breath. There was no missing, however, the struggle he had with keeping a smile out of his eyes.

With a smile of her own, Elizabeth leaned back against the cushions, relaxing in the ease that always seemed to surround this couple.

"What's the building fund for?" Elizabeth was curious. "They aren't adding on, are they?" That old church hadn't changed in all the seasons they had come here. Same congregation, only a few new faces in the summer when weekend places were in use. Other than that, nothing seemed to change.

"It's for the new handicapped ramp out in front of the church. I've been helping to raise money for it."

"Bravo." Elizabeth was impressed. "I think that's wonderful."

"Then would you like to make a donation?" Adrienne never missed an opportunity.

"Sure." Elizabeth grinned. This woman, whether in a wheelchair or using crutches, certainly made things happen. She couldn't believe that old, tradition-bound church would agree to something so modern and . . . useful.

Not only did Ian bring in a tea service, but also some hot scones. Butter and jelly were already on the wicker table. "Help yourself," he encouraged as he poured a cup of hot tea for each of them. Then he sat down and nodded toward Elizabeth.

"So, Elizabeth, since we've already touched on the subject, did you ever decide on what you wanted your husband, er, Michael, isn't that his name? Yes, what do you want him to do?"

Elizabeth nibbled at the sweet buttered scone and considered. She thought immediately of the essay by Lynne Howard. Even now she could feel the small stab of envy—what were those words?

"I want," she tried to remember, "a husband . . . whose presence intensifies the good moments, yet remains steadfast despite the very bad ones." She thought she had gotten everything.

"Ohhh, I like that," admired Adrienne. "Don't you, Ian?"

He nodded and then asked another unanswerable question. "How are you going to achieve this?"

Adrienne grabbed his hand. "The same way I'm going to get you to do it. Nag, nag, nag." She threw back her head and laughed as he groaned.

Still clutching his hand, Adrienne fixed a radiant smile on Elizabeth. "So. How are you going to get your husband to toe those lines?"

Elizabeth threw up her hands with a helpless grin. "Nag, nag, nag." She added with a mischievous glint, "Actually, I'm going to move up here and watch a master like you, Adrienne, perform your magic on your husband, and then I'll know what not to do." She sat back with a satisfied smile that was contagious.

"She's good," both Ian and Adrienne said at the same time and then yelled "Jinxed!" This was followed by some mumbo jumbo that was comprehensible only to themselves. Elizabeth watched, fascinated. When they finished, they sat with folded hands and looked at her with perfect innocence, as if what they had just done was totally normal.

Elizabeth leaned forward. "You two are the most fascinating people I've met in a long time."

Ian gently squeezed his wife's arm. "At least she didn't say crazy. That's a step up, I'd say."

Adrienne snorted and punched him back with her elbow. "Speak for yourself, old man." Then with a grin she explained their shenanigans to Elizabeth.

"Our godchild was with us all last week, Thomas Edward Smith. He's ten and very much into superstitions and unjinxing and all that. Let's just say he put us through our paces, and we haven't gotten over it yet." She chuckled. "He is the dearest, funniest child. I hope you can meet him sometime this summer."

"He certainly is a pistol." Ian grinned. "Here, let me show you some pictures."

The next thirty minutes were spent showing pictures and chronicling Thomas's life. By the time they finished, they all had laughed so hard tears fell. Even though Elizabeth had never met this boy, she felt as though she had known him forever.

She dabbed her eyes with a Kleenex from the box Ian had brought to the table. "You've got to let me know if he visits you this summer. I would love to meet him."

They chattered on happily for a while longer, until Ian said, "All irreverence aside, would you like to come and see the church? It's a beautiful old place with a huge arched sanctuary. The wood is fine and old, the stained-glass windows are just as elderly and beautifully made. Or perhaps another time? I wonder if we haven't tuckered you out with our ramblings."

Elizabeth assured them she would love seeing the church. "Maybe the next time I'm down here, I can attend a service with you," she offered, adding, "When we first started coming here in the summers, we went there once, but it was a frigid place. They didn't seem to like children, so we never went back."

"That's why this church nearly died—all these old folks who didn't care to bring in new families. When it was drawing its last feeble gasp and nearly ready for last rites, some of the old people realized that children were precisely what that decaying old place needed."

"At least that's what we've heard," said Ian, wanting to be sure to set the record straight.

Elizabeth looked out at the sky. "Have you happened to see any . . . sun dogs since you've been here?" she asked casually, hoping they wouldn't know what a sun dog was so she would be able to tell them.

"Saw one today, as a matter of fact," Ian replied.

"No! You did?" Elizabeth said, feeling a sudden burning in her eyes. Why hadn't she looked up at the sky today? She certainly could have in all the time it took to drive here.

"Well, yes. Close to midday." Elizabeth was obviously upset, and both Ian and Adrienne glanced at each other, puzzled. "Why?"

"Because of a sermon my rector gave last year." She told them about it in an abbreviated form, smiling at their reaction.

"How charming!" Adrienne exclaimed. "Don't you think so, Ian?"

He nodded, adding, "Someone should write that down. That's a gem. But it doesn't explain your reaction over not seeing it today."

"I loved his story, and I've been looking to see a sun dog ever since." Elizabeth felt foolish trying to explain, not totally understanding herself why it was so important. "But I haven't."

"Well, we will call you the very next time we see one, won't we, Ian," announced Adrienne. "Now, not to change the subject, but to change the subject, guess what I'm going to try to start this fall?"

Elizabeth smiled back, finding her lightness contagious. It seemed Adrienne was always up to something.

"I don't have any idea," she said truthfully.

"A support group," Adrienne said, hauling out some brochures and flyers she had made with her computer.

"A support group? You mean for other people who have your illness?" Elizabeth was surprised there was anyone else around who had this rare condition.

"No. A neuromuscular support group. How about that? Then people like you can come, people with arthritis—there's a bunch of different kinds, and people with any of the other dystrophies."

"The criteria," explained Ian in an amused monotone, "is anyone who has a chronic, incurable disease. That covers it, doesn't it, dear?"

"Yes, thank you very much." Adrienne turned to Elizabeth and said, "Ian doesn't think it's a very good idea. He wonders why anyone would come to something so depressing."

"I would," Elizabeth said loyally. "It might be fun."

Adrienne beamed and then looked at Ian as if to say, See? "Have you been to any of the support groups in Richmond?"

Elizabeth grimaced. "Once. I went to one of the 'minimally symptomed' ones, you know, for people who don't look like they're sick?"

"Sure, that's the kind for cowards who don't want to see the possibilities," Adrienne said pleasantly.

"I am so glad you understand," Elizabeth said drily. "I went to one that had just started, but no one knew the lady leading it was this evangelical creature who was convinced we all had to save our souls in order to be healed. You know, 'We wouldn't be sick if we were right with God' sort of stuff."

Adrienne closed her eyes, shaking her head. Ian grimaced, thinking how unfair and unkind some well-meaning people could be. He tried not to recall their own encounters with these types. "Heaven help them, is all I can say. I take it you didn't go back?"

Elizabeth shook her head. "Now tell me about why you're starting this, ah, neuro-what group?"

"Neuromuscular support group," Adrienne enunciated very clearly. "Because I went briefly to one in northern Virginia, and it was so cool. We all had a blast!"

"Really?" Elizabeth asked, surprised to hear the shading of doubt in her own voice.

"Absolutely. Why, I remember the last meeting; it was a picnic, a kind of farewell for Ian and me. They knew we were leaving. Do you remember, Ian?" She looked at her husband expectantly.

"How could I forget?" He turned to Elizabeth, a smile twitching the corners of his mouth. "The majority were in motorized wheelchairs, and someone had the bright idea to find out who had the fastest—"

"So we all lined up in the road in front of the house. Ian had some lady's scarf in hand, and he stood in front of the pack and yelled, 'People, start your engines; on your mark, get set, GO!'"

"And they did," Ian continued, in the tone of a man who is forever being forced to do things he knows he should not do. "As a matter of fact, they did three carts at a time, so there were several heats, if you will. And then"—he looked sternly at his wife, who was bubbling over with laughter—"and then the police came. It seems the lady across the street was very disapproving of our turning her road into a drag strip. She thought we were all crazy and irresponsible."

"That lady had no sense of humor," Adrienne scoffed.

"Neither did the police, they agreed with her," Ian reminded her. "They let all of them go with a harsh warning," he told Elizabeth, and then grinned. "I have to admit, she wasn't nearly this much of a daredevil before she got this thing," he added, patting the steel chair.

Adrienne pushed his hand away. "How quickly he forgets. Elizabeth, will you come to the first one? It'll be at the health club over near the hospital. It's all accessible, and they've got a big meeting room we can use for free."

"Let me know when it is, and I'll do my best to be there," Elizabeth promised.

Chapter Seventeen

Elizabeth arrived at her own river home later that afternoon. Inside, she looked over the brochures Adrienne had insisted she take, chuckling. Maybe this support idea would be fun. Michael, she was sure, would have a hard time understanding. She glanced at the wall clock and saw that he and Kellan would be arriving within the hour.

They had picked this weekend, the end of May, to come and officially open the house.

Last summer they had rarely used this place at all. It had been a hectic and busy time for everyone—even Elizabeth. Her hours at the library had increased, and since they desperately needed her to fill in for the vacationing regulars, the city was where she remained. Michael had continued to travel and expand his business, so it was also hard for him to get away.

She already knew the next several months would contain international travel for him; Elizabeth had taken a leave of absence from volunteering, but she didn't want to tag along with her husband. She wanted to spend as much time as she could with Kellan, which was looking to be precious little.

Kellan had decided to enroll in a six-week artists' workshop in the mountains of North Carolina. Although she wasn't planning on pursuing painting as a career, it was very much an avocation. Kellan had loved watching her mother create visual feasts on canvas when she was growing up and enjoyed trying to do the same.

Elizabeth thought she might visit her daughter at least once while she was away, and then Kellan would come to stay at the river. Elizabeth sighed, thinking even those casual plans were always subject to change. She wouldn't be surprised if Kellan decided to join her father for a jaunt across the ocean. But that still held no allure now that Elizabeth had met the Moores; the river held much more interest.

She checked the refrigerator and smiled. Thank God for Mehalia. For years, Elizabeth had used a relative of her housekeeper in Richmond to help during the summer, as well as to clean and check on the house during the times it wasn't in use.

Mehalia King was conscientious and unflappable—nothing fazed her; she was supremely capable of getting any and all jobs done. She helped keep the place sparkling on the inside and cooked food plentiful and delicious when needed. Like today.

For the last six years, a granddaughter had also come with Mehalia: Serenity Brown. The child, taken to Jamaica by her mother when she was very young, had come back to live with her grandmother when she was eight years old. After years of living closer and closer to the edge, her mother had finally slipped and landed in prison for drug distribution and prostitution.

Serenity had grown elegantly tall and slim, her features exotic. And according to Mehalia, in the last six months her attitude had become insufferable. It was that treacherous middle ground of no longer being a child yet not an adult, all coupled with newly raging hormones. Elizabeth commiserated with her when they talked last week, wondering how society could get rid of those years. Everyone she had ever known had disliked that time of life. Except for the ones who made it insufferable for the rest, the so-called popular ones.

Elizabeth poured a glass of tea and waited for her family to arrive.

By the middle of the summer, Michael was so encouraged by what he didn't see, he couldn't keep it to himself.

"She's doing great!"

Michael sipped the wine, his happiness bubbling from the inside out. God, he was happy. Jubilant. The long weekend he had spent with Elizabeth had left him deeply satisfied that whatever his wife was doing was working. Kellan had also been there, and it had been a perfect weekend.

Stunned, Carol, who was seated on his left, looked at Gordon. They had just been talking about Elizabeth before Michael arrived and the words out of this man's mouth could not be further from the truth.

"She's hardly using her cane at all. I don't know what it is about the river, but Elizabeth is thriving. I really think she's got this thing beat," Michael enthused.

Gordon listened in silence as Michael spoke at length about how great his wife was looking—her energy level was up, she was even painting a little. "I think my Elizabeth is coming back. It may take a little bit more time, but I believe she's going to be able to throw that cane and the brace away."

There was a small pause. "Michael, you haven't been to the river very much this summer, have you?" Carol tried to keep her voice neutral and failed. Her disbelief twanged like a fiddle string. She kept her eyes on her salad.

"I've been there often enough," Michael said, his voice clipped. When he had invited Gordon to lunch, he hadn't known Carol was going to make it a threesome, but that's just what happened. (Gordon had arrived early for a change, ran into Carol coming to grab a bite to eat by herself, and had insisted she join them.) Michael knew good manners dictated he be gracious and include her in their conversation, but the two always grated on each other. They could be talking about the weather and end up arguing.

"But you have been traveling a lot for work, right? I mean, that's what Elizabeth told me," she pointed out carefully. How could he not get it? He was allowed to see only what Elizabeth wanted him to see.

Annoyed, he glanced impatiently at her. "What exactly are you getting at?"

"Nothing. Not a thing." How, she wondered again, could Michael be so successful in business yet so dumb in life? She chewed the spinach with crumbled feta cheese and concentrated hard on not talking.

They were eating lunch at a Greek restaurant near the hospital. August was keeping its tradition of being as hot and humid as the inside of a sauna. No one who had the choice ventured very far from manufactured coolness.

Gordon was finishing up the last of his Greek omelet, trying to quell misgivings over what Michael was saying. In the ten minutes since the food was served, Michael had dominated the conversation. He was on a roll, his pleasure at how well things were going in his family's life, and particularly with Elizabeth, was too immense for him to notice his friend's silence. And except for Carol's few comments, there had been no interruptions.

"How's Kellan?" Gordon finally asked during a break.

"Great, great; she's staying busy and having a blast at Virginia Beach with friends. She'll be home next week and then go on to Charlottesville."

"I'm glad to hear about Elizabeth. I hope she continues to do well," Gordon said mildly.

"Same here," Carol mumbled, trying to keep her attention focused on finishing this meal as fast and as quietly as possible.

It was finally over when Michael stood to leave. Gordon insisted on picking up the tab for the whole table. "It's the least I can do. I love hearing good news," he insisted to Michael, who grinned. It was not just good, it was the best news.

Carol waited until Michael cleared the exit. "He doesn't know what he's talking about! She's not doing any better. I've seen what she does when he's around. Instead of using the cane, she walks around touching everything so lightly it doesn't look like she's doing anything out of the ordinary, like maintaining her balance. She uses that brace almost all the time! She says she's gotten used to it enough she doesn't need the cane all that much, but try to get her to walk several feet without anything around to touch—she can't do it."

"I know." She blinked as she heard Gordon's resigned tone.

"Then why didn't you set him straight?"

Gordon shook his head. "Carol, he sees what he wants to see, just as Elizabeth does what she needs to do. It's called coping."

"It's called denial," she insisted hotly.

He held up an admonishing hand. "Which you yourself have experienced, so you know what it's like. The coping will change when they are ready, not when you or I think they are."

Brought up flat against such common sense, there wasn't anything she could say. But she tried anyway. "How did you get to be so smart?" she grumbled.

"I'm not saying I'm smart, just realistic and empathetic," he said mildly. "There's no reason to be anything else."

She looked at him again sharply and then sighed. She hated it when she was wrong, especially when it felt so right.

～

The heat was unbearable. Intense. Draining. Elizabeth was smothering even as she fought to take another breath. She was struggling and couldn't understand why. She felt like a hose that had sprung a leak; every bit of energy had dribbled out.

Could she move? It was a question that had no sure answer. She struggled to take in a deep breath. Eyes closed, she prayed her eyelids wouldn't burn. That it was ridiculous was beyond thinking, but couldn't it happen?

Why had it seemed like a good idea to come out here like this? Because sunbathing was something she'd done hundreds of times, thousands of times. It was something she had always enjoyed.

After a lazy, late breakfast, the lure of relaxing in the sun to get more color had been enticing.

Since spending the last few months living here, she'd learned to laugh at the idea of anyone coming to this place to retire. Initially, that's why she and Michael had bought this place, and now she understood what a joke it was. You didn't come to the river to retire; there were simply too many things to do. There was always something going on, some worthy cause, a parade, a fund-raiser for the library or for the restoration of a historic building, something that could take up all your free time.

So this Tuesday was hers. The river house was slowly being put to bed for the winter months, but on this day she was completely alone. No visitors, no housekeeper, no one. Summer was ending, but the weather was still downright hot.

Relaxing was the only thing on her agenda. Except now she didn't think she could move.

She was covered with sweat. The heat was baking her, no, steaming her, the moisture in the air suffocated like a wet rag. It made breathing hard. She felt drugged and weak and very, very scared.

Fighting back panic, she slowly, oh so slowly raised the watch she had taken off her wrist and with dismay saw she must have literally fallen asleep. It had been almost three hours and with that slight movement she felt the tightness of her skin: Her flesh had shrunk.

Mentally, it took long, comforting minutes of convincing her body that indeed she could get up; she must get up and she could make herself move. Eventually, she finally forced herself to sit up and then almost dropped back on the beach towel because she felt so dizzy.

Please, God, no more of that. No, this can't be happening. It just cannot. So. All right, I'll be okay. God, I was such a fool to do this, too much sun isn't good for anyone, I know that. Oh, please, please, let me be fine, please, please, please . . .

Her prayers were as disjointed as her body felt. Moving very, very slowly, almost crawling, she eventually made it back into the house and collapsed on the rug in the family room. Thank God for air-conditioning.

Although it had taken what seemed like hours to crawl the small distance back into the house, it took only about ten minutes to cool down once she was inside.

What was remarkable was that after her body cooled, she was back to normal. She really was fine. No dizziness, no weakness. Still moving thoughtfully, she took a cooling shower and actually felt chilled. She dressed quickly and then tried to go back outside with a small lunch. It took scant moments for her to begin wilting like a parched plant. She retreated inside.

For several days afterward, she was very conscious of the heat and slowly realized that this wasn't going to change. Sun and heat had never bothered her. Never! Before this summer, she was the only one in the family who was a self-described sun lover; there were a vast collection of memories to support this. The many times she had switched the air conditioner off, enjoying the warm breezes, feeling it was so much more natural. *Wholesome* was a word she remembered using to Michael and Kellan, who had both strongly disagreed, but usually acquiesced to her desires.

Now she got up in the mornings and checked the indoor thermostat, making sure the temperature hovered at a cool sixty-five degrees. She was deeply puzzled that this sensitivity to the sun had only happened now, after nearly two months of hot weather. Puzzling and distressing, this new observation was one she kept to herself.

It was fairly easy to rationalize: She was getting older; perhaps menopause was on her doorstep. This was certainly something she didn't feel was worth mentioning to anyone, so she didn't. Then some literature came in the mail one day that discussed heat sensitivity and MS. One more change on top of all the others, she thought, wondering how many more there might be to come—but no, surely God wouldn't let anything more happen. Surely.

God, thank You for . . . Elizabeth stopped, wondering what exactly she should be thankful about. After a long, thoughtful moment she finally concluded, *for not letting it be even worse. And could this be the end of it, please?*

Chapter Eighteen

Elizabeth was leaving to go back to Richmond, Kellan was already in Charlottesville, and Michael would be flying home this weekend.

Before pulling away, though, she was taking Adrienne and Ian a gift basket of cheeses, breads, and wine. She had discovered an excellent wine shop in Kilmarnock. She wanted to surprise them.

Because of them it had been a wonderful summer. She didn't know what she was going to do without their almost daily conversations. She did know she'd be back next month for the meeting, that support group Adrienne wanted to start.

Once a month would have to be enough. Of course, there was always the telephone. She wished idly that the Moores could come visit her, but the city house wasn't accessible, not at all. As she pulled into their driveway, she wondered how hard it would be to put in a ramp. She'd have to look into it.

She left the basket in the car, thinking she'd ask Ian to run out and get it for her, but when she knocked on the door, there was no answer. She rang the bell once, then twice. Nothing.

Odd. They knew she was coming. She walked back down the ramp and looked around, wondering what to do. The trees made a canopy over the house that blocked out the sun's heat, making it bearable, but she didn't intend to stay out long.

She was turning back to her car when she heard a muffled noise. The door was opening and there was Adrienne, tears streaming down her face, a handkerchief pressed to her mouth as if to contain her grief. She didn't say anything, but motioned Elizabeth inside. Alarmed, Elizabeth tried to walk quickly back to the house, but the quicker she tried to move the more disjointed her movements became.

She stopped, took a ragged breath, and then moved to a self-imposed slower tempo and finally was inside. By this time, Adrienne was sitting at the table in the back closest to the glass wall overlooking the river. Her head was in her hands, and Elizabeth could see her chest rise and fall spasmodically, enormous sobs wrenching her body.

Speechless, Elizabeth sat down next to her and laid a gentling hand on her friend's back. What on earth had happened? Had Ian suddenly taken ill? If so, why was Adrienne still there? But if she was still here, Ian must be all right, so then what on earth had happened to break her into pieces like this?

Ian suddenly appeared in the doorway of the kitchen. It was obvious he had been crying, too. His eyes and face were red and puffy, but he was in ragged control. "Elizabeth." He nodded, and ever the gentleman, said, "May I get you some . . . thing to drink?"

Numbly, she shook her head. The incongruity of his appearance and polite gesture while his wife was sobbing offered a surreal sense of the absurd. It was disorienting.

"Ian, what happened?" she begged, rubbing and patting Adrienne's back helplessly. He raised his hand and then dropped it. Slowly he walked into the room, a man shrouded in disbelief, haggard with the weight of horrific news. Suddenly, Adrienne's head came up and she took a deep, noisy breath and blew her nose, mopping up the tears again with the wet cloth. "Ian," her voice sounded strained, as if it had just been sanded and scraped, "c-could you get me some m-more tissues? I think . . . I've used up all these."

She was still trembling, but the weeping seemed to be slowing. The breathing was uneven, and there were irregular catches of her breath, but Adrienne had calmed down. Ian brought a large box of Kleenex, grabbed several for himself, and sat down heavily on the other side of the table.

"It's Thomas." The words dropped like a stone on the table with a heavy thud, and Adrienne pressed a clean tissue to her eyes. Elizabeth felt a cold finger of dread. Thomas was their godson. They had talked about him so many times this summer. The child had been away at different camps, so he had not appeared at the river. But Elizabeth had seen all the most recent pictures, heard their pride, their love . . . What could have happened?

"What about Thomas?" Her voice was almost a whisper, as if a quiet question couldn't hurt as much.

Ian shook his head, struggling.

Silence draped a cloud over them, and Elizabeth's thoughts conjured up all sorts of ugly, horrible possibilities. Instinctively, she knew she wouldn't speak; when they were ready, they would talk.

Outside, the sun was embracing all it saw, caressing the river, making it dance and sway with a constant melody that played ceaselessly and soundlessly. Looking on such a scene, Elizabeth was unsettled by the beauty outside and the hurting inside. How often was this same incongruous drama played out over and over in houses each and every day?

Elizabeth swallowed hard, at a loss. Suddenly there was a nudge to her spirit, and she lifted her face up, closed her eyes, and began to pray.

It was much later when, resignation mingled with a calmness born of exhaustion, they were able to finally tell what had happened.

As if she had never spoken of him before, Adrienne explained who he was. "Thomas Edward Smith was born ten years ago to a very dear friend," Adrienne began, her voice as gray as her face.

"Ian and I had just gotten married. Danielle is younger than I am with two older children. Thomas was a surprise, but everyone loved him so. Never had a child been so welcomed. Thomas was born near the time of our wedding, which is why Danielle wasn't able to stand up for us. Instead, she asked Ian and me to be his godparents. It was an honor. God, such an honor." A half sob broke from her.

Ian's hand gripped his wife's as he spoke. "I've never been particularly interested in babies, but Thomas was different. We had promised to be there for him, to be connected with this child and help raise him." His voice caught, and he passed a hand over his eyes but kept on going. "As he grew into a bright, insightful boy he was a delight to us, who have never had children. We would plan trips with him, activities to expose him to the beauties of the world—its plays, theater, music, stories . . . He had an artist's heart but a soul as big as the outdoors."

"His family chose to homeschool him, as they had done their older children. Years before, Danielle and her husband had purposefully moved to a small farm in a rural community where they could instill in their children the quality and love for life they both shared." Adrienne wavered for a moment and then continued. "Early this morning Thomas was out bird-watching. It's something we love to do, and we had also shared this with him. We took him with us on several occasions, to identify birds, learn more about their nesting habits, things like that. Danielle told us he would often go into the forest and silently climb trees, binoculars around his neck, to get as close as he could to observe."

The pain filled her eyes with tears again, but Adrienne made herself stop and look fully at Elizabeth. "This morning . . . this morning he was out early, climbed a tree, and somehow he slipped . . ."

She couldn't go on and Ian, now clenching her hands in his, finished, "He was wearing the binoculars we gave him for his last birthday, and when he slipped and fell, the cord was around his neck. The other end, it caught on a branch, and . . . it hanged him. Thomas, he . . . he's . . . dear God, our wonderful boy is dead!"

It was another hour before Elizabeth felt she could leave them. She took it upon herself to make coffee and then sandwiches for them. She had never seen them nonfunctional, but when she considered why, she had to stop for a moment and press a firm hand on her heart to quell the hurting she felt for them. Her sorrow also included the poor family. Elizabeth carried that darkness with her as she got into her car and left for the city. The basket stayed in the backseat, forgotten.

Chapter Nineteen

It was the weekend following Labor Day, a holiday known to schoolchildren as the last hurrah of summer. Elizabeth had decided not to attend church this Sunday. Michael was flying home today, and she planned to be at the airport to pick him up. She was tired and still unsettled about what had happened to Thomas. It was tragic and awful and she couldn't let go of it.

After a very small breakfast, she went into her library to read and think. Randomly, she pulled out a few books to look through, hoping she could find something comforting, something that would make sense of the senselessness.

She glanced through a book by Oswald Chambers, put it down, then opened a book on grief by C. S. Lewis and finally realized that nothing was going to help. She got out her journal and sat, tapping a pen on the table, thinking of how to put into words this swirling confusion of emotions that was setting her on edge.

She prayed. It didn't help. She moved around the room, trying to walk away from this uncertain place.

By the time Elizabeth pulled up to the airport to get Michael, she was exhausted. It seemed to be the premise underlying life now—being worn out. And it hadn't helped that she couldn't let go of what had happened to Thomas. That darkness kept shadowing everything she did, pulling on her and keeping her from seeing anything clearly.

She vaguely wondered how she was going to manage to shield Michael from this, when he was going to be home for several days. It was what she had done all summer. She had tried to rest earlier, but the tension of trying to handle all the recent events wouldn't allow it.

Of course she had missed her husband, that hadn't changed, but she also wanted to keep him from what he shouldn't have to see. The weight of that burden also wouldn't go away, one more brick to add to the load on her shoulders.

They had seen each other infrequently over the summer, and when they did meet it was expected; she had been able to plan for his arrivals. She rested, she made sure things were done beforehand. In that way she knew she was ready to face his scrutiny and it had worked. According to Carol, he actually thought she was getting better—and why not? Even she believed in those good moments that of course she would get better. After all, Father Wells had just said that all things are possible—with God. But if that were true, what about Thomas?

Later, after they had arrived home, they made love. After all, they had not seen each other for several weeks. Michael left her resting with her eyes open, but he couldn't lie still. His business done in Canada, he was feeling energetic and buoyant. This summer had been excellent for his firm, and expansion seemed limitless.

Michael emptied his suitcase and garment bag, sorted out clothes for the washer, and gathered things destined for the dry cleaners. While he did this, he often went to check on her. "How are you feeling, Beth?"

Elizabeth had no idea what she should say. She didn't feel all right, but she didn't have a fever, she wasn't hurting . . . What was the correct response? A small wave of her hand seemed to suffice.

He came back a little later. "Stay there as long as you like," Michael urged. "I'll order some pizza. Wouldn't that be good? I noticed the salad in the refrigerator. I'll get that out, too. Is there anything else you'd like?"

She shook her head slightly, not wanting to make the effort to speak.

It seemed like mere seconds had passed when Michael was again sitting on the edge of the bed.

"Elizabeth, do you want me to bring you a plate?"

She moved slightly to look at the clock on the bureau; she couldn't believe it was that late. Where had the time gone? She shook her head and began to creep out on her side, but Michael was right there, a hand under her arm—the *wrong* arm—and she suddenly knew she didn't want any of this. "No. No, Michael, I'm not hungry. Truly."

She rested back against the pillows and looked up into his anxious face, and for a moment it was almost enough to make her try again to get up. She was making him very worried. She knew it, wanted to erase that look from his face, but the idea couldn't make her move. His feelings didn't matter at this moment because she needed every bit of effort for herself.

For the first time, without realizing it, Michael's happiness and concern were not her priority.

She was.

Michael left her, worry chasing him like an itch; he went into the kitchen but couldn't eat. How could this woman, so weary now, be the same woman who was in his arms mere hours ago? A woman who had filled him over and over with desire and completion, participating and giving and giving until he not only thought he would explode but did—with her. The difference was like someone had hit a switch so abruptly she had shut down. He wondered if this was *his* fault. Had he been too demanding? But she was so responsive, . . . so . . . He shut his eyes, trying to quell a wave of fresh desire. No, no, he knew it was this rotten disease; he knew it caused fatigue, yet it seemed surreal, so . . . wrong. And suddenly he was swept away by the burning question that had no answer: What in God's name could he do for his Elizabeth?

The whisper of the answer—*nothing*—slashed him harder than any knife blade. Restless, he kept quietly returning to the bedroom, being careful not to disturb her, but wishing, hoping, he could find a way to help.

With her eyes closed, Elizabeth could hear every time the door was pushed open; the light from the hallway brightened the dark under her eyelids. She knew it because she couldn't sleep.

Fatigue and sleep had nothing to do with each other; she wondered if he knew that. Probably not. The bone-deep weariness that had nothing to do with physical activity didn't respond to rest—all she could do was stop, keep breathing, and hope.

He had come yet again to stare down at her, then reach out to touch her shoulder, but she was relieved when she heard the door finally shut. She should have been warmed by his concern, but how could she feel a closeness that wasn't there? Perhaps his concern and worry were real, but wrapped within them was an edge, a hardness she didn't try to understand.

Instead of feeling cherished by his attention, she felt exposed and vulnerable; all she felt when he looked at her now was—damaged.

～

Michael woke up at his usual 6:00 a.m., immediately alarmed at the empty space beside him. Concern pounding his heart, he grabbed a robe and went in search of his wife. *Please let her be all right, please* . . . Words tumbled around in his head, disjointed and erratic. He pushed the door open to the kitchen and found her.

Piano music from a CD filled the air and there she was, mixing eggs and sautéing vegetables for an omelet. He could already smell scones in the oven. His frown wasn't from anger, though it looked like it. Damn, this made no sense at all. She had been exhausted last night. Of course, he was relieved she wasn't hurt, but the adrenaline pumping inside him had nowhere to go. He breathed hard and finally said something.

She jumped at the stern "Good morning" that came from the doorway. Then she laughed, throwing back her head. It did nothing to ease the conflicting emotions wrapping him like a prisoner. "Hey sleepyhead, you finally got up." She set the bowl down on the counter and held out her arms. He moved in closer to hug her and even tried to smile, but failed. He was completely baffled. Michael had a hard time comprehending things that made no sense whatsoever.

"Me a sleepyhead? You're the one who never gets up before I go to work! And what's all this? You never ever cook me breakfast during the week." He tried to keep his voice clean, but even he could hear the clip in it.

She lifted her chin a little higher. "So enjoy it now."

She turned back to the oven, and all Michael could do was shake his head. It made no sense. Intellectually, he tried to blame the disease. Tried to, but he had to wonder what was real and who was really in charge. He knew it wasn't him and resented that more deeply than he could admit.

Chapter Twenty

The first meeting of the Northern Neck Neuromuscular Support Group was called to order by a wonderfully composed Adrienne Moore. Elizabeth was amazed at her friend's resilience. Adrienne and Ian had only just returned from the funeral and visiting Thomas's family. She found it incredible there were no smudges of sadness on their faces. Elizabeth thought them remarkably stoic.

The fitness center had a large open room with the front desks staffed by healthy, muscled attendants. Situated on the other side of the building was the indoor pool. The chlorine smell attested to its health. Adrienne had pointed out on the way to their room that the club offered water aerobics. "The doctors said that would be very good for me. Would you like to try it, too?"

Elizabeth shrugged, not really listening; she was trying to push away the absurd nervous jitters suddenly making her heart race. She fervently hoped there would be somebody here for this new group Adrienne wanted to start. What if there was only her and Elizabeth?

It was the third Tuesday of the month, and when they opened the door to the designated room, she was relieved to see people at the long rectangular table.

A bright, welcoming smile was bestowed all around, and Adrienne looked with approval at the thirteen people who presented themselves this morning. Some in wheelchairs, others with canes, some looking as fit as the people using the exercise equipment beyond the door of this room.

"I am delighted you all could come. My name is Adrienne Moore, and I would like to go around the room and let you introduce yourselves. I'm also sending a pad and pen around for your names, phone numbers, and addresses, so we can keep in touch. Let me assure you, this information is confidential and will not be allowed to go outside the group. Here, Elizabeth, you start."

Elizabeth nodded, wishing her face wasn't flooded with color like a red neon sign. "Hello, um, I'm Elizabeth Whittaker, and I have MS." Laughter suddenly sputtered. "I feel like I'm at an Alcoholics Anonymous meeting." Nervous titters eased the nervousness of new people meeting for the first time. Except for Adrienne and Elizabeth, no one knew anyone else.

As everyone introduced themselves, Adrienne was making notes: three people with MS plus Elizabeth, two with fibromyalgia, two with post-polio syndrome, Adrienne with SMA, two with various forms of arthritis, two with Parkinson's. There on the far end of the table was a very handsome and obviously athletic young man.

"Uh, my name is Gregory Jamison, and I'm not here for myself. I have an uncle who has ALS; you know, amyotrophic lateral sclerosis. He saw the story about this group starting and asked if I could come and, well, check it out for him."

"That's kind of you," Adrienne said, puzzled. "We're glad to have you in proxy and we'll be glad to have your uncle when he comes, but what exactly are you supposed to check out? See if we're legitimate?"

She watched, intrigued, his face coloring. "Well, um, to see . . . if you're upbeat, or . . . uh, depressing. Yes, I think those were his words."

Adrienne threw back her head and laughed so fully, so broadly, that it demanded participation; within seconds the room was roaring. "Well, let me assure you, the last thing this group will be is depressing. I'm hoping we can be activists, leading the charge for change, for awareness, for understanding from people like you who are"—she paused dramatically—"merely temporarily-abled." That startled a smile from him; this woman had no idea of how right she was about that.

"Welcome." She looked around at the others, hoping this group could be what she had just described. "This area needs a lot of change. For the ones who use the handicapped parking spaces, are you tired of people who invariably leave their shopping carts right smack in the middle of the space because they're too lazy to walk them back into the store?" The nods were unanimous.

"How about that huge discount store in town that mashes all its merchandise together so even if you don't need a wheelchair, you can barely get from one department to the other?" Ethel Carden asked with a good deal of indignation in her voice. She sat in a trim motor-ized cart as she looked around the table, frowning hard enough to go do something about it right now. She was one with MS and had not taken kindly to it, or to the way it had changed the people in her fam-ily. The way they treated her now, as useless as a piece of dried-up old wood, kept her grumpy.

"Good! One of the things we can do is to write to these stores and let them know how we feel. Another thing is to write to newspapers and complain. It's the squeaky wheel that gets the attention and be-lieve you me, I intend to sound like pure rust."

"Did you ever happen to consider," an amiable man in a wheel-chair pointed out, "that it's also the squeaky wheels that get re-placed first?"

Giggles rippled the room and only increased when Adrienne sat up straight and said smugly, "I'm irreplaceable"—Adrienne checked her notes—"Mr. Albert Stoddart."

"Uh-oh, she's got my name, there could be trouble." His face fell easily into familiar laugh lines, as if it was something he often did. He held out his hand. "Peace. I'm perfectly happy to have you as my leader, dear lady."

Gregory watched as strangers soon relaxed into the ease of old friendships and wondered why that was. Adrienne was discussing strategies and speakers, and there was no end to discussions and ideas for topics.

"What about health insurance?" a young woman asked. She had no diagnosis, still going through a tumult of tests because of dizziness, numbness, and temporary blindness and, as yet, all the doctors could do was speculate. There was not enough evidence clinically for any firm diagnosis. She had a high deductible and it was costing too much to find nothing.

"Ah." Adrienne shook her head. "I was a lobbyist on the Hill for over twenty years, and we could never, ever get Congress to focus in on the need for reform. How many people here have some sort of health insurance?"

Roughly half held up their hands. Adrienne nodded knowingly. "What do the rest of you do?"

"Pray nothing else happens," muttered a construction worker crippled by arthritis. "All the companies want to exclude the arthritis because it's a preexisting condition, but hell, that's why I need it."

Pearl Smith, who had fibromyalgia, raised her hand to speak. "Well, I don't know if this counts, but I'm on Medicare through Social Security disability and my husband makes too much to be eligible for any other assistance. The supplemental insurance I've been paying for out-of-pocket has been going up so much each year I can hardly afford it. No other company will insure me because of *my* 'preexisting condition.' Don't you hate that phrase? Talk about discrimination. Every cent I get from disability goes to insuring my family. I'm just hoping the rates don't go up as bad as they say they will next year."

Elizabeth listened to the undercurrent of anxiety in their voices and was amazed she had never, ever once considered how fortunate she was. Michael's company was profitable and all employees had excellent coverage.

Tammy was a young mother with an autoimmune disease affecting the organs; the costly drugs she was taking helped control it. She was among the fortunate ones who respond to treatment, though she stayed very tired. Her two-year-old son was playing quietly nearby with a bagful of toys. "My husband has a good contracting business, making a comfortable living for us. Up until this year, he was able to provide health insurance for his two employees, but with my getting so sick, and we have a major claim on our workers' comp, we are seriously looking at bankruptcy."

"That is awful, just awful," Adrienne said, frowning intently. "I think it's a disgrace that our politicians have let us get into this situation while they enjoy the best health care in the world—at our expense. It used to drive me crazy because we couldn't get enough support from the public and business world to push some sort of mandate through that would provide health coverage for everyone. Every American should have a right to purchase health insurance at affordable costs with the risks spread out over the majority, but that's not how it works. You get a policy that may have a pool of only several hundred, while the larger corporations and state and federal governments have hundreds of thousands in their pool."

Red-faced and passionate, Adrienne shook her head. "Insurance companies actually make a tidy profit on every health premium dollar. The pharmaceutical companies are making huge profits, and it's the consumer that is getting squeezed more and more."

She paused, trying to quell her anger and then said, almost apologetically, "I was extremely fortunate my husband put me on his insurance policy before I got sick. Otherwise, I wouldn't be able to afford any of the care I get now. Let me tell you, this is not a country to live in if you get sick and disabled. With Medicare"— she nodded toward Pearl—"you have to pay for your own medication, which again costs more in this country than anywhere else in the world. And if you get any state or federal assistance, they make you jump through so many hoops you'll be too exhausted to even seek medical care. And if you do qualify, that means you have to remain poor for the rest of your life to keep it. It just makes me insane," she said, glaring around the table.

Albert Stoddart started clapping. "You've got my vote!" Murmurs of agreement hummed as everyone began to clap.

Finally, Adrienne broke into a smile and began holding up her hands. "Okay, okay, I know I get carried away, but that's also something we can at least write letters to Congress about."

"What was it like working in the Capitol?" Pearl Smith wondered.

Adrienne thought for a moment and then her eyes started twinkling. "A friend at the Pentagon once described our government perfectly. Picture this huge log floating down the river, and on that log are a million ants, all racing in different directions"—she paused for effect and looked at each one of them—"and every last one of them thinks he is in control."

Laughter, interspersed with disgusted snorts of agreement, filled the air. Finally, when there was silence, Elizabeth spoke. "Adrienne, tell that marvelous story about what your last support group did when you left."

As soon as she finished, Mr. Stoddart started pushing the buttons on his electric cart, moving it back and forth. "Whenever you little ladies are ready," he offered.

"I'll give you a run for your money, Stoddart," an older man challenged, bent deeply inside his own electric cart. The others hooted their approval.

Gregory couldn't keep from grinning. Dr. Meade knew what he was talking about. When the old doctor had called him last week and told him he should stop by this new group and see what it was about, he'd been right on the money. Since he had found out about the results of the blood test, his life had changed. Gregory had been dealing with it alone, feeling like a marked man.

Instead of telling his fiancée, it had been simpler to break off the engagement. He did not want anyone else to know what his future held. Knowing that made him concentrate more on his work, which wasn't hard; he was used to that, he was an overachiever. With the future haunting his present, he had also begun to exercise with a determination borne of the fact that if his muscles were destined to atrophy, they would first be as fit and strong as possible, to make the dying take longer. Hell, maybe he could make it impossible. The medical community, Dr. Meade kept assuring him, didn't know everything. Each person was unique.

Perhaps he could siphon off information from the people in this group, especially this Adrienne woman. Useful stuff. Like maybe how to find some courage. God knew this disease stuff wasn't for the fainthearted. How do you handle the worst news you'll ever be given and survive?

Adrienne checked her notes. "Did you know that fourteen million Americans have an autoimmune disease, with women holding the lead? That when this affects men, they tend not to fare as well? I'm looking around, and there's a seventy-thirty split right here. Not all the women are in wheelchairs or carts, but all the men are. Well, it's a little slice of statistics showing up right in our group." She shuffled some papers around and then looked up.

"As I was preparing for this meeting, I started making notes, jotting down things to talk about, and it suddenly occurred to me what we all are. Anyone with a chronic, incurable illness is a plugger. We aren't heroes; not for us the drama of a cancer patient surviving not only the disease but also the god-awful treatments, then finally attaining remission—a cure! We don't have that. All we can do is hold on long enough to get through, day by day. So we keep plugging. We keep plodding and sometimes all we can do is keep crawling, but the important thing is to keep on and not give up hope. We are pluggers extraordinaire, if you will. As a matter of fact, I was up late last night plucking through a thesaurus trying to come up with appropriate words to make up the acronym PLUGGERS. I couldn't come up with anything logical. I tried People Living Under God's Grace, but I got tired so I went to sleep instead."

A man at the other end of the table held up his hand. "Excuse me?"

Adrienne glanced at her notes. Post-polio syndrome, with lots of pain, wheelchair. "Yes, Mr. . . . Sanders, Carl Sanders."

His smile became a wince as a small tremor traveled across his face. "I don't mean to be difficult or anything, but I must point out, we all may not share the same religious beliefs as you."

Adrienne clapped a hand to her face. "You're absolutely right! I immediately apologize. Is this offensive to anyone here?" She looked around, abashed at being so insensitive.

No hands were raised but Carl Sanders's.

"Yes? This offends you? Are you, um, Buddhist? Muslim? Or—"

He shook his head. "I'm not anything. I'm an atheist." He glanced around at the surprised looks and then held up a weak hand. "But harmless."

"Well," Adrienne said, "it is very important we respect our differences, and we certainly will respect yours. We don't really have to have a silly acronym for ourselves, but if anyone wants to fiddle with it, be my guest." She smiled, her face angling to one side. "Nonetheless, I do like the word *pluggers*, and as long as we know who we are, everything else falls into place."

"What happens if you can't plug anymore?" Sally Trotter asked fretfully. She wanted to know. She was an older woman with fibromyalgia, and the pain she felt was worn on her face. The lines were deep and unrelenting.

"Well," Adrienne considered for a moment. "I think that if you can't plug along physically, then all you can do is plug along emotionally, if you are Mr. Sanders, or spiritually, if you are like the rest of us. I mean, what else could we do; is there anything left?" She looked around with an inquiring look.

"Are you always so positive?" Claude Nolan asked, suspicion scraping his voice. "Optimists can be a real pain in the tail, if you know what I mean." He was in a manual wheelchair, shaggy white hair matching a long beard. His demeanor was weathered and irritable.

"Adrienne keeps things in perspective," Elizabeth offered helpfully.

"Perspective?" He grunted. "Don't tell me, the glass half full or half empty crap?"

"Mr. Nolan, why don't you tell us how *you* cope with having an incurable, chronic illness such as post-polio syndrome?" Adrienne leaned over, and all eyes were resting solely on him.

He didn't like being the center of attention. His face reddened and he started breathing hard. He finally wheezed out, "I don't. Can't you tell?"

"Then that's the way you handle it. By not handling it. So maybe you might want to try a different way, because no one is right or wrong in this," she cautioned. "We are all finding our own way. Our own way, in our own time. Don't forget that."

Then she smiled brightly at Mr. Nolan, who blinked several times before attempting one of his own.

Sandra Little, her shiny black-wheeled walker resting behind her chair, was one of those who shared Elizabeth's disease. She looked over at her. "Elizabeth, does she always have this much energy?" Then she looked at Adrienne. "Do you?" It was an accusation. Although Sandra looked wonderful, she was mired in fatigue that had been unrelenting for a week. This wasn't helped by the intense jealousy she was feeling at this moment.

Elizabeth glanced at Adrienne. "She usually does; she's very focused and motivated. And organized . . . as for me, I'm not." She said this apologetically. Sandra gave a little nod of approval, and Elizabeth was touched by the empathy she saw in others also nodding.

"I would like to say one more thing," Carl began, with a rigidity to his jaw that spoke of constant discomfort. "I've already told you I'm an atheist. I will respect your right to believe anyway you choose, and I'll count on you to respect mine. I don't want you to think I'm rude, though, when I excuse myself if these meetings get to be . . . What did you say earlier?" He frowned, and then found the word. "Spiritual."

"Thank you." Adrienne made a note beside his name. "I find this fascinating, your views. I don't think I could get through a moment without knowing God is real and alive. I'd like to understand your viewpoint, if I may. A thought occurs to me: Does this merely mean I am more needy than you?" She watched him try to shrug.

The word jogged Elizabeth's memory. "If you need something, you look for it. Perhaps Mr. Sanders doesn't need anything?"

His smile was brief, twisting at the end. "I think I need to be taken out and shot. This damn body is falling apart."

"Oh, no, surely your doctors can come up with something," Adrienne urged gently, relieved to see the tension finally roll off and his shoulders relax.

"You don't believe in nothing?" asked Nicole Anderson, who had a mane of long auburn hair and looked normal—until she stood up and you saw the cane. Her face was plain, and these were the first words she had spoken beyond introducing herself. She had relapsing/remitting MS.

Hard blue eyes grazed her and she flinched. "You sound like there must be something wrong with me," he said sternly. "And you've used two negatives that negate your question," he added, a hint of superiority coloring his words. For a brief second before his mouth tightened, he was the arrogant son of a bitch he used to be—in his other life.

"Culturally, she sounds like 99.9 percent of America today," Adrienne interjected, dismayed at the embarrassed color on Nicole's face. Adrienne's husband was a master of the English language, and she wasn't about to let this man make anyone feel bad about words.

"True." Carl grunted. "If I believed in anything, I'd agree this country is going to hell in a handbag . . . but since I don't, I won't." The smile that briefly found his eyes was almost amused before it disappeared in a grimace.

"Yes." Adrienne's voice was as dry as day-old toast. "Well, we will indeed respect each other's differences, certainly. Not only with respect but"—here Adrienne shot him a hard, chastising glance, her eyebrows raised—"we will treat each other with courtesy and kindness."

Her glare didn't affect him much, although he did nod and say, "Yes, ma'am."

"Fine. Now, please forgive my curiosity, but may I ask if you have always been an atheist? Is that how you were raised?"

He shook his head and shifted in the chair; that slight move seemed to settle his body in an easier pattern. "No, ma'am. For the first thirty years of my life, I was a Christian, went to church most Sundays when I could."

"What happened? That is, if you wouldn't mind telling us?" Adrienne was fascinated, but was mindful of not prying too much.

"I saw personally what mankind can do to each other, its women and even children. I was part of the military task force that detailed massacres throughout the world—the ethnic cleansing, tribal conflicts; it was our job to sort out the details of the dead. How many, how they were killed, etc." Dark, terrible memories haunted his eyes and he grimaced, whether in pain or something else was known only to him. "After the first year, I knew there was no God. All that church stuff, feel-good loving God crap was just that. No merciful, caring God could allow people not only to kill and torture each other, but to do that to innocent children, too. Nope. That's why I know there's nothing beyond these known facts: We get born, we live, we die. Period."

It was a harsh assessment, Adrienne thought, but one borne of knowledge that shouldn't exist.

She could feel his anger, his disgust, but she couldn't contain her questions. "You said what mankind does to itself. Why do you believe God had anything to do with any of those awful things? Now, I'm not saying you're wrong," she hurriedly assured. "I just want to understand."

She saw the look of pity he gave her. "The way I was taught, the way I remember it, God's supposed to be the One in control, the One who decides what'll happen, right? Look around the world. There is nothing in control except people . . . most of them doing a damn poor job." Suddenly weary, his shoulders drooped. "Can we talk about something else?"

"Of course, of course. I didn't mean to be so curious, Carl. Perhaps we'll talk later. Now, let's see." Adrienne immediately shuffled through her notes and gave a brief summary of what she would try to plan for next month's meeting.

She looked around the room with a smile for each person. "Anything else? No? Then we are adjourned until next month. A notice will be in the newspapers, but it's the third Tuesday of the month. I'll try to give everyone a call or e-mail. Thank you so much for coming."

Everyone but Elizabeth wheeled, walked, or shuffled past as Adrienne glanced at all the notes she had written. An older man slipped into the room and fell in step with Carl Sanders. Elizabeth later learned he employed aides as he needed them and drivers.

Adrienne was already making plans to get the speakers they had talked about, such as a physical therapist, one local doctor offering acupuncture, and perhaps someone to talk about the Americans with Disabilities Act. Several of the people who came were still working, albeit part-time. Knowledge is power, Adrienne had stated, and they all agreed.

Elizabeth was impressed. Things had gone very well, and she insisted on taking Adrienne out to eat.

Restaurants are as abundant as the fresh fish in the rivers hugging this northern peninsula, and although all are supposed to be handicapped-accessible, some are more so than others. Adrienne knew, by practical experience, which was which. The two had ridden together, so they drove back toward their homes and stopped at Café Latte.

While they waited for their food, Elizabeth ventured to ask about the funeral. Adrienne's eyes suddenly misted, but she remained composed.

"It was beautiful. Everyone had a special memory to share about Thomas. It was beautiful and sad. It helped us heal, a little, I think." Adrienne paused to sip some water. "It reaffirmed what an incredible, loving child he was, yet so adult at times. He cared for other people; he was the most empathetic child I have ever known. The stories were happy, sad . . . His brother and sister spoke of how much he meant to them. It was a poignant gathering filled with laughter and tears."

Elizabeth waited as a few quiet moments slipped by before she could put together the next question, her voice tentative. "How are the parents holding up? Ever since you've been gone I've been thinking, carefully and very gingerly, how I would feel if something happened to Kellan. The thought makes me cringe. I don't think I'd be able to live with such a loss."

Adrienne looked at her thoughtfully. "Actually, if it happened you wouldn't have a choice. Just as they have no choice—no, that's not right either. What they have decided is not to let this cripple them, but to instead strengthen them. I can tell you honestly that their faith is allowing them God's grace to deal with losing Thomas."

Faith—always faith . . . "Compared to all of you, I don't think I have any," Elizabeth said flatly. "You all seem to be handling it so well, and I—there's all these questions, all these hurts, I . . . what if I were to lose Kellan like Danielle lost her son, how you lost your godchild? I . . . how can God let this happen?"

Adrienne's eyes narrowed. "You sound like Carl. Do you think God lets or makes these terrible things happen? Have you asked yourself how God could let this happen?" Her gesture encompassed the chair and her body. "Or this happen?" The motion encompassed Elizabeth, her cane, and her weakened leg.

Elizabeth rolled her eyes. "Of course I have; haven't you?"

"In the beginning, yes. We had some strenuous discussion over it, God and I." Adrienne's face clouded with past memories. "But I have to say I believe He doesn't let anything just happen. It's part of . . . some magical master plan. It's up to us to choose if we are going to be players or not. Don't forget, we are the ones with free will. You are perfectly free to disbelieve if you choose. That's the premise of our faith."

Pretty words, Elizabeth thought. "Doesn't it all make you crazy?"

Adrienne waved her hand again in a broad gesture encompassing everything. "Sometimes."

Elizabeth pushed aside the plate of food. "Then how? How do you deal with it, live with it, and on top of everything else believe God has our best interests at heart? What *is* the point?" On one level, Elizabeth was dimly aware she was stranded at a crossroads; on another level she saw the easy beliefs of a lifetime start to smolder under a dark flame. And yet . . . there was something she couldn't let go of. How could Adrienne, whose health was far worse than her own, whose godchild was dead because of a senseless accident, keep such a strong faith?

Adrienne leaned closer and touched Elizabeth's arm. "Because to do otherwise is truly and absolutely unthinkable, unbearable. I meant what I told Carl a little while ago. I find it fascinating he is an atheist, but even more so that after a lifetime of belief he has chosen to disbelieve because of what people with free will choose to do.

"I think it's easy to forget that there really is an evil one, the evil force that rips and devastates and ruins life. That's the force behind all of the horrible things he has seen." Adrienne sipped a little water and then flattened her hand on the table. Her eyes were clear, intense. "After I found out about the SMA, when my back was figuratively and literally against the wall and life was so frightening I could hardly breathe, I discovered something I had never known. In desperate times, some people look down and that's where they stay, letting the weight of their circumstances cripple them even further. Perhaps others are like Carl; they look straight ahead and accept each moment as merely finite, without meaning." Adrienne looked at Elizabeth intently. "Me? I was too desperate to look anyplace but up."

More than the words, Elizabeth heard the assurance wrap like steel bands around each word with solid certainty and wished she could embrace it without hesitation. Elizabeth sat quietly, her face sad.

But Adrienne wasn't finished. "One more thing occurs to me. It's that marvelous story your good priest told about the sun dogs. Everyone needs a sundog moment, when things become so clear you can almost see the other side of life, circumstances blossom into something extraordinary and the impossible becomes possible."

Sun dogs! Elizabeth shivered. "Do you know I still haven't seen one?"

"Keep looking up, and you'll find everything you need," Adrienne advised.

That's what Father Wells had said, Elizabeth thought.

With a sudden, intense longing, Elizabeth looked toward the windows of the restaurant and noticed clouds had drawn curtains around the sun, casting a gray net without end, and she sighed.

Chapter Twenty-one

You enjoyed yourself?" Carol tried not to sound doubtful. Personally, she couldn't see it. Why would people who were sick want to get together with other people who were also sick? It sounded like a prescription for depression.

Elizabeth had stopped by to see Carol before going on to the state library to help in the catalog department; they were still updating everything to a new, more advanced computer. "It was great and," she said, reading easily the expression on her cousin's face, "no, it wasn't depressing, not in the least. You should come and visit. We meet once a month."

"You're going to drive all the way up there just for one meeting?" Carol was incredulous. "Don't they have support group meetings here?"

"It's not the same. I told you, Adrienne Moore is the force behind this, and I like her very much. You said you wanted to meet her. Remember?"

"Well, sure, one of these days," Carol said vaguely, feeling uncomfortable about the whole thing. Why did Elizabeth want to be around people in wheelchairs with diseases and such? Regardless of what she said, it *was* depressing, and Carol couldn't imagine willingly going. She'd rather go see her dentist, which now that she thought of it, had been postponed to the point that it was inevitable.

Carol simply pushed the idea of the dentist and the group away from her, ignoring the discomfort she felt, not realizing it had more to do with an undercurrent of fear. These people were tangible proof of what could happen, and there were enough things in the world to worry about without subjecting one's self to this on purpose.

She changed the subject. "Didn't Kellan look great on Friday? That girl just keeps getting more and more gorgeous; I don't know how you can stand to let her out of your sight. How come she doesn't have any boyfriends?"

Elizabeth picked up her purse, keeping an eye on the clock. "She says she'd gone out with a bunch of guys this summer but threw them all back. None were keepers. She is very discriminating, I am happy to report."

Carol walked her to the sidewalk where her car was parked. "She deserves the very best, so I'm glad she's being careful. I know what she means about keepers, though. They are hard to find."

"Uh-huh," Elizabeth murmured noncommittally and got into the car, but Carol held the door open.

"I'm surprised you aren't regaling me with how wonderful your husband is and how you knew he was a keeper the first time you laid your blue eyes on him."

Elizabeth merely smiled, not surprised at all. She said good-bye, closing the door firmly.

～

"Father Joe, I've got a question for you, if you don't mind?" Elizabeth had stopped at the church on the mere chance he might be here and not busy. For the past two weeks she had been mulling over Adrienne's comments. Since she had no idea if her priest would be available to talk when she had stopped by without calling first, Elizabeth took it as a good omen he was even there this early afternoon.

"Come in, come in." He waved her to the upholstered chair and sat down opposite her. "Your timing is perfect. I finished one meeting and have no one else to see until the vestry meeting tonight. Would you like something to drink?" He held up a tea bag and a jar of instant coffee, but she shook her head.

"No, I wanted to ask you. . . . How can God let terrible things happen?"

He whistled silently, shaking his head as he got up. "You might not need anything for a question like that, but I do—a very strong cup of caffeine."

"Sorry," Elizabeth murmured, watching him heat up water in the microwave he kept in his office.

Within moments he stirred two heaping teaspoons of instant coffee briskly into the microwaved water, took a sip, and looked over the Styrofoam cup at her. She glanced down and saw his brown shoes matched nicely with the khaki pants, black shirt, and priest's collar. "How's Estelle?"

"Staying so busy she and I practically have to make an appointment to see each other. Now," he said as he focused on her. "Your question: Why does God let awful things happen? There are several possibilities, the least of which is that bad things happen because of the bad choices we make—" He stopped as she held up her hand.

"Let me tell you something that happened recently, to a friend's godchild," she began.

When she finished, Father Joe's face was saddened in sympathy. "God be with that family," he murmured. His eyes closed, as if in a brief prayer, and then he looked hard at her. "Accidents happen, Elizabeth."

"Isn't God supposed to be in control of everything?" she countered.

He nodded. "But it's more than that. Things happen, and we can't understand, but we survive by God's grace. And, frankly, sometimes we need our hearts broken soundly. Sometimes that's the only way we will ever know how much God loves us."

She rubbed her neck, weariness suddenly undermining this quest for answers. "Surely you can understand that makes no sense."

"It does," he insisted. "But if you've not been through it, it may be hard to understand. It sounds like a paradox, but trust me, it's vibrantly true. As far as bad things happening, we're not in this world alone. Just as there is a God of mercy and blessings, there is a Satan of evil."

"The devil?" She wrinkled her nose even as she remembered what Adrienne had tried to explain. Before she could stop it, an image of a cartoon devil popped into her head.

Her rector was unfazed. "Absolutely. There is God and there is Satan—good and evil—and with faith in God, we can overcome anything. Or at least endure. Look at the example of Job. Look at the psalmists. Their faith and their hope in God were enough. More than enough, Elizabeth. By remaining faithful, it will always be more than enough."

He could see he wasn't getting through to her and stopped. He thought hard and then finally offered, "I have a story about good and evil that might help just a little. Years ago, when my grandson was nine years old, he was spending the weekend with us. Saturday night he came and curled up on the bed beside me and told me he had been talking to God. 'Papa,' he said, 'I just told God I would become a vegetarian, not watch television for the rest of the year, do one chore a day, and not be mean to anyone if He lets me have magical powers.' He was dead earnest, and he wanted me to tell him God would make such a deal with him."

Father Joe chuckled, and even Elizabeth's face wore an amused look. "What did you say to him?"

"I told him in my experience, God didn't really work that way. He doesn't expect us to give up a bunch of things in exchange for His doing something for us. Face it, God doesn't need or want anything from us but our love. Needless to say, that didn't set too well with him. 'Papa, you said I should pray to God for everything.' 'Well,' I said, 'I could be wrong, but let me tell you something I have learned. If God gives you a wonderful gift, be it magic, wisdom, the ability to help people, whatever it is—make no mistake—along with it comes a great responsibility to use it wisely and carefully. Because the moment you get such a gift from God, Satan will be right there wanting to snatch it away.'"

He said this with such force, Elizabeth felt his certainty spread over her like a blanket and for a moment, she agreed without reservation.

"I bet he's never forgotten that story."

"No, I don't think he has. And as for being blessed with magic, he's been blessed with helping to heal children who have been abused by the people who were supposed to love them. He's a pediatric psychiatrist and believe me, he has performed some mighty strong magic. With God's help."

She nodded doubtfully. "I see."

But he wasn't quite finished with her yet; he clasped her hand, seeing her confusion.

"Elizabeth, when you try to put God in a box, you limit not only Him but also yourself. The world's rules don't apply. So listen with your heart, pray with your heart, and listen carefully for God's answers." He thought briefly of what C. S. Lewis had once written: *We*

*are not necessarily doubting that God will do the best for us; we are won-
dering how painful the best will turn out to be.*

He kept that thought to himself because she wouldn't understand, couldn't understand . . . not yet.

There was nothing more to say, and Elizabeth was too restless to
hear anything. She stood up and was gone before anything else
could be said. As soon as she was through the door, he bowed his
head in prayer for her.

She walked out to her car with all the uncertainties back in place.
This had never happened before and she wondered, vaguely, why.
She looked up at the church as she stood in the parking lot by her
car. There was sadness that kept her torn, and she didn't know
which way to turn.

Dinner was a silent affair. Michael had come home weary; she
had not been up to fixing very much. Weekend leftovers filled their
plates along with sandwiches. There was little conversation. *How
many times and in how many different ways can you ask, "How are
you,"* Michael wondered, watching Elizabeth out of the corner of his
eye. She looked tired. And depressed. He had asked her about her
day, and she had mentioned the usual things—said that everything
was fine. Maybe it was because *he* was tired; maybe it was his fault
the evening seemed so . . . flat.

"Would you like anything else?" she asked, beginning to pick up
plates.

He stood up and took the dishes away and waved her off. "Don't
do that, Elizabeth, I'll clean up. After all, you fixed it." She gave him
a brief smile and left the room without saying a word.

He sat back down, thought about making some coffee. He also
wondered if, in a few minutes, Elizabeth would sail right back in
here, somehow magically rejuvenated and ready to clean the entire
kitchen, top to bottom. It had happened. She'd be tired, bounce
back, then be fatigued for days and then become energized. It made
no sense, and Michael was discovering how much he hated things
that didn't make sense.

⌒

"How do you handle this without a script?" he complained to Gordon a week later. Michael was irritated. These days he could never
second-guess his wife.

They had met for lunch and, thankfully, Carol had not in-truded. She was in New York. He knew Elizabeth was spending the day at the river, packing up clothes and odds and ends to bring back home.

"Just when I'm worried sick that she's getting worse, she'll surprise me and be back to almost normal. What am I supposed to think?"

Gordon looked at him without sympathy. "Consider yourself lucky she has these reprieves. It could be a whole lot worse, trust me." Gordon had heard this complaint in different forms more than once; he spoke automatically, as if he were distracted. If Michael hadn't been so preoccupied, he might have noticed Gordon seemed to have something on his mind.

"How do you know what you're supposed to do? There's no rhyme or reason; she gets mad when I try to help, yet gets upset when I don't, and I can't read her mind." Michael fumed, running a hand through his hair.

Gordon shrugged and lifted his drink in a mock salute. "Have you told her you can't read her mind?"

His face tightened when Michael merely shrugged. "She doesn't listen anyway."

"I know husbands who'd kill to have the problem with their wives you're fussing about. Maybe you two should get counseling to learn to communicate better. I've got the name of a wonderful ther-apist—" He stopped when Michael shook his head.

"We don't need to talk to anybody; we just need to . . . get used to things." He bent down and picked up his sandwich and began eating.

Gordon looked at him, a deep frown creasing his face, and won-dered how they were going to get used to things when the premise of their lives now was change. "Michael, let me ask you a question."

"What?"

"What would you do if your roles were reversed? What if you had the disease, not Elizabeth. What would you be doing?"

Michael didn't hesitate. "I would avail myself of the best and lat-est information and then do everything the doctors advised me to do. Wouldn't you?"

His voice held a smugness that was erased when Gordon shook his head.

"Come on, Gordon, of course you would." Michael didn't believe him.

Gordon rested his hand on either side of his plate and leaned forward, rigid with fury over what he was about to say. "No. I would keep up with all the research, but at this point I wouldn't follow standard advice for myself."

"How can you say that?" Michael demanded. Gordon's jaw clenched at the information he had learned earlier that day, devastating news that had wrecked his life, his past, and forever his future.

"I've been practicing medicine for over twenty years; my father was a doctor for over forty years before he died; my grandfather, another forty. They each confirmed the same thing that I've also discovered to be true. Every patient will respond to the same medication differently. Sometimes it's a big difference, sometimes small. Why do you think there is such a wide range of possible side effects listed on most prescriptions? Because the drug companies have to cover their tails; they don't know how it will affect everyone. The therapies that Elizabeth won't use? No one knows how they work, what the long-term side effects are, and frankly, that scares the hell out of me." And that wasn't all, he thought, his chest tightening. That wasn't all.

Yesterday afternoon he'd opened one of the many AMA journals he hadn't had time to scan before. Glancing through the index, he saw the term *bone-marrow transplant*. He immediately turned to the story and crashed into a nightmare. He took a deep breath, shifting back to this moment

"If they don't know how it works, then how do they know it *does* work? Because it does—I've seen the reports." Michael's patronizing tone grated and fueled Gordon's anger, making him dangerously precise.

"Statistics. Statistically speaking, patients become about twenty-nine percent less disabled over a ten-year period, give or take a few points, with the therapies."

"Well that's a damn sight better than doing nothing!"

"My patients aren't statistics. I've got an MS patient now who has been on one of the therapies for years, has gone blind in one eye because of optic neuritis, is in the hospital as we speak, being pumped with steroids while continuing the therapy, and it's been three weeks. No sight has returned. Statistically speaking, it won't."

"That patient is still doing the absolute best thing," Michael insisted, frustrated when Gordon shook his head.

"The bottom line is, no one knows. I tell you, between managed care telling me what I can and cannot do and the pharmaceutical companies pouring money like water into advertisements to get my patients to buy only their brands, it's become a crazy, unbalanced playing field. And the drug industry pouring its money into research laboratories? Did you ever consider the incredible pressure to make the results pan out the way the guys who are footing the bill want it? Did you ever consider the possibility that pressure could slant and skew results? What is this world coming to when every tiny scrap of research is motivated solely and purposefully by money?"

Michael was affronted. "So now you're saying we shouldn't have a capitalistic society? What's with you, Gordon? Without the massive amounts of money those horrible companies pour into research, you wouldn't have better and better drugs to help your patients. Put things in perspective, man."

"I'll put it in perspective for you; I'll be damn happy to put it in perspective." Gordon's anger boiled over, and he couldn't contain it.

"Guess what I found out yesterday? When Allison was still alive and we were grabbing and clutching at straws, we relied on the best and latest information. She was in the last stages of breast cancer, and the only hope we had was high-dose chemo followed by a bone-marrow transplant. Research said it prolonged survival better than conventional treatment." He stopped abruptly, averted his face and tried not to be overcome with the anger hammering at him. God, this was killing him. He wiped away sweat from his brow.

"Gordon, you did everything you could," Michael began impatiently, but Gordon held up a hand.

He breathed deeply and fought to keep the words steady. "I just found out the research was bogus. Wrong. Results had been misreported; there is no benefit from that dreadful procedure. But I talked her into it. I talked her into going through hell because I thought it would help. All it did was make the last several months that much harder, a thousand times more painful."

Struggling to control his emotions, Gordon stood up abruptly. "Excuse me."

Michael watched the doctor leave. He couldn't understand. Gordon had done everything, literally everything possible, for Allison. So what if the research was proved wrong *now*? Gordon had made the best decisions based on the information available at the time. Michael shook his head, wondering why some people made things that much harder on themselves. Like Elizabeth was doing to him.

When Gordon didn't come back, Michael paid the bill and left, his mind fully engaged with what was happening that afternoon at his business.

He wasn't aware he had a mind that could compartmentalize, because it was something he had always been able to do. And since it was part of his inherent nature, he could not understand the majority of people who were not able to compartmentalize their thoughts and feelings.

Gordon Jones was one who could not . . . not when his heart had been smashed to pieces. Again.

⁓

The hint of salt clung to the moist air, and breezes off the river cooled anyone near it on this day in late September. It was Indian summer, the season's last performance before bowing out formally to autumn's legitimate claim. The crowd of girls banded together was a multiracial gathering; two of the girls were white, another dark, one light skinned, and another whose skin was a beautiful mixture of dark cream and polished mahogany. This young woman was the star of whatever group she found herself in. Black rippling waves of hair cascading down her back, Serenity Brown demanded attention simply by breathing. Tall and regal, she could never be anonymous.

Her face held the mixture of all the best of several nationalities. Her cheekbones were as high and defined as any princess's from India, her lips the best mixture of African and Greek features. Serenity Brown's eyes, large and surrounded by lush dark lashes, were a mixture of browns and blacks and moods. Her body had an inherent grace that years of ballet lessons could never teach. School was finished, part-time jobs had been completed this late afternoon on Thursday.

These friends were hanging out at the Freeze, the only fast-food joint in the area.

Serenity's anger was eloquent, her low voice pleasant even while spouting steam. "I will not tolerate such behavior either from her or from my grandmother." Her words were spoken with precision. It was the way she had been taught by her grandmother, each word and syllable clearly heard, and at this moment, quivering with fury.

Then she snapped to a low-class southern twang, notching the alto up higher. "That rich bitch is going to get it. I'm gonna make sure she gets hers; you be assured I get even with her. She be sorry for firing me."

She seethed, recalling the afternoon. She had gone with her granny after school to clean up and help pack things away for the season. Sure, the lady had been all sweetness when Serenity first started working there in the summer, but now that white cripple had turned awful. She was missing some things and asked—oh, her voice had been the sweetest fake thing imaginable—"Have you seen any of my jewelry, Serenity? Did you happen to move my rings, Serenity?" The suspicious bitch had already convicted her, made all those snide insinuations! She felt anger flare up and burn all over again inside her, hands clenched in fists.

No one—not even her grandmother who had raised her for the last six years or these girls who thought they were her closest friends—could imagine what her life had been like before she came to this country. America, where so many had so little and yet there was this abundance of *stuff*. Pretty things, valuable things, all reaching out for her attention.

"What'd your granny say when she fire you?" Kasey asked, snickering. This outburst of temper was not unusual because Serenity was always getting herself into some kind of trouble. The fun was watching her get out of it.

"You mean when that rich bitch said I took her stuff? That fool of a woman, who calls herself my flesh and blood, *agreed* with her! Took her side against me, and we are *kin*." She added a southern drenching to that last word, turning its meaning into a two-syllable slur. "I said I didn't take anything, and then my grandmother made me turn my pockets inside out, didn't give me one little minute to do anything else."

"What happened when you did that?" Kasey persisted.

Serenity's mouth firmed into a slash of disapproval. "There it was, *her* gold necklace. I tried and tried to explain I had no idea how it got there, but would they listen? Noooo, just kicked me out, and now Granny says I have to clean up my act and stay out of trouble or she's turning me over to the cops as a juvenile delinquent."

The other girls twittered with sounds of admiration as Serenity suddenly pulled out another gold necklace with a diamond and emerald pendant from her bosom. "Now tell me why that witch needs this down here in slum town. There's nowhere she's gonna wear something like this." She draped the necklace against her throat, modeling it with disdain.

"So you did her a favor." Kasey cackled, slapping her leg while the others applauded.

Quick as a cat, Serenity flicked the necklace back into her bra and grinned. She liked their admiration; the applause made her feel important.

As suddenly as a spring thunderstorm, her triumphant smile turned into a fierce frown. "That sick old witch still's gonna pay. She made my granny turn on me; it's all her fault. I'm gonna wait, be patient, but she's gonna pay. Big-time." She heard the girls giggle in support and Serenity held her head up even higher. She, Serenity Brown, was never going to take any crap off a rich person again.

What she left unsaid was that her granny had also threatened to send her back to Jamaica, back to the authorities to wait until her mother got out of jail. For a moment, Serenity had been fearful her granny might actually do it, but after she left that stupid place and thought about it, she was sure that it wouldn't happen. For one thing, her grandmother would have to reach down and dig deep into her pockets for the cost of sending her back, no easy task.

The other thing was that Serenity knew her granny really loved her; she knew the old woman could never send her back to that hole in the wall with her mother hopelessly addicted to that moment's chemical of choice—whatever she could find to shoot in her veins.

Reassuring herself, Serenity calmed to a regal innocence that belied her clear thought about revenge. She realized how she was going to have to manipulate the truth to eventually succeed. And that would mean doing something totally distasteful—but necessary.

While she planned her strategy, her grandmother and Elizabeth were commiserating in their worries about the girl. Inside her house, Elizabeth sat at the kitchen table, trying to be consoling.

"I'm sorry, Mehalia, I simply cannot call the police about this. She's just a child." Elizabeth was earnest and patted the old woman's hand.

"I know, Elizabeth." The housekeeper's sigh was painful. "I know, and I do not want you feeling bad. I plainly do not know what to do with this child. She is so good in so many ways. Bright, good at school, but she has gotten this attitude lately that the world owes her." Her voice was deep and smooth, forming each word specifically and correctly. Mehalia had always spoken her words precisely and taught all her children to do the same. She was an uneducated woman, but the words she spoke always sounded as they should. It was how she lived her life. She wore an honest dignity like a mantle and made no pretensions about herself.

It grieved her that Serenity seemed to have slithered away from that example. Mehalia's steadfast demeanor was creasing with despair.

"She's a beauty, but that's just on the outside," she slowly considered. "Maybe that's what makes her so . . . needful. Beauty is nothing if it's not on the inside, too, but how do you make a child discover such a thing? I'm worrying myself to pieces—what is going to happen if—when—she steals from someone who's not as nice as you?"

Elizabeth shook her head. "I wish I had answers for you." She insisted that Mehalia stay sitting at the table while she got up and made tea for them both.

Elizabeth wondered why she had decided to come here today. If she hadn't, no one would have known anything was missing. It just seemed the right time to come back and pack up the expensive pieces, to take them home tomorrow or the day after.

If she had called Mehalia earlier, would Serenity then have had time to put those pieces back? Calling Mehalia and her granddaughter had been as much for company as it was for the help. What a mess.

"Here." She set the steaming cup of tea in front of the older woman, patting her arm gently. "I wish I had some easy words for you, knew what to tell you to do, Mehalia. I don't have a clue. But you are right, she is one of the most beautiful young women I have ever seen. That sure complicates things."

They shared brooding sighs and worried thoughts as they offered possible solutions that—once spoken—didn't seem possible after all. Finally, Elizabeth walked her part-time housekeeper to her old Chevrolet, offering to think hard about the problem. "Surely we can come up with some sort of plan for the child." Elizabeth said this earnestly, leaning down to give Mehalia another consoling hug.

Chapter Twenty-two

When Gordon walked out of the restaurant, he wanted to escape. From everything. Without thought, he called his office, feigned illness, and told them not to expect him for the next several days. Ask one of the associates to cover for him, he'd told his assistant, and if that doesn't work, cancel appointments until further notice.

He drove the gray Lincoln, his mind fogged with grief and guilt; he was the doctor in the family. Bad enough he couldn't even save his own wife, but to have done that to her, to have failed to look at the research more carefully, scrutinized it before talking her into doing it . . .

He returned home by way of the liquor store, stopping to load up with a variety of bottles to ensure his escape.

The first bottle didn't do much to assuage the guilt but blurred it, pushed it back.

By the time he had opened a third bottle, his heart was no longer hurting because it was numb. There was an absurd delight in beating himself up intellectually. He, the big know-it-all doctor who got blindsided because he trusted the research. God, what a fool he was.

He was well into that last bottle, knowing the anger was still there lurking but mercifully detached, when he heard the doorbell chime. Startled, he jerked up; splashes of liquor stained the chair and floor. *Damn. Who could that be?* he wondered as he slowly made his way to the entry. His home had a large foyer that was practically empty. He had gotten rid of all family pictures as well as Allison's possessions after her death. Those reminders were too painful to have around. Now, as he stumbled past the bareness, he was aware of sorrow that he'd even done that, in a confused, jumbled sort of way.

He peered through the glass and saw Carol Stephens, looking very New York in black leather pants and a matching long trench coat. She looked like the modern version of an old western gunslinger. The idea of her being a shootin' chick bubbled up a hilarity that got caught in his throat and he opened the door in a spasm of coughing.

She strode in, immediately pounding him on the back. "Good grief, Gordon, what did you do, swallow a fly?"

She'd meant it as a joke; her brows rose at the smell of liquor and his jagged movements. "My, my, must've been a rough day," she murmured as she tried to take his arm and help him into the living room.

He was hiccupping now and his mind was riveted on snatches of an old, old childhood song. "I swallowed a fly, I sure as hell don't know why . . . There was an old coot who swallowed a . . . a . . . bird to eat the damn fly, . . . Swallowed a fly, I don't know why . . . Maybe I'll die." He flopped on the recliner as he said those last words. He looked around, momentarily confused about where he was, then he looked up and smiled. "Where are my m-manners? Wanna drink?" He started to get up again and she pushed him back gently.

"You've had enough for both of us, thank you." She said this with such a kind smile, he grinned then burped loudly.

The force of it sprawled him backward against the chair. He sighed and rested his head comfortably against the cushions and closed his eyes. Within moments he was snoring.

Carol sat across from him. "Oh, Gordon." She spoke softly, wondering what had pushed him over the edge. There had been plans to go out tonight. But she had come back from New York earlier because of how he sounded yesterday when they had talked on the phone.

He had sounded . . . odd. For a man who maintained a carefully neutral emotional state, he sounded like he had slipped off the deep end but was fighting to keep his head up.

He had agreed to get together tonight, but in a distracted way, and she wondered if he had even remembered to write it down on his calendar, which was the only way he kept track of where he was supposed to be. She went into the kitchen and checked it herself.

What had happened? She frowned as she saw where he had been yesterday and today. And then she did something she had never done before. She didn't even have to look the number up; she knew it by heart.

"Michael, this is Carol. No, nothing's happened to Elizabeth. I just wanted to know, have you talked with Gordon lately? You had lunch. Today? Oh, I see."

She listened intently for several minutes, grimacing as she had to listen to Michael's whole account of the conversation instead of what she had asked about.

"How did he seem when he left? Depressed? I see . . . Well, we were supposed to get together tonight, but he seems a bit . . . under the weather."

Carol didn't like talking to Michael, but since the two men had been together today, she thought he might know something. For some reason, Gordon had claimed Michael as a best friend over twenty years ago.

"Really? He said that? And you told him . . . Oh, okay. That's certainly enlightening. No, I'm not being sarcastic, I'm just trying to . . . okay. Fine. Bye." She hung up the phone, feeling angry. Her dislike of Michael was reinforced yet again. The man had no heart.

She walked back into the living room. Gordon hadn't moved a muscle; he was snoring loudly. She got a blanket from a linen closet and draped it over him, then picked up the two empty bottles and looked at them; she was impressed. He should be sleeping a long time. She took the bottles to the kitchen and put them in the recycle tub. She tidied up the room a bit. She was glad to be doing something constructive, although she was finished in moments.

She wanted to do more. Carol understood his pain; she knew

how devastated he must feel about Allison, but . . . there was nothing he could do about changing the past. He had done the best he could do for his wife at the time. That was fact.

But emotions, as she well knew, don't listen to logic. She wondered what she could do to mute it, soften it for him. After several moments of reflection, she nodded to herself. With purpose she went to her car, retrieved the laptop, found a space at the kitchen table, and plugged it in. The next few hours were spent searching the Web for information that might not even exist.

Evening drifted away into early morning.

Like an internal alarm, Gordon woke up instantly, immediately aware of the intense quiet surrounding him. The sun was several minutes from gilding the eastern sky with color. Completely alert, palpable silence embraced him; for a long moment he was inside it, part of it, and it made him invisible, only it didn't last long enough.

As the moments stretched forward, the inevitable memory also slid to the forefront of his mind and he squeezed his eyes shut. When he could stand the darkness no longer, he opened them and was startled to see Carol curled up on his couch; a sudden thought made him sick: Weren't they supposed to get together . . . sometime? Thoughts fluttered in disarray as the confusion mingled with the aftereffects of the booze.

How had she gotten in? He had no recollection of yesterday after he left the liquor store and arrived home. Damn. He was in no mood for company; he wanted to be alone. Completely alone, to continue drinking toward nothing but a soft oblivion. He must have made some unconscious noise because suddenly she was awake. He watched her legs swing to the floor, her hands stretching overhead, and then she was walking toward him.

"Gordon." She stopped in front of him, eyes warm with sympathy he didn't need or want.

"Carol." He was surprised he had a voice at all. "How, uh, did you get in here?"

"You let me in."

"Oh." He squinted up at her. "Hmm. I don't really remember much . . . What happened last night?"

She sat on the edge of the hassock, pushing his feet over. The small smile was provocative, her voice low and amused. "You mean after we consummated our friendship? Or before?"

A hand snaked up to rub his face. "Aw, hell." He was dismissive. "We didn't do any of that; I never get sick when I'm drunk. I have a cast-iron stomach."

Her face was the picture of innocence, her voice soft, insinuating. "That's not what I meant." Startled eyes met hers. She watched as clashing emotions slid over his face, easily reading his thoughts.

"We didn't . . ." He looked at her, not sure of anything. Seeing her lift a seductive brow, he asked uneasily, "What—what *exactly* do you mean by consummate?" The last thing he wanted in this world was any more emotional baggage. His shoulders were simply not wide enough.

Carol let the moment lengthen substantially before finally patting his hand. "Nothing physical."

His sigh was so full of relief, it made her chuckle. "That's just the way you made me feel, so consider this payback."

"Thanks," he murmured feebly, trying to sit up and then wincing. His head was splitting.

"So I take it you were upset enough to get sauced last night?"

"I don't want to talk about it. God, my mouth stinks. Move, let me get up." She stood, letting him pass.

"Go get cleaned up; I'll make coffee," she instructed him, even escorting him to the back stairs.

Humming, she fixed not only coffee, but also pancakes from a mix. By the time he came back down, his hair still damp from the shower, she had a place all fixed up for him at the table. He stopped at the bottom stair, taking in the food, coffee; she had even gone outside and plucked some colorful flowers that scented the room.

He wasn't hungry. His head still hurt and while he boasted of an iron stomach, it was letting him know how little it appreciated last night.

What he really wanted was a drink.

She pulled out the chair for him. There was nothing left to do but sit. He wondered how quickly he could get rid of her.

It was then that he noticed a folder filled with papers next to the plate, which was heaped with pancakes. Butter and syrup were on the side and a big mug of steaming coffee.

Carol sat down next to him, her own cup half full, looking like she was settling in.

"Carol, thanks, but I wasn't expecting all this. To tell you the truth, I'm not this hungry." He waved a hand at the plate.

"Then just eat what you can," she said reasonably.

"To tell you the truth, I'd rather . . ." He bit the inside of his lip, wondering how to carry this out. She did it for him.

"Be alone, right?" She watched him nod, then waited for him to look her in the eye. "Not a chance. Not until we talk. You owe me."

He put a hand to his thudding head, wondering what he had ever done to deserve this. "You barge into my house, spend the night un-invited, and now you won't leave when you know I don't want you to be here, and *I owe you*?" He was incredulous.

She smiled sweetly. "Now, you know how I felt when you barged into my house last year, bringing food to wile your way in, promising to leave on your *Scout's* honor, when you were never a Scout, and then staying even after I told you to leave. Have I got it right?"

He gave her a beleaguered look and wished he could say she was wrong. He took a quick sip of coffee. "You forgot to mention I had your very best interests at heart." The two situations were not alike at all.

She smiled and touched the folder next to his plate. "And I have your very best interests at heart. But that's not why you owe me," she said softly.

He sighed, knowing he was not going to get what he wanted. "And why not?"

"You owe me because when I got here last night you were three sheets to the wind and very soon you passed out on the recliner. I saw on your calendar you had lunch with Michael. I figured if anyone knew why you got loaded last night, it would be him."

"Yeah. So?"

She grimaced. "So I had to call him and talk to him. And found out more than I wanted to know. You don't want to live in a capi-talistic country anymore, you're beating yourself up over something you had no control over, and you think Elizabeth is doing the right thing—boy, that really pissed him off." She watched him rub his eyes vigorously before peeking around to look at her.

"I said all that?"

"And more. So why don't you want to live in a capitalistic country anymore?"

"What I meant—and I thought I said this—was that this is a capitalistic country without a heart. Only the bottom line is valid, and that's just not right."

She watched as amusement started to dance in his eyes.

"So Michael was pissed?" She nodded. "Hell, you should just take me out and shoot me." He took a gulp of coffee, feeling a little more human. The thudding in his head was getting softer. "I guess it comes as no surprise that I don't remember anything that happened after I got home last night?" With raised eyebrows, he watched her shake her head.

"Doesn't surprise me. I saw what you were drinking. Very strong; very expensive. When you tie one on, you do it with style."

"Thanks."

He set the coffee down and then noticed the folder again and began to pick it up. "What's in this, anyway?"

This was the part she wasn't sure about. How would he take her digging up other cases where bone-marrow transplants had been successful? Since she wasn't sure what kind of cancer Allison had, she knew it might not be accurate, but would it be worth anything?

"It's what I spent my time doing while you were snoring last night," she said lightly, watching intensely as he glanced through the pages she had printed from several sources on the Internet.

He finally collected them all and put them back into the folder. "Thank you," he said softly, "but this has nothing to do with Allison's situation. It's like comparing a . . . an oyster to a water chestnut."

"I was afraid of that," she admitted, "but I wanted you to understand . . ." Her voice trailed off as she thought hard about how to say this.

"Understand what?"

"That you and hundreds of others might have been duped by the research, but you did the best you could with what you had . . . And there are plenty of people who have had their lives saved by this very thing. And, as I recall, Michael kept saying over and over how you hate statistics, your patients don't fit into tidy molds, etc. Allison *was* terminal. Whatever you both decided to do was probably not going to work. And besides that, what right do you have to wallow in self-pity when you have other patients who need you now? Your office administrator called last night, hoping you were feeling better because they really need you. Today. Or sooner rather than later."

He looked at her, surprised. He hadn't thought of it that way at all. And besides the words, her caring touched him. Staying with him while he slept off the alcohol, making the effort to get this information, and then not leaving when he wanted to be alone. Damn, he hated it when she was right.

With a reluctant smile, his hand covered hers. "We really did consummate our friendship last night, so now we're *really* even. So. Thank you."

Her answering smile was relieved. "My pleasure."

And suddenly his appetite returned. As he helped himself to the pancakes he asked about her New York trip. "Do you have the television series?"

She fiddled with her coffee cup. "Maybe. The powers that be are interested. Actually, I have an oral agreement. They're putting things in writing, but the one thing we haven't agreed on is talent. I want to pick an unknown for the lead character, and so far she doesn't exist anywhere but in my head. They want a known star, but—" She looked up at him and smiled. "We'll see."

Of that, he was certain.

⌒

Serenity Brown watched Elizabeth's car pull into the driveway of her river house. Right on time. She let out a long sigh of relief. She knew she could pull this off.

It was an early release day at school on this Monday. Serenity remained hidden behind a swatch of shrubs and greenery a few lots down. It had almost been too easy, the girl mused, anxious about all the things that could go wrong. Days before, she had written Elizabeth a brief but very polite note asking for this meeting. Her granny didn't know anything about it. Serenity had been waiting twenty minutes, and during that time she had purposefully recalled a moment from her past that always provoked tears.

She kept that memory in place until her eyes and face were

swollen. She checked her image in the mirror one more time before she replaced it into the backpack. She looked miserable, disconsolate, and repentant. Perfect.

A pair of huge reflective sunglasses hid her face as she stood up, her shoulders hunched over as she walked sadly the several yards to Elizabeth's front door.

∽

"When she took off those sunglasses I thought someone had died," Elizabeth exclaimed. She was sitting in Adrienne's kitchen, talking about what had just happened in the last hour. "That poor little girl was miserable. She said, 'Mrs. Whittaker, I want you to know I talked to Preacher Sammy Deitz at the church and he told me I had to ask God to forgive me, and I did. Then he said I had to ask Granny to forgive my evilness and I did.'"

Elizabeth tried to tell it as vividly as it had happened.

Serenity gulped in some air, her pale face suddenly flooding with color, eyes starting to water again. "Then he told me I had to ask your forgiveness and say how sorry I am and . . ." She tried to swallow a sob back and fell into a spasm of coughing.

Elizabeth immediately poured her some water and set it on the table in front of her, gently patting her back. "It's okay, Serenity, take small sips. And small breaths of air." Elizabeth felt like crying, too, but she forced herself to remain composed until the apology was finished.

"I'm s-sorry," Serenity had finally managed to whisper. "Please. W-will . . . you forgive me?" Without hesitation, Elizabeth offered forgiveness freely, praising Serenity for her honesty and courage.

∽

"I was impressed, Adrienne, I really was. She was sincere and humble; I think she is going to be just fine. I'm so glad for her and for Mehalia. I told her how worried her grandmother has been." Her smile was relieved. "Mehalia wanted me to call the police and scare Serenity when we found the jewelry in her pocket; I just couldn't do it. But everything seems to be working out anyway."

"I'm glad that you're glad." Adrienne nodded. "Does she ever hear from her mother?"

Elizabeth shook her head and glanced at her watch. "No, no one's heard from the mother since she's been in jail. She has at least another two years to go. And speaking of going, I've got to do just that. Michael didn't know I was coming here today, so I need to get back."

Adrienne glanced at the wall clock. "But you won't get home until well after dinner. Won't that be too late?"

Elizabeth shook her head, standing up. "Normally it would be, but he has a dinner meeting with the MS Society tonight. He's helping with one of the fund-raisers."

"Good for him," Adrienne said, her cart following Elizabeth to the front door, pleased to know the man was doing something practical and positive.

Chapter Twenty-three

Dr. Meade, I've heard a lot of wonderful things about you," Adrienne said, extending her hand to a man who looked ancient. Yet her doctors said this man would be able to monitor her condition and keep them apprised. And he could do this without having any diagnostic tools in his small office.

"We will keep seeing you every three months, but this way he can monitor you monthly for us, and if need be send you back to us or send you to one of the local hospitals in that area," one of her doctors had patiently explained. "Don't be misled by his age or brusque manner. That man has eyes and a brain that can see things we mere mortals can't." He described this small-town doctor as a "legend at two state medical colleges."

With those accolades, she had finally set up this first meeting. Driving to Maryland for monthly routine maintenance was too time consuming, too exhausting.

"Well, I would advise you not to believe everything you hear," he said gruffly, but there was no mistaking the pleased twinkle in those dark eyes. She relaxed.

Dr. Meade was looking at the copies of the charts that had been sent to him. When he looked up, his words floored her. "You've been through hell and you're not done yet. This is awful."

She suddenly felt her eyes burning. No doctor had ever said anything like that to her. There had been no validation of the awful shock. "Well," she said weakly.

"I just want you to know I can only imagine how hard this has been for you, but I'll do my best to look after you and keep my ear to the ground, along with the bigwigs up at—where? Johns Hopkins, good school. Anything worthwhile comes out of the pipe, I'll let you know. Now let's check those muscles."

He was kind and gentle, and made what was usually an uncomfortable exam bearable, talking to her quietly the whole time, explaining and saying encouraging things when he found them.

Back in the small office, he told her what he was going to write to her doctors in the big city. The whole visit had taken only twenty-five minutes, and he had charged a pittance compared to what the others charged.

"Now, I don't bill insurance companies; that's something you'll have to do. I'll tell you the truth. I'm darn glad I'm not starting in medicine now with all these insurance rules and regulations binding up a doctor so tight he can't do squat for his patient."

They commiserated a bit over the sad state of health care in this country, but before she left, Adrienne had a totally unrelated question.

"Dr. Meade, how is Charlie Jamison?"

Dr. Meade looked at her blankly. "Same as he's been for the past—what—two years?"

"So he hasn't gotten any worse?" she said, her voice relieved, wondering why he hadn't come to the support group with his nephew during the past few months.

"I sure as hell hope he's not any worse. Dead is about as bad as it gets, I think."

It was Adrienne's turn to stare at the doctor blankly. "I don't understand . . ."

And they talked a little more, without either one of them initially knowing what the other knew. By the time she left, however, they each knew all they needed to know.

⌒

"Are you going to say anything to him?" Elizabeth wondered out loud as Adrienne pulled up to the long table. The support group would be meeting soon, and Gregory often popped in to chat or sometimes to listen to a speaker. The two women, who had ridden together, had come early to ready things.

Adrienne shook her head. "No, I don't think there's any reason. If he wants to keep coming, that's fine. No one else needs to know. Don't you agree?"

Elizabeth nodded. "It's so very sad, don't you think? I couldn't imagine what it would be like to be young and know such awful things will probably happen." Pity settled on her face; Adrienne glanced sharply at her.

"My dear Elizabeth, *you* are living with such knowledge. Think about it. You're still young. You know you have a crippling chronic illness, and you don't seem to be doing too badly." As a matter of fact, she looked the picture of health in a deep burgundy jacket, a lightly shaded gray crisp cotton blouse, and gray slacks.

"I never thought of it that way," Elizabeth said slowly. "I guess because even now, it doesn't seem real, does it?"

"Nope." Adrienne reached inside the metal basket attached to the front of her scooter and hauled out a sheaf of papers that included home addresses, phone numbers, and e-mail addresses of the members of the group. "This way we can keep in touch with each other," she explained, handing one to Elizabeth. She then wheeled herself around the table, leaving a folder at each chair.

There was no specific program planned. Instead, Adrienne had thought they would discuss some political issues and any other topic that came up. She also had preprinted letters people could sign to send to Congress to support health insurance reform. There were at least five members who had no insurance within the group, and while there was a free health clinic miles away in the next county, the care that was provided took hours to receive.

Almost everyone was there when Nicole Anderson walked in,

using a cane. Although they had known her only a few months, it was obvious the woman had changed. Her haircut was the same, she wore blue jeans, battered tennis shoes, and a nondescript cotton shirt, a zippered sweater—but she was much, much smaller. A belt was cinched tight to keep her baggy pants from falling off.

A month ago, the weight of extra pounds had added soft rolling creases to her diminutive frame. But now, her small bones were emphasized by leanness.

"Nicole." Adrienne was astonished, and watched as the small woman's face turned red.

"What?" she asked softly, averting her eyes.

"Did you not eat a bite of food since we last met? Good God, how much weight have you lost?"

Nicole smoothed a hand over the piece of paper in front of her, surprised. "You think I've lost weight?"

"Don't you?" Elizabeth asked and then saw the sheepish smile.

"Sure I do."

"Then how?" Pearl Smith wanted to know. She had some pounds of her own she'd like to get rid of.

Nicole raised shy eyes. "Well, you have to promise not to tell anyone. It's kind of personal."

"You're not bulimic, are you?" Adrienne asked, distressed. Surely this woman had enough problems . . .

Nicole shook her head. "Of course not. I'm not crazy." She paused and glanced at Carl apologetically. "Well, you see, I really believe in God . . ."

Adrienne, ever watchful, immediately cut in when she saw those fretful glances. "You don't have to apologize, Nicole. Carl has his beliefs and you have yours, and both are just as valid. So. You believe in God. Okay. So do I. Go on, please."

Nicole stretched a hand up to her neck, angling her face away from Carl's observation and began.

"About eighteen months ago a good Baptist introduced my husband and me to red wine, touting the good health benefits to the heart and all. I never grew up with any sort of alcohol around, nor did my husband, so it was a new experience for us. My husband didn't like it, but I kept trying it. And trying it. And before I knew it, I was buying bottles and bottles and consuming gallons. I never really liked it, but it made things hazy, softer . . . easier."

She paused, frowning as if this was still too new a discovery for her. "I've never ever told anyone how much . . . I hate this." The cane moved. "It was about the time I started drinking that I had to start using the cane. At first I actually had to work up the nerve to go out in public with it. It was awful; I was so self-conscious."

"I know exactly what you mean," Sandra Little said, surprise making her voice shrill and she blushed. "I had this walker for six weeks before I found the nerve to use it in public. I felt as naked as a jaybird that first time. But you know what?" She looked around the table for answers.

"What?" Pearl asked timidly, not certain she wanted to know.

"*No one noticed!* Here I thought I was going to be such a spectacle, but everybody was so wrapped up in their own little world, nobody bothered with me."

Adrienne nodded. "Yes, I think that's very true. But Nicole, please tell us what happened next."

"Well. I just kept needing a drink. It wasn't a physical craving, I knew it wasn't, but I had to have it. If we didn't have a few bottles in the house, I'd get edgy. But a few big drinks or several little glasses of wine would take that edge off. Sometimes after I consumed as much as I wanted, I'd get really angry over the least little thing. My kids started avoiding me, saying Mom gets really cranky when she's had too much to drink."

She looked around, disbelief wrapping her face and voice. "I couldn't stop it, but somehow I knew I wasn't an alcoholic, it was something else. I started questioning why? There were moments when I'd wake up in the middle of the night not remembering how I'd gotten to bed. Or I wouldn't remember to do something my children had asked me to do. I would feel awful, but by the middle of the day, I'd need a glass of red or white—chardonnay, Chianti, Shiraz, zinfandel, cabernet, merlot, I got to know all the ones I liked. But it didn't explain the need."

"You said you didn't think you were an alcoholic, but did you ever consider that going to AA might help?" Carl wondered, then waited for a small spasm of pain to leave.

"No, I never did. My husband commented a few times that maybe I should cut back. I started hiding things from him," she admitted.

Adrienne tilted her head and asked, "What finally happened?"

Nicole's voice got softer and she continued to keep her eyes away from Carl. "Several months ago I started praying. Every day. As I bought my wine, as I drank too much of it, I prayed. I couldn't understand why God let me have a need like this, such a desire to make the world unfocused every day. There were a lot of moments I was really messed up, but I kept asking and praying. Last month I got my answer—in a dream."

Elizabeth glanced around and saw that everyone—even Carl— was as captivated as she, waiting to hear more. After a moment, Nicole continued. "In this dream, I was with the husband of one of my dearest friends, and he intimated he was ready to take me up on my offer to have an affair with him." A hand crept over her heart. "I have never, ever entertained a sexual thought about this man, but in my dream he was insistent that I had approached him, and I realized it must have happened in my, uh, inebriated condition. He got a little angry with me, then I told him something I hadn't realized myself. I didn't really understand about alcohol, I mean intellectually I knew it could affect you, but I never felt drunk so I thought I wasn't. I never felt it impaired anything, but of course it did.

"When he demanded to know why I was drinking so much I said"—she paused, astonishment shining in her eyes—"I said, so I wouldn't have to see the changes. I wouldn't have to see the changes." She repeated the words slowly. "Until that moment, I didn't realize that emotionally I wasn't coping with this disease at all. I've never admitted to myself that I've gotten worse, that I hate what it has done to me. All this time I've needed to drink to keep everything fuzzy to . . . handle it. It gave me a buffer, I guess. Well, once I realized why, the desire disappeared. The weight I gained from it, well, it disappeared along with the need." She shrugged, too shy to look around.

"What a marvelous story. Talk about an answer to prayer. Thank you for sharing." Adrienne beamed. Even as Nicole received smiles and nods of approval from everyone else, Carl cleared his throat.

"I don't doubt you believe God gave you that dream, but did you ever consider that your subconscious, which has been working on your question for a year, finally came up with the answer?" It was a reasonable question, but the answer Nicole gave was equally so.

"I can't speak for anyone else but, frankly, my subconscious just isn't that smart."

"Oh." He realized she was probably right. "I see."

Adrienne looked around the room. "Has anyone heard from Tammy? The woman whose husband was having a lot of insurance problems?"

Pearl answered with a frown. "They lost everything. They had to move in with her husband's parents in North Carolina. His lawyer didn't get the papers filed about the bankruptcy or some such thing. Tammy was not up to talking to me before they left; she was pretty upset." She shook her head.

"Which is awful for her health," Adrienne said grimly. She felt helpless and didn't know of anything else to say and so remained silent, letting others speak.

Although she kept an eye out for Gregory Jamison, he didn't make it to the meeting that day. Which was just as well. Although she had sounded confident to Elizabeth, Adrienne wasn't sure if she should say something to him or not. This gave her more of a chance to think about it.

◆

"Boy, she nailed that one!" Carol had just heard Nicole's story from Elizabeth, although Elizabeth had not used a name. They had arranged to eat together at a Cary Town restaurant and were waiting for their food, taking advantage of the outside patio to enjoy a mild day.

"You think? Is that why you were drinking so much when you got back from California?"

"Emotionally I was a wreck, but I didn't consciously realize I was using alcohol to stay numb. It just made me feel better. When your reality isn't pleasant, it's comforting to keep things fuzzy." Carol shrugged. "Gordon has had his own emotional lapses, poor guy, but I think we both have a much better handle on things."

Elizabeth looked thoughtful. "I wonder why I never overindulged? I mean, I think I've had some pretty crappy things happen here at midlife, but alcohol holds no allure. Frankly, too much and I go to sleep."

Carol laughed. "You never needed it because you're perfect. Remember? You could never disappoint your fan club."

Elizabeth looked at her strangely. "What do you mean?"

"When we were growing up, do you have any idea how my mother and your mother held you on a pedestal for all the world to see—especially me. 'Oh, Carol, why can't you be more like Elizabeth? She would never do such and such; she would never say such and such. Oh dear, why can't you . . .' It used to make me want to gag, hearing how all the adults raved about you."

Elizabeth's face grew hot. "That's not true! They never did that, and I was never perfect."

Carol looked over the tall glass of iced tea she was holding and challenged, "Name one time when you were grounded for doing something awful all by yourself."

Thoughts raced back in years and Elizabeth could think of numerous occasions of being grounded, but each had Carol involved. Her cousin watched, smug and amused, as flickers of memory danced over Elizabeth's face. Several times she opened her mouth, only to close it again. "I know it happened; I just can't come up with anything right now," she said, irritated. "After all, we are talking about a lot of years here."

"Keep thinking about it, and call me when you come up with something," Carol said, maddeningly self-assured.

"Maybe I just handle things differently, is all," Elizabeth pointed out. "And how can you say I'm perfect? That's so unfair."

Immediately Carol became serious. "But you are. You were the perfect child, the perfect teenager—God, that's an oxymoron—and then you even married the perfect man—for you. You had the perfect child, the perfect life, and now you are handling having a dreadful disease, perfectly."

"Don't call it a disease; it's an illness," Elizabeth murmured, her face distressed. "Disease sounds . . . contagious."

"Fine, fine, illness, whatever. Same difference." Carol shrugged and then smiled. "And you're wonderful. And I love you. So that's all there is to it."

The food came and they picked up their utensils and began to eat. Elizabeth was still unhappy about how her cousin had branded her. Then she remembered Virginia Mae and suddenly realized she *had* always acted in whatever way would make her mother happy. She did the same thing for Michael . . . and Kellan.

She wondered, as she slowly chewed the excellent food that now tasted colorless, if that was why, more and more, *she* was so unhappy.

⌒

They had no plans for the holidays. Michael was gone the month before Christmas; Elizabeth was too tired to mind. She wasn't volunteering anywhere anymore, just intent on being quiet. She was keeping any energy for herself and knew it was something she *had* to do.

Later she wondered if perhaps she should have been doing something else. In hindsight, would it have made a difference?

It happened one morning in early December. She woke up, feeling an awful aching in her hands, as if something had crushed them during the night. In a very short time, they started refusing to do what she wanted. Before the day was over she was thanking God that Michael was out of town, because everything got worse. It was only by very carefully watching exactly what she was doing that she'd been able to call Carol.

Hearing the panic in Elizabeth's voice, her cousin had raced over and immediately taken her to the neurologist's office. Once there she had demanded the doctor see her cousin.

"I don't care that we don't have an appointment; she is in trouble NOW!" Carol's voice was dramatic, loud, and authoritative. Everyone sitting in the waiting room quickly found out who Elizabeth Whittaker was and that "her hands are not working, she is in pain, she's not going to wait a week or a month, she has to see Dr. O'Day TODAY!"

Elizabeth was too frightened to be uncomfortable with the scene Carol was making. Besides, it got her in to see the doctor with little wait. Once inside the small examining room, she couldn't find any words to describe the pain; she had never experienced anything as horrible as this.

The doctor, however, knew exactly what was going on. "Painful paresthesia. I know, burning and freezing, isn't it? Close your eyes and try to touch your nose."

Carol's hands clapped over her mouth as she saw Elizabeth miserably fail such a simple task.

Dr. O'Day's face held no surprise. "Yes, I can get rid of the pain for you, but you will have to use physical therapy to get back as much dexterity as you can."

"How long will it take? And will she get everything back?" Carol asked with urgency, anger erupting as the doctor sat back and shrugged. "I don't know. We will hope for the best."

It was as unsatisfactory an answer as she had ever heard in her life. But he had already turned to Elizabeth and begun speaking of the therapies available that would perhaps slow down the progression. *Progression?*

Elizabeth listened intently, clutching her hands together, frantic that this had to be over before Michael returned and before her mother found out.

Although she didn't understand it at the time, her fear was magnified because she knew she had to keep this hidden from two of the most important people in her life. They would be too upset to see her like this. She had caught sight of Carol's shocked face, but at the moment she knew she couldn't do anything about it.

Thank God, Carol had not mentioned herbs or low-fat diets.

Once she was back home taking oral steroids, she consistently tried over and over again to establish communication between her brain and fingers. Over and over again she did the central nervous system exercises. She extended each finger and then curled it into a precise zero touching the tip of her thumb. Over and over and over. It took days before she started to feel a bubbling of hope. At last, she was actually seeing small improvement, a little bit each day.

The lie Carol told Virginia Mae was that Elizabeth had a dreadful cold, one that lingered for several days and then weeks. Her mother seemed content to call her several times to make sure she was mending. Michael also checked in regularly, and Elizabeth assured him each time she was getting better.

She discovered lying was exhausting, but it was what she had to do to get through this. Even though Carol had helped immensely, it was Elizabeth's decision to see the specialist, her decision to take the medicine, and her decision to start one of the drug therapies.

Her decision, and hers alone. Without Michael's insistence or her mother's badgering. Taking control was frightening, yes, but at the same time—empowering.

She wanted to share these thoughts with someone and suddenly remembered Lynne Sears Howard. Elizabeth decided to write her a letter. She flexed her hands again and realized she wasn't up to using her own penmanship—yet. Refusing to give it any more thought, she turned to the computer and booted it up. At the same time she sent up a prayer of thanks that she could still do this and smiled.

When she was finished, she checked the calendar to see which day she was supposed to see the doctor and start the new therapy. It would be the day before the first support group meeting of the New Year. At the last meeting, they had changed the date to the second Tuesday of each month. Good. She would take an aspirin that afternoon before the shot and then everything should go perfectly. She should be fine, just fine.

Singularly and collectively, she again stretched each finger. Central nervous system exercises—who would have ever thought there were such things?

Chapter Twenty-four

Sandra Little was going to be late on purpose, something that was not in her nature. This would be the fifth support group meeting, the first one of the New Year, and it was going to be a shocker. Today she had a secret that could only be shown and she was shivering with excitement.

At all the other meetings she'd come carrying complaints, lugging around the hopelessness of seeing her MS get worse. This despite being on a therapy that was supposed to slow these bad things down. So they said. In all fairness it had helped her younger cousin immensely. The therapy had kept her running and jumping and working and doing everything a twenty-five-year-old wanted. She often wondered if it was the fact that her cousin had started taking the medicine *before* there were any problems—was that what made the difference? Sandra had started taking the weekly shots after things had already started breaking down. The difference between her and her cousin usually made her feel sick with envy, but not to-day. Today she felt like she was on top of the world and could not wait to share the good news.

She giggled to herself. It was almost like she'd had a religious conversion . . . only better.

Her nerves were jangling with impatience and she checked her watch yet again. Twenty more minutes before it even started?

Darn. With muffled derision at having that second cup of coffee, she headed for the restroom for a third trip and hoped it would be the last. At the very least, it would eat up some time.

Thirty minutes later, she edged toward the closed door and reached for the handle. Taking a deep breath and wishing her stomach wasn't fluttering like a tangle of hummingbirds (which were the meanest creatures God every made), Sandra Little squared her shoulders and yanked open the door.

She strode in briskly, legs strong and steady, arms swinging in perfect rhythm from side to side and felt every pair of eyes on her. "Sorry I'm late." Her voice was high and breathless and she finally made it to the chair but instead of sitting down, she stood there with a hand on the chair and smiled like a lit-up Christmas tree. She was show-and-tell today, although no one knew it until she walked in.

Mouths dangled open. Shocked faces stared. Everyone leaned toward her, trying to fathom the sight. All of them knew the score: A person with a chronic, degenerative disease does not get better.

Finally, Adrienne found her voice. "Sandra?"

Sandra's satisfied grin split even wider, and she pirouetted gracefully before bowing deeply, "Ta-dah!"

Spontaneous applause and questions erupted as Sandra Little, the star of today's show, finally sat down.

Adrienne finally hushed everyone by putting fingers in her mouth for an earsplitting whistle. Elizabeth stuck her hands over her ears. "I didn't know you could do that," she marveled.

Adrienne didn't even spare her a glance but kept her eyes on Sandra. "Sandra Little. Explain. Immediately. How on earth did this happen?"

The small woman leaned forward and let her eyes race over all the eager faces. "You will never guess in a million years what I did."

Impatiently, Adrienne agreed. "You're right. And you won't be so unkind as to make us try. Now tell."

Sandra took a deep breath, brought her hands in front of her and clasped them. "Two weeks ago, my neighbor came to see me and saw that I wasn't doing well at all. I had been lying on my sofa all day, I was sooooo tired." She suddenly glanced at Elizabeth. "Don't you get blasted tired of saying how tired you are all the time?" She waited for Elizabeth's quick nod and then continued. "Well, my friend took one look at me and left, saying she'd be right back. Did I tell you we've known each other since the first grade? She is my dearest and closest friend. She wanted to do something for me." She paused for a quick breath.

"Sometime today, please, Sandra," Adrienne impatiently prompted.

"Sure. Well, she came back and brought me a joint. And I smoked it." She sat back proudly.

Adrienne frowned. "Is that all? You haven't done anything differently?"

Sandra leaned toward her with an urgent voice. "What I think is this. You know I'm taking one of the therapies for my MS? Well, after I smoked about half a joint, I started feeling different. And before my husband got home for dinner that same night, I didn't need the walker. I did not need a cane. I started walking a little faster, Heck, I went outside and ran to the mailbox. And back! I had such a good time doing that I kept on doing it until I got a stitch in my side. It was glorious! I waited a few minutes and then did it all over again. The last run I made, my husband drove into the driveway and about had a heart attack. His mouth dropped to the ground and when he reached me I started doing jumping jacks—just cause I could. He about passed out."

Adrienne's intense frown turned into one of concentration as she thought hard. "You mean that the therapy you're on worked synergistically with the dope? Is that possible?" Her tone was hushed; she felt as if they were on the precipice of an enormous discovery.

"That's what *I* think," declared Sandra, her head nodding emphatically.

Adrienne had another question: "Have you been back to see your doctor?"

"The neurologist? No, but I called his office, and they said it would take about two months to get an appointment so I told the secretary—not about the marijuana, but about how I could suddenly do all these things I haven't been able to do for years."

"Did they say anything? Did he call you back?"

Sandra shook her head and rolled her eyes. "Are you kidding? She told me that in this disease there is always the possibility of a total, spontaneous remission. Forget that I've never had one in my entire life, but she insisted that's what probably happened. She said the doctor did want to see me and suddenly they had an opening in three weeks."

"Are you going to go?" Elizabeth asked.

"Yes, I'm going, but I don't think I'll tell him what I'm doing because he'll tell me to stop." Sandra's brow wrinkled up with worry. "And I can't. I won't. Not as long as I'm doing this good, no way Jose!"

Adrienne nodded. "I think that's wise." She gnawed her lip in contemplation and then turned to Elizabeth. "It's something you might think of doing. I know you've been reluctant to try one of these therapies because no one knows how they really work, but—"

Elizabeth colored, and interrupted. "I already have. I started shooting myself up yesterday."

"Well, that was providential," Adrienne said.

"Coincidence," muttered Carl.

"You mean a God-incidence." Adrienne chuckled, then held up her hand. "Just kidding; I couldn't help it." She started giggling. "You might say the devil made me do it. Oh, dear, I think Sandra's news has addled my brain. Forgive me, Carl?" She waited for a grudging nod and then snatched a breath. "Elizabeth, I'm excited for you; this might work out very well. Can you imagine? If you have the same results as Sandra, we could be making medical history."

Elizabeth's nod was distracted. Her mind was racing. To do this she would have to stay at the river for a while. She didn't think Michael would be too understanding of having an illegal drug used in the house. As a matter of fact, she shuddered at what his reaction would be to this entire meeting. She had no plans to tell him.

While she mulled over differing possibilities, Claude Nolan suddenly spoke up. "Why just her? I say, Why the hell not all of us?"

He looked around and glared at what he first thought was hesitation, but was, in reality, speculation. Pairs of eyes met up and down the table, eyebrows raised in question marks. Within seconds an upsurge of hope crushed all tentativeness, and first one and then another and soon everyone was nodding, murmuring assent. Nolan turned triumphantly to Adrienne, his face a challenge. "Are you going to start squeaking?"

Startled out of her inward pondering, fired up by a rush similar to the ones she used to feel on Capitol Hill, Adrienne sat up, looked hard around the room, liking what she saw. "Why the hell not?"

The rest of the meeting centered on how to make this happen. There were a million details to work out, such as where to meet, how to get the illegal drug, how much it would cost . . . It was the sort of thing Adrienne relished. Such logistics tired Elizabeth out completely. Adrienne was in her glory.

At the end of the meeting, when everyone began leaving, Gregory walked in. Greetings of hi and bye met him as Adrienne motioned him over.

"I don't think I should tell you the context of today's meeting. It's, ah, well, complicated—maybe next time," she said, coloring at his curious glance. And then he smiled.

That normally serious face changed; he had a killer smile. Elizabeth wondered why he hardly ever smiled and then immediately answered her own question.

"It must have been some meeting to make you speechless." He laughed. "I got held up down the road, that's why I'm so late. I just wanted to come by and say hello. So, maybe next month." He lifted his hand but Adrienne stopped him.

"I wanted to ask you about your uncle," she began softly. She saw the smile drop away and the slight flush. He didn't lie well, she thought.

"He's about the same," Gregory said, glancing at his watch and starting to move away.

"Gregory." Adrienne's compassionate voice stilled him. "I want you to know I met Dr. Meade. And if you ever want to talk to me about it, I'm here. That's all." She smiled. His face remained blank, not giving anything away.

She touched his arm. "Have a great day, and I hope we'll see you next month," she said, and then moved her wheelchair away toward Elizabeth. Gregory shoved his hands in tan pockets and left without saying a word. Elizabeth frowned.

"Adrienne?"

"Yes, dear?"

"I thought you said you weren't going to say anything to him about his uncle?"

Adrienne nodded. "I know."

Elizabeth waited. She watched Adrienne pack up her briefcase and tuck it into the compartment in the back of her chair. And waited while she maneuvered the cart toward the door. "Then why did you?"

"Actually, I was trying to compose an answer for you." Adrienne looked up, a little sheepish. "I've thought about this a great deal since last month. I finally decided that sometimes keeping something awful inside you can be as bad as the secret. I have found that if you can say it out loud, it helps diminish the fear. At least it does for me. So I offered, just in case it might do the same for him." Adrienne shrugged. "How about you?"

Elizabeth's mouth twisted and she gave a little laugh. "I never get the chance to have any secrets."

"It's probably just as well," Adrienne said. "Now, come have lunch with me," she demanded, "my treat."

Elizabeth was feeling worn out and lunch didn't sound appealing. Not nearly as enticing as a nap and she said so.

"Please," Adrienne said. "I have something to tell you. Couldn't you come to my house and rest afterward?"

The restaurant was a new one, hooked up to a new eighteen-hole golf course. Although well into January, the winter had remained mild and the course was busy.

They were seated in a formal dining area overlooking the green. Gourmet delicacies graced the pages of the restaurant menu and with the smells from the kitchen, even Elizabeth felt hungry. The prices made her eyes widen. "Adrienne, you're not treating, not with these kind of prices. We'll go dutch today."

"No, no. I've been here before so I knew what I was getting into, don't worry. At least it's not dinner." She chuckled. "Do you want a drink while we wait for our lunch?"

Elizabeth shook her head. "It'll only put me to sleep, and I have to drive back to the city this afternoon." Her voice was not enthused at the prospect.

"Stay here," Adrienne urged. "Do you *have* to go home today? There's so much to talk about."

Elizabeth shrugged, touching the ice water glass and feeling the wet condensation. "I suppose I do. Michael's in town, but he'll be leaving in a few days—will be gone for a couple of weeks. I know he'll want me home."

Adrienne ordered a glass of chardonnay, reasoning, "I'll have coffee for dessert and that'll keep me alert."

"What do you think about Sandra's news?" she asked.

Elizabeth shrugged. "I don't know. Are we really going to try to use it, all of us?"

"I don't see why not. I'll get on the Internet and get as much information as I can, see about the medicinal uses. Then we can go from there. I must say I was flabbergasted with her waltzing in. She is so much better it defies explanation, don't you think?"

"I agree and wouldn't it be wonderful if . . . Do you think it's possible?"

"With God, all things are possible," Adrienne stated and then leaned over. "And do I have a story to tell you."

"About what?" Elizabeth suddenly noticed how vibrant Adrienne had become, animated, as if she had been colored in neon. She had such a . . . presence.

"Thomas."

Elizabeth stared at her. What more could possibly be told about a dead boy? Of course there was only one response.

"Tell me."

Adrienne smiled. "Well. It's quite a story. And an emotional one, so I reserve the right beforehand to break into tears."

"Then wouldn't you rather do this at home?" Elizabeth asked anxiously, not desiring such a public display—not like when she burst into tears that day long ago.

"Don't worry, I'm teasing . . . sort of. It's such a wonderful, absolutely joyous story that I'm honored to have a part." Elizabeth could see her friend already misting.

Joyous, she had said? Elizabeth thought not, but was poised to listen stoically—she did not want to get involved emotionally; she had already shed too many tears over a child she didn't know.

The waitress brought their food and left. Adrienne sipped some of her wine and suddenly Elizabeth motioned the waitress back. "I'll take some white wine, please." She might as well be fortified, too.

"I spoke with Thomas's mother, Danielle Smith, before Christmas and she was having a hard time. She said she was trying hard to give Thomas back to God, but it was hurting, she was missing him so. She found herself searching through the house, looking, hoping to find something that belonged to Thomas that she hadn't found before. She was searching for . . . something. And then she finally put it into words; she wanted to find a *scent* of him, of his life, something new, something tangible to hold in her hands, crush to her heart." Adrienne looked up as the waitress placed a small napkin and then the wine in front of Elizabeth.

"Thank you." Elizabeth was glad for the distraction because reluctant tears were threatening, and she didn't think she wanted to hear any more. "Can I get you anything else?" the young girl asked, her smile bright and energetic.

The women shook their heads politely. When they were alone, Elizabeth spoke. "Adrienne, I'm not so sure I want to hear any more; this is all so . . . terribly sad."

Adrienne held up a hand. "Wait. Trust me, just let me finish."

Elizabeth hastily took a big gulp of her drink. With a great deal of misgiving, she nodded.

"Just two weeks ago, I had a very vivid dream. Filled with color and emotions, it was like a family reunion. Ian was there nearby, although I didn't really see him, just as I knew there were others there, but not in focus. It was Thomas's family and friends. We were in a cafeteria-style room, with long tables and chairs, and there was food being cooked. We were all waiting and talking and laughing. The only one I could see clearly was Thomas, sitting just a few feet away from me. He looked at me, and even though I knew he was dead, it was the most natural thing in the world that he should be there. His smile showed me he was happy, he looked healthy and well and so very pleased to see me. When I looked around I realized no one else could see him or even knew he was there, but I was fine with that because I knew somehow if they were supposed to see him, they would."

"You mean you didn't grab Ian and force him to look?" Elizabeth's smile was faint.

"No, which shows you this was indeed an extraordinary dream. Now, after I finished dreaming about Thomas, I had other dreams but there was one constant thread throughout the night I kept trying to remember. It was a verse from the book of Thessalonians, and something about that line kept repeating itself. Although I didn't remember the other dreams, I kept telling myself over and over again to remember this from Thessalonians because I had to tell Danielle. It was very, very important for me to do this.

"When I awoke the next morning, sunshine was streaming through the windows, which I found odd because the weather forecast had been for rain. I immediately remembered the dream and could see Thomas's face as if he were right there. I also remembered he looked amused at finding himself in my dream. I called his mother before I even got out of bed, before I even told Ian.

"Danielle was quiet, and although I kept gushing on and on about how well and happy Thomas looked and how something from Thessalonians kept threading through all my dreams, she didn't say very much. When I hung up, I wondered at her quietness, and then thought about how I would feel if our roles were reversed."

"I'd feel awfully jealous," Elizabeth said, second-guessing a woman she had never met, the mother of a boy she had also never known. This was taking on a surreal quality, and she wondered how much longer this story would go on. She took a bite of food and surreptitiously glanced at her watch. She would have to be leaving soon.

"Stop with the learned responses," Adrienne said sternly.

"Excuse me?"

"The learned responses of our culture. Society tells us this is supposed to be this way because our culture says so. Our culture and advertisers, that is. Of course you'd be jealous, because our society says you should be jealous in a situation like this. Get over it. And listen to the rest of this story before you jump to preconceived notions. Will you do that for me?"

Elizabeth felt diminished, although she wasn't sure why. "Go ahead," she said stiffly.

Instead of answering immediately Adrienne touched her mouth

with a napkin, then placed it on the left side of the plate. "Would you like some coffee?" she asked, as she beckoned their waitress over. "Two coffees," she ordered, without waiting for Elizabeth's answer.

As soon as the girl left, Adrienne started talking. "During the next few days I was having a rough time of it. Things were a little off and I fell, bruised up my legs, and Ian was very angry with me for not waiting for him. I was feeling depressed, wondering just where the heck was God when I needed Him. I forgot all about my dream and Danielle. The next Sunday after church, I got a call from her and I could hear in her voice something wonderful had happened. There was brightness that hadn't been there the last time we talked. I assumed it would be about her other children or perhaps something good had happened for the entire family. Well!" Adrienne took a deep breath and patted the vicinity of her heart. "Danielle told me that when I called to tell her about my dream, it was her birthday. I had completely forgotten and felt terrible. She brushed aside my apologies, saying they had not planned to celebrate this year.

"That day she was experiencing an even deeper sorrow because Thomas, more than anyone else in the family, always made sure she had a birthday card. After I told her about my dream, she went to her room and cried, knowing her son was gone and he would never again be able to give her a birthday card. It was one more loss she had to endure. Later that day she thought about what I had said about Thessalonians. Even though I couldn't remember the exact verse, she got out her Bible and opened it."

Adrienne's face was shining with a wonderment that couldn't reflect what she was talking about, and Elizabeth felt a ripple of irritation. She stared down at the coffee.

"Danielle said, and she was half laughing and half crying, there on a sticky note was a drawing Thomas had made for her about three years ago. They were at some meeting and she gave him some sticky notes to draw on. So"—Adrienne closed her eyes tightly, trying to control the tears in her voice—"she suddenly realized that Thomas had indeed provided her a birthday card, just like always."

Elizabeth's eyes began to fill, and she blinked rapidly, feeling her throat close. Breathing hurt, and she looked away at a group of golfers hitting balls outside. Her heart cracked as she realized how much this must mean to Thomas's mother, good God . . . And suddenly she knew that God had provided this moment . . . what an extraordinary story—but it wasn't over yet.

Adrienne dabbed at her own eyes. "She said that Thessalonians is the only place in her Bible that has something from Thomas." She blew her nose. "Then yesterday she called me. 'You will never believe this,' she said. 'Someone just sent me a newsletter. It's called *First Thessalonians 4:13*. It's for families who have lost children. I immediately looked it up and this is what it says: 'We do not want you to be unaware, brothers and sisters, about those who have fallen asleep, so that you may not grieve like the rest, who have no hope.'" Adrienne lifted her hand. "That verse was on the very page where she found Thomas's drawing."

Laughter and tears tangled as Elizabeth visibly tried to keep her composure. The barrage of emotions battered and uplifted and filled her with a new knowledge. Could she believe? How could she not? But if she did, then God had also taken this wonderful child away in a senseless, tragic accident. The tragedy juxtaposed vividly against this extraordinary story, one that was years in the making . . . Therein was the rub. A nagging memory of the vitality of a bit of morning sunlight made her wonder again about the music that made it dance. Where *did* that music come from?

Chapter Twenty-five

Michael was waiting when she wearily pushed open the back door. She had decided to stay at Adrienne's to rest and actually fell asleep. She already knew she was late but figured they could call for takeout or see what was in the freezer.

She felt like a cluttered bag of mixed feelings, churning and changing with each second. All the way home she had pondered that wonderful story shadowed by the needless accident. She was edgy and certainly didn't care for Michael's tone of voice when he started in on her the moment she walked in.

"Where have you been? I've called everywhere looking for you—why didn't you leave a note?" Accusation strained his voice and matched the anger on his face.

She hung the black purse on the chair and sat down. "I was at the river, at the support group. I told you I was going there this morning."

He frowned. "No you didn't; I would have remembered."

She looked at him, stung by the certainty in his voice because she *knew* she had told him.

"I did, but fine," she said, her voice clipped. "I'm home now, so it doesn't matter."

He sat down across from her, taking her hand. "What's wrong, Beth? Did something happen at that meeting? Did somebody upset you?"

She looked at him, feeling his concern was a sham. "Actually, I was fine until I walked into the house and you started fussing—"

"I'm not fussing, okay? I'm not. I worry about you when you're not where you're supposed to be. My God, anything could happen; you might have fallen somewhere, you might be hurt. That shouldn't make you mad; you should be happy that I'm concerned." Her face was a total blank, and that irritated him even more. More and more lately she had turned a cold shoulder to him, as if she could not care less about his worries, his concern for her.

Elizabeth stared. Was he earnestly sitting there waiting for a pat on the back? It was ludicrous and she was in no mood to be patronized by anyone, especially her husband. How could this have gone on for years without her noticing it before? Anger tumbled over inside her and then out.

"Do you really want to know how you make me feel?" she asked. Michael, stiffening at the anger he heard, nodded.

"You make me feel damaged."

"*What!?*"

The unfairness of that statement propelled him out of the chair. "I do not! How dare you say that. I take damn good care of you, but you don't appreciate anything I do for you, what any of us do for you. You just don't give a damn, do you?"

She was standing now, fingers perched on the table for balance.

"Look at that. You can't even stand up by yourself anymore," he said hotly, "and you're not doing one damn thing to help yourself. You delight in making us crazy."

"There is nothing I can do," she cried. "Don't you understand that?"

"There is. One of the new therapies—you could be in physical therapy, there's a lot you could do, should do, but you're too busy with these new friends of yours. What do you do at the support group, wallow in each other's sickness and disease?"

Her hand shot out on its own and slapped him hard. It was a moment frozen in time as they looked at each other, anger and shock marking their faces. Elizabeth, white and trembling, was appalled she could do such a thing.

Michael felt the sting vibrate over his cheek and down into his heart. The explosion reflected the months and weeks of buried hurts, and anger over how each perceived the other.

The long moment hung over them silently, icily . . . destructively.

Finally, Elizabeth, her voice shaking, spoke. "Michael . . . I—"

"Damn you, Beth. And damn me for being a big enough fool to still love you." His anger was dreadful to watch, his hands clenched into fists, but before any more words could be spoken, he turned and stomped away. She heard the front door slam shut and for the first time in her life, she didn't care that he was gone.

This enmity had been building for a long time. Tonight, it had finally erupted. She wondered what would happen now. Would they both tamp the relationship back into a respectable box so they could go about the semblance of a normal life?

She realized she couldn't do that anymore. Wouldn't do it. She was too upset to eat and instead went to bed, far beyond tears, far beyond regrets.

Sleep came in fits and turns, but with the glimmer of dawn, she had made a decision.

They could not live together anymore. They were on opposite sides of a door, each trying to open it, inevitably pulling in the opposite direction.

Michael had not come home, but that didn't concern her. There was a couch at his office. A shower, too, and he kept a change of clothes there. Those were provisions in case he had to pull an all-nighter or if he had to fly out at an ungodly hour. It had never before been because he walked out of his house or away from his wife.

Elizabeth waited until she knew Carol would be awake and called. Her cousin listened to the clipped instructions, not daring to ask questions, but instead hurried over to help her cousin pack.

Elizabeth decided she was moving to the river. Permanently. Or at least until things between her and Michael cooled enough for them to talk. At this moment she had doubts about that ever happening.

She left a note for him on the kitchen table, so he would know where she was and also what not to do.

Dear Michael,

I want to say I'm sorry about last night, but I realize I can't. You are angry at me, and I with you, and I see no resolution. Perhaps a time to reflect about what we both want is what is needed now. You said last night you still loved me. I still love you, but I don't like you very much right now. The weight of your worry is simply too great a burden for me, and it seems to get heavier each time we are together. I am sorry for getting sick. I never, ever meant for this to happen, but now that it has, I have to deal with it as I see fit.

It puzzles me why that makes you so angry.

I plan to stay at the river indefinitely. If I need anything, I will contact you through your secretary, Sheila.

My hope for the future is that things will turn out for the best. What love I have is yours, but understand, I must be alone right now.

Elizabeth

Much later that day, after she got settled in at the river home and Carol had left, dusk was just casting its shadows. She leaned against the doorframe, looking out at the river. Her shaking hand crept up over her mouth and she briefly closed her eyes, trying to shut out the pain, but there was nothing she could do about hearing the sound of her heart breaking . . . yet again.

⌒

When Michael opened the back door of his home and found it empty he was only puzzled. Thinking Elizabeth must be resting he started walking that way but noticed something white on the kitchen table. It was the letter written by his wife. He read it once, then again and sat down, rereading it once more.

He was incredulous. He thought it was a joke. He had been miserable all day and was determined to make things right this evening. With a bouquet of flowers in one hand, he was fully prepared to do any amount of groveling. He just wanted to make things right.

Letter in hand, he glanced around the room, disbelieving. The events of the night before ran though his mind. So he had gotten rattled last night. So what? Couldn't she see he was desperately concerned about her, he was in agony about her? Looking at the letter again before crumbling it up in a shaking hand, he realized this was all he got for the grief he had endured.

She had left him.

He couldn't believe it. He searched the downstairs, ending in the bedroom; when he saw the pieces of luggage missing, he began to get chills. He rubbed the back of his head, walked to the back door, saw the car was gone and wondered what he should do.

The shock, which began to dissipate after several minutes, was soon replaced by anger. He was furious at how unfair she was being. How could she treat him this way? How could she betray him like this? Restless, he ran down the steps to the backyard and immediately turned and ran back up when he heard the phone ringing, hope crushing his chest.

"Michael?" It was his mother-in-law. Damn. He rubbed a hand over his eyes.

"No. She's not here. Where? At the river, Virginia Mae. You've got the number? Good. No, I don't know how long . . . Well, you will just have to ask her."

He listened a few more moments, frowning. "I can't comment. As I said, you'll just have to ask her." And before she could say another word, he hung up.

He walked into the living room and dropped to the sofa, elbows propped up on his knees, hands raking back his hair. He didn't know what he should do. Elizabeth didn't want him to be around her.

And he could not fathom why she felt the way she did. *Damaged?* He suddenly wondered if the disease could impair her mind. He had never done anything to provoke that feeling. Nothing! Never! It made no sense.

He grabbed a pillow and curled it under his head.

He stayed there for a long while, barely noticing as streetlights came on outside and brightened the darkness. He ignored the phone ringing twice more. It would not be his Elizabeth. He knew that without a doubt.

And he could not understand.

⌒

Virginia Mae impatiently punched in the number to the river and drummed a hand against the table, waiting for her daughter to answer. When she finally did, Virginia Mae demanded an explanation.

"I just got off the phone with Michael. He said you weren't home, that you're staying at the river—for how long he didn't know. What is going on, Elizabeth?"

A tone of disapproval resonated through those words but Elizabeth, tired but calm, didn't care. "I don't want to talk about it."

"What?" Her daughter was refusing to talk to her? She didn't understand. All she wanted was a simple answer. "You may not care to discuss this, Elizabeth, but I am your mother. I have a right to know what is going on with my daughter. Look, you sound tired. Just let me know when you're coming home and I'll come over and we can talk then, okay? That's reasonable."

It couldn't matter less. "I have to go, Mother. I'll call you next time. Until then, don't call. And don't come here. I need to be alone."

Virginia Mae pulled the phone away from her ear, dumbfounded at hearing a click and then the dial tone. Her daughter hung up on her. Elizabeth had never done that in her life! What was going on? Feeling the first scrapes of panic begin to claw, Virginia Mae punched a new set of numbers into the phone.

"Carol? When was the last time you saw Elizabeth? Today? Good God. You were the one to help her move?" she accused. "Why? You think I should ask her? Well, I just did and she hung up on me. Now, are you going to tell me, or am I going to have to get in the car and drive all the way down there at this time of night?"

Virginia Mae listened as her niece told her, using the nicest and fewest words possible, that it was none of her business. "If I could be of more help, I would, Aunt Mae, but Elizabeth didn't explain anything to me. As a matter of fact, she made me promise not to say anything to anyone. And that's why I'm saying good-bye now."

Again, Virginia Mae glared at the dial tone emanating from the phone. She vented a tiny bit of her anger by slamming it back onto the receiver.

Who else to call? Kellan? Maybe if she called Michael back and threatened to call Kellan for some answers . . . Better yet, call her daughter back and threaten the same thing. Her hands flew back to the phone and then paused. It *was* late, and Elizabeth had sounded very tired. Could this wait until morning? After all, if her daughter was in any danger, Michael would never have permitted her to go away. This simple truth gave her a great deal of solace and made her decide to wait until morning. But come morning she was going to get some answers.

What she didn't know then was it would be useless to call Kellan because her granddaughter already knew.

Elizabeth had called Kellan that afternoon after the move and did most of the talking.

⌒

Kellan hung up the phone, frowning. This was unreal. The premise of her life had just broken apart. Her parents—the only two people still married in her social circle—were separated?

She sat there overwhelmed. Why couldn't they deal with this together? Why apart? Why couldn't they talk about their differences? She slumped back in the kitchen chair, shaking her head. She was glad her housemates were out. She didn't want anyone to know about this yet.

It was several weeks before the country would discover whether the groundhog would see his shadow. Early spring or a longer winter? She shivered, looking at the snow outside. Kellan used to think spring the most romantic time of the year. But only if you were in love . . . as her parents had been.

Kellan was glad she had never been in love.

Restless, she got up, walked toward the kitchen window and with crossed arms leaned against the sink. Most of her friends' parents had divorced long ago. Some collected the legal documents like worn-out trophies. The fact that her parents were still married and so much in love had been almost a novelty. But it had also been strength, a reality not only to hold on to, but also to aspire toward.

Most of her friends had multiple lovers and relationships, all with an ease similar to trying on and discarding makeup or accessories. Entanglements that were emotionally rootless had never appealed to her. When she thought of loving someone, it was in the way she saw her parents behave—they wanted to be together, they enjoyed each other and therefore enjoyed their lives together. Together their love embraced Kellan, wrapped her in a blanket of security that made everything possible.

Where had they gone wrong?

Kellan wondered fretfully if it was possible to really love someone forever.

She checked her watch, slung a purse over her shoulder and, with a backpack in one hand, she went out, started the car, and headed for the library.

Ultimately, her parents would simply have to fix things up themselves. Kellan pushed aside the heavy weight of disappointment and forgot about springtime and romance. That was the stuff fairy tales were made of and anyway, she was far too old for make-believe.

⌒

Sipping coffee and settling in after her first night there, Elizabeth realized the argument between her and Michael had been serendipitous. She had been aware of the anger slowly churning between them for quite a while. She wasn't sure how or even why it started. She, for one, was glad it had finally spewed over the top. It allowed her to make an honest escape. She could stay here and conduct the experiment with her friends and not be fearful of interruption. And she wouldn't be weighted with Michael's worry every time he was around. Thank God.

There was one exception, of course: Virginia Mae. She had

called again this morning, fussing and fretting and worrying about Elizabeth.

"Think of all the horrible things that could happen to a woman alone," her mother begged. It was a familiar weapon. Fear used to be a great deterrent to doing anything, Elizabeth recalled.

When Elizabeth was a teenager, Virginia Mae made certain Elizabeth knew of all the break-ins, rapes, and violent crimes that ever happened in the city. She had been on pins and needles the whole four years Elizabeth had been in college, and took extra pains to inform her daughter of the real and supposed dangers that awaited her in the actual world—which just so happened to be any world without her mother standing guard.

The day Elizabeth married Michael had been a moment of vast relief for Virginia Mae. She was able to hand her daughter to someone else for safekeeping. To a point.

Eventually, whenever Michael was out of town Virginia Mae took it upon herself to call Elizabeth every night to ask: "Are all the windows locked? The doors, too? You're sure? All right, darling, then sleep well. Oh, and make sure you lock your bedroom door and keep the phone right by your bed. Good night."

It was years before Elizabeth finally shed the fear her mother had draped over her. It took her that long to finally realize that her mother lived alone, and went out and about with nary a thought to the dangers she constantly paraded in front of her daughter.

That was the day Elizabeth started drawing a line in the sand. A very polite one, because Virginia Mae's feelings were so easily hurt, but no longer would she answer dumb questions or listen to the horror stories her mother seemed to keep at her fingertips. It was then Elizabeth started making jokes and laughing at it, pushing it away with humor her mother didn't find amusing.

"No, Mother, I've got the front door open with a sign out front, inviting all sexual predators to come in."

Virginia Mae complained to Michael, who was of no help. He joined in the fray, laughing and joking in a way that caused Virginia Mae to accept the fact her daughter was indeed an adult.

But she wasn't taking this new tone her daughter was using very well. Elizabeth had actually slammed the door shut on their conversation—she would not discuss with her own mother why she had left

Michael. That didn't bother her as much as Elizabeth's not moving back in with her.

When Elizabeth took the morning call from her mother, for the first time she refused to carry any of the guilt her mother was trying to throw on her.

"Mother, stop it right now. If you want to waste your time worrying about me, that's your problem. I can't control what you do. But neither do I have to listen to you fuss and complain about it either. I'm fine, this is what I want to do right now, and I don't want to discuss it further. I've already talked to Kellan, so don't you bother her. And do not come to visit without making sure you've discussed the time with me so it will be a time I'm here. Uh-huh. I'm sorry you feel that way, Mother, but that's the way it's got to be for right now. I love you. Good-bye."

As soon as she hung up Elizabeth called Adrienne. "Want some company? Yes, I'm here . . . for a while. Yes, I'd like to discuss specifics. I've talked to Mehalia. Good, I'll be right over."

Elizabeth walked into the Moores' house filled with purpose and direction. She hadn't felt so good in a very long time.

She marveled once again at the lightness of this house, not only because of the sun streaming in from the large multitude of windows, but also because of the easy and relaxed atmosphere the occupants created. Or usually created.

"Come, come sit down and partake of some of our coffee and low-fat Danishes," Ian implored. She stared at him, surprised. Normally he was dressed in nice but casual clothes—khaki pants, short-sleeved shirts with sweaters draping over the shoulders, very collegiate.

Today, however, he was dressed . . . scruffy. A baseball cap turned backward, baggy navy workman pants, a long-sleeved T-shirt with a long ski jacket that had rips in it. At her look, he announced he was going fishing. *Fishing?*

"Yes, ma'am. I am going out into that wet wilderness, casting my lines into the deep blue to catch food necessary for the nourishment of my lovely, but nonetheless highly worried, lady."

Adrienne rolled up to the table. "Huh! I'm not worried. I'm terrified. You should see this relic that he and Father Jacobs are planning to use. They are actually intending to get into it and then expecting to come back alive. I say, if Ian wants to bring back fish, he can go to the market. I can just see this wooden boat sinking before they even get out of the dock—capsizing. Then the river will spit them out miles down on the shoreline, and nobody will find the bodies until they've been picked clean by birds and animals."

Her cheeks were ablaze with color as she spoke. She could see everything as clearly as if it were happening in front of her, and she didn't like it a bit.

"Then why are you going? Ian, you're not going to worry your poor wife like this, are you? I've always thought you were such a gentleman." Elizabeth found Adrienne's worry contagious.

Ian shrugged, winking. "A man's got to do what a man's got to do."

"I never thought I'd hear such rubbish from your lips, Ian Moore; you are being absolutely ridiculous. And so is Father Jacobs." Adrienne heard the truck pull into the driveway. "And furthermore, I'm going out there to tell him precisely what I think of this harebrained idea. And he with a young wife and children; I swear, I should take a stick to both of you."

She was still muttering angrily as she opened the front door and rolled out onto the porch.

Ian and Elizabeth joined her, and he had the satisfaction of watching Adrienne's face drop in complete surprise.

"Well, Ian, I—you—this is not the boat you showed me."

Sitting grandly behind the pickup truck was a gleaming fiberglass cabin cruiser with an inboard/outboard motor. Father Jacobs, dressed in even more-battered clothes, waved from the truck, his smile wide and happy.

Ian dropped a kiss on her head. "Now are you still worried?" His grin was contagious, but she was having none of it.

"Go on, get out of here. And with a boat like that, I'll expect some impressive fish for the grill tonight."

"Your wish is my command," Ian called back as he sauntered toward the truck.

Adrienne turned her back on both of them and she and Elizabeth went back inside. "That man," she fumed and then started laughing. "Oh, Lord, he probably showed me a picture of that heap of decayed wood so I'd get all the worry out of my system. Did you see that gorgeous boat?" Adrienne continued to chuckle, maneuvering her chair into the family room.

"So how come you're back here so quick?" Adrienne asked, picking up her coffee cup. Her eyes became round with surprise as Elizabeth told her all that had happened since yesterday. "Wow. That was bold. Are you sure you want to do this?"

"He and I have been needing some space for quite a while," Elizabeth said evenly.

"Did you really tell him that he makes you feel damaged?"

Elizabeth nodded, adding, "I don't want to talk about it anymore, if you don't mind. It'll work itself out, one way or the other. So. When are we going to meet to talk about this drug experiment?"

Adrienne looked carefully at her friend's closed face and decided not to pursue her own curiosity. At least not today. Instead, she tapped her fingers against the cup. "This is happening fast. I haven't even told Ian about it." She thought hard for several minutes and then a smile crept over her face. "Well, I guess we'd better call a special meeting and figure out how we're going to do this. It will need a lot of careful planning."

Elizabeth was merely glad to have something else to think about.

Chapter Twenty-six

Claude Nolan greeted everyone with conspiratorial whispers of intrigue. "Keep your back covered and stay alert." As they were all sitting on Adrienne's massive wooden deck on the back of her house, overlooking the Potomac River, it was a hard thing to do. Claude, however, was having a great time. "The walls may have ears," he whispered as seagulls honked overhead.

"I guess we should shoot the birds in case they're carrying microphones in their bills," Carl snapped, weary of the old man's antics. Carl was tired. He had not slept well for the past several nights. His doctors had changed his medicine again, concerned that he might actually get addicted. This new stuff didn't do squat for the pain; if anything, it seemed to enhance it.

He was cranky and in no mood for stupid people, but it seemed those were the only ones he encountered.

Ian brought out tea and wafers to the tables and encouraged everyone to partake. Heading back to the kitchen he squeezed his wife's arm, wondering for the umpteenth time whether they had all lost their minds.

Promptly at 10:00 a.m., she rang a bell and brought them all to attention. It was the Friday after the support group meeting.

"The reason for this special meeting is that I didn't want to wait a full month to meet. I've been doing research and wanted to apprise you of it."

"Is Sandra Little coming?" asked Albert Stoddart.

Adrienne shook her head. "No. She talked to her neighbor, who was aghast that she told anyone. The neighbor also refused to name the supplier and, rather than take the chance of that drying up, Sandra promised her neighbor she won't have anything to do with our experiment. I am happy, sort of, to report Elizabeth has talked to her housekeeper's granddaughter, who is asking around to get us what we want."

Adrienne looked around. Besides Elizabeth, Adrienne, and Albert, Sally Trotter, Ethel Carden, Nicole Anderson, Claude Nolan, Pearl Smith, Carl Sanders, and Herbert Allen were there. Herbert, who suffered with arthritis, had started coming only the last two months. Everyone, except Carl, was in high hopes fueled by Sandra Little's story.

"Now, let me tell you what Ian and I found. Marijuana eases pain, it can increase appetite, can ease nausea, can create a sense of well-being, it can help with muscle spasms. There are volumes of anecdotal stories about how this drug helps in many different ways. Unfortunately, there are plenty of medical studies that refute all these claims. For the first time in years, though, there are actual clinical scientific trials going on to discover just what is real and what's not with this drug. But I have to tell you, given the political climate of this country, I personally worry about bias." Adrienne sighed, pulling out even more papers.

"Talk about a political hot potato! Several states have passed laws making the medicinal use of marijuana legal. But federal laws negate state laws. We are pitting states' rights against federal rights, and it's chilling. There seems to be a lull about prosecuting, though. Everyone on both sides of the legal issue seems to be looking the other way. That's the good news. But the question remains, for how long?

"Like I said, when it comes to this particular drug, our country seems to be schizophrenic. Right now in California, Alaska, Arizona, Colorado, Hawaii, Maine, Nevada, Oregon, and Washington state, they have medical marijuana laws that allow people with AIDS, epilepsy, MS, and glaucoma, as well as those undergoing chemotherapy, to grow it or buy it and use it. The newest wrinkle is, last year the United States Supreme Court ruled definitively that there is no legal basis for medical marijuana.

"Yet, in the most recent twist, the Supreme Court has rejected federal prerogatives that wanted to snatch away a doctor's license for even discussing pot with patients. Now the court is allowing, *allowing* doctors to discuss using this drug with their patients as well as prescribing it. This is clear as mud, right?

"Let me see . . . Yes, I wanted to share this story because I found it very distressing. In June of 2000, a young playwright named McWilliams was sentenced to death by a federal court for using marijuana."

"Death? That's not possible; you don't get death for *using* drugs, not in our legal system," sputtered Albert Stoddart.

Adrienne held up a hand. "Let me finish. McWilliams was dying of AIDS and cancer. Marijuana allowed him to keep eating, kept him from vomiting, and relieved a lot of his pains. Under the California *state* law of medical necessity, state and local police could not touch him. However, federal law could and did. He was convicted of possessing an illegal drug. The judge gave him a choice: jail, or home—as long he agreed to weekly urine tests to prove he wasn't using the drug. He chose to stay home and started taking Marinol, a legal prescriptive substitute allegedly containing only the active ingredient of marijuana.

"It didn't work. It didn't keep him from vomiting every bit of food that entered his stomach, as the home-grown marijuana he smoked did. He died choking on his own vomit."

Shock rippled across the faces and she shared their dismay. "That's why I'm worried about these so-called clinical trials— what are they actually testing? Already, several reports from English scientists have found nothing to support these anecdotal testimonies."

Silence reigned as Ian moved back and forth refilling glasses.

"That's a damn shame," Carl stated, eyes downcast for a brief moment. "My pain is increasing because my doctors are reluctant to give me enough of anything to make it bearable. I know they are regulated heavily, but I don't really give a damn about that." He stopped as a spasm rippled through his back. "All I care about is getting rid of it. If it keeps on like it has been, if they can't do squat because they're too busy watching their back to keep from getting in trouble with the powers that be—well, in the next few months I'll be doing something drastic."

He left unsaid what that might be. Adrienne sighed. "This country, its legalities, so politicized. Sometimes I think our laws . . . How is it helping by denying hope to those who have none? I just don't know."

Elizabeth spoke up. "Carl, like Adrienne said, this drug might help diminish your pain. I hope so," she said fervently. You could almost see the rippling of pain when it hit him. She felt so bad for him. "My housekeeper's granddaughter has said she can get it for us, but she's going to deliver it to me, so I can deliver it to the rest of you; no one else will be directly involved."

"So you don't have to tell her about us, do you? We can remain anonymous, right?" Nicole Anderson asked. She was jittery about the whole thing; she had never done anything illegal in her whole life. Good Lord, she had children in the school system and hadn't they both completed that state Don't Take Drugs program? She had even gone to see them receive their certificates. Her stomach clenched again and she thought she might be sick.

She watched Elizabeth shrug. "I can call tonight and get the ball rolling. I'll find out how much, and we'll let everyone know."

"Well." Adrienne was again caught off guard at how quickly this was happening. "Well, then I guess we have to decide when we will be getting it and where we are going to use it and"—she paused, flustered at all the unknown details—"my goodness, what am I leaving out?"

"Are you all going to use it together? I think that would be unwise." Ian spoke for the first time. He was sitting behind Adrienne and had listened to everything.

He started laughing. "I have to admit that the thought of what might happen if you did inhale en masse and got busted has crossed my nimble mind. What would they do, handcuff your wheelchairs so you couldn't roll away? Or could you all outrun them going in different directions?"

Chuckles joined his as imaginations conjured up ludicrous scenes. "Can you imagine their faces? The faces of the cops, thinking they were busting up a huge pot party?"

"What if they thought we were a gang lighting up and they burst in like they do on television, with dogs and guns and whistles and knocking the door down—" Ian started and Claude finished for him, wheezing, "and then they see *us!*"

"We'd get on the six o'clock news, roaring with indignation, and state that what we were doing is medically necessary, and then we'd haul out Sandra Little to prove it," Adrienne gushed, liking these thoughts. Then it hit her. "Strike that. We can't let anyone know about Sandra. I promised her yesterday." She looked around. "That would have been one whale of a story."

"Yes, well." Ian sighed and shrugged philosophically. "So now let's concentrate on a plan so that no one will get caught. I think Elizabeth, who already said she would, should buy it and then bring it back here. It can be dispersed throughout the day and each can individually use it in your own homes or wherever you deem appropriate. Does that sound like a plan?"

Nicole Anderson interrupted the nods and murmurs of approval. She got up hastily, apologies falling from her voice and filling her face. "I'm so sorry; I just can't do this. I'm sitting here, and all I can think about is what if my children learn about this. It would break their hearts. I just can't do it. I wish you all the best of luck, but now I've got to leave." Ian was already ahead of her opening the front door as good-byes chased her out.

"Poor thing. I certainly understand," Adrienne murmured, then looked back at the others. "If anyone wants to back out at anytime, just say the word. It'll be fine."

"I'm here for the duration," said Carl tightly. "And I'll buy her share."

Claude and Albert gave the thumbs-up signal and everyone else nodded. Adrienne looked around. "So. It's all systems go. I guess this is a wrap."

⌒

Serenity Brown maintained a neutral face as easily as if she were a car idling. Her grandmother talked at length about bad influences. About people pulling you down in the gutter with them; look at the example of her own daughter, Serenity's mother. Is that what her granddaughter wanted for herself?

"No, Granny," she answered demurely, pretending to listen attentively even when her insides were flapping up and down in childish glee at the money she was going to make. Her instincts had been right on the money to go and apologize to that Whittaker woman! Forget revenge, she had been given the opportunity to make a bucket load of money.

Still, she stood there inside the kitchen of the concrete house, the picture of innocence as Mehalia lectured. There were no new arguments, just the same-old same-old that school offered. And not very convincingly either. She knew how much money her grandmother made cleaning the houses of the well-to-do. And she found it ludicrous that a teacher who earned a pittance comparatively had the gall to say anything about dealing drugs. Society clearly showed how much real value it put on that occupation.

All this was going through her head while she stood presenting the correct visage, which only made her grandmother keep talking. Mehalia was relieved almost to tears that for once she was getting through to this headstrong and willful child. Finally, she was seeing some maturity. Although she didn't like the idea of Serenity buying drugs for Elizabeth, it was such a good and worthwhile cause, and Serenity must see it that way, too, because the child was getting nothing out of this for her troubles.

Serenity made up the perfect lie and then maintained a face that looked as sincere as it was false.

"By the time I get the stuff, it will have gone through three middlemen, each making a cut," she explained carefully and earnestly. That was why each joint, or each "little gentleman," as the girl liked to use as a code, would cost forty dollars instead of ten.

All the while she was saying this, she knew precisely what she would be doing. She would go to the dealer directly. Through the grapevine she would know where the dealers would be each Friday night. Then she would show up at, say, the Get 'n' Go gas station at the corner of Bleak House Road and Clareton Station. That was one of the places she could easily bike to and, once there, stand around—and wait. Maybe for hours after dark. It might be real late because the dealers cruised constantly, leery of staying in one place too long.

She'd have to wait for the car to come up and for a brother to lean out and grunt, "Ya lookin'?" That was the signal to say what you wanted, money changed hands, and it was a done deal. Serenity would pay a hundred dollars for the ounce that would make ten joints, and pocket three hundred dollars; it was capitalism at its very best.

Serenity was all smiles as she let herself into the small house. When she called to find out for sure that the group wanted to do this thing, she held on to the door ledge to keep herself from dancing wildly about the room as she listened to Mrs. Whittaker. "Yes, there will be four hundred dollars ready by next Friday morning. Yes, thank you, Serenity, so very much. You don't know how much I appreciate your help. Please be careful," Mrs. Whittaker gushed on the phone.

The support group was being very cautious. They were going to do exactly what Sandra had done. Once a week seemed to be keeping her wrapped in the same miracle they wanted.

⌒

Saturday morning, in the busy parking lot of an independently owned grocery store, Serenity stepped out of her grandmother's used Chevrolet and trailed behind the older woman to the door, eyes darting back and forth through the cars and trucks. In her hand she held a brightly colored gift bag, red tissue paper peeking out the top. She stopped when she finally saw what she was looking for: Elizabeth, sitting in her shiny Volvo station wagon. The woman was huddled in the front seat, clutching the steering wheel, eyes hidden behind huge black sunglasses. Serenity yawned. She had been up till after midnight last night. She had spent the night at a friend's house so her grandmother wouldn't know just how she was getting this stuff.

And then, to top it all off, *she'd* had to get up early this morning to roll the stupid things. She had earned her money; she only wished she had charged more.

The sun had slipped behind a bevy of clouds that were gliding in from the south, white bellies filled with dark patches of moisture that would soon be pelting down on their heads.

White folks were as dull as they were predictable, Serenity thought, stifling yet another yawn. She summoned up a smile as she reached the car window. "Hello. Happy birthday, ma'am." She held out the party bag.

"Serenity, I appreciate this so much," Elizabeth murmured, uncomfortable and feeling conspicuous. She felt the girl's amused eyes.

"Yes, ma'am. Anytime." She strode away to find her grandmother.

Elizabeth gulped a ragged breath. Now all she had to do was deliver this to Adrienne's without incident.

She put the car in gear and slowly pulled out.

⌒

Anger was a ribbon around the box that contained Michael's emotions. He got into his car and drove to the cottage to talk to his wife, to tell her he'd do whatever she wanted him to do.

He was prepared to beg. He had all sorts of scenarios playing in his head as he drove the hour and a half to get there. The only problem was, no one was home.

So he waited. He made coffee and checked the refrigerator.

It was two hours later when he heard the front door open. Elizabeth was just walking into the kitchen; she had seen the car and was not pleased. "Michael."

"Elizabeth. We have to talk." His voice was urgent. Hers was cool.

"You should have let me know you were coming. I have plans for tonight." The brightly colored bag she had left on a table in the foyer contained the reason she wanted to be alone.

Stunned, he looked closely at her. He couldn't believe it. "Can't you cancel?" Incredulous, he saw her shake her head. "Elizabeth, we have to talk, we can't let things stay like this—"

He stopped as she held up her hand. "We both need some time apart to . . . sort things out. Michael, I know you're not happy. You haven't been for a long time. Well, neither am I. I need this time alone. And so do you. Good Lord, it's only been a week. Go. Let it be. Because"—and she started turning away—"because there is really nothing new to say right now."

She walked out of the room, leaving him there, angry, alone, and scared.

⌒

Now it had been over a month.

Elizabeth was still gone, had not once called and it had shut him down emotionally. The only way he could function was to pour his concentration fully into business during the day, go home to eat, and then go to the gym to work out, tiring his body so he could go home and sleep.

Routine kept him from having to think beyond the moment but, eventually, it wasn't enough. He arranged to travel as often as possible, taking trips with senior sales executives even when he wasn't needed.

He was running away from the only situation he had no control over—his wife. Of course, it didn't help that Virginia Mae stayed upset about her daughter, didn't understand anything, but blamed Michael for it all. She had taken to calling him often at night and fussing so much he had finally left the answering machine on, letting it screen the calls.

Finally, after one restless Saturday when he seriously considered driving out again to the river, begging her to come back or at least tell him what the hell he had done that was so wrong, he came to a conclusion: Enough was enough. He put on casual clothes, called on some friends and went out, determined to have a good time. And he did. The food was good, the company easy, and he consciously put Elizabeth out of his mind. By the time he got home, he felt as if he had finally turned the corner; now he would start living his own life. She had made her choices, and he was finally learning to tolerate them. He would be all right.

Later that night when he entered the kitchen, the heavy sigh was as dark as the night when he saw the red blinking light of the answering machine. He was more than certain who the one phone call would be from—who else but Virginia Mae? He flicked on the switch, hunkered down in a chair to listen, finger poised to punch the erase button, when he heard Carol's voice. Chills ran over him as he got the shock of his life.

~~

Each time Elizabeth received the merchandise from Serenity, she drove slowly and carefully to Adrienne's house. The others would come there throughout the next few hours to pick up their share and then Elizabeth went home. The next morning she would travel again to Adrienne's house, and out on the back deck they would light up and smoke for the twenty minutes it took to finish just half a joint. Then they would bag the unfinished portions, and Ian would collect the tiniest scraps and flush them down the toilet. "No evidence is good evidence," he would quip. He was always there to ensure things went right.

During and afterward, Adrienne and Elizabeth waited. Hoped. Tried to feel a difference, tried to move legs and feet, wondering if what happened to Sandra Little would happen to them.

Then Elizabeth would take the smaller joint home and take little puffs throughout the week, always outside and always alone.

One thing Elizabeth could say was that filling her lungs with smoke produced a lot of coughing, but when it was over, a hazy peace floated over and through her, as if she belonged right where she was. There was no worry, just a delicious hopeful joy. A kind of . . . serenity. She grinned at the word.

Adrienne had described much the same, but was dismayed at how much her appetite increased on the day they did their main experiment.

"If I keep this up, I'll be a round ball and won't need this bloody cart because Ian can just roll me from one place to another," she snorted one afternoon, trying hard to sneak another pastry to her plate.

"Not to worry; I'll starve you for the next few days," Ian promised, taking the plate off the table altogether.

"Have you felt . . . anything change for the better?" It was the end of the fourth week, and Elizabeth's hopes were dimming. What happened to Sandra Little had not happened to her. At the same time, her spirits were up, so she knew she felt better and sometimes she thought she was moving better, but . . . not like Sandra. Would it be more gradual for her? Or was she deluding herself? Hope was a rare commodity in her world and she shared it only with the other support group members.

Sandra was the benchmark for all of them. Carl Sanders had reported relief from the pain, so he was more than satisfied. Claude Nolan also reported relief, but the smoke was clogging his sinuses, so as far as he was concerned it was a wash.

Albert Stoddart said that even if it was helping, the tension he felt each time he inhaled the illegal drug was overstressing him. Whatever happened for Sandra Little just was not happening for them. Ethel Carden had taken one sniff of the pungent sweetness and never came back. She said she'd never smelled such a stink before and knew there was no way she could inhale it.

Elizabeth looked at Adrienne. "She'd rather inhale tar and nicotine?"

"She's scared," Nolan said, who seemed to know the family quite well. "Her husband's got a controlling nature and a god-awful way of looking at right and wrong. I'm surprised she's been able to come to this as many times as she has." Carl took over buying her portion, too.

Pearl Smith loved it but could barely afford it. "Ask that little girl if she can get me some cheaper ones. I can't hardly lay my hands on so much money each week."

"But Pearl, is it making you better?" Adrienne asked, a little concerned. This was a potentially addictive drug, but she had to admit the woman was smiling a lot more and the fibromyalgia didn't seem to be hurting her as much.

"I *feel* better," Pearl snapped, "and that's all you need to know." She counted out the money, first in two ten-dollar bills, two five-dollar bills, then the rest in dollars and change.

Elizabeth and Adrienne frowned at each other. Could this cause more problems than it seemed to be helping? It was a thought that remained unspoken as each hoped the miracle of Sandra Little would somehow be re-created.

⌣

Serenity had twelve hundred dollars in an envelope pressed between the mattress and box springs of her bed. Although she knew she'd be adding another three hundred dollars to it Friday morning, she was not happy. She had figured these people would keep her busy forever, but that wasn't going to happen. Nope, it was over this Saturday. She would never get a job making this much money again.

Greed was quickly replaced by revenge. The grievances were plenty: This woman, after all, had once fired her. It seemed to her that Elizabeth Whittaker, who had never known a rough place in her life, should be shown what life was like for the rest of the real world. It didn't matter the woman was sick—or that a bunch of her friends were sick. They were adults who were supposed to play by the rules and not use a poor teenager to make illegal deals for them. Serenity felt righteous indignation start to smolder.

She had come to dread the Friday night adventure. She was getting a rep for hanging out at that intersection. It was a place where more than one white (and black) man offered to be her sugar daddy. Of course she had glared and said no, but she couldn't leave until she got what she wanted and sometimes they wouldn't leave either.

Serenity gave a great deal of thoughtful consideration to Saturday's ending. She had enlisted two of her most trusted companions to help her make this scene happen as she so directed.

Soon. It would be soon, she thought, exiting the school bus that had pulled in front of the little concrete house, feeling the wind on her back pushing her toward the future.

Chapter Twenty-seven

Saturday morning, Elizabeth was sitting in the parking lot of the supermarket, eyes closed. So absorbed in hoping for a miracle like Sandra Little's, she had never thought to specifically pray about this. Would it make a difference?

She was going to find out.

Thoughts flickered in and out as she talked with God. *Please let it be different for all of them.* Maybe this time nerves and muscles and magic would somehow click into place. A smile curved her mouth as her imagination soared along with her hopes.

Her eyes were still closed when Serenity rapped the window. The girl smiled with bright energy and handed Elizabeth the pretty bag. She left, and Elizabeth slowly pulled out of the parking lot, not seeing anything else.

Serenity walked toward a group of people huddled at the picnic tables under the cover of maple trees. It was chilly on this blustery March day, and Serenity knew precisely who was there. She stopped about ten feet short, turned slightly and flicked the side of her nose, the cue for action. Immediately someone got up and headed for the public phones.

Serenity then walked to the other side of the building, stood motionless for a second and then flicked her hand up to her brow in a quick military salute. Immediately a person sitting in an old convertible Mustang picked up a cell phone and punched in some numbers.

⌣

Elizabeth was nearing the turn toward Adrienne's house at Newman's Neck. There had been no traffic, but she had still driven well below the speed limit, wanting to be invisible.

She reached down and turned up the radio and when she raised her eyes she was jolted by what she saw in the rearview mirror.

A sheriff's deputy was right behind her, no sirens but with lights flashing. Her heart started pounding. What had she done? Hands shaking, she pulled slowly off the road, praying she wasn't the one wanted, that the car would pass her in pursuit of someone else.

He pulled in directly behind her. He slowly got out of the car. Instinctively, she pushed the colorful gift bag to the floor of the car, frantically trying to remember if her state tags were current. She knew the car had been inspected recently, she could see the current city decals on the windshield, even as she racked her brain. What did he want?

"Ma'am, I need to see your license and registration." He was a young man, looked younger than Kellan. She tried to keep her face relaxed.

"Of course," she murmured, fumbling with her bag and having

trouble getting her license free. It took even longer to open the glove compartment and find the registration, which was tossed casually in with a mix of papers. Finally, she turned and handed them to him, with what she hoped was a puzzled, innocent smile.

He took the documents back to his car, radioing in the information. She sat, waiting, wondering, and trying to think calm thoughts. She kept glancing at the rearview mirror, wondering what the protocol was in a situation like this. She had not a clue.

He finally came back, handed her the documentation, and for one fragile moment she thought it was that simple and sagged with relief.

"Ma'am, we got a tip; someone called to let us know they had seen a drug transaction involving this car. May I have your permission to search this car?"

Her heart was slamming so hard in her ears she thought surely she had heard wrong. "You got a what?"

"A tip, ma'am. I repeat, may I search your car?"

She was trembling. Suddenly she had never felt so tired in her whole life. "Officer"—she passed a hand over her eyes—"I am not feeling . . . well. Could I go home and rest and then you'd be welcome to come and search my car." She really did feel like she was going to collapse—pins and needles were engulfing her legs; she didn't think she could walk.

"Wait here." She dropped her head back against her seat and wondered what on earth she should do? If she had been schooled in the ways of dodging the legal system, she could have tossed the bag out the window, but it never occurred to her. In the emotional state she was in, Elizabeth could barely connect one thought to another.

Then the officer was back. "Ma'am, since you won't give me your permission to search your car, I've called for a drug-sniffing dog." He looked down the road at a brown-and-gold police vehicle with its lights flashing its suspicion for all to see.

"A drug-sniffing dog?" Elizabeth's voice was faint. Never in her entire life could she have imagined herself in a situation like this. She had never even had a speeding ticket! Good Lord, what was going to happen to her? And it was all so innocent . . .

She watched the massive golden retriever barrel out of the car, lunging full throttle against the leash its handler held.

Immediately it went to the driver's side door and lunged, barking to let its handler know it found a hit.

The other officer nodded and started pulling Bud away as the first officer instructed Elizabeth to get out of the car.

"Why? What's wrong, Officer?"

"I now have probable cause to search your vehicle, ma'am. The dog has detected an illegal substance. Ma'am?" He held the door open.

Trying hard not to dissolve into absolute terror, Elizabeth turned and shakily reached into the console to pull out a new collapsible cane that she kept neatly folded in a small, dark leather case. The top of the sleek handle was the only thing the officer saw—a glint of dark steel; the curve of the handle looked ominously like the butt of a gun.

When she turned back to the open door, it was to see the barrel of a gun pointing directly at her. "Drop it; get out of the car, hands on your head, NOW!" he barked, both hands stretched out, the gun leveled straight at her.

"All right! All right, I'm coming, I'm coming," she screamed, panic making her movements jerky and awkward. She was trying to put her hands on her head, at the same time struggling to get out of the car, unsure of what was happening, all among the backdrop of a fierce dog barking and growling. She tried to move quickly, which only made things worse but she didn't want to do anything to antagonize this clearly demented young man. And what if the other one let the dog go?

She struggled to get out of the car. She had to lean against the door for stability but he ordered her to turn around, which she did, again almost losing her balance. When she tried to speak, he ignored her, intent on cuffing her hands behind her back. "Officer, you can't—I need my ca—Why, you can't do this! Please, will you just listen?"

He was turning her around just as a news photographer jumped out of a car and started taking pictures. The sudden movement knocked Elizabeth farther off balance. She was shaking so hard, her legs were like jelly; she started falling even as the officer tried to pull her back by jerking up on her arms.

Instead, the force propelled her back into him, and they both began teetering awkwardly from one side to the other, Elizabeth yelling and the officer cursing. For a long, horrible moment they floundered against gravity but ultimately lost.

Elizabeth fell forward with the officer inches behind still standing, trying to pull her away from the road. Just as the side of her face grazed the asphalt, a series of pictures was captured that would go over the AP newswire later that day. The pictures would be published, not because of what happened, but because of her name. It was the very last thing in the world she wanted.

Father Wells could have told her, you don't always get what you want, but with God you always get what you need. At that moment in time she would have considered him a damn fool.

After the sheriff's deputy helped her up, apologizing, he took her to the station, administered first aid, and then charged her with drug possession with intent to distribute. And on top of that Elizabeth heard she had paid four hundred dollars for ten joints worth one hundred dollars. But wait, hadn't Serenity explained all that? She was too shaken to think clearly.

Ian had come and picked her up as soon as she called. Adrienne stayed home to alert everyone not to come and why. Ian waited as the warrant was issued and charges filed. She was released on her own recognizance.

～

Ian served tea and an ice pack, setting both in front of Elizabeth. "Are you sure you won't go to a doctor, Elizabeth? It looks wicked. Something could be broken." He tried not to wince as he looked at her.

"I don't want to go anywhere, Ian. My face is just bruised and skinned. The deputy almost was able to pull me back before I hit. It really looks much worse than it is."

"What was that young man thinking of when he pulled a gun on you like that?" Adrienne shook her head, disgusted.

Elizabeth tried to sip the tea and grimaced at the movement. "Could I have some aspirin?" She waited while Ian got her several.

"He had been shot at last week, by someone who looked like a grandmother. When I made a move to get that new cane and pull it out of its case, well, all he saw was the big bright handle and thought I was pulling out a gun," she said dully.

Adrienne sputtered. "Like you look like someone who's waiting to pop a cop? That's ridiculous. And why did he stop you, anyway? What cause did he have?"

"A tip. Someone called in, gave them the make and license number of my car, said they had just seen a drug transaction go down and were reporting it."

"Who was it?" Adrienne was suspicious.

"Anonymous." Elizabeth really didn't feel like talking.

"Convenient," Ian noted, meeting his wife's eyes, sharing his suspicions. "But why did they charge you with distribution? There wasn't enough to warrant it." Adrienne was indignant.

Elizabeth just shrugged slightly, feeling suddenly limp and worn from the day. "It had something to do with . . . Serenity packaged each joint in a plastic bag with . . . a tag on it. Something like that, anyway."

Elizabeth pushed back the chair and began to get up. "Thank you both for coming to my rescue. I really appreciate it, but I need to get home. I need to rest."

"Elizabeth, please spend the night here," Adrienne implored, not liking the white pallor of Elizabeth's skin or the shocking multicolored bruise. Talk about police brutality—not letting a poor woman get the cane she needed and then making her fall. Good grief.

"I'll be fine. I'll call you in the morning." Elizabeth's promise was faint. "I appreciate your taking me home, though. They said my car would be impounded probably until next week."

The ride to her home was silent, Ian sensing her fatigue. He insisted on walking her inside the house and making sure she had everything she needed. He checked her refrigerator, pointing out some ideas for a simple meal later.

"Call us if you need anything," he urged, wishing she would let them do more.

"I promise. I'll call you both tomorrow. And thank you for coming and getting me," she said, trying to smile and then stopping as the muscles protested.

What a mess, he thought, driving back home.

Adrienne was thinking much the same thing. He sat next to her at the table. "You know what I think?" she asked him, eyebrows arched.

"An inside job," Ian said. "Not only did Serenity make a tidy profit, she set her client up for a very nasty fall—figuratively and literally."

Adrienne nodded. "I don't think Elizabeth's put it together yet."

Ian smiled, touching his wife's hand. "But you'll help her do that, won't you?"

Her smile didn't quite reach angry eyes as she squeezed back. "You bet I will."

~~

The first thing Elizabeth did after she rested was call Carol. She knew she would need a lawyer and at this moment, she really didn't want to have to explain anything to Michael.

It had been an eye-opening conversation.

After she explained why she needed a lawyer, Carol demanded, "Why didn't you tell me? I could have gotten you great stuff delivered to your door and no one would have ever known!"

"Carol," Elizabeth's voice was hushed with shock, "you do drugs?"

"Not anymore," her cousin said impatiently. "Now, tell me—"

"You *did* drugs?" Elizabeth was floored. "When did this happen?"

"Another lifetime ago, okay?" Elizabeth could sense her cousin's eyes rolling with annoyance. "Now tell me what you need me to do." The subject was definitely changed.

~~

"She what?"

Carol, scowling on the other end, held the receiver away from her ear. Then did some yelling of her own. "Michael, stop screaming in my ear and just listen. Are you sitting down?"

She waited for him to grumble a yes. In the next several minutes she explained what Elizabeth had told her. It had been hours since she had talked to her cousin, but "you weren't home. She needs a lawyer, Michael. All the lawyers I know are in Los Angeles. I figured you would know who to call better than anyone and besides, Gordon is out of town at a conference."

"I've got to see her. She's at the house now, isn't she? She's not still in jail?"

"Michael, she doesn't want you. She needs a lawyer. And right now she's at a friend's house. Okay? She told me to call you and see if you would get her a lawyer."

Michael stood very still, trying to keep this from cracking him open. She didn't want him? How could Elizabeth do this to him? He took a ragged breath. "I'll get her one; don't worry. I'll look around and call you as soon as I have one lined up." And he hung up the phone, leaning against it, feeling tears squeeze out of his eyes no matter how tightly he shut them.

⌒⌒

It would be the end of the following week before the pictures of her began to appear in several of the local county papers that came out weekly. Those didn't matter. What did matter enormously was that it appeared on the front of the city section in Richmond. She cringed when she imagined all the people she knew seeing it and then reading the caption.

The wife of city businessman Michael Whittaker, former member of the Richmond City Council, was arrested last Saturday for possession of marijuana with intent to distribute . . .

She forced herself to read the rest of it quickly. The picture made her shudder, and she wondered where they had gotten their information. She never said the first word about why she had marijuana in her car and yet unidentified sources said she suffered from MS and was using it for medicinal purposes. Those words had never come out of her mouth!

Her nose wrinkled at the words *suffers* and *victim*. Who said she suffered? Whoever said she was a victim? These two words had also never come out of her mouth; she had never used them in her entire life. Why couldn't they all just leave her alone?

As if on cue, the phone began ringing again, and she waited for the answering machine to screen it. This morning so far had brought voices she'd ignored. Either friends expressing concern or media outlets wanting comments. There were also shocked friends, either from here or the city. "How could you, Elizabeth?" or "How long have you been a drug addict? You taught my daughter in Sunday school; were you using then?" The voices of outrage and righteousness rankled the most.

One voice called her name and she snatched up the phone.

"Mom?" Kellan's voice.

She grabbed it. "Kellan?"

"Are you all right? A friend who gets the Richmond newspaper just showed me her copy. I saw the picture. What have you been doing out there? Is that why you left to go live at the river?"

Elizabeth closed her eyes, wondering how to answer such a complicated question. "That and for other reasons. You see, there is a woman who lives here who . . . has the same illness. She'd been on one of the therapies available, but was still feeling awful. One of her friends brought her a joint to smoke and she's amazingly better. She's even running, Kellan. Think of it! So, we—the members of my support group, some of us anyway—decided to try it ourselves. There are volumes of anecdotal information about marijuana that offers . . . hope. That's why we were doing it, just hoping it would help . . ."

"Did it?"

Elizabeth grimaced and wished with all her heart she could shout yes! "No, not like it helped our friend. One man who is in a lot of pain says it has helped him, but that's about it. When I got stopped yesterday, we were using it for the last time. Ironic, isn't it?"

"Has Dad called?"

"No. I don't know if your father even knows—well—I'd be surprised if he hasn't heard yet, but no . . . he hasn't called." Oddly, she felt a pang about being ignored. Perhaps she had hoped he would call, but after all, he was only doing what she had asked him to do months ago—leave her alone.

"What can I do? Surely I can come to help with something. Moral support, if nothing else." Kellan was insistent. "I really need to see that you're all right, okay?"

"Don't you have classes?"

"I can take off tomorrow. Look, I'll leave in just a little while, spend the night, and get back here tomorrow afternoon. I'll still be able to make the evening lecture. And if not, then I can get the notes from a friend."

Kellan wouldn't take no for an answer so Elizabeth finally gave in. It would be wonderful to see her daughter, after all.

The next phone call was one she really didn't want.

"Elizabeth? If you're there, pick up. If you're not I'll call the hospital, which is where you should be after that fall—"

"Mother? I'm all right, don't worry." Elizabeth tried to sound soothing, but her mother was already out of control.

"What on earth is going on there? Who ever forced you to buy drugs for them? My heaven's, Elizabeth, do you have any idea how awful this is? I've never been so humiliated in my life, seeing my poor daughter's picture on the front page. Everyone in the world I have ever known has called me this morning, and I don't know what to tell them!" Her mother's excited chatter turned Elizabeth to ice.

"What bothers you the most, Mother? Being embarrassed or not knowing what to say?" Elizabeth quietly hung up.

Virginia Mae looked at the phone like it was a mistake. Their conversation must have got cut off. This was too important! She dialed the number again and got the answering machine. This did not make sense because she knew Elizabeth was there. She dialed the operator and asked that her line and her daughter's line be checked.

It was only after the operator had patiently checked the numbers twice and assured her everything was working perfectly that Virginia Mae suddenly considered the astonishing idea that her daughter had actually hung up on her . . . again.

It lasted just for a moment. It was too ridiculous; something else must have happened. And she called Carol and got no answers to her questions. She called Michael and got an answering machine.

Virginia Mae continued to field phone calls for the rest of the morning from her friends who wanted to know about Elizabeth. She finally turned her own answering machine on and went out to visit her sister, feeling indignant about her life at this moment and eager to confide in someone with an understanding ear.

Chapter Twenty-eight

Kellan arrived by mid-afternoon, an expectant smile fading when she saw her mother's face. "How could they have done this to you?"

She hugged her mother gently, hoping there had been no other bruises, before pulling back and scrutinizing her. "Have you seen a doctor?"

Elizabeth shook her head.

"Why not?" Kellan asked, concern sharpening her voice. "Something could be broken."

Elizabeth hooked her arm around her daughter's and walked inside the house with her. "Because it's better than it was yesterday. Truly. So don't worry. Tell me what you've been doing."

Kellan flopped down on one of the kitchen chairs, looked at her poor beat-up mother, then grinned. "Nothing as exciting as you. Same old college grind. Papers, books, reading, projects, exams. Now, let's get back to this drug deal—do you have a lawyer, or are you going to plead guilty or what?"

Elizabeth tore a piece of a paper napkin into little balls and rubbed them around on the table, enjoying the feeling of something underneath her fingertips. It gave her something mindless to do while she put together an answer.

"I talked with Carol. She said she would call around and see what she could find. She offered me one of her lawyers but they're all in LA, and since I'm not going to pay a lot for a legal defense, she said she'd find someone local."

When the phone began ringing again, Elizabeth listened to the machine. When she heard Carol's voice on the other end, she picked it up. "Hi, Carol, guess who's come to see me. No, not . . . Kellan, yeah. Someone showed her my picture in the paper and she insisted on checking up on me. Sure, I'll put her on. What's that? Oh, you talked to Michael? How was he—upset?" She listened intently, frowning. "I never said I didn't want to talk to him; I said I didn't want to bother him. There is a difference. He found me someone? That's great. Sure, here she is." Elizabeth handed the phone over, murmuring, "Your fairy godmother."

She heard them talk without listening to what they said, thinking about Carol. Michael was upset because he thought she didn't want him to call her, but it wasn't true. She would love to hear from him . . . but she didn't want to see him, not yet. Especially not with a bruised face; she shuddered thinking of his reaction. Still, memories and feelings suddenly swamped her and she felt her eyes burn with a wetness she would not let out. The past was the past. She could deal only with the present.

Would things always be this complicated?

Elizabeth mouthed she was going to the bathroom and left. After a few moments of chatter, Kellan hung up the phone and was rooting around the refrigerator for a snack when the doorbell rang.

"Kellan, get that please?"

"Sure." She shut the fridge and walked quickly to the foyer.

She opened the door, and for the rest of her life Kellan would never forget this defining moment. Hearing the door open, the tall man turned to look at her from the bottom step.

Blue eyes met brown ones and time stopped. A hush swelled between them, a moment of anticipation. A humming started as two unique melodies waited to meet for the first inevitable time.

Kellan and Gregory had both done a dangerous thing. They had put shutters on their souls, an act of control that is only an illusion. It's an act of will that in reality only exposes the most vulnerable places. By refusing all the gifts that love has to offer, they allowed its surprise to cut right into their hearts.

Kellan, standing very still, fell into his smile with a wonder as new and old as time itself. Gregory's heart was thumping wildly, tangling with emotions he thought were under his control.

Elizabeth looked over Kellan's shoulder. "Gregory? Hello."

The startled shock on his face made her hand reach up to cover the bruise. "It's getting better."

His breath came out in a rush. "Elizabeth, I'm sorry. If there's anything I can do—" He felt awful; her cheek was swollen, an angry mottle of purples and blues.

"No, I don't need a thing. Won't you come in? Oh, and this is my daughter, Kellan. Kellan, Gregory Jamison."

Kellan shivered at the brief touch of his skin and then the handshake was over. They followed Elizabeth into the kitchen and sat around the table. "Can I get you anything?"

Gregory blinked; for a moment he forgot why he had even come.

"Um, no, thank you, ma'am, no. I was visiting my mother and while I was at the store for her, I saw Dr. Meade. You know him, don't you?"

Elizabeth nodded.

"He saw the story and the picture about you and said to tell that little girl he'd be glad to testify on her behalf if she needs anyone from the medical community to back her up on the use of medicinal marijuana."

"He did?" She was touched. "Thank him for me, please. I'll certainly tell my lawyer about his offer. Everything is . . . a jumble right now. I won't be sure of what I'll be doing until I see the lawyer my husband has found for me."

He smiled.

"Who's Dr. Meade, Mom?" Kellan thought it was time she got into this conversation.

As Elizabeth explained, Gregory kept glancing her way and tried to ignore this tug at his heart that had started the moment their eyes met. He sternly reminded himself this was Elizabeth's *daughter*. One person in the family with an awful illness was more than enough.

He forced his eyes elsewhere while he got his thoughts under control. As soon as there was a lull in the conversation, he rose to leave.

"Well, that's all I came to tell you. Let me know if you or your lawyer wants to talk to him. You've got my number, right?"

"Yes, I believe I do. It's on the membership roster, right?"

He colored slightly. "Right. Call anytime."

"Do you have to go?" The words flew out of Kellan's mouth before the thought had even formed. It was important he not leave. Not yet.

Elizabeth agreed, wanting to do something for this young man who was nice enough to go out of his way for her.

"Yes, Gregory, you have to stay. It's certainly close enough to dinnertime. I'll order pizza and you and Kellan can go pick it up. I've got a salad in the refrigerator, and I'll toast some garlic bread." She rummaged in her purse for cash and then picked up the phone and began dialing.

"I didn't come to eat," he protested. He didn't think this was a good idea, but he stopped abruptly when Kellan's hand pressed his arm. That pulled him around to look at her, and his heart danced and skipped into a new rhythm.

"Maybe you didn't, but you are now." Her smile was welcome, and he suddenly felt himself relax in it. What could one meal matter?

He was pulling out of the driveway when she asked him where

he lived and he told her. "I've never been to Fredericksburg," she lied. "I'd love to see it." Her lovely face looked expectant.

"Sure . . . we'll have to plan on it," he said vaguely, knowing it would never happen. "Elizabeth has mentioned that you're at UVA?"

"Yes. I'll have to go back tomorrow afternoon." He pulled onto the highway and headed east. He could feel her eyes on him and was glad he had to keep his on the road.

"How do you know my mother, Gregory?" She wanted to know everything about him and more.

His hands clenched the steering wheel tightly and then he forced himself to relax. *This is where it all hits the fan*, he thought. He knew honesty would be his protection, but he was surprised as he tasted the hollowness of regret.

He told her everything, not holding anything back because he knew this was where it all ended. "Now you know more about me than my own mother."

"Does *my* mother know?"

He nodded. "Only her and Adrienne Moore. And Dr. Meade. That's it."

She couldn't speak for a moment; she felt honored.

They went in and got the pizza. Back in the car on the way home, Kellan was still tingling with brightness that he trusted her with this knowledge. But now she wanted to know everything about him.

He pulled the visor down to block the western sun, displaying a picture.

It was of an infant. "Is that your baby?

He shook his head. "Of course not. It's my sister's."

"Oh." She reached over and took it, feeling vastly relieved. "He's adorable. How old?" She liked his smile.

"Six weeks. And both sides of the family are so excited, they can't see him enough. Nancy and her husband hardly have time to be alone with him. His name is Jacob, but they're calling him Jake."

"That's great." He took the picture from her and tucked it back into the visor. "Your sister? Was she tested?"

He nodded. "But they're not telling that around."

Kellan nodded. "Does this mean—she can't get ALS?"

Gregory shrugged. "She has the same chance as you, I guess."

"Do they know what causes it?"

He shook his head.

"How to prevent it?"

Again, another shake.

"Well, since you have this . . . defective gene, does this mean you definitely will get it?"

"A better than average shot, I'd say."

"Meaning a less than average shot you won't get it?"

He shrugged.

"Are you doing anything alternatively for it? I mean, anecdotal stuff?"

"Not really. I work out, eat healthy, I'm insured to the hilt in case anything happens, and I try not to think about it."

That all sounded reasonable, but she didn't share his concerns for his future. "Research is exploding. I'm sure they'll come up with something long before you need it."

His lips tightened. "Yes, that's what they told my uncle."

"You're not your uncle."

He made no response.

She decided to change the subject—she wanted to know more about him, not his future possibilities. "Where do your parents live, Gregory?"

"Fairport. About ten miles from here, but it's only my mom now. She and my father retired there about five years ago, on the Great Wicomico River. As soon as they moved here, he was diagnosed with a rare form of vascular disease that attacked his lungs. Within a month he was dead."

"I'm sorry." Kellan paused, absorbing all this. "How is your mother; is she doing all right?"

He shrugged. "She stays busy, she volunteers at the hospital. Now there's the new baby, so Mom's often up in Baltimore visiting them."

"That must be hard, to retire and lose your husband," Kellan said softly, thinking about her parents. They were both alive—yet in a way lost and apart. She started asking him about college and work.

She found it fascinating he had a dual degree in horticulture and business from Virginia Tech, and he, along with three partners, had created a booming business. Not only were they a full landscaping service for burgeoning planned communities, they also catered to the corporate communities, inside the buildings and outside on the surrounding grounds. The more he spoke, the more she was attracted.

They were nearing the driveway when she asked, "This rare form of vascular disease your father had—is it hereditary?"

She saw his quick look of surprise. "Um, well, I don't know. I don't think so." He put the car in park and turned off the ignition.

"But you're not sure," she prodded. He shook his head, his face suddenly white.

"So you could possibly end up dying from that rather than ALS. Isn't that possible?"

He didn't answer for a long time, obviously stunned by what she had just asked. His thoughts were weaving into a tangle while his heart raced. Could what happened to his father happen to him? Would it?

He finally looked up. "God knows," he murmured.

He almost jumped when he felt her hand on his arm while she waited for him to look at her. "My point exactly. *Only* God knows—so stop deciding your future when you only have *this* moment in which to live. You may get hit by a truck going home tonight—"

"Now that's cheery thought," he said with a weak grin.

"So don't project into what may happen and what might be, because you're going to lose the here and now—and that would be the real shame, the real loss. For everybody." She watched as a myriad of emotions chased across his face and saw the moment he finally relaxed. She started to pull her hand away when his covered it. She swallowed hard.

"Have you ever thought about going into psychology?"

He watched her bright eyes sparkle, her lips start creasing into a mischievous smile. "As a matter of fact," she drawled sweetly, waiting for his eyes to come back to hers before uttering a succinct, "No!"

They burst into laughter and it was healing and oddly bonding. A connection was being forged, whether or not it was wanted or desired.

"Let's get this pizza in before it gets too cold," she suggested and they were inside within minutes, where Elizabeth had set out the salad. Ice water and a bottle of red wine were also on the table along with garlic bread, which was giving off a mouth-watering aroma. It was a feast.

When they were finished, Gregory insisted on washing and Kellan insisted on drying. "I love a man who's domestic," she cooed, elbowing him at the sink.

"And I love a woman who is respectful of her elders," he mocked, snapping a wet dishrag at her.

"Children, children," Elizabeth murmured, smiling as she put the leftover salad away. Then she excused herself and went to watch the evening news.

"Do you want to take a walk on the beach?" Kellan suggested, putting away the last glass. She looked up, her eyes suddenly focused on his lips. They were strong and full. He was ringing out the wet dishrag and wasn't looking at her. Kellan blinked. *Get a grip*, she admonished herself.

"It'll have to be a short walk; I've got to get home," he said, struggling to be casual. A nice short walk, maintaining a friendly banter would be all right. "Do you want to ask Elizabeth to join us?"

Kellan shot him a wry look. "In case you haven't noticed, my mother doesn't just take *walks* anymore."

"Oh." He felt like an idiot. He had completely forgotten, but it was hard to remember anything when her glances dissolved all his good intentions. "I guess you're right."

She led him through to the family room and told her mother what they were going to do. "It's a beautiful evening; have a nice time," she encouraged, smiling. "I'll be going to bed soon, so if I don't see you when you get back, Gregory, thank you again."

"My pleasure, ma'am."

The night was a canopy of black velvet, a perfect foil for the half-moon and a cascade of winking diamond stars. The moonlight draped an intimacy over the world. Kellan slipped her arm through his, the softness of the dark making her brave.

"Gregory?"

He stopped at the tension in her voice and she moved to face him. Moonlight framed her and he felt himself wanting, while trying hard to pull back. He took a deep breath and finally found his voice. "Yes?"

"Do you have a girlfriend?" Kellan waited. She didn't think he was involved, there were no subtle overtones that hinted he belonged to someone else, but she had to know.

He thought about lying, but somehow couldn't bring himself to say the words. "Not anymore," he finally said.

"What do you mean? What happened?" Because she was listening so carefully, she heard the pain so faint, so subtle he didn't acknowledge it to himself.

"Last year I was engaged. Now I'm not."

"What happened?" Her words were soft, hoping to gentle the answer from him.

"I told you. I'm defective."

She caught her breath at the anger that ripped through her. "She broke up with you because of *that*?" Kellan was incredulous. What a shallow, worthless—the biting words and anger slammed to a halt and then veered into the opposite direction at his explanation.

"No, she didn't break it off. I did. I told you, only three people, and now you, know. I never told her. I couldn't let her marry into the kind of future I'm going to have."

"What?" All the anger she had directed at the unknown fiancée was now aimed at him. "How *dare* you decide for her? How could you be so *unfair*?"

She heard the resignation. "I wasn't unfair, Kellan. I know her. Believe me, if I had told her we certainly wouldn't have gotten married. Melanie . . . is beautiful and wonderful, but she could never handle an illness like this. And I couldn't allow her to make the choice anyway, so it's moot."

She grabbed both his arms and tried to shake him. "The choice wasn't yours to make. You should have told her."

"I disagree, but it doesn't matter anymore. It's the way I live my life now. No relationships." Even he could hear the regret, but it didn't matter.

"It's not for you to decide." Kellan was so adamant it puzzled him.

"Of course it is. It's my life."

"No, it's not just your life. Not anymore," she whispered with a certainty as strong as her arms growing around him, pulling his head down to hers.

Stunned, he felt her body imprinting his; startled arms reflexively wrapped around her waist and back and then he was participating in the sweetest, hottest kiss. Reality was suspended, like a balloon hovering.

Breathless and dazed, they finally broke apart, overwhelmed at the magic they had just created. Kellan felt her heart wrapped in a newly discovered joy, knowing there was no going back. Gregory felt his resistance draining and tried hard to keep it from slipping away entirely.

"Kellan," he moaned, "you are probably making the biggest mistake of your life—"

"Our life," she corrected, her mouth hovering over his. "And don't you believe it." Then their lips met again and again, as the music they were creating danced around them, their souls melding and soaring without boundaries, without limits.

Chapter Twenty-nine

Elizabeth checked her watch once again and knew that Michael and the lawyer would be pulling into the driveway very soon. She took one more moment to look out over her river and tried to pull some of its peace into her, willing herself to stay calm.

In the kitchen Mehalia bent over the oven, carefully placing a tin sheet filled with yeast bread bowls. She set the timer for precisely one hour, fifteen minutes, and proceeded onto the next project. Iced tea, with a special blend that was her own, then vegetable snacks and, of course, the crab bisque with sherry, simmering on the stovetop now, would fill those crusty bowls.

When she stood, she placed a floured hand on the pit of her back and stretched. The morning was still young, but she wasn't; she had been up for hours. Some of Elizabeth's jitters had become her own. In truth, she felt responsible for this whole mess, although no one knew. She and Adrienne had talked for a long while last night, each discovering things they needed to know. She would be glad when this day was over, but God Almighty, she didn't even want it to start.

She thought about her granddaughter and what she might have done. Adrienne would be hauling out lots of questions, throwing them right at Serenity before this day was over.

Trying to shove back those scratchy thoughts, Mehalia decided on the spur of the moment to make her homemade chocolate éclairs. Mr. Michael liked them best of all.

Humming snatches of hymns from her Baptist church helped pass the time and keep bad thoughts out of her head . . . or at the very least from staying too long.

~~

Michael had been dozing in his car, waiting for the lawyer. The plan was to meet at his office and he would drive her to see his wife. Kate Wilkins had family at the river who would pick her up later in the day. As was his nature, he had arrived early and had actually fallen asleep.

It seemed as if no time had passed at all when the sharp rap on the car window startled Michael Whittaker awake. As his eyes swung to the window, he took in the time on the car clock; he had been asleep for nearly an hour. Anger boiled up in him as his first thought exploded—inexcusable.

He motioned to the passenger door and unlocked it. Moments later an older gray-haired woman in a trim navy blue suit entered, placing a heavy leather briefcase on the floor in front of her. Before he could open his mouth, a stern voice devoid of apology informed him, "Your office gave me the wrong address. I took the precaution of being at the address given me thirty-five minutes early. I take being prompt very seriously. When no one showed up I finally found a service station and looked up your advertisement in the yellow pages and discovered the mistake. I'm Kate Wilkins. My son talked to you this past week."

She held out a sturdy hand toward him and Michael had a premonition the day was bound to get worse. "Ms. Wilkins."

"Please call me Kate. We will be working intensely this day, and Ms. Wilkins is simply too many syllables."

"Kate, then. And I'm Michael. Are you ready to get started?" He saw the brief nod and started the car. She waited until they cleared the city traffic before she spoke.

"My son, Edward Griffin Wilkins, as you know, informed me about your wife and this case. I must say I'm fascinated. Of course, I saw the picture in the paper and the follow-up report. What can you tell me about Elizabeth Whittaker?"

A rippling of images flickered through his mind, and he wondered where on earth to start. What could he tell her about Elizabeth Whittaker? Was a lifetime long enough to even skim the surface?

Kate Wilkins's eyes narrowed, waiting. She decided to be more specific in her questions. "Has she broken the law in the past?"

"No! Not Elizabeth. She never even goes past the speed limit. She has never had an overdue library book, she . . . she has always played by the rules. I remember once in college we were heading up to another floor in the library and I wanted to take a shortcut through the staff entrance to avoid the crowds. She stopped me and pointed to the sign that said STAFF ONLY. That was that. We went with the crowd."

"Except on March 10," the lawyer observed, opening her briefcase and pulling out a small thermos of coffee. "Would you care for some?"

He declined and remained silent. After she sipped some steaming coffee, Kate began to probe.

"Can you tell me what happened before March that would prompt her into breaking the law?"

The shake of his head was decisive. "No, I can't."

"It's my understanding you two are separated. Is that correct?"

She watched the thinning of his mouth before he said, "No. We simply . . . live apart. For now."

"How long?"

He thought for a moment. "About seven weeks or so."

"Can you tell me why?"

His voice was clipped. "You'll have to ask Elizabeth."

Her curiosity quickened, but she moved on. "Tell me how you two met."

She saw his surprise. "It helps to know the people I may be representing, on a somewhat personal basis."

He considered that for a moment and then began to speak.

"It was in college, our senior year. We both had electives to fill and ballroom dancing sounded fun. Elizabeth was getting a degree in art; I was in biology and business. We hadn't met or even seen each other until the moment we appeared for class. The ballroom was filled. The moment I laid eyes on her, I knew she was going to be the one I wanted to spend the class with; even as the professor told us to choose partners I was zeroing in on her. Unfortunately, so were several other guys; she was—is—a beautiful woman. I wasn't bashful. She was my partner."

Kate waited but he said no more, so she murmured, "And the rest is history, as they say?"

He didn't blink. "For me it was. We started dating and by the time we got our degrees, we were married."

"She is an artist?"

His pride was obvious, she could tell. "Oh yes. Well, was. Oils. She's had several shows over the years, but now she doesn't do so very much. Strike that. She doesn't let me know, really, what she's doing. You'll have to ask her. I do know she tires very easily now. She . . . has been frustrated by that in the past, but then we haven't talked in a while so that might have changed."

"You have children?"

"A daughter, Kellan. She'll be at the cottage later today."

"Pretty name. What about the other members of this . . . What did your wife call it?" By keeping her eyes on him she could see the subtle pieces of body language that spoke volumes.

His mouth tightened, as did his hands on the steering wheel, and he cleared his throat—perhaps dislodging something distasteful? "A support group."

"Ah, yes, a support group. But what kind of support group? It seems it was one I have never heard of before."

"A neuromuscular support group."

"I see." But she didn't. She wanted to know why he was uncomfortable talking about it; she was also curious as to who was responsible for their living in two separate places. It was obvious he had deep feelings for his wife. It was also as obvious there were negative emotions about what she and her friends were doing together. Curious. From what she had heard about Michael Whittaker, he was a strong, ethical man who had accomplished much in the business world. He was also a strong player in the undercurrents of state politics and was admired by many in the upper social echelon of Richmond City, as had been his father years ago. Kate wondered idly what Michael Whittaker Sr. would have thought of this lively situation his son and daughter-in-law found themselves in.

He turned the car onto the bridge and she saw the waters rippling, flexing muscle, and an unbidden thought made her suddenly glad this was one of the structures the state had been regularly checking to make sure it remained sound. Had there not been other bridges in other states that had actually collapsed because of years of neglect? She pushed away those thoughts with another question.

"Will members of this support group be there, too?"

"Later this afternoon, I believe. Elizabeth has it all scheduled. It's something she's good at, always has been." He thought also of the other people who would be there this day, the ones he believed didn't need to be. Once Carol had found out the lawyer would be coming with him to see Elizabeth, she had invited herself and Gordon. Somehow Virginia Mae had also found out, and decided without discussion that she should be there, too. It would be quite a mix, Michael thought grimly.

Kate Wilkins took a sip of coffee as the car glided safely off the bridge, and she decided to rest her mind before the day of work would begin.

When presented with this case last week, she had been mildly intrigued. Medical marijuana had always interested her—the rights of individuals butting heads with not only state laws but now with federal. And, of course, six states with laws regulating medical marijuana were currently directly clashing with the U.S. Supreme Court ruling declaring there was no such thing.

However, bottom line, Elizabeth Whittaker had broken the law. But these circumstances were extenuating.

Kate Wilkins at this time of her life was quite willing to try stretching and pushing the law to include humanity when it was lacking. It would also make people sit up and take notice, maybe even make them think—really think—about why they believed so adamantly one way or another. How long she would remain intrigued had everything to do with this meeting.

⌒⌒

When the knock at the river home broke the quiet, Elizabeth was ready; she was carefully positioned in the family room. With a serene smile pasted on her face, she waited for Mehalia to bring the guests to her. It would save her a little energy, and she took the extra seconds to breathe deeply, to quell last-minute jitters dancing up and down her body like hysterical butterflies with tap shoes.

"Good morning." Kate Wilkins was surprised. She had not expected this: a regal and erect woman, leaning slightly on two magnificently carved canes. As the lawyer moved closer, she watched as

Elizabeth easily moved a cane over to the one hand and held out the other. "I'm Elizabeth Whittaker."

"Kate Wilkins. So pleased to meet you." The handshake was strongly received and given, she noticed.

Kate put down her briefcase next to the chair Elizabeth indicated and declined a cup of tea or coffee, instead asking directions to "freshen up, please."

After she left the room, Elizabeth finally found the courage to glance up at Michael and felt her heart leap. He was looking at her with a smile that in the past had melted her.

But that was then, and so much had changed. "Michael, it's good of you to come and help," she murmured as he put one arm around her for a gentle hug. It slid through his mind that she might be bruised so he was careful to be very gentle.

"No place I'd rather be, Elizabeth," he said, sounding as if he meant it. "You look wonderful. Your face—it's much better, isn't it?"

She nodded. "The bruising is almost gone." His reaction caught her off guard a bit. She was expecting him to be upset because she was back to using two canes, but he was acting as if he hadn't noticed. Her smile was warmed by his apparent acceptance. What she didn't know was he was so mesmerized just by seeing her for the first time in several weeks, he had not noticed any changes. There was always that initial gladness between them, that first encounter that only remembered better times.

Within moments, though, his eyes raked over the double set of canes and the frown was firmly creased on his brow. Without comment and only the whisper of a sigh, Elizabeth turned to sit down, telling him to do the same.

"Mehalia has spent all morning baking your favorite pastries."

The lawyer came back into the room, draping her jacket on the side of the chair. She sat down and opened the briefcase on the ottoman. She smiled brightly at Elizabeth. "I have heard a great deal of complimentary things about you from your husband."

Elizabeth's eyes widened. "Well, I haven't heard the first thing about you. As a matter of fact, what I was expecting to see was someone about twice the size of Perry Mason, burdened with the appropriate ego, as well as carting the requisite bad habits—like drinking and smoking."

Kate's lips twitched. "Smoking . . . what, exactly?" There was a fraction of a second before shocked silence split with Elizabeth's laughter. Kate's smile widened. Elizabeth's laughter was unrestrained and contagious. Even Michael chuckled a little.

"You're quick. I like that, Ms. Wilkins—" The lawyer held up a hand. "Kate." Elizabeth's voice, still amused, "Kate, then. Can you help me?"

The microcassette recorder was being propped on the table between them. "That's why I'm here. I need to ask a lot of questions to get a feel for why this happened and how we can put together the best possible defense. Agreed?"

Michael watched his wife pale, then take a deep breath before nodding. "Agreed."

"Perhaps we should start at the beginning. The diagnosis. Can you tell me about that?" In addition to turning on the recorder, Kate also held the legal pad that was halfway filled with notes from the drive. Before she could even look up from the pad, she felt the atmosphere cooling and wondered why.

"Since Michael was the first to find out, perhaps he should begin," Elizabeth said briskly, keeping her eyes on Kate.

The lawyer shifted her gaze to Michael and waited. She saw the glance he gave his wife, and saw sadness. After a few moments, presumably gathering his thoughts from the past, he spoke of that night in the hospital, of all the possibilities the doctors had put on the table, all of them awful.

"Then Dr. Gordon Jones came and told me what they had found. What it was, what they could do for it, what they couldn't, but he also offered a great deal of optimism and hope, as well as sympathy. The next morning I was with Elizabeth when he told her."

The room was heavy with memories. Michael turned to Elizabeth. "What happened that morning when you woke up? Do you remember?" The look on her face left no doubt that she did.

"When I opened my eyes the world had stopped revolving, and I discovered I could move my legs. It was wonderful. Then I fell back asleep. Michael came and, as he said, Gordon came in later and told me." She shrugged, thinking but not saying anything about that little bit of light that had mesmerized her that same morning.

"What happened afterward? Were there any impairments?"

"A little weakness that didn't last very long. I was fine for a long while." Elizabeth wouldn't talk about the occasional problem or other things that kept happening intermittently. If it wasn't permanent it didn't count.

"It must have been hard to believe you were sick, I would think?"

"Absolutely. The doctors kept saying all these things, but I was in the hospital only once and very briefly and then everything was back to normal."

"Not exactly back to normal," Michael interrupted, not sharing that memory. "You had some trouble with high heels, as I recall." He turned to Kate. "The day she was due to be released she was wearing very high heels, and when I opened the door to her room I caught her before she hit the floor."

Elizabeth shook her head. "I stumbled on something. I told you that then, Michael." She turned to Kate. "It was nothing. Nothing. And later—"

"And later, the very next day to be precise, she could barely walk because her left foot kept twisting back."

Elizabeth sighed. "But it got better the *very* next day. And I was fine for several more months—why, until the next year. Then it crept up on me. These little things that would come and go ganged up to become a problem."

"Don't forget the fatigue," Michael interjected. Mehalia brought in a plate of steaming scones with honey butter. "Thanks, this is wonderful." He smiled at the housekeeper, who nodded and left.

"Fatigue?" Kate made a note.

"Being very, very tired. It comes and goes and it's unpredictable. It's why I don't commit to anything anymore. I never know how I'll be feeling."

"But you are committed to this support group," Michael was quick to point out, deaf to the resentment in his own voice.

"It's not the same. We—the people in my support group, they understand. They don't make you feel like you have to live up to . . ." She paused and looked away.

"Live up to what?" Kate asked gently.

"Live up to expectations," she said softly, not looking at Michael. Then she sat up, sipped her coffee. "Any other questions?" Elizabeth asked in a voice that invited none.

While Kate was forming several, Michael surprised even himself when he said, "I have one, Elizabeth. What did you mean by expectations? I've never expected anything of you; you know that."

Elizabeth saw that he already knew the answer to his own question and wondered why he even bothered to ask. Well, since he asked, she emphatically shook her head. "No, I don't."

"What do you mean?" This time it was Kate who wanted to know, and Elizabeth wondered why something so obvious had to be explained. How could she find the words to really explain when they had no reference point to understand?

She took a breath of resolution and tried. "Expectations of the way life used to be. If you're tired, then you rest and become refreshed; isn't that what you think, Michael? But it doesn't work that way for me anymore. I can sleep all night and wake up in the morning as exhausted as when I went to bed."

Mouth compressed into a thin line, Michael shook his head, thinking this was so unfair. She didn't know what he was thinking. When she was tired he never bothered her. When she slept he checked on her countless times because he was concerned, but he never expected anything from her.

Elizabeth turned to Kate. "I need to have a lot of empty spaces to maintain my energy, so I can do the things I want—like being a part of this support group. We usually meet once a month, that's all. I can rest up enough for that. Although I do have limitations, I don't dwell on them. As long as I'm careful, this illness takes up a very, very small part of my life."

Kate was impressed, but still pushed. "That's admirable. But do I detect a slight bit of denial there? How can it take up only a tiny part of your life when it's changed so much?"

"If that's what you think you're hearing," Elizabeth said archly, "I would suggest you have your ears checked."

Kate chuckled. "Just wanted to be sure. Frankly, I'm impressed."

"Perhaps you can explain it a little better to me, then, because I don't think I understand too well," Michael said impatiently.

Elizabeth pushed back into her chair, finding comfort in the softness of the upholstered cushions. "I'm not in denial about anything. Good Lord, every time I take a step I'm reminded of its presence.

But my way of handling it is to limit . . . the emotional impact. To push it away, Michael. I can't explain it any better than that."

"She makes fun of it. She turns everything into one colossal joke, and she doesn't care who she laughs at either," a new voice sniffed.

"Mother, I didn't hear you come in." Elizabeth's voice was a murmur as Virginia Mae Bartlette swept into the room, her face reflecting her mission—to make her daughter see the truth as only a mother can do.

"I came in through the kitchen. I quietly crept in to surprise you. Did I manage it?" Her mother bent down and gave her daughter a kiss.

"Totally. Did you get some of Mehalia's pastries?"

"Do fish swim? Of course, they're divine."

Elizabeth introduced her mother to the lawyer, who asked, "What did you mean she makes fun of the whole thing?"

Virginia Mae shook her head, disapproval creasing her face. "She certainly doesn't take it seriously, like a normal person. Several weeks ago she came to Richmond to do some shopping. It was a few weeks after I had sprained my ankle; I was using a cane myself. Do you remember what you said, Elizabeth?" Her mother frowned at the smile lifting her daughter's lips.

"We hadn't gone to the first store when she started to simply dissolve into laughter, saying, 'Good Lord, Mother, we look like runaways from the nursing home; keep your eye out for the cops.' Nursing home indeed," Virginia snorted, clearly displeased.

"Mother thought I was vulgar for suggesting she might be an inmate at a nursing home," Elizabeth tried to explain through a sputter of laughter.

"They are not called inmates! Really, Elizabeth," Virginia Mae scolded, helping herself to some coffee from the carafe. "You don't take any of this a bit seriously. You joke and jeer about it; you make it all—"

"Harmless."

Elizabeth's word hung awkwardly in the air like a crooked picture in an otherwise well-appointed room.

Virginia Mae shook her head, pity pulling down her lips in dismay. "Oh, Elizabeth, is that what you think you're doing? Open your eyes, child." To emphasize this, she put down the almond tart she had just picked up and felt tears begin to swell.

The lawyer cleared her throat, a smile playing about her mouth. She looked at her client with respect.

"Tell me, Elizabeth, if you can, how has this affected you emotionally?"

Elizabeth tried to remain neutral and not let her eyes roll, although an ironic smile hovered. "I know exactly how it has affected me emotionally, physically, every which way. I have this wonderful friend who has taught me to put things in perspective." She wanted to change the subject "Now, tell me, has Michael mentioned the babies?"

Her husband made an impatient sound. "For God's sake, Elizabeth. We did it because we knew you wouldn't. And it was not only for your sake, but those babies', too. Everyone agreed on that."

His reaction was familiar and easier to take than being told she wasn't handling her own life appropriately.

"Babies?" Kate asked, frowning. "I thought you had only one child, a daughter."

"Mehalia," Elizabeth suddenly called, "may I have some iced tea?" She waited the few moments it took the housekeeper to bring her a tall glass clinking with ice. Not until she had taken several sips did she begin to speak.

She told about being there for the babies, how important that had become to her. "I missed it very much while I was in the hospital. After I got home, it took a while to get my energy level up, so weeks went by before I was able to get back to them." She smiled at the excitement she felt, the anticipation on the day she knew she could resume that part of her life. "Imagine my shock when I got there to be informed that my services were no longer needed. My husband and doctor had decided for me that I should no longer do this thing I loved." The hurt was a subtle, silky thread that wove easily through her voice, almost overshadowed by the harshness of the words. "They took my babies away without asking."

Every person in the peaceful sunroom of the river house could feel the hushed silence pulsing around; no one felt inclined to say a word, instead replaying the story Elizabeth had just told so poignantly.

"Excuse me," Elizabeth said, standing up in a smooth fluid movement, using the canes as an extension of herself. No one spoke until she left the room.

Virginia Mae reached over and touched her son-in-law's arm. "She's so lucky to have you, Michael, always looking out for her. She worries me to death, that child. I just wish she would listen to reason." The older woman blinked away the sudden moisture blurring her vision and lapsed back into her own thoughts.

"Is she in remission now?" Kate finally asked Michael.

A jaw muscle tensed. "I don't know about now. After the diagnosis, she was seemingly fine for the first several months. Then there was this painful numbness. It weakened her foot; ergo the brace and cane. But she would get a little better, then relapse a little. After that she began refusing the steroid treatments."

"Why?"

"She said it was because she was scared to use them, afraid of what they were doing to her. The side effects. I think it was mainly because it made her puff up so. These drugs tend to make you retain fluids and often give what the doctors call a 'moon face'; the whole body becomes puffy."

"Have the attacks continued?"

Michael shrugged. "I don't know. That's when she stopped talking. I think probably so. Sometimes she wouldn't need any assistance; then she would, sometimes all in the same day. I started noticing bruises on her legs and arms. Her explanation was either that she didn't know how she had gotten them or she must have walked into the corner of something, or bumped her shoulder going through a doorway. I was damn worried. I still am." The anger simmering under the surface was controlled. Its focus was only partly his wife but more so himself. For not being able to do anything. For not being able to make his own wife better. Even he didn't realize what a burden it was.

Kate had another question. "Do you make most of the decisions for your wife?"

"No, of course not," Michael said, his voice adamant. He turned as he heard Carol's snort of astonishment as she came into the room. "How long have you been here?" He frowned at her as she walked in with Gordon right behind her. He nodded in his friend's direction.

"I've been here long enough to know you're not telling the truth," Carol said, ignoring Michael's glare. She held out her hand to the lawyer, introducing herself and Gordon.

"I've read a lot about you, Ms. Stephens; nice to meet you," Kate said formally and also shook Gordon's hand. "Doctor."

Michael waited until the two had barely sat down before he demanded to know, "What the hell was that comment supposed to mean?"

"It means you make all the decisions concerning your wife. You always have. Have you forgotten the shoes?" Carol glared right back at him.

"That wasn't just my idea. Virginia Mae and I both wanted—"

He stopped as Virginia Mae waved a hand, interrupting. "Actually, as I recall, Michael, it really was your idea and I thought it a good one, after all, but for the most part, yours." She said this softly, avoiding his eyes.

"Whatever," he growled, dismissing it.

"The shoes?" Kate asked, eyebrows raised slightly. Carol leaned forward and told the whole story. As much as she knew of it. When she finished, Michael was furious.

"You're trying to paint me as the bad guy here and I'm not. All I've ever tried to do is protect my wife and help her in any way I can. You're trying to make it look like I'm controlling when I'm just trying to make things easier for her. I'm not controlling, I'm just trying to help in any way I can." His sincerity was absolute.

Astonished, Carol looked closely at him. He really meant what he said. She wondered fleetingly, *Then why do you keep doing the wrong thing?*

Kate was wondering the same thing, but then Mehalia entered with some small bite-size quiches, followed by a platter of small round hash browns. There was no more conversation as appetites were assuaged.

⌒

Elizabeth escaped to the bedroom to compose herself. She drooped on the bed, feeling worn. After a moment's indecision, she reached for the phone.

"Adrienne?"

"Hello." Adrienne looked at the clock. "Is everything all right?"

"Yes. No. I don't know. I know I asked you to come over later, but could you get here sooner. I need . . . someone on my side."

"How soon do you want me there?"

"Now?"

"I'm on my way. And Elizabeth?"

"Yes?"

"Sun dogs, for Pete's sake!"

Elizabeth laughed with relief into the dial tone. Of course. Why did she let herself get so unbalanced? Just the mention of the words sun dog calmed her spirit. It was easier to let the sad memories that had been conjured up for all to see to slip away. Even though she had yet to see one, the mere thought of a sun dog filled her with hope.

Another thought occurred to her; recently, Father Jacobs had been preaching on faith, *not* feelings. She might feel like giving up . . . but she had to believe in what she was doing and have faith things would be all right. No matter what.

And whether or not she had that much faith was something she wouldn't, couldn't consider.

Adrienne hung up the phone and turned to see Ian shaking his head. "I'm sorry, sugar, but there aren't any sun dogs out right now; the sky's as blue as a robin's egg. Not a cloud in the sky. Maybe you should call her back and tell her."

She felt a wellspring of love. "Ian, no, not real sun dogs, the sermon of the sun dogs, remember? Elizabeth knows what I meant. She needs me, wants me to come right now."

He nodded, then asked, "Want me to go with you?" She shook her head and started gathering her things. He followed behind her trying not to lecture.

"Promise me you won't take over and try to fix everything?" He meant it. He knew his wife through and through, even as she laughed and protested.

"Me?" she said, pressing a hand to her heart. "You've got to be kidding. I'll just be there holding her hand, I promise."

Head cocked, he gave her a look of wry disbelief. She held up a hand, her face now serious. "Okay, I promise. Besides, they have this lawyer there. I'll just keep the others from beating up on her too much."

"Okay." He brightened. "Go, then, Dree, and you'll kindly ignore the fact I'm hearing the lure of the river creatures. Instead of hopping on those chores you wanted me to do, I'll be going fishing in your absence. I'll do my best to bring back supper; how's that?"

"I'll be counting on it," she said as he knelt down to give her a hug and a kiss.

Then he sat back. "Are you sure you don't want me to come with you? We have fish in the freezer."

She looked at him fondly, knowing how much he enjoyed fishing, but he still was willing to join her if she needed him.

"You're a sweetheart," she said, even as she shook her head, offering a grin. "No. You'll only remind me I should be tactful and behave myself. Go and enjoy."

She was still smiling as she loaded herself into the van. She refused to think any further than the moment she was in and hummed as she worked the gears and pulled out onto the lane.

Elizabeth heard the van and met Adrienne at the door. "Come. Everyone is eating. I hope you're hungry."

"I'll manage to eat a bite or two, thanks."

Adrienne rolled behind Elizabeth to the family room and cheerily said hello as Elizabeth introduced her.

Virginia Mae, recognizing the name, asked stiffly, "Are you the one Elizabeth told me about who instituted a drag race with your friends in motorized carts?" Clipped disapproval underlined every word.

"Why, yes I am." Adrienne chuckled. "And I'm so glad to see you up and about. I understand you sprained your knee, poor thing! That must have hurt."

This was said with such empathy, Virginia Mae immediately brightened and eagerly spoke about herself. "Oh, it was my ankle, and the pain was intense, my dear, intense. I was coming down the stairs of the front porch and the banister rail I was holding popped right off. I couldn't believe it. I fell down three steps and my ankle was twisted under me. If it hadn't been for my neighbor seeing me, I probably would still be sprawled out there on the ground."

"Neighbors are wonderful," Adrienne agreed. Elizabeth, trying to keep a smile from taking over her face, sat down next to her friend. Adrienne turned and winked. Then she looked with interest at the lawyer, who looked more like a grandmother.

"Kate Wilkins . . . Kate Wilkins, where have I heard that name before?" Adrienne mused out loud, tapping a finger against her mouth. Then it dawned on her.

"You helped free that man on death row last year! Yes, because of evidence you discovered that the prosecutor withheld. Bravo." Adrienne beamed while Kate merely shrugged.

It was only then Elizabeth suddenly realized who she was. "You're Mark Wilkins's widow! I've heard about you; I don't know why we never met." She looked at Kate Wilkins with new respect. The story had made it in the Washington, D.C., papers as well as state papers, and she easily remembered it.

After Mark Wilkins's death, Kate, who had worked alongside him for over forty years, realized she didn't want to fade into history. It would have been easy letting her sons run the law firm her husband had built. Mark Wilkins had created the class-action lawsuit to save citizens from big corporations; huge fees and settlements had made it one of the largest firms in the East, known for its aggressiveness.

When Mark Wilkins died, Kate grieved and then took stock of her life. She enjoyed her grandchildren, but she enjoyed law just as much and discovered she wanted to litigate. So, at age sixty-five, she read for the law, having learned more than enough by being her husband's legal assistant as any Ivy League law school graduate. She took the bar and easily passed, then set out to change the course of history where she could.

To her mind, the humanity of law had got lost in the shuffle and she saw, too often, people who didn't get the kind of representation they needed. She aided several mothers who had lost their children simply because the men who left them had more money and power. Where she could, she leveled the playing field.

Of course she had seen the infamous picture of Elizabeth and learned a little more about the Whittakers from her son; she was interested enough to come and visit. She already had some ideas of what they could do, but it would all depend on Elizabeth.

Kate Wilkins sensed Elizabeth might have the heart to go the distance, but wasn't sure her body could take the strain. If she took this case to court, stress would stay tight and taut as a rubber band hovering at its breaking point. Moral fortitude couldn't keep the physical body from wearing out, no matter how hard someone believed.

"You got someone off death row?" Virginia Mae didn't think too much of that and looked at this woman who was of her generation but certainly didn't act it. *She should be home playing with her grandchildren, baking cookies,* she thought. *Doing genteel, womanly things.*

"He was innocent," Adrienne pointed out, wanting to make sure Elizabeth's mother understood.

"If someone is innocent, how do they get to be on death row?" Virginia Mae thought it ridiculous. Innocent people didn't find themselves in such a situation. If he hadn't done the crime he was convicted of, surely he had done something just as awful. It made perfect sense to her.

"Yes, well, his family was pleased," Kate said drily. She focused on Adrienne. "I understand you started this support group?"

"Guilty," Adrienne quipped.

Michael's eyes narrowed at her casual irreverence. He had heard about her, of course, little bits here and there. For some reason their paths had never crossed before today. He knew how much Elizabeth liked this woman, as well as her husband, so it was with interest he sat back to listen.

"Why?"

"Why did we start the group?" Adrienne asked, wanting to be clear. Kate nodded. Adrienne thought for a moment. Eyes twinkling like stars, she couldn't resist. "Misery loves company?"

"Good grief!" Virginia Mae's eyes glared with accusation at her daughter, who had brought this uncouth person into their midst.

"Aw, I'm kidding. I'm kidding," Adrienne hastened to explain to the older woman, thinking Elizabeth's family definitely did not have a sense of humor about these things. "I started it because there wasn't anything around here like it. And the Northern Neck is so large geographically, we figured we'd get more people by opening it up to people with different problems. We all can relate to the same issues."

"Such as?" Kate probed. Virginia Mae had averted her head, as if she wasn't listening. Michael was frowning, but with concentration. He was trying his best to understand the attraction this group could have for his wife.

"Such as abuses of handicapped parking places, of entering stores that are so filled with merchandise you can't shop with a cart, much less a wheelchair." She shrugged. "People who like to tell us what we should be doing—that's always rich. And others who insist that perhaps if we tried a little harder, we'd do better, perhaps our lives would be a little different; you know, mind over matter crap. Like people using semantics to tell us disease is really dis-ease. You get rid of the 'dis,' and you will presumably be at ease." Adrienne rolled her eyes, disgusted.

"You see"—she motioned to Elizabeth—"we relate. We know how maddening it is to know you used to be able to do something but now you can't. Sometimes you have to either get really, really mad or just sit and cry, get it out of your system to go on."

She looked at Elizabeth. "Have I left anything out?"

Elizabeth nodded. "That we are pluggers extraordinaire."

"Well, that, too. Those of us who have chronic illnesses the doctors can't really treat, well, we plug along as best we can." Another thought struck her. "Oh, and once you lose something, you tend not to take anything else for granted." She thought of Carl and clarified, "Well, you shouldn't."

Kate nodded. "Now, can you explain to me why . . . you began this little experiment in which Elizabeth has been charged with possession, with intent to distribute?"

Adrienne clasped her hands in front of her. "At our first meeting in January, one of our members, who has MS and had been using a walker, someone who had complained vigorously about being so sick and tired of being sick and tired, came to the meeting and astonished us." She glanced at Elizabeth.

"She came in walking, then running, then doing jumping jacks, all the things she couldn't do the month before." Elizabeth was still buoyed at the memory.

Adrienne nodded but then looked straight at Kate. "But we can't use her name. She had nothing to do with helping us get the drug or anything."

"Couldn't she have gone into remission? A complete remission? I'm sure that's what her doctors say happened," Kate wondered.

Again, Adrienne nodded. "Of course, because that's the easiest explanation. Now, she didn't tell them she was smoking a joint, but what she thinks is that the drug therapy she's on worked synergistically with the marijuana and, at least for her, did something miraculous."

"Did it help anyone else?"

Elizabeth and Adrienne looked at each other. "It helped me gain some unneeded weight." Adrienne frowned. Elizabeth just shook her head and shrugged.

"Elizabeth's not on any of the therapies," Michael felt compelled to point out, looking at her quizzically. "Why did you think it would help?"

Elizabeth wouldn't look at him, irritated she could still feel her face burn with color. "I have been on one of the therapies. Since January."

He was floored. "Why didn't you tell me? This is wonderful," he said, ecstatic that she was finally taking care of herself. The moment was short-lived.

"I've discontinued it." It was a lie, she knew, but she couldn't bear to see him gloating. Why did he always have to think his way was the only right way?

"But why?" He couldn't believe it. In scant seconds he had been slammed between hope and despair: She finally did something right and now she quit? Why did she have to be so recalcitrant, so unreasonable, especially when the stakes were so high?

Elizabeth merely waved a hand, dismissing his concern. "I don't want to talk about it now."

His face reddened and he bit his lip to keep from saying another word. Adrienne was fascinated. So was Kate Wilkins.

Virginia Mae, however, was as unhappy as her son-in-law. Why had her daughter become so headstrong, so unreasonable? The old woman wondered if it was something *she* had done as a mother. She couldn't think about it now. Instead, she grabbed a tiny quiche and shoved it into her mouth, blinking away tears.

Bored, Carol looked around. "When is Kellan getting here?"

"Anytime," Elizabeth said, glad to change the subject. She grinned at Adrienne. "She's coming with Gregory."

Adrienne's eyes widened. "How on earth did they meet each other?"

"She came to visit me after the—ah—encounter with the police, and he stopped by to tell me that Dr. Meade said, and I quote, 'Tell that little girl I'd be glad to testify on her behalf about what medical marijuana can do.'"

"Dr. Meade?" Kate took notice. "But I know him! He saved my life once."

"What?" All eyes turned to look at her even as Virginia Mae wondered disparagingly, "Who is this Dr. Meade?" Her voice implied he couldn't be much.

Kate spoke to the room at large, ignoring her. "It was several years ago. The whole family was at our place at Lewisetta, and my leg suddenly started throbbing. This all happened before he had to cut his hours back. I knew if anyone could help, he could. I drove myself over, thinking it must be a pulled muscle. As soon as he looked at my leg, he fixed me with those piercing dark eyes and told me, 'Kate, I'm going to call the rescue squad. You have got to get to the hospital immediately. You've got a blood clot.'

"By the time I got to the hospital it was hurting so much I couldn't walk. They immediately started pumping blood thinners through my veins, and within twenty-four hours I was able to go home. My husband took Dr. Meade a huge box of candy and told him how much he appreciated being able to bring me home in his car, rather than in a casket."

"It was that serious?" Virginia Mae asked doubtfully, trying not to be impressed in spite of herself.

The lawyer nodded. "It was. And as far as I'm concerned, he is one of the best."

"I agree." Adrienne nodded vigorously.

Elizabeth smiled. "I think I need to plan to go see him myself."

Michael wondered why and almost said so, since she didn't listen to medical professionals anyway, but he stopped himself. It would be better all around if he kept his mouth shut. It was a fact that didn't improve his mood. *They don't understand*, he thought.

Nor do I, he suddenly thought. Looking around at everyone seated in the spacious room, he wondered what thoughts were going through their heads. He looked at Elizabeth, and was comforted and irritated in the same moment at how relaxed she appeared.

Adrienne suddenly leaned forward to speak to Kate. "I meant to tell you before, everyone in our support group is completely behind Elizabeth on this a hundred percent . . . a thousand percent. We'll help raise money for her defense any way we can. The reason we haven't come forward to admit to our culpability in this is simply because one, we don't want to make things worse; and two, none of us have very deep pockets."

Startled, Elizabeth turned to Kate. "As a matter of fact, I don't have deep pockets either. You know I had never thought about the expense. I'm astonished to say I don't know how I'll pay for this."

"Don't worry about it, Elizabeth; arrangements have been made."

The flatness of Michael's voice discouraged questions, but Elizabeth paid no attention. "What arrangements?"

"We can discuss this later," Michael said tersely, not wanting a lengthy dissection of their finances in front of strangers.

Her lips thinned as she heard the finality there. Of course Michael would take care of it, Elizabeth thought angrily, never thinking to apprise his wife of the details. He had always been like this, and she had allowed it, fool that she was.

Michael could see Elizabeth was upset, and was surprised, but it made his own irritation level start to rise.

"What has happened to the gentleman you said gained some benefit from smoking the drug?" Kate asked Adrienne, who seemed to know most about the situation.

"As a matter of fact, I got a phone call this morning. I'm afraid he's in the hospital. The pain got unbearable last night." She looked around at everyone else. "You see, he has no family, just an aide who comes in daily."

Her sad eyes met Elizabeth's equally concerned ones. "When I leave here, I'll be going to see Carl."

Kate, ever the astute attorney, never displayed emotion unless it was effective. Her face was a mask, her voice toneless. "Sorry to hear about that. You don't think he'd be able to testify at a trial if it comes to that, then?"

"Well, the pain isn't life-threatening, I understand. He had a nurse call me this morning. She said he was stable and they were trying to figure out just how to keep him that way. She said he would be there no more than a few days. It's possible he could testify."

"Do you think we could talk this woman who had such startling results into testifying? That could be very crucial. It justifies Elizabeth's motive very strongly."

Adrienne and Elizabeth looked at each other. They had no answer. "We could ask her," Elizabeth said doubtfully.

"Yes, we could *ask* her," Adrienne echoed thinly.

"Why don't I call her?" Kate offered. It was evident the lawyer thought she could sway her into making the right decision, and Elizabeth didn't like it.

Before she could say a word, though, Serenity walked in, right behind Kellan and Gregory. "Hello, hello," Kellan greeted the room at large.

Standing nearby, Serenity nodded pleasantly to each of the people there as Kellan leaned over and gave her mother a hug and a kiss, even as her grandmother stood up, protesting.

"Your mother just saw you weeks ago, Kellan, and I haven't seen you in months," the old woman complained, but Carol had already jumped up and claimed her godchild before Kellan could get to Virginia Mae and then, last, her father.

Following that, introductions were made all around, with lots of handshakes. Drawing Serenity in closer, Kellan explained, "We saw Serenity walking up the road and offered to bring her with us. She said Mehalia was here and besides, she wanted to say something to you, Mom."

All eyes moved to the very pretty young girl, dressed in a flowing yellow skirt and simple white blouse topped with a colorful sweater. Her face, glowing from the briskness of the pleasant day, was captivating.

"Yes, ma'am," the low voice spoke elegantly and Carol, impressed, thought that this was one self-assured teenager. But looking like that, what else could she be?

"I wanted to say how very sorry I am for what happened. I thought we made everything look so . . . ordinary, so . . . so natural. I am very sorry also that you fell."

Serenity shook her head sadly, which caused the long rippling mantle of dark wavy hair to dance.

Elizabeth was nodding and smiling at the pretty apology, but Adrienne wasn't buying it.

She focused intent eyes on the child and asked in a direct, hard voice, "Serenity, do you know how much the ten joints you gave Elizabeth are worth?"

With a clear, uncomplicated face, Serenity answered, "Four hundred dollars."

Elizabeth's eyes dropped to the floor as her face reddened. She hated confrontations and even now could not believe this child was capable of any real mischief.

Adrienne shook her head. "The police valued those joints at one hundred dollars."

Serenity merely shrugged. "I explained everything to Mrs. Whittaker. Perhaps she did not explain it to you?" She paused and waited for Adrienne to say something. When she did not, she patiently explained again. "The joints were passed through three other dealers before they came to me. Each wanted their cut, including the original dealer. I'm sorry, but it was the best I could do."

Adrienne wasn't finished. "Why did you put each joint in a separate plastic bag this time? You had never done that before."

Serenity didn't particularly like these questions, but she forced herself to remain unperturbed. With remarkable casualness a tiny smile lit her face. She motioned to Elizabeth. "She told me it would be the last time and I wanted to be make it easy. A little more special."

"But you marked them each with a number. Why?"

Again the girl lifted a graceful shoulder. "Just to be different. Make it a little different."

She was perfect, Adrienne thought. Perfect inflection in her voice, face casting just the right amount of certainty to make everything she said so plausible. But Adrienne knew something Serenity didn't. She and Mehalia had talked yesterday. Now it was time to bring this farce to an end.

"Mehalia, please come in here." Adrienne never took her eyes off Serenity. Serenity's grandmother had been hovering just out of sight, hearing everything, and she immediately walked in.

Carol, chin resting on a hand, wondered what was going on.

"If what you are saying is true," Mehalia said, her back as erect as her innate sense of right and wrong, "then explain how you have precisely the amount of money those other three dealers should have?"

She flung out the hidden hand, holding several one-hundred-dollar bills. "Fifteen hundred, to be exact."

Carol saw the slight ripple, the tightening of Serenity's mouth, but only because she was watching so closely. This unexpected drama was fascinating.

"You know where I found this?" Mehalia demanded.

Serenity nodded slowly. "In my room. Between the mattresses of my bed."

"And where in this world would you get fifteen hundred dollars?" Mehalia's angry face suddenly tumbled into worry and sadness, and her strong shoulders began to sag.

"Granny, that is the money I've been saving all my life." These words were spoken with such honesty Mehalia faltered. But Adrienne Moore did not.

"Come on, Serenity. Give it up, girl. You've been caught. You charged Elizabeth, well, all of us, thirty dollars more each time we bought a joint from you. Three hundred dollars for five weeks too conveniently adds up to exactly the amount of money Mehalia found."

The young girl looked around, gauging their reaction. She tossed her head, her demeanor haughty. "I see you're not going to believe me if I deny it; you've already made up your minds." Then she seemed to change course as deftly as if she were steering a boat through treacherous and deceptive water.

She looked at her grandmother. "What do you want me to do, Granny?"

Startled that her granddaughter was actually asking her advice, Mehalia put the money down on the table in front of Elizabeth. "Get down on your knees and apologize to this fine lady for what you did—apologize that you are a cheat and a liar."

The girl looked seriously at her grandmother as if absorbing those words and within a long moment of consideration, literally became them.

Trembling, as if gripped in a clench of repentance and shame, Serenity fell fluidly to her knees in front of Elizabeth, tears beginning to pool in her eyes then gently cascading down her face. It took several moments before she was able to talk.

"Mrs. Whittaker," she said, her voice filled with anguish. "I am so very sorry . . . You must think I'm awful, and you're right. I am a terrible, terrible person like my granny just said. You have no obligation to do so (sob), but please, ma'am, I ask (sniff) . . . I ask, no, I beg . . . please, could you (sniff) please forgive me?" The girl was in misery and Elizabeth's soft heart couldn't stand it, listening to her cry.

She reached out and touched Serenity's bowed head. "Serenity dear, please, it's okay; of course I forgive you."

The words were barely out of her mouth when the elegant head shot up, the beautiful face cleared. Elizabeth's words had eliminated any more need for a performance. There was no more sniffling; the tears stopped. Serenity flung off the image of a sincere apologist and rose, turned slightly to look at her grandmother. "Happy?"

Startled at the smooth impudence she saw in those clear eyes, Mehalia was too stunned to say a word. Everyone in the room stared, motionless.

Serenity's hand shot out, snatched the money cleanly off the table. With graceful ease she turned and walked away. Although her steps were swift, she managed to retain an elegance that seemed perfectly natural.

Mehalia, a hand over her mouth, sank into the closest chair, trembling. She was beyond anger; she was filled with a fatal hopelessness. What in the world was going to happen to this child?

The older woman was not crying, but her eyes were moist and she blinked rapidly. Elizabeth, wanting to go and comfort her friend, got up a little too quickly and reached out to steady herself on Adrienne's chair.

At the same time, Adrienne was trying to apologize to Mehalia and everyone all at once. "I am sorry. I didn't know this was going to happen, Mehalia; I just wanted to make her see that what she had done was wrong."

Kate was watching the entire scene, wondering if anything could be used to help the defense. Michael wondered if he should just call the sheriff's department and turn this girl in and be done with it all. He also wondered just where Serenity was taking all that money.

Elizabeth by now had reached Mehalia and put her arms around the old woman, murmuring words of comfort.

"What am I going to do, Elizabeth? I don't have any earthly idea what I can do to make that child understand what she's doing. I just don't know . . ."

"Shhh, we'll work it out. She's not a bad person, Mehalia, she just needs some . . ." She floundered briefly before finally saying, "We'll find someone who can help her."

Carol, who had watched the performance from start to finish, was glowing and although she had not yet spoken, Serenity was barely out of the room before she mouthed one word: Wow.

Virginia Mae was appalled. "I cannot believe that child. Well, she's hardly a child anymore. She should know better. I bet she's a—what do you call those people who have no conscience—a sociopath? Like Ted Bundy; yes indeed, that girl is a sociopath. Mehalia, she's going to murder you in your bed if you don't do something about her," she admonished the old woman, waving a finger in her direction, which finally caused tears to flow over and out. Mehalia fished out a handkerchief from a pocket and buried her face in it, her sobs quiet and desperate.

Carol finally found her voice and stood up. "Mehalia." Her voice cut through the nonsense and caught the old woman's attention. "We have to talk. Let's go into the kitchen."

No one had any idea what Carol could possibly want with the old lady, except Gordon. Although he, too, had been appalled at the girl's duplicity, he had also seen Carol's reaction. What seemed like aberrant, even immoral, behavior to some, Carol saw as great talent.

Go figure, he thought. Carol was part of the world of make-believe, and that girl certainly had a knack for it. He followed the two women into the kitchen.

Kellan was barely listening to what was going on around them; she was too busy exchanging glances with Gregory.

Since they had met just weeks ago, they had talked every day on the phone. Last weekend and last night they had spent together.

But it wasn't a typical lovers' tryst. This was a man she could entrust herself to, she knew it intuitively; he would not hurt her or take advantage of her. He had a guest bedroom. At the end of each evening they had stood in front of that door, he kissed her, said good night, and left for his own room.

It was so honorable, she had told her mother just a few days ago. "He's treating me with such respect. And we're learning about each other in small, wonderful ways . . . We're becoming intimate with our feelings, rather than jumping into bed and losing ourselves in a fit of physical passion that might not go anywhere. It's really special."

Elizabeth had been so happy for her. And Kellan had never been more radiant. Gregory, too, smiled more but was still conflicted.

Kellan kept telling him to stop worrying and then did her best to chase away all the fears. She had succeeded too well in making him forget . . . It had been idyllic. They created a harmony that made them complete. And there was the expectancy, the anticipation of waiting that made everything brighter and more intensely real.

He was learning, slowly, that the future would have to take care of itself.

Michael, too, had noticed the glances between his daughter and this Gregory person. The young man seemed to be nice, though Michael hadn't heard the first word about him. That would change before this day ended.

The phone rang and Elizabeth went to get it. With a brief good-bye, Carol had driven off with Mehalia to find her granddaughter and taken Gordon with her.

Virginia Mae was disgusted with the whole situation. They had turned everything into a carnival; once Carol had left, she walked into the kitchen to clean up and perhaps have another plate or so of the delicious food.

Moment's later Elizabeth came back, holding the cordless. "That was Albert. He talked with Pearl and Sally. They all planned to be here this afternoon"—she said this to Kate, glancing at Adrienne—"but everyone is feeling really lousy and they send their regrets."

"I see." Kate sat, thinking for a long moment.

Adrienne and Elizabeth looked at each other, wondering what was going to happen now. Again, Adrienne murmured softly, "I am sorry about Serenity."

Elizabeth just shrugged and smiled. "It doesn't matter."

Kate Wilkins spoke up. "Elizabeth, may I speak with you privately?"

"Of course," Elizabeth said, uneasy. "We can go sit out on the back deck. It's adjacent to my bedroom."

Kate nodded to the others and followed Elizabeth through one of the sliding glass doors.

Michael frowned, not liking this at all, but he felt powerless. He looked over at Gregory with curiosity and spoke. "Now, you are . . . Gregory? Am I getting it right?"

"Yes, sir, Gregory Jamison." The young man held out a hand.

Michael approved of the strength he felt there and then he eyed his daughter. "How come I've never met this young man?" He said this with a quizzical smile and watched Kellan's face beam as though she'd won the lottery.

"Because I only met him a few weeks ago. I haven't had time to bring him home. Mom knows him, though."

"Oh?"

"Yes, sir. She's a fine woman." Gregory wondered how far he should go with this. Should he tell Mr. Whittaker everything now or what? What was the protocol in a situation like this? He looked away and saw Adrienne smile.

She moved over to where he sat and began talking. "I think Elizabeth has shown amazing courage through this whole ordeal. I know you must be very proud. And it is a pleasure to finally meet you, Mr. Whittaker. She has told me such good things about you." Adrienne's smile was wide and inviting.

"I've heard a great deal about you, too, Mrs. Moore," he said solemnly, "and it's Michael."

She extended a hand. "Adrienne."

The doors were open and Kate and Elizabeth walked back in. Michael frowned when he saw how pale his wife looked.

"Is everything all right?"

He was deaf to the harshness of his worry, but Elizabeth felt it, and it made her own voice curt. "Everything's fine." She turned away before she saw the hurt in his eyes.

Kate Wilkins was putting things back into her briefcase as she spoke.

"It's been a pleasure meeting all of you." She nodded to the room at large and then pulled out a cell phone from her briefcase. "Michael, I'm calling my son to come pick me up." She glanced around and explained, "The family's at our river place this weekend; my son is waiting for my call." A few moments later she switched the phone off. "He should be here in about ten minutes. Michael, perhaps you could keep me company out front and we can chat a bit?"

And then she and Michael were gone. "What did she talk to you about?" Adrienne was curious but Elizabeth shook her head.

"Kellan, are you and Gregory planning on spending the night here?"

Kellan shook her head. "No, we planned on going back to Fredericksburg. Gregory's promised me the grand tour."

Elizabeth saw the happiness brimming in her daughter's eyes and refused to think beyond that one thought.

"If that's all right with you, Elizabeth," Gregory added earnestly. He didn't want to do anything upsetting.

Elizabeth smiled. "Just take good care of my daughter."

He smiled and she was struck again at what an attractive man he was. "You have nothing to worry about." She could see the matching joy in his eyes and for the briefest of moments, envied them.

Kellan slipped her hand inside his larger one. "Thanks, Mom."

Virginia Mae walked into the family room after finishing putting away the leftovers.

"Kellan, how would you like to go with me to the shop down the road? I saw some beautiful dresses in the window as I was driving here. They would look wonderful on you." Her grandmother sat down and looked at her expectantly.

"I'm sorry, Grammy, but I'm going to Fredericksburg with Gregory. We're leaving in just a little bit."

"Oh, no," a disappointed Virginia Mae exclaimed, her voice hurt. "I see you for barely three seconds and you're leaving. Why, I expected you to spend the night. I never get to see you, and certainly your mother wants to spend time with you—"

"Mother." Elizabeth's tired voice was firm. "They are going to Fredericksburg." Then she stood up, cueing the young couple to stand up and make their getaway.

At the front door Kellan threw her arms around her mother and whispered, "You're the best, Mom. Thanks."

Elizabeth smiled and watched as the two young people went to say good-bye to Michael. She turned to go back inside and found her mother standing rigidly in the hallway, hands on her hips, glaring at her.

"Who is that young man, and how can you just let your daughter go off with him? They're probably going to be *sleeping* together, Elizabeth! How can you allow this?"

Elizabeth smiled at her mother. "I trust my daughter. That's all I need to know." She walked past Virginia Mae to sit with Adrienne.

Virginia Mae was left gaping, absolutely shocked at how her daughter was behaving. It took several seconds before it dawned on her no one noticed her anger. She closed her mouth, straightened her back, and walked into the kitchen, thinking she, too, would get in her car and leave. After one more cup of coffee. That would show them all. They would be sorry, especially Elizabeth. She would deprive her daughter of the pleasure of her mother's company.

Chapter Thirty

Everyone was gone except Adrienne. Kate's son had picked her up, and Michael had come inside to see if Virginia Mae wanted to follow him back to the city. The older woman brightened, suggesting they stop at the Rappahannock Gourmet store to eat and pick up some cheeses and wine before heading home.

"Whatever." His glance was cool as he said good-bye to his wife. "If you need anything, Elizabeth, you know how to get in touch."

"Thank you for everything, Michael," she said softly and watched them leave. Her mother was trying to plan the rest of the evening for herself and her son-in-law, but was not getting any response.

Elizabeth could hear her mother's voice getting softer and softer and then the cars were started and first one and then the other pulled away.

Elizabeth and Adrienne sat in the silence of the family room. Slits of western sun lit a wall and for a long moment the room was gentle, toneless. Elizabeth welcomed the emptiness, embraced it as she closed her eyes and tried to shed the pressure of the day.

Eventually Adrienne spoke. "Ian's supposed to be fishing for dinner right now." Adrienne eyed the perfect day and the lazy river.

"That's nice," Elizabeth said. Adrienne looked at her friend, saw shadows in those blue eyes and waited. If Elizabeth wanted to talk, she would.

Adrienne, for once, was behaving herself and not prying, despite the intense curiosity she was determined to ignore.

Moments floated on and the peace of the house tucked around them like a blanket. Adrienne was almost nodding when Elizabeth finally spoke.

"Kate said I had a choice. She said for me to think this over very carefully because I would be the one who would have to live with the decision."

Adrienne nodded. That made sense. She wondered what the choices were.

"We can go for the big bang; you know, the medical necessity defense, even though this state doesn't have one. If we go that way, we will want a jury trial because, well, a jury can come back with any verdict they please. She thinks she could get them feeling sorry for me." Elizabeth wrinkled her nose at the thought. "And there would be a lot of publicity. Newspaper interviews, television, all aimed at leveraging our side."

Adrienne cocked her head. "I wonder if we could get Sandra to change her mind? Or if we could use her anonymously, you know, to validate what you, well, what we all did."

"Kate said it would make my case stronger if she would come out, so to speak." As she spoke, Elizabeth could feel her shoulders tighten, tension knotting up in her stomach.

Adrienne didn't notice. Indeed, she was warming with ideas. "I know some people at the *Post*. We could probably get in there; well, I could write our own press releases. We could make this whole thing a media sensation. I can see it all, the whole thing. We could map out a whole PR campaign. Do you realize by the time this trial is over, you, Elizabeth Whittaker, will be famous? The possibilities are endless." She shook a fist in the air, a smile of triumph already on her face. And then she looked at Elizabeth.

Her friend's face had drained of color, a shaking hand was placed against her heart, and her eyes were desperate.

Adrienne, chagrined, immediately reached out a hand. "Or maybe not," she said soothingly. Her mouth had been in gear before she'd thought twice about how Elizabeth might react. If Ian were here . . . Adrienne shook her head, a faint glimmer of a smile in her eyes as she imagined the lecture she would get.

"You don't have to do any of that, Elizabeth, absolutely not. You tell your lawyer you don't want to do that, okay? I'm right behind you. Here, let me get you a drink, maybe some wine. That will calm you down."

She was back in a moment not only with a glass of wine, but with a basket of crackers with odd bits of cheese. She waited until Elizabeth nibbled some; it was with relief she saw color come back.

"What's the other option?" Adrienne asked gently. Elizabeth nodded and finished swallowing.

"She can arrange with the commonwealth's attorney at the preliminary hearing in a few weeks that I plead guilty to a lesser charge, simple possession. Then I can go to some drug classes, keep out of trouble for a year and if I do, I get my record cleared. This will go away easily and simply."

Elizabeth could tell Adrienne was disappointed in her, although she didn't say a word. Elizabeth felt the need to explain.

"Adrienne, I just can't do it. I could not live with that sort of notoriety you were talking about, which is just what Kate said earlier. I shudder every time I think of that picture in the paper. It's horrible; I abhor it. I'm a very private person." She finished those last words with her chin up. It was short-lived bravado. Tears started welling up, her shoulders sagged, and a tremulous sigh escaped.

Immediately Adrienne offered complete support. "Then you are doing exactly the right thing."

"But it's not what you would do," Elizabeth said glumly. Why couldn't she be a stronger person?

"No, it's not, but that's why you are you and I am me. Or is it I? I need Ian." Elizabeth didn't share her laugh, so Adrienne pointed out what was so obvious.

"Elizabeth, I don't get one-hundredth as tired as you do and you know it. If I knew, from the start, that I would have to handle not only all the details of a media campaign where I was the center of attention, but also do it knowing I would have to live with the kind of fatigue I have seen drain you . . . Well, let me tell you, I would simply crawl under the bed and stay there. No one would be able to get me out."

Elizabeth's face finally held a tentative but sad smile. Or was it just relief? "Not even Ian?"

"Especially not Ian," declared Adrienne. "Now, why don't I scoot and let you get some rest? I'm going to stop at the hospital and see Carl."

"Let me know how he is. Tell him I said hello," Elizabeth said, walking Adrienne to the front door.

Elizabeth watched her friend roll to the van and leave. The silence was welcome, she was grateful for the respite from this relentless day. Elizabeth closed the door and then sagged against it as the heavy press of tension rolled off. Now that the decision had been made to take the easy way out, she marveled at how limp she felt. Relaxing for the first time since the deputy had stopped her, she went to her room and snuggled into bed, asleep almost before her head met the pillow.

Chapter Thirty-one

The irony wasn't lost on Carl Sanders, and in brief painless moments he could almost chuckle. Hospitals were buildings dedicated to making sick people get better.

He had come here to die.

It was that plain and simple. At least now it was. It had taken him a while to puzzle out why he did not want to die alone. He marked himself an atheist and he believed that death ended life and that was all there was to it. But without at first understanding he knew he did not want to die alone.

It had taken several weeks of inspecting that feeling to figure it out. And his answer had come in, of all things, a dream a few nights ago. A smile tightened his face as he thought of Nicole Anderson. The difference there, he knew, was that he could trust his subconscious mind. It made perfect sense.

He had seen too many bloated dead bodies; he had seen what insects and roaming animals could do to dead human meat. He had lived in this body for over fifty years. Although he believed after his death there would be nothing, he wasn't about to let the physical part of him die alone.

It was as simple as that.

The pain roared through again, like a cat clawing out his insides, and Sanders caught his breath to wait it out. The only reason he wasn't screaming was that this long spasm would not allow speech. The disks in his lower back were wearing away, so he had been told, but not the nerves, no. They were very much alive.

After Elizabeth had been caught and the supply of marijuana cut off, the pain, which had been dulled for the past month, began screaming almost nonstop. There were occasional moments when the pain stilled and he could almost think clearly. It was during one of these moments he had made his decision, irrevocable and precise. He could no longer live like this.

He wanted to die. He was glad he had no family. Old friends had fallen away over the years due to his inattention. As his health worsened, he pushed the rest away; he simply shut them out. So now here he was at this stage of his life, and glad he could take complete control over its ending.

That's why he had insisted the doctors put him in the hospital. The pain was unbearable, they had to do something, he insisted.

"Hello, Carl." Adrienne wheeled into the room. She kept a bright smile pasted on, trying hard not to allow her face to reflect her shock. Carl Sanders looked awful. What had the hospital done to him? His face was lined, haggard as if he had not slept in days, darkened with stubble.

"Is there anything I can do for you, get for you?" Adrienne wished there were something tangible she could do for this man; it broke her heart. *God, why?*

She already knew an answer would come in its own time. She just wished . . .

"Adrienne." The voice was a harsh whisper and she saw the effort he made to get it out.

"Oh, Carl, dear, I wish—isn't there anything they can do for you?"

As if on cue, a nurse came in wielding a needle "Why hi, Mrs. Moore," she greeted Adrienne with ease. Marianne went to Adrienne's church.

"Marianne." Adrienne tried to smile but couldn't get past her concern for Carl. "Please, isn't there anything more you can do to make my friend comfortable?"

"You bet." She grinned and then addressed Carl. "Good news, we finally caught up with him on the golf course."

"What was the score?" he rasped, knowing his doctor's lack of skill. They had actually joked about it in another lifetime. Hell, they had played together then, too.

She cocked her head at him while rubbing alcohol on his arm. "He told me I couldn't tell you and since he wouldn't tell *me*, he made it a moot point. But he did say we could increase the dosage throughout the night and he would be by to see you bright and early tomorrow."

Carl grunted, the pain of the needle sharpened by so many out-of-control nerves screaming for attention.

"Marianne, how long will it be before it takes effect?" Adrienne asked anxiously. Carl looked in such distress.

"Oh, about twenty minutes or so, not too long," Marianne assured cheerfully, and then trotted off to fulfill a myriad of duties before she came back to check on him.

After she slipped out of the room, Adrienne rolled close and put a gentle hand on his, eyes warm with compassion. "Carl, is there anything, *anything* I can do for you, anything at all?" She felt so helpless; his suffering was so immense she could almost feel it herself. She could not understand why he had to suffer like this. Why couldn't they just give him something to let him sleep? At least then he wouldn't have to feel the pain.

"As a matter of fact," he began and then clenched his teeth through a bad one. When it was over he breathed out all the words in a rush. "Could you go to the front and buy me some bottled water? The water here smells like bleach and tastes as bad."

"Of course I can," Adrienne said, turning the chair around eagerly, thankful he had asked.

He motioned to the small metal bureau near the bed. "There's money in there," he bit out as she shushed him.

"My treat, I'll be right back."

He heard the humming of the cart's motor, the soft tread of her wheels as she left.

From underneath the sheets he pulled out a vial, an old prescription container he had brought with him when he checked in. In it he had smashed more than enough pills to end his suffering. He carefully unscrewed the top. A multicolored array of pills he had taken throughout the last months, leftovers as the doctors tried first one medication, then another that did little to quell the pain.

His right hand began raising this promise to his lips. He wanted all of this in his mouth before Adrienne got back, then he'd drink them all down with the water.

Closer and closer his hand moved toward its final destination when suddenly a spasm of pain shot through him, paralyzing him. "Dammit," he swore, and watched helplessly as his right hand, no longer under his control, began to tilt and push toward the side of the bed. And he couldn't make it come back.

Sweat broke out, the pain lingered, drifting lazily away, as slowly as it could. His hand was precariously tilting ever so slightly and he knew his one chance was slipping away. He wasn't going to be able to pull it back before all those damn pills were on the floor instead of his mouth.

He was helpless, desperate; amid scattered thoughts he suddenly recalled the story of the sun dogs Adrienne had shared with him. There had been long talks between the two of them, philosophical discussions, the premise being they agreed to disagree. She had also told him about her godchild, Thomas. He had talked of coincidences, of seeing what you wanted to see . . .

Now he was seeing his only hope of leaving this life slipping away from him. Seized with an urgency, his eyes squeezed shut, he shouted a silent challenge: *Dammit, God!* If You really exist, You will let me do this one thing. If You are real, You will—"

Before his mind had finished the thought, his eyes opened and he watched his hand, still not under his control, suddenly right itself. Hardly daring to breathe, he watched it turn and move toward his face.

Tears of relief sparkled his eyes as every last pill was dumped into his mouth just as he heard Adrienne greet someone right outside his door. He slid the empty bottle under the covers.

"Here you are, Carl," she said brightly, bringing two bottles toward him. "I brought you back another one in case you get thirsty later on."

Without waiting for him to ask, she unscrewed one, put a straw in it and held it up to him. With relief, he was able to lift it with his left hand and drink greedily, feeling the clump of tablets vying for space in his throat. By the time the last one had slid down into place, he had finished the entire bottle.

"My goodness, maybe I better go and buy you a case." Adrienne immediately wondered if this man was becoming dehydrated. She would have to ask before she left.

Concern turned to astonishment as he put the bottle down and gave her a smile that immediately softened his face, and she felt a little blip of hope for him. Maybe things would turn out all right. She had never really seen Carl smile before.

"That shot must be working, Carl. You look like you're feeling a whole lot better," she exclaimed, encouraged for him. "Are you?"

"Yes. I am," he said, easing back into the pillows. "Everything's going to be just fine now. Thank you, Adrienne. You've been a good friend. Would you do me one last favor?"

"Of course, Carl, as many as you need!" she said without hesitation. She was so glad the pain finally seemed to be slipping away, she would do anything she could for him. And if she couldn't, she'd call Ian. "What do you want me to do?"

He closed his eyes briefly. "Would you stay here until I fall asleep? It won't take long, I just took a sleeping pill." Already his words were slurring slightly.

He felt the brief touch of her hand as she said softly, "Of course I'll stay. Sleep well. I'll stay here, and then I'll come back to see you tomorrow."

He smiled. There would be no tomorrows, thank God or whatever. As he slowly felt the pain dissolve and his body begin to relax, he thought fuzzily that she would never know. Was this one of those sundog moments she had talked to him about? Or more likely a coincidence . . . But then again, if she were right, maybe she would find out, and he could tell her . . . much later. With a sigh of contentment, he sank deeper and deeper into the blessed relief of a dreamless eternal sleep . . .

Chapter Thirty-two

For over an hour, Carol sat on the small faded couch, waiting for Serenity to come home and talking to Mehalia King.

Gordon listened silently, his long limbs folded under a very uncomfortable kitchen chair. Once again Mehalia was shaking her head, clearly disgusted.

"You are trying to tell me you think what my granddaughter did was *wonderful*?"

Carol closed her eyes at the shocked and outraged voice, trying to think of another, gentler, way to say the same thing to this conflicted woman.

"No. What Serenity did was wrong; I agree with you on that. But what I'm saying is the *way* she did it was . . . extraordinary." Carol looked at Gordon. "You tell her."

He half smiled and looked at the agitated old woman. "What Serenity did was wrong, but the way she did it was marvelous. And marketable." He saw Carol's frown and merely smiled in her direction. Then he sat up, elbows resting on his knees and focused completely on Mehalia. "Mrs. King, from what I've seen your granddaughter is like a lot of teenagers these days—mixed up, wanting everything they can get their hands on, too young to realize that won't make them happy. So Serenity is pretty normal in that regard. What we saw her do at Elizabeth's was, yes, morally reprehensible, but her acting ability was . . . extraordinary in someone that young. You've watched television. You know what most actors on TV are like today—not very good. Given the right material and a little training, I think Serenity could really make a success of her life."

Mehalia's sigh was deep and long, full of confusion and despair. "I don't think that child knows where playacting lets go and reality begins." She was weary in every bone in her body. Her sorrow was deep over the fact that this child, this beautiful young woman, was heading straight to hell. She looked at the doctor again. He was a good man, he was a doctor helping people, and she felt she could trust him. He knew a lot more than she did.

"What would you do, Doctor?" Mehalia asked, her voice catching.

He looked deep into those worried eyes and was as honest and direct as he could be. "I'd let Carol talk to her. Carol would not let anything bad happen to her, rest assured. As a matter of fact, if Serenity decides to say yes"—he glanced at Carol—"I see no reason why you couldn't go to New York with them both, keep an eye on Serenity and assure yourself everything is as it should be."

"Of course I would want you to go, too," Carol said, chagrined. "I thought I made myself clear about that."

Mehalia frowned, shook her head helplessly. "Good Lord, child, I can't afford a trip to New York. With the little pension I get, I still have to clean houses to keep this roof above our heads and food in the cupboard."

For the first time, Carol actually took notice of her surroundings. The home was clean and tidy, but worn and tiny, inhabited by people living on the edge of their money. Suddenly she felt ashamed of herself again, for not making things crystal clear. "Mehalia, I'm sorry. I mean you would come as my guest, both of you, of course. My production company would pay all your expenses as well as a monthly stipend—"

"That's a monthly paycheck," deciphered Gordon, wanting Mehalia to understand completely.

Red with anger at herself, Carol shook her head and wondered where her brain was. "Of course, a monthly paycheck to keep all your bills here paid and to keep you in spending money in New York. I promise you would lack for nothing."

Exhausted, Mehalia sat back in the rocker stuffed with pillows she had bought used over the years. All this was coming too fast and furious for her; it was muddling her mind. But the question was, Did she have a choice? No indeed, her grandbaby was out of her reach and control, and Lord God only knew how to bring her back. She wondered if these people really knew what they were getting into, because Serenity had been able to fool her for a long time. The child was so good at changing into whatever personality would be most beneficial to her. The back door slammed shut and they all heard the quick footsteps and the call, "Granny?"

Carol leaned over to Mehalia. "Say yes."

The old lady nodded, passing a hand over her eyes, despair dropping over her as surely as the years had chipped away her own youth.

Serenity stood in the doorway, suspicion holding her erect and poised for flight. She had seen the car parked out front, the shiny sports car.

"What are you two doing here?"

"They want to talk to you, Serenity," her grandmother began.

"About what?" Chin up, defiance outlined every muscle as she eyed them both with contrived dignity.

Carol bit back a smile and stood up, her face and her own manner suddenly changed into a maternal drill sergeant. "About offering you the deal of a lifetime."

Serenity snorted, her eyes rolling, and folded her arms across her chest. "Sure. Right."

"Serenity, will you please shut up and listen to what she has to say?" Mehalia pleaded, hating the airs her granddaughter wrapped herself in with the unconcern of a queen bee.

The girl leaned against the doorjam, a sarcastic smile playing over her lips. Her money was hidden in the woods where no one could find it, so these people would not be able to trick her out of it, no way. She wasn't going to lose anything by listening. "Okay. Shoot."

Carol's words were cool and professional. "I am a writer, and I have an agreement with one of the television networks to start production on a new series I've developed. I've been looking for a new, fresh talent and I think that maybe—just maybe—I've found what I'm looking for in you."

Serenity ducked her head to hide her surprise, but Carol was much too observant not to see. "I want you and your grandmother to come to New York for an extended stay, at my expense."

Serenity couldn't hide the triumphant gleam in those beautiful eyes, but Carol wasn't going to let her think it was that easy. Oh, this brat was going to have to want it so much and then work her tail off for it.

"The first thing we have to do is film you. Frankly, if the camera doesn't love you, if you don't photograph well, we can just forget it, and I'll bring you back here and we can forget the whole thing ever happened." She watched with perverse satisfaction as the girl's face paled.

"I think—I hope—that won't happen. And for the record, I did not like what you did to my cousin," she said sternly, "but I was impressed with the way you did it. You may have a natural acting ability. I'll have to get you under the tutelage of one of the best acting coaches I know, and let me tell you, it will be rigorous and unrelenting training. Think boot camp, and you might get a faint picture of what your life will be like."

"What's that word, *tootlidge*, mean?" Mehalia whispered to Gordon.

He whispered back, "Teaching—you know, tutoring."

He smiled as she shook her head, murmuring, "Why can't she say what she means using words people *know*?"

He covered her hand and gave it a soft squeeze. "I wish I knew."

By the time Carol had finished talking, Serenity was sitting cross-legged on the floor, a nervousness starting to jitter inside her that she was trying hard not to show. She almost succeeded but it showed in the way she chewed her lower lip.

"What do you think, Granny? What should I do?" Serenity was seeing a bright dream suddenly placed on a silver platter in front of her. What girl hadn't thought of going to New York and becoming a big star? But now that this had been presented to her, she was terrified. What if she got there and couldn't open her mouth to speak? What if she stunk? What if she was so awful they had to come back home? Then she and everyone else would know she was a . . . failure.

Serenity pressed a hand over her racing heart and realized she was trembling.

"What do *you* want me to do?" Those beautiful eyes were unguarded and, for once, as young as their handful of years.

Mehalia looked deep into her granddaughter's soul and could have cried at the alarm she saw there. The child was scared, which was a good thing. Fear could make you humble as long as it wasn't the dangerous kind.

She slipped her hand over Serenity's and felt the child clutch hers for support. Suddenly, in that instant, Mehalia was the grandmother, the rock in the swirl of change, and her words would carry the authority this child needed.

"We'll try it together, child. Together, we'll see."

⌒

The next day, just as visiting hours began, Adrienne motored into the hospital, picking up some water bottles in advance for Carl. She turned a corner heading toward his room and nearly collided with a nurse.

"Oh, Mrs. Moore!" Marianne was startled. "What are you doing here?"

"Why, I've come to see Carl Sanders. I told him yesterday I would."

Adrienne watched the girl's face flush red. "But, but . . . Mrs. Moore, I don't know how to tell you this, but Mr. Sanders died last night."

Adrienne blinked. *Died?* Stunned, she looked at the girl again, shock momentarily sweeping speech away.

She finally found her voice. "What happened?"

Marianne shook her head and shrugged. "We don't know, but the doctor thinks his heart might have given out. You know he was in a great deal of pain. It's not unusual, and we were having a real hard time medicating him."

"Yes, I recall." Adrienne shuddered, thinking they had hardly done anything at all until the doctor authorized that last shot.

"Will there be an autopsy?"

The girl grimaced. "I don't think so. Ma'am, excuse me, but the doctor's waiting on these papers."

And then she was gone, leaving Adrienne to wonder what she should do next. Carl dead? Its very newness made it unbelievable. She had just seen him yesterday. Less then twenty-four hours ago.

Sighing, she turned the cart around and slowly made her way back the same way she had come. Thoughts flickered like lit candles—would there be a funeral? A memorial service? She knew he didn't have any family, but what about friends? She wondered what Ian would say and the rest of the support group. Carl's personality was sometimes as grating as sandpaper, but she liked him, and they all had gotten used to his sharp edges. Pain could do that. Still, she had enjoyed conversations with him. Pain had not erased his wonderful memory and he was able to pull out quotes of philosophers, even at times Scripture, to defend his disbelief.

She was near the front desk before it suddenly dawned on her that she and the others *were* his friends. She turned the scooter around and headed back to find out whom she needed to talk with about arranging a funeral.

Chapter Thirty-three

The Northern Neck Neuromuscular Support Group met for its April meeting. Wearing a low hat and dark eyeglasses, Elizabeth arrived just as the meeting started. When she ducked into the room, her face blazed scarlet as spontaneous applause erupted from her friends gathered there. She froze, the door half open, uncertain what to do.

She had hoped to slip inside unnoticed, but as soon as she pushed the door open, Claude Nolan motored up to escort her to a seat of honor next to Adrienne, who was grinning from ear to ear. Elizabeth had just talked to her friend yesterday, and there had been no mention of any such activities. As a matter of fact, Adrienne had known explicitly about Elizabeth's wish to be as private and anonymous as possible.

Elizabeth glared at her friend, whose grin only widened. *Rat*, Elizabeth mouthed and then glanced down at a sheet cake in front of her that was frosted with red, white, and blue icing and held the inscription: Thank you, Elizabeth! When the going gets tough, so do you!

She couldn't help grinning. They saw it and applauded again. She waved them off. "Stop!" She laughed. "You are being so foolish!"

"No, we are not," declared Adrienne, clapping her own hands even harder.

Everyone nodded and applauded for a long time before they finally quieted down.

"We are really sorry you ended up being the fall guy for the experiment," insisted Albert Stoddart.

"Indeed we are," Claude Nolan said. "Do you know what's going to happen, what you're going to do?"

Nicole Anderson, quietly sitting at the other end, shuddered slightly at how close she had come to being involved in this. She was sorry Elizabeth had been caught, but so extremely thankful her children would never know. Relaxing enough for a smile to slip on her face, she hoped Elizabeth wouldn't have any repercussions healthwise from all this stress. It was good to see her.

"Yes, I know what I'm going to do," Elizabeth said firmly. "I'm taking the coward's way out—"

"She is not!" Adrienne interrupted just as firmly. "She's doing the most intelligent thing she can do."

The two women smiled at each other, and Elizabeth waved a hand toward Adrienne. "She's my legal adviser. Maybe you should just ask her."

"What I want to know is, how I can get me some more?" Pearl's face was determined. "Can't you give me the number of that little girl who was getting it for us?"

"Why, Pearl, was it doing that much good for you?" Adrienne

asked, surprised. Frankly, she could see nothing different about the woman at all.

"Made me feel better," asserted Pearl, "and that's a long shot better than my doctors can do."

"Is that really enough, just feeling better? I mean, you could get caught, just like I did, Pearl," Elizabeth said, concerned.

"It don't matter to me if I do. I liked the stuff; I liked the way it made me feel. I didn't half listen to the old man after I smoked it."

Adrienne thought Pearl had a lot more issues to deal with that couldn't be smoked away. For once she was pleased to realize she couldn't help on this one.

"I believe that source, that young girl who helped us, is no longer living in the area," Adrienne began, looking toward Elizabeth, who immediately nodded.

"That's right. She and her grandmother are in New York City for . . . an extended period of time. I have no idea when they'll be back."

Pearl wasn't going to give up. "Do you have her phone number? Maybe I could call her and ask her where she got it from, then I could just go . . ." Flummoxed, her voice trailed off as all the shaking heads were unanimous. She didn't care a hoot for what anyone thought, but still . . . It didn't look like she was going to get any help at all. She kept a frown fixed on her face for the rest of the meeting, thinking hard about any other source she could investigate. Who knows, if Sandra Little could get it from *her* neighbor, maybe it would be a good time to go visit and check out who lived next door. She started making plans in her head while the rest of the group discovered what Elizabeth's plans really were.

"I think you are doing the best thing"—Albert Stoddart nodded—"absolutely."

Everyone else also concurred with Elizabeth's suggestion for the end of the year meeting in May. "I think a picnic would be nice, perhaps at the new state park near Lively," she suggested.

"Let's all bring something to eat. Here, I'll send a sheet of paper around. Write down what you can bring and I'll supply the drinks," Adrienne offered.

She listened to the chatter as she sat back in her chair and wondered for the umpteenth time whether she should share what else was in the letter that Carl's nephew had sent. She had received it earlier in the week and had been carrying that secret around like a bruise that wouldn't heal.

On Uncle Carl's desk was a letter almost finished, written "To whom it may concern" . . . It was an explanation of what he hoped would happen in the hospital. "I just didn't want to die alone," he wrote over and over in capital letters . . .

I don't want to die alone. Those words chilled Adrienne as she kept replaying those last few moments they had been together. Carl had asked her to stay until he fell asleep and she had done so willingly, glad to be able to do anything for this poor man who was in so much pain. Had he taken something more than a sleeping pill?

If so, she was partly responsible for his death, which was devastating. It meant she had been instrumental in his death. She had to keep reminding herself again and again that guilt over which you can do nothing is masochistic; it kept haunting her.

At the same time she was glad he was out of pain, but . . . Ian had chided her again last night not to dwell on this. "It's like a dog chasing its tail—you'll keep going around and around in circles, and you'll only make yourself sick about it."

He also thought this should not be made public. "Will it do anyone any good, Adrienne? I can't think of how it would, so let's just keep this quiet. Just be glad the poor man is no longer in pain."

She heard a shriek of laughter at the other end of the table as Albert had just finished telling an Irish joke. She had been too distracted to hear any of it.

Shaking off all the bad feelings for once and for all, she asked him to repeat it, apologizing for her inattention. He immediately donned an Irish brogue again, enjoying the retelling as much as the first time.

"Well, listen up, then," Albert said, his voice lilting with an Irish cadence. "It seems there was this Irishman who was at the bar drinking late one night. Finally the bartender said no more and began closing up. So the man got up and turned to walk away and fell flat on his face. 'Oh, well, I've had a mite too many, I'll just crawl outside and get a breath of air,' he said. He did so and pulled himself up, breathing in the cool chill air. He turned to walk and fell flat on his face. Not to be deterred, he crawled to his house and pulled himself inside. Thinking surely he must be a little bit more sober now, he stood up to walk into the bedroom only to fall flat on his face once again. *Well, blast it to the devil himself,* the man thought. And he crawled into his bedroom where he stood up one last time, and then fell flat onto his bed and went fast asleep.

"Well, the next morning his missus was standing over him, face like a thundercloud, arms crossed in anger, and she bellowed out, 'So, you were at the bar drinking again last night, were ya?'

"'What makes you say that?' the man asked quickly, unwilling to fess up.

"'The bartender called,' his missus roared. 'You left your wheelchair there again.'"

Adrienne laughed until tears started streaming, thinking Carl would find this just as funny, and she hoped—somehow—he was listening.

Chapter Thirty-four

Kellan drove the now familiar path to Fredericksburg, her spirits floating and bubbling, so wrapped in romance. Life had taken on an opulent grandeur since she had discovered and donned the fabric of love. It was too magical and wondrous, and at the same time she knew these words were corny and nonsensical, but she didn't care. She was in love and was loved, and there was simply no help for it.

God, she was happy!

Had it been a mere two months since Gregory Jamison had enveloped her life? How had she lived before without knowing him? The simple truth was she had not. She had merely been skimming a surface that had no depth, no layers—until now.

The humming that started in both of them the moment they met swelled into something so rich and wonderful words did not exist to describe it. It was a new discovery, mystical and magical, that belonged only to them.

There were dim memories of past relationships that paled quickly because they were so inconsequential. All those relationships had started the same way; bright little moments that sputtered and ended for a lack of something crucial.

Now she understood what had been lacking.

Love. Trust. These two powerful energies between her and Gregory melded to create a bond so valuable, so enduring, it took her breath away. She was still using the guest bedroom, and there was that invisible line he would not cross as he had done with Melanie, but there were no doubts that the future would belong to them. She knew hers was the only heart in the world right for this man. And she knew he felt the same way.

This afternoon she was on a quest he didn't know about. She was supposed to be at his town house tonight for dinner, but she had come to Fredericksburg this morning. It was Friday, and she had been able to shift things around to free up some hours.

She intended to check out Mary Washington College, an old and well-respected school of higher learning just minutes away from where he lived.

It was with relief and excitement she discovered all her credits would transfer. Kellan could hardly wait to tell him her good news.

It had never dawned on her that there had not been any real discussion about the future. It didn't matter. She knew there could be no future unless, hands entwined, they forged one together. She sat in the library of her soon-to-be school, spinning plans, waiting for the time when she would see him.

⌒

"Thanks for doing this, Al," Gregory said as his cousin came through the back door into the kitchen. "I appreciate it."

"Don't call me Al."

"Right. You know what you're supposed to do?"

Warily, his cousin nodded. "Save your butt from someone who doesn't hear the word no." His cousin frowned. "You didn't seem to have much trouble saying no to Melanie. Why is this one such a pain?"

"She's spoiled, definitely used to getting her own way." It pained him to lie, but he couldn't see any way out.

It sounded logical, until Al really looked at Gregory's face. Haggard and white, this man was not a bit happy with what he was planning on doing this night.

Why?

Al skimmed him with skeptical eyes. "Right. When have you ever needed my help to break up with someone? What's really up?" Suspicion darkened his cousin's face.

His head was pounding again and he felt his stomach lurch. This had been the worst two days of his life.

He heard his own feeble answer and hated himself even more.

"She just won't take no for an answer," he insisted and then looked away, not wanting his cousin to see the lies burning in his eyes.

"When she gets a look at you, when you tell her *we* are a couple and for her to get lost, it should make things real simple. And clear."

Then he turned back to offer a sick grin. His cousin Alex, short for Alexandra, was tall, slim with waist-length blond hair, and gorgeous. She was the definite beauty in the family. If she had been an only child, she might have ended up being obnoxious, but with two younger and two older brothers whom she idolized, she had turned out sensible. One of the guys. Growing up as a tomboy, she had always disregarded her looks.

She certainly earned their respect, Gregory thought, hating himself for using her like this.

Then again, since he had done the same thing for her last year, he figured this would make them even. The bottom line was, he and Kellan could no longer see each other.

He knew it without a doubt, but, frankly, he didn't think he could look into that beautiful face and say those words, because he could never mean them and she would know it and see the lies.

Alex was still suspicious, but she had agreed to help her cousin. After all, he had done the same thing for her. But the whole thing stank. She had discovered it was always harder to break off a relationship if you were a girl. It seemed, in her wide experience, men were like little boys who hated to let go of anything they wanted. She never realized it was because no one ever wanted to let go of her.

She shrugged.

Looking at her cousin objectively, she could understand why someone would not want to let go of him. He was attractive, had a killer smile, and was just so damn nice. But she had never known him to have trouble ending a relationship. Look what he had done to Melanie. Poor girl, she was still devastated. She cried tears of real sorrow whenever she saw Alex, sniffling that the sight of her was too vivid a reminder of what Gregory had done.

She tapped fingers on the table restlessly, eyes darting around. "You heard about Mark?"

It shouldn't have been possible but Gregory's face turned whiter. He nodded.

Disgusted, she shook her head. "Our family's got a curse on it or what? I swear, when Mom called to tell me the news I almost stuck my head in the gas oven right then and there." Her eyes rolled, and her small grin reflected the foolishness of her statement.

"Have you thought of being tested?"

The words slipped out before Gregory could stop them. He really didn't want to talk about it. Her reaction, though, caught him off guard.

She vehemently shook her head, the long blonde hair swinging across her shoulders.

"Nope. No way." She was so sure about it, so adamant, he couldn't believe it. How could she not want, not need, to know?

"Why not? I mean, how can you plan anything not knowing what might happen?" He was incredulous.

She tilted her chin up, her face stubborn. "I'll be damned if I'm going to live my life making decisions based on what might be and maybes. Even if I carry the defective gene, it doesn't mean I'll actually get it. Look, I could walk out of this door, get on the interstate, and get creamed by one of those crazy truckers who think they own the road—"

"Or you could end up with this damn disease and become nothing but Jell-O, not being able to do anything for yourself." His face was grim, thinking of their uncle Charlie and now his son, Mark, who was only ten years older than he, who had just been slammed with the diagnosis. ALS. The kiss of death.

Alex stared, her eyes suddenly clearing.

"You got tested! You know!" Her voice was breathless, as if he'd done something extraordinary, but her next words knocked that notion out of the park.

"You're an idiot. You may die before anything happens. Or it may never happen. Besides, there will be treatments sometime soon, certainly within our lifetime."

"There weren't any for Charlie." Gregory's voice sliced the air like a knife.

"We are not our uncle. You are letting this whole thing get out of hand and besides—" She stopped as another thought suddenly made her livid.

"*That's* why you broke Melanie's heart! And that's why you're going to break up with this girl, too, isn't it?" She stood up and started advancing toward him, hands clenched and fury shaking her.

He stood also, wanting her to understand.

"Alex, how can I ask anyone to marry me, to commit to me with this shadow, this . . . God, it's worse than a death sentence. How can I expect anyone to take this on?"

His voice was hurting as much as he was and that stopped her. Anger drained away as she realized he really meant what he said.

She put a gentle hand on his shoulder. "You let them make up their own mind. That's how you do it. You didn't ask Melanie; you made up her mind for her, and that wasn't fair or right. This girl you're trying to get rid of tonight—does she know?"

He averted his face as he whispered, "One of the few who do."

"And she's still coming around to see you?"

He nodded.

"Then what does that tell you? Can't you see it doesn't matter to her? Besides, who's talking commitment here—has she mentioned marriage?" She waited for him to say something, but he remained silent. "So what's the problem?"

"The problem is"—he rubbed his face with a weary hand, wondering if he could trust his voice to say it—"the problem is that I already love her. But I can't ask her to marry me. Not with this . . . curse, like you said, hanging over me like a shroud."

Alex hit him so hard on the arm, he yelped. "It's not your choice to make. It's hers." She had never thought of her cousin as positively stupid before. Now she faced him with an ultimatum. "Do I stay here and make sure you're honest, or do I just leave and believe you'll do the right thing?" Her stance was belligerent, one foot tapping the floor with impatience.

Even as his thoughts raced furiously for a logical way out, he knew there was none. He tried one more time.

"I think it would be easier just to break it off now. Before she and I get too involved. Besides, what if she wants to be with me . . . out of pity?" His voice had dropped and was so low Alex almost didn't hear it.

"Gregory." She waited for him to look at her. "I have always figured you for a fairly intelligent man. You, of all people, should be able to tell the difference between pity and love."

He just stared at her, his mind numb from too many disturbing and distressing thoughts colliding like a pinball machine run amuck.

Making a quick decision, she walked over and sat down on the sofa, crossing her legs.

"All right. That does it. I'm staying. I see you need someone to keep you honest. And keep you fair. Oh, and just to make it easier on you, I'll try to grill this girl and see if *she* knows the difference between pity and love." She grinned wickedly. "At least I'll try to be subtle."

With both arms stretched out on the back of the sofa, she gave him a clear look. "This should be one interesting night."

Gregory sat down glumly in the recliner, thinking that was not the way he would describe this evening at all.

‿‿

An hour later the doorbell rang and Alex jumped up to get it. "Stay," she commanded Gregory, who had started to rise. "I'll bring her back."

When the door opened Kellan was only mildly startled to see this beautiful blonde standing there. "Hi, I'm Kellan Whittaker. I'm here to see Gregory." Her smile was confident and embracing.

Alex liked her on the spot. They shook hands. "I'm Alex, Gregory's cousin. Come on in. It's a pleasure to meet you; Gregory has told me so much about you."

Gregory, hearing shared laughter as the two women came into the family room, stood up and tried to smile. His legs were shaking, his stomach was flipping out of rhythm with his heart; this made him unbalanced, and he knew he had never felt worse in his entire life.

Kellan stopped at the doorway, her smile fading like dusk as she saw the love of her life, his face drained of color, looking like he had just escaped from a horror film in which he was the victim. She couldn't get to him fast enough.

"Gregory, what happened? Oh, God, not your mother? Sister? What?" Her arms around him, she was shocked at his coldness. What terrible thing had happened?

"Are you going to tell her or should I?" Arms folded, Alex leaned against the doorjam, stern and impatient.

He couldn't speak because he was drowning in Kellan's anxious eyes, feeling a rush of love that was so real his heart stopped hammering, his legs stopped shaking, and somehow his stiff mouth tried to smile. Shoulders straightened and arms wrapped around her, he desperately wanted to clear those beautiful eyes and bring light and laughter back to them. God, he had been thinking only about himself, he suddenly realized with a shock. But what else could he do?

Suddenly he was overcome by shame for what he'd almost done to his wonderful girl. Using Alex had been a ridiculous, cowardly idea. He hadn't trusted Kellan, had never thought about telling her the truth and making her understand why they could have no future. He had never felt like this when he had made the decision for Melanie. This story had nothing to do with that one.

Suddenly he was touching her face, smiling into her eyes, and he somehow knew that whatever happened this night, everything would somehow be all right. But he still needed to make her understand and somehow try to live without her.

"No. I'll tell her." The words were spoken like the man Alex knew her cousin to be. As the couple sank down onto the sofa, she made herself quiet and comfortable on the recliner, eagerly waiting to see what would happen next.

The silence was long but comforting. Finally Kellan picked up his hand in hers.

"I went to Mary Washington College and found out all my credits will transfer. They have a great school of social work and I can start an internship in the spring if I want. Isn't that great?"

Instead of saying a word, he gently took back his hand and looked at her without expression.

"There are some things you have to know," he began and then told her everything. About the cousin just being diagnosed, even about Alex and what he had tried to make her do, about his right and strong feelings that told him they should end this relationship now—for her sake.

He told her he loved her but that he knew sometimes that just wasn't enough. "I cannot and won't ask you to take this burden on. It would be unconscionable for me to expect you to do that—"

Her hands slipped over his mouth to stop him from saying anything more. She smiled into those anxious eyes, knowing the strength of her love would endure anything for this man.

"Then I'll ask." She made certain he was looking as deeply into her eyes as she was his. "Gregory, will you marry me?"

The question was simple, sincere, and direct, and he wanted to say yes more than anything. The unfairness washed over him like acid and he closed his eyes, trying to think of a way to make her understand the true reality of what she was asking. "Do you realize what the hell you're getting yourself into? Bedpans and diapers, for God's sake, making the decision when to put me into a nursing home, because I'll need twenty-four-hour-a-day care, seven days a week. I won't be able to help you do anything. You'll need to do everything for me."

"Let me correct you right now," she said fiercely. "You *may* need that kind of help. The fact is, you may never develop it. There's a fifty-fifty chance—"

He interrupted her. "I can't stand those odds."

She faced him, and the look she gave him made him know he was a coward. "But I can," she said forcefully. "No one knows if you'll ever develop the disease." In the background she could hear Alex whispering a triumphant "Yes!"

"Kellan—" he tried again.

"Will you marry me, Gregory?" Kellan looked at him with a stillness that demanded attention.

He opened his mouth and then shut it, trying to figure out precisely what he should say. "I want to, Kellan, God knows I want to—"

"Then it's a yes," Kellan declared, giving him a bear hug that was never going to end. Alex was shouting and jumping up and down.

Gregory was desperate and put his hands on Kellan's shoulders to force her to look up at him. "Dammit, Kellan, you don't know what you're doing or asking me to do. You don't—"

Then she stepped back, hands on hips, glaring. "Oh, yes I do. I know precisely what I'm getting into; I've done my research. I've visited two ALS patients in Charlottesville; I've talked with their caregivers. And I know what I want."

Her hand reached out to touch his face. "And I would rather have a few days of you now and thirty years of living with you and ALS than a lifetime without you at all. That's as cut and dried as I can make it, Gregory. Now . . . will you marry me?"

Alex was beside herself. Tears brimming, she looked over at him. "Well, I think we can all forget about pity, don't you, Gregory? This woman knows exactly what she wants."

She saw his eyes start to glisten and sparkle at Kellan, and Alex caught her breath. This was better than any romance novel or movie she had ever seen or would ever see. She jumped up and clapped her hands.

"Why are we wasting time? Let's go find a justice of the peace," she urged, not wanting them to let any more moments slide by.

Startled, Kellan started laughing. "Uh, I can't do that. My mom would probably be fine, but my grandmother would disown me." After those words were said, Kellan added thoughtfully, "That might not be such a bad thing."

"No, we can't tonight. I have to talk with Kellan's parents, lay everything on the line and"—he turned to Kellan, his face sober and dead serious—"we have to get both of them to approve of our marriage, with them knowing everything. Agreed?"

Kellan nodded with ease, secure in the absolute knowledge her parents would agree to anything that was so necessary for her happiness.

Alex moved toward them, arms held wide, laughing through tears, and wrapped them both in an intense hug. "God, I just love happy endings."

Chapter Thirty-five

Serenity Brown was as emotionally precise as a rubber band, Louis D'Angelletti thought darkly. Pull her one way, you got the desired response. It was his job to pull those strings and make her dance because he was one of the best acting coaches in the world. He had waiting lists and his fees were legendary. The highest bidder usually bought his talents. On occasion he had been known to take on an assignment for the challenge. This was one of those times. He was here because of his friendship with Carol Stephens, and because he was intrigued and wanted to get inside this child's head.

Her timing, the nuances, the emotions were impeccable. Her face was so fluid, expressions so real, it was like she was talking to the audience instead of just curling her lip, cocking an eyebrow, narrowing those stunning eyes to dangerous slits.

The problem was, she was essentially unavailable to him; he had not been able to snatch out her real self. So far he had not seen one honest feeling that spoke anything about her essence.

Everyone he had ever helped to learn the fine art of acting fell all over themselves letting him inside their heads, their hearts, their *fears*.

What was wrong with this girl?

As she finished one more scene with a young actor, he thought again about the way she treated him. It was as if there was this underlying snort of amusement; the girl just didn't seem to get it that this was extremely serious business.

He was right. He did not impress Serenity at all. She felt that this playacting was meaningless. The love of money was the only motivation she needed to keep doing whatever she was told to do.

The money let her and her grandmother enjoy walking the streets of New York, going to the theaters, museums, taking in the culture that everyone said was so important. Serenity was tutored three hours a day, and with this kind of one-on-one supervision, her excellent mind absorbed and retained more than enough to zip far past where she would be if she were still in the public school.

At work and in acting class, Serenity observed the world of egos and hopes and dreams that kept colliding in this city that never slept. She had a practicality to life that had been borne of time spent with her mother. Living meant minute-by-minute survival, a chase always for food and her mother's attention, and then knowing instinctively when to disappear into the background.

Comparatively, what was expected of her now was a piece of cake. When she went to meetings at the television studio with Carol, she could see biting envy in the eyes of other young actors. She could read their thoughts: They resented that it had come so easy for her.

They hadn't a clue. She looked at them and saw shallow, pampered souls who would never have survived the eight years she spent with her mother in Jamaica. They had no sense of actual deprivation. They had only book knowledge, which had nothing to do with the knowledge of the gut. That was reality; this stuff they wanted her to create was fairy tales and spiderwebs.

She and her granny, an invincible duo, were also unimpressed with all they had seen and the people they had met. They liked Carol, but their complete trust was only in each other.

For really the first time, Serenity had come to appreciate the solidness of her grandmother. She was a rock that could not be swayed or intimidated by how many utensils decorated a plate or how much money slipped out of someone's wallet—all the fancy window dressing designed to impress.

Serenity kept a distance between her and all these new fragile people. Only with her grandmother was she beginning to come to know herself. And to slowly realize that she, Serenity, was worthy and, consequently, all the self-important people around her were no better—maybe not even as good. Mehalia, simply by surrounding her granddaughter with the security of her love, allowed her granddaughter to ponder what she had done to get to this place.

She had lied and she had cheated a very nice woman, all because she had this want burning her up inside. She had grieved her grandmother, and for the first time she was feeling the twinges of guilt, perhaps even remorse. These were odd, foreign sensations that made her feel unsettled, vulnerable.

If Serenity had been a little older, she might have understood why she was having these sensations: Her heart was growing bigger. If she'd had the words to even explain to Mehalia, the wise old woman would realize the prayers she had heaped over this child from the moment she knew of her existence were finally growing into an answer.

She and Mehalia shared a whole lot of laughter about their new lives, the kind of inbred humor only their closeness would understand.

In the spacious apartment Carol had provided them, they encountered their first bidet. It was one of many mutually shared jokes. At odd times they would catch each other's eye and without warning they would both think the same thing and begin to snicker: *Can't these people do anything for themselves?*

Chapter Thirty-six

At the preliminary hearing, as promised, Kate Wilkins tied up all the loose legal ends and Elizabeth, relieved, accepted it as a gift. They left court after Elizabeth entered a guilty plea and accepted a sentence of probation, with stipulated drug awareness classes to be taken at the community college. They walked outside and Elizabeth inhaled her first worry-free breath of air.

For the first time in several weeks, Elizabeth felt free enough to actually go out and be seen in public. She also felt sanctified enough to know she could return to church the next Sunday.

"Thank you." She shook Kate's hand, chatting for a few more moments before they left, each heading in different directions.

Elizabeth joined Adrienne for lunch, marveling at how lightened the absence of stress made her feel. Before entering that guilty plea, she had felt far too conspicuous to venture anywhere. And oddly ashamed. She knew using that drug was wrong, even if it was for the right reason; guilt had kept her isolated. Now, absurdly, after saying a few words, promising to do a few things, simple penance had set her free.

And on top of that, there was such good and exciting news to tell.

"You're beaming," Adrienne said, "it must have gone just right."

"Yep. You're looking at a free woman. And if I do what the judge says and stay out of trouble for a year, my record will be free and clear, too."

"I hope this means you're coming back to church." Adrienne shook her head. "I've never understood why you stayed away. Hardly anyone has said one negative word about you. Besides, church is for sinners, after all, not saints."

"I can think of more than one saint-in-training there." Elizabeth's mouth thinned, recalling a few phone messages from those souls who had been vocally astonished . . . outraged. . . . disappointed . . . and other words that were less than kind.

"Well, now it doesn't matter," Adrienne said happily, glad things were finally over. "Carl's nephew sent the nicest thank-you note about the funeral. He said he was very sorry he had no idea what was happening to Carl. He thought it was very kind of his friends to take care of the arrangements. He also sent a check covering expenses. His estate is being settled." She said nothing else, determined to keep things positive.

"And it was very nicely done." Elizabeth still couldn't believe the man had died in the hospital. She also couldn't believe they still didn't know why. The doctors had all agreed it had to be from natural causes. Elizabeth hated that they didn't know which one.

Elizabeth sighed briefly, then looked up with a broad smile aimed at Adrienne.

"Guess what?"

Adrienne looked and blinked. Elizabeth's smile was sparkling with sunshine. She wondered what had happened to make her friend so happy; she could probably light up a dark alley with that smile.

"I promise you I can't guess, so just tell me. No, wait, you're moving back to Richmond because you've made up with Michael, right?" *What else could light up her face like that*, Adrienne wondered, watching this make the smile dim.

"No, not that," Elizabeth said. Funny, she had found herself missing Michael a lot recently. Or, more precisely, missing what they once had.

"Well, then what?"

"They're getting married! Kellan and Gregory!"

"You're kidding!" Adrienne looked blank. "They're getting married? But that's wonderful." Adrienne was still shocked. "How did this happen? I mean, how long have they known each other?"

"Obviously long enough." Elizabeth chuckled. "They spoke to Michael earlier in the week. Gregory told him everything about his medical condition, about his financial situation, how he intended never to be a burden to Kellan."

"That must have taken a lot of guts." Adrienne's respect for him rose a few notches.

"Kellan said Michael listened to Gregory for a while, then held up his hand. 'Gregory,' he asked, 'do you love my daughter?' And of course, Gregory dropped the papers he was holding and said emphatically, 'Yes!'

"Then Kellan said her father turned to her and asked, 'Do you love this man? Do you want to marry him?'

"She said, 'Absolutely!' and he gave them both his blessing, provided, 'your mother agrees.'" Elizabeth laughed. "Gregory told her later he was so nervous he felt like he was coming out of the closet, really. She said he did a great job, though."

"I'm surprised but pleased Michael gave his blessing."

Elizabeth thought about what Kellan had told her. "If he's feeling any misgivings, he also knows his daughter has a mind of her own. And he does want her to be happy. Kellan was very relieved."

"'When is the wedding?"

"June fourteenth."

"You're kidding?" That was a little more than a month away. "That's just weeks," she said out loud. Adrienne thought of her own wedding, simple and small, and yet it had taken at least six months to get the details firmly under control.

"They want just family and they want to have it at the river, at our house. That's where they met, after all. I'll just arrange for the catering, and flowers. She's already bought a dress, and they've used the computer to design and print their invitations, so there isn't much to do. Amazing, isn't it?"

"I'd say so." Adrienne shook her head. High tech could certainly make things faster and easier, but in her admittedly old-fashioned way of thinking, taking away the stress from such an undertaking took away some of the magic. She smiled as she heard what Ian would say to such a thought.

"You've turned into a real old lady fuddy-duddy," he would har-rumph with disapproval.

"Anything I can do to help?" she offered, smiling.

Elizabeth reached out and touched her hand. "I was hoping you'd ask."

⌒

That Saturday night Elizabeth slept hard, making up for the fitful snatches of slumber she'd chased and lost during the last few months. She had been tired and gone to bed early because she wanted to get up early. Sunday would be the first time since this whole mess started that she would enter church.

As she slept, a dream began swirling closer and closer to the edge between what was real and illusion. It churned closer and closer, un-til she heard something clattering in her room, inside the closet. Along with the sound came the awareness that something was very wrong. There was no fear, but concern made her careful. As she moved closer to the door, she was relieved to find a flashlight in her hand. She opened the door slowly.

At first there was nothing to see as she chased away darkness with the light. Everything looked normal but the concern grew larger.

Something was not right. She heard this snipping sound behind her and turned quickly, but as soon as she did, the noise stopped. It started again from a different direction and this time she very slowly turned toward it, not wanting to surprise it. A seam-ripper was methodically destroying the threads that held her clothes to-gether. Pieces of pants, sleeves, a jacket bodice littered the floor. Another sleeve from a coat joined the pile as the seam-ripper con-tinued. She immediately pushed forward and grabbed the coat, try-ing to knock away what should be an inanimate object with the light she held. It dodged and immediately launched into another shirt. She pulled that away and for the next several minutes, she was panting and yelling, grabbing clothes and screaming at this thing to stop and suddenly she was amazed to hear herself yelling for Michael.

Michael?

The light extinguished, the room fell to darkness, and sleep filtered out images, allowing Elizabeth to rest easily, peacefully, until the glimmers of the early morning sun broke through the night.

Her awakening was gentle. Eyes opened to the small normal sounds of day beginning. She stretched while in bed, knowing it was the safest place to pull out the muscles that had been still for hours. Hands clasped over head, muscles were pulled luxuriously from one side to another. *Thank You, God, for stretching.* She enjoyed the pleasant sensations a while longer before she focused on the day.

It held mostly empty spaces, which was fine with her. But this morning included church, something she'd missed like an old habit. She got up, put on a white robe, and hummed her way to the kitchen.

Breakfast was a bowl of cereal and apple slices. She ate while looking through the paper that had been left on the front porch. She was relieved to find no mention of anything to do with Michael Whittaker's wife. Any story about her had died of disinterest because she wouldn't talk. Kate had managed to steer any interest about her away to something else she was working on. Elizabeth wondered if the media were always so easily herded in one direction or another. Kate Wilkins sure made things happen, so of course people would listen carefully to anything she had to say. Elizabeth was just glad all this legal mess was over for her and she could slip back into boring anonymity.

When she got up from the table and set all the dirty dishes in the sink, she stretched again, carefully leaning against the counter, keeping her knees slightly bent, keeping the balance steady.

She couldn't remember a time when stretching had ever felt this good. She was so glad she could still do this. A deep, cleansing breath and then she headed back to her room, slowly touching the furniture, walls. Thoughts glided into seamless, easy venues as she prepared the shower.

Pricks of water splattered as she stood under the soothing spray of at first hot and then more moderate temperatures for a long time. The lesson of being heat sensitive was not forgotten.

Finally, when the water was almost temperate, she pulled out the body gel and applied it to a sponge. She knew she had plenty of time to get ready for church; she detested being rushed.

It wasn't until she moved the sponge to her legs that the feeling that something was not right finally splintered into reality. When she first got up this morning she hadn't noticed anything being immediately amiss; it was more like haze on the edges of consciousness.

She dropped the sponge, staring down at the water drenching her legs. Everything looked normal.

Maybe she was imagining it? Gathering up courage like a weapon, she ran her hand down each leg lightly.

This didn't make sense.

She touched harder, sliding a fingernail up and down first one leg and then another, back and front, side to side.

She stopped and thought hard, looking for a reasonable solution. If she could only think clearly. Her thoughts were already jumbling with the emotions she was trying hard to ignore . . . Surely it had to be something simple, rational. After all, she'd just gotten up; she wasn't fully cognizant.

Impatiently, she turned off the water, sat on the side of the tub and let sharp fingernails rake up and down again slowly and then faster until, finally, she knew she wasn't wrong. Ribbons of feeling around her legs had been sliced away during the night. First there was feeling and then nothing, then a sliver of feeling and then nothing. Elizabeth's mouth dried, her breathing became ragged.

No, God, please, no, no, no! She got up and stood, shivering. What could she do?

Get dressed for church, her mind suggested. That would be a normal thing to do; yes, she could do that. She carefully stepped out and grabbed her robe. She hugged its warmth about her as she took tiny, uncertain steps to the bedroom.

She saw the clothes she had placed last night on the small valet. She clasped the top of the robe around her throat, thoughts whizzing around too fast for logic. *What if . . . ? What should . . . ? Could it . . . ? How bad . . . ?*

God, don't let this happen to me; please, not now, her heart was pleading, and suddenly the sky shifted and light tumbled through the patio doors leading out onto the deck. Ripples of fear swept up and down as she tried to walk the few steps toward the light and discovered with horror her legs didn't exactly belong to her. "No, please, no," she heard her voice murmuring incoherently.

Please don't let this happen, she begged again, pleading to a silent God. *Please, no, not anything else. Please, no. . . .* The refrain suddenly mocked. She wondered how much more she could take. The fear was horrible enough, but this one-sided conversation, this sense of isolation, was . . . unbearable.

If this new ugly thing was going to happen to her—if she was once again going to have to live through the knowledge that her body was breaking apart—then maybe it was also time to stop believing in anything. Maybe it was time to let go of a faltering faith that had done so little for her.

Maybe it was time, or past due time, for this child not to believe in fairy tales anymore. This was real life at its worst. But as these thoughts flickered, she emotionally recoiled. When she slowly understood what this meant, coldness seeped inside like a death; she had never felt so completely alone in her life.

If she didn't, couldn't, believe in anything, what on earth would she do? How could she live? Memories swept over and in her, swirling around her, fragments of pictures that held the past. Her history.

Her marriage, the formal and holy ceremony embraced within the church, kneeling at the Communion rail, having first Communion together with her new husband . . . the christening of her tiny baby . . . glimpses of the hours, of the weeks, of the years she had spent helping and nurturing and laughing and praying . . . This was the fabric that held her life together. A sob pushed out, and it tore her heart in two to think that it had all been for nothing—no purpose, no reason.

In anguish she sank to her knees, ignoring the silent scream in her legs and squeezed her eyes shut. She had reached the patio doors, vaguely aware of the light outside.

The child who was the woman realized the danger, the grave danger, of moving the wrong way at this crucial moment, and she remained still, letting her heart pray for her, letting it utter a song she had never before been desperate enough to sing.

God, please. Please listen to me. I realize . . . now . . . there isn't a choice. I believe—I have to believe—You are real because if You're not, I think I would, no, I know I would die. Because if You don't exist, if You aren't real, it's worth nothing. My life is worth nothing.

The mere contemplation of the possibility that God didn't exist had touched her briefly with a darkness, a despair, that was even worse than discovering the numbness encircling her legs. She shivered violently and knew with certainty this wasn't a choice, not for her. She could no longer dangle precariously on this fence. Her only choice was to jump into a world that demanded a stronger commitment than she had ever made in her life.

God, thank You . . . I believe . . . I have no doubt because it is not possible to live in this world without You. I believe . . .

Blinking away tears, Elizabeth, resolute, slowly stood, pressing her hands on the patio door for support, inch by inch, until she was finally standing. She kept one hand on the door for balance and brushed her hair away from her wet face. Looking out over the river, her eyes were drawn to something shimmering in the distance and she caught her breath. She blinked and there it was again.

A sun dog!

Chapter Thirty-seven

Michael woke up shivering. After a moment of disorientation his rigid body relaxed against the bed, a sigh burst from his lungs loud and hard, like the whoosh of an airplane landing. He looked at the clock and saw it was early. And yet the angle of the sun would suggest it was later. Odd.

A hand scraped through his hair, and he pondered what he should do. It was Sunday. Go to church? Sleep in? Go out? Stay in? He shrugged off aimless thoughts, righted himself, and waited for everything to become solid again.

He was dimly aware he had been awakened by something hard and intense having to do with his wife, but he couldn't think of her on an empty stomach. Or without a boatload of coffee to clear away the cobwebs. Bracing himself against the world, he stood up and went to take a shower.

Later, with the coffee brewing and his thoughts clearing, Michael warily entertained the question of why he had been thinking of Elizabeth. Did he have a dream about her? Or had something happened to her? That thought clenched.

No, he couldn't think that. She had an army of people looking after her in that river community. Plus, if anything bad happened, he would be the first to know. Bad news always traveled at light speed. Good news generally had the pace of a snail.

After he got dressed and retrieved the paper from its box, he went back to the kitchen and waited for that first cup of coffee. He opened up the front section.

He stood as he ate a few slices of toast and downed a couple of cups of coffee. He was restless, antsy, shifting from foot to foot. It was as if he was waiting for something to happen, like a kid waiting for a trip to the toy store. Elizabeth kept crossing his mind more and more frequently. It was probably just the stress and relief of finally having that situation over. He knew everything was set in place because Kate Wilkins had told him. It was over, done with.

Maddening, too, that a picture of Elizabeth's lovely face kept appearing in his mind, haunting him. He shrugged and concentrated on what he was reading.

He quickly finished eating, then picked up the rest of the paper and went into the library, placing another cup on the table. He sat down in the La-Z-Boy, the one she had gotten him for their fifteenth anniversary, and sat back in comfort. Before he could pull the paper up to read, he found that he was at eye level with Elizabeth's desk and the locked armoire where she kept her journals. In all the years she had kept them, he had never thought about what was in them. They were private thoughts, and he'd always respected her privacy.

If he was restless before, he was positively on edge now. The newspaper held no interest for him. All he could think about was her journals. What if there was something in those journals that might help him understand? Understand why she felt she had to leave him.

At first maybe she had left to go there and try pot without him looking over her shoulder. But that was all over, and she had said nothing about coming home. He stared at the cabinet for a long time, weighing all the considerations, the pros and cons, just as he would a business decision.

The inner debate was long. Beads of sweat dotted his brow as he wrestled with the idea of invading her private writings.

Finally, he got up slowly, numbly hearing the paper crumple to the floor. He hardly noticed his hands were shaking as he opened the drawer to the desk and saw the key.

Unlocked, the cabinet door swung open easily. Almost in slow motion, his hand was reaching and pulling out the long notebook on top, the last one she had written in before she left him. It was for both of them, he reasoned with his conscience, for a hope of understanding.

~

Walking slowly, carefully, Elizabeth moved inside the sanctuary, following at a distance behind the vested choir that had just filed in.

After her small miracle this morning, Elizabeth didn't want to talk to anyone. She had planned on getting here and sitting in the back, then leaving before the choir recessed.

From the moment she had opened her eyes and seen her sun dog winking back at her, there was a newness in her she didn't want to disturb. She eased into an empty pew at the back and settled down at the edge, looking at the bulletin and waiting for the service to start.

Encircling her like steel bands was an icy resolve, a certainty that something powerful had happened to her this morning, and she was holding on to it for dear life.

She couldn't think beyond this moment. Intuitively, she knew if she did, then logic, rationale, would intrude and snip away this remarkable moment and she would dissolve into despair.

This new faith was simply not that strong.

She stood as the choir joined with the congregation, voices swelling the air with a confident song of hope and grace. She kept her legs slightly bent for balance, her knees pressed against the pew for support. And willfully ignored what she could not feel.

After the readings of the gospel and the rector's prayer, the young priest stood before them, his smile sheepish.

Father Jacobs held out his hands. "I should apologize to you, and

I know my wife wants me to apologize to her, but I hope you will understand that the matter was taken out of my hands at about 2:30 this morning." His face was beseeching and earnest; the congregation perked up with interest.

"I had my sermon prepared fully by this past Friday, everything written down and ready to go, just the way Kelly likes it. But all I can tell you is that God has something different in mind for today. Early this morning I was awakened with an urgency I have never felt before, with a certainty that today's sermon was not right. I sat up in bed, almost shivering in anticipation of . . . something. When I got out of bed, Kelly woke up and wanted to know where I was going.

"She didn't like hearing I was on my way to the study to write another sermon." He looked out at his blushing wife, who was busily shaking her head and holding the bulletin up in front of her face as dozens of amused eyes glanced her way.

The rector continued, "You see, if I'm not completely prepared well in advance of Sunday mornings, it makes her nervous. I wasn't nervous, but I was a little sorry, because I really liked the sermon I worked on all last week." He lifted his hands, face comical in its asking for their understanding. There were plenty of smiles and nods.

"What was put on my heart so heavily last night that I had to get up and write it down?"

His face was sober as he looked at each of the faces turned toward him and asked one simple question.

"What if there was no God, what if He didn't exist? How would you live? Could you live if there was no God?"

Many faces pondered the question, while others looked out the stained-glass windows, and children were scratching out pictures on the bulletin quietly.

But in the back, tucked in the corner of a pew, a miracle was happening.

Wonder enveloped Elizabeth. Caught in such complete surprise, she was mesmerized by the immensity, the grandeur of this moment.

It was her epiphany . . . her validation . . . her personal sundog moment.

She sat there while a light embraced her that would brook any darkness, a joy filling within her as she realized she had already answered that very question for herself this morning. (Only this morning? It felt like a lifetime ago.) Within this knowledge she felt something begin to melt away: the hard resolve she had manufactured to get through this morning. She felt her soul opening to welcome a spring, a season of faith that can come only after a frigid season of uncertainty, of doubt.

For the very first time, she not only understood the lines from the Book of Common Prayer, but her soul knew it with a clarity that had never been known. *"The peace of God that passes all understanding . . ."*

And the words from the essay by Lynne Sears Howard *". . . now that I'm listening through a broken heart, I hear what has always been playing."*

Yes!

Finally, she knew and heard the melody that made that little bit of energy dance, that slip of light she had seen move with such vitality on the hospital wall years ago.

Michael was in a fury, his face red with explosive emotions as he read portions of Elizabeth's journal. He felt indignant. How could she have ever felt this way?

He had always been there ready to help her in any way she needed, but did she ever ask for help when she did need it? Never! That was what was so damn maddening about the whole thing, so bitterly unfair—her blaming him!

He had always wanted to take care of her. Always! But she would no longer let him. Even before she left, she was keeping secrets; she wasn't telling him anything. He had been shocked that day with the lawyer to hear she had finally taken the doctors' advice and was on one of the therapies, which had always been the best thing she could do for herself.

And when he showed his pleasure about it, she shrugged off his concerns like a distasteful garment and said she wasn't continuing it.

Why did she have to drive him out of his mind?

He had read about her desire to see a sun dog and also about her conversation with Father Joseph after the shoe debacle. And of course those people, Adrienne and Ian Moore. They seemed like a pleasant couple who knew how to relate to each other; he could sense the wistfulness in Elizabeth's writings about them and this woman he had never heard about, Lynne Sears Howard.

So each one of them had cried on their husbands' shoulders; big damn deal. Had Elizabeth ever let him see her pain? No! She was too busy pushing it all way, denying anything was wrong.

He was clenching his jaw and saw his hands tremble and forced himself to calm down. His anger, however just, would change nothing. All it would do was completely spoil his day.

He took a deep, relaxing breath and let it out as a sigh, forcing himself to relax. Then he began reading again.

I can't believe this happened, I am so angry I want to scream! Whatever have I done to deserve this? Why are people so stupid?

The morning was good. The day was bright and brisk and so I decided to take a walk. The brace was on my left leg, the cane in my right hand, and I started off. I've taken short walks before and I've always felt self-conscious, but today it didn't matter. The sunshine and weather lured me out with a smile.

Everything was going great. Even with the aids (or maybe because of them), I was walking great.

I was three blocks away from the house coming back when I heard someone calling my name. I turned and there, running across two busy interchanges, was Helen Lyndon. She was running, her legs and arms in perfect harmony, and I was so jealous I could barely breathe. Suddenly I wanted to scream out to the world that I could do that! I could do that very thing once, too!

When she finally reached me I tried to put a pleasant smile on my face because I hadn't seen her for months, but the first words out of her mouth were a slap.

"Elizabeth, my God! What have you done to yourself!?" The pity in her eyes made me want to hit it away. (Yes, that was precisely how I felt!)

"Nothing, Helen," I said.

"For God's sake, you're using a cane, Elizabeth. Why?" Her voice had risen as if I must be hearing-impaired as well.

*I shrugged, feeling my pleasant face start to fall. "Because I need it."
I made my voice sound as if my answer was completely reasonable
and turned to continue my walk, but then she grabbed my cane arm
at the elbow. "Elizabeth, I don't know what's going on, but here, I'll
help you back to your house."*

*By this time any pleasure I had found in taking a walk by myself
had shriveled up, and I literally bit my lip the whole way back to
keep from either screaming at her or crying, Why are people so
stupid?*

*By the time I got home I had a headache. My stomach is still in
knots, but writing this down has helped. At least I didn't hit her. Helen
actually walked me all the way to the front door and waited until I
unlocked it and stepped inside.*

*"Call me anytime you need my help," she said with a sappy smile
and ran down the steps, a hand waving backward.*

"Why?" I muttered under my breath. "I didn't ask this time."

*What is just as infuriating is this: If Carol or my mother heard this
story, they would take me to task for not simply explaining everything
in the first place. They certainly would not understand why it made
me feel the way it did.*

Michael frowned. He knew Helen Lyndon, and he wouldn't be
inclined to give her the time of day either. Thinking of Carol and
Virginia Mae, he could hear them fussing already. There were a lot
of stupid people indeed, and for the first time he connected with
Elizabeth's side. He'd be damn angry, too. He found himself shaking
his head out of sympathy and skimmed the next several pages before reading again . . .

*Something happened today that was startling. Actually, it shocked me
because it showed vividly how much things have changed.*

*I was at a restaurant and bar in the Slip waiting for Carol to come.
I ordered white wine and was sipping it, minding my own business.*

*A man seated at the bar kept turning around and looking. I caught
his eye once and smiled vaguely and then politely kept my gaze
averted, mostly toward the door, waiting for my truant cousin.*

*My heart leaped up to my throat when he walked over and sat
across from me. I looked at him hard, wondering if I knew him.*

I did not.

He was attractive, a man about Michael's age, light hair cropped close, and then he smiled. My heart tumbled over itself in a way I haven't felt in a very long time.

"I saw you looking toward the door. I was going to say that I hope whoever you're waiting for doesn't show up because I would dearly love to buy you lunch." There was a dimple on the left side of his mouth and his eyes were frank and admiring.

I smiled and when I did, dammit, I could feel a blush start so I looked down and said, "I'm flattered, but my cousin will be here any moment. And besides, I don't think my husband would understand about me having lunch with a stranger . . . especially one so attractive."

I couldn't believe that came out of my mouth, but I looked up to see his smile deepen and then he chuckled. "I should have known someone like you would be married, but I believe in always hoping."

We were smiling at each other when Carol came up suddenly, looking from one to the other. "Hello?" She was very polite, but also puzzled.

The stranger looked inquiringly my way. Heart pounding, I knew I had to be firm. "Hello, Carol, please sit down. This nice man was just leaving."

He got up, still smiling and said, almost under his breath, "I hope he deserves you."

Then he was gone. Although Carol had a lot of questions, I didn't have answers. It was just a brief encounter but later as I thought about it, I realized the way he looked at me made me feel something I haven't felt in a long time.

Pretty.

And attractive. And it suddenly occurred to me that was the way Michael used to see me. With loving, admiring eyes, he would flirt and make me feel pretty.

Now his eyes are disapproving, almost always glaring these days.

I don't know how to change this. I don't know how to reach back and bring forward what we used to have. I wonder if he notices, too, and just doesn't care . . .

Michael put down the pages slowly, stunned. He wanted to be able to say vehemently she was wrong, but how could he? Suddenly, in an awful moment of self-realization, he knew that wasn't possible because she was right.

It had never occurred to him that *he* had changed. He was so wrapped up in what was happening to her, he never thought about it changing him.

A memory several years old came rushing toward him, hitting hard. It was something that had taken place when Kellan was a young teenager.

It seemed almost overnight she had changed from his easygoing and lovable daughter to a depressing, cynical, self-centered brat.

She had driven him crazy. He had yelled harshly over the things she had conveniently forgotten to do and disapproved of those she did do.

On this particular occasion, he had been yelling because of neglected overdue library books and countless other things until finally, in tears, she lashed back.

"Why do you have to yell and scream at me to do what you want? Why are you forever scolding?"

He was about to say that was the only way he could get her attention these days, but she kept talking.

"When you yell at me the last thing it makes me want to do is anything that'll make you happy." She was crying so hard it was difficult to make out her words, but the next came out loud and clear.

"Why can't you encourage me to do better? Why can't you tell me when I've done something right instead of always yelling and fussing about what I've done wrong? Why can't you?"

These words had bit into him then because he realized she was right. He had been so focused on what she was doing wrong, anticipating it, it had never occurred to him to help her, encourage her to focus on the right things.

He felt sick. For the first time, he understood with a horrible, sinking realization this was what he'd been doing to his wife.

⌒

Carol was slipping chocolate chip cookie dough into the oven when the phone rang. She picked it up as she saw car lights moving out of the drive. Gordon was going to the store to get some more coffee.

They had spent this Sunday together, going to church and then brunch. It had been an easy, restful day, something Carol needed. She'd spent the last three weeks in New York, supervising the endless details of putting together a thirty-minute television show. No one outside the business would ever see the mindless hours of often drudge work required to create those few moments of magic that ended up on the small screen.

But that's what it took, and Carol was determined to make it shine.

It was over brunch Gordon had asked, "How are our girls doing? The King/Brown duo?"

Carol laughed. "They seem to be thriving. D'Angelletti said at first he had to tell Serenity how to play a part, what to do, how to inflect her voice, but I think she's getting some confidence about what she's doing. She's starting to vocalize what she thinks. There have been some disagreements, to put it mildly, but she's growing. I think Mehalia is thrilled; the two of them are inseparable. She's being tutored, and I've been told the girl is frighteningly smart."

Gordon nodded. "I'm glad it's working out. For Mehalia's sake, especially."

"Me, too. I really want Serenity to play a part in this series, but I'm still talking with the network. They would prefer to use someone with an already established name as the lead. I'm thinking about rewriting it to include a strong supporting role for her."

They had come back to her house to read the Sunday paper or maybe watch the news. It had been restful and pleasant. They decided, after a small dinner, to watch a movie. She found cookie dough and decided to bake them some dessert, while he volunteered to get the coffee.

"Hello?"

Ragged breathing.

"Hello?" She almost hung up.

"Carol? This is . . . Michael."

She made a face but kept her voice pleasant. "Hi."

"Is Gordon there by any chance? I tried his home, but—"

"Actually, he just left to go to the store, but he should be back any minute. Have you tried his cell phone?"

"No, I . . . didn't want to bother him on the road. I thought . . .

well . . ." Michael actually sounded unsure of himself, which was to-tally out of character.

"Do you want me to have him call?"

"Please." The relief she heard was as vivid as the delicious smell of baking cookies. It was so out of the ordinary she felt a stab of worry. Was something wrong?

"Michael, is everything all right? Is Elizabeth all right? Kellan?"

He paused, trying to formulate an accurate response. "As far as I know, Carol. I'm just calling because I need to speak to Gordon about . . . well, some things he suggested a while back, that's all."

"Oh. Well, I'll have him call as soon as he gets back then." Curious. Something was different, but Carol couldn't put a finger on it.

"Good." That relief again. "And Carol, thank you."

Now she knew something was up. Michael had never treated her with that much politeness. Worry started churning and she couldn't wait for Gordon to get back. She punched in the number for his cell phone and belatedly heard it ringing in the other room. He hadn't taken it with him.

She was putting the cookies on a cooling rack when Gordon walked in. She didn't wait for him to say a word. "Gordon, you have to call Michael. He's at home and something really weird is going on."

He set the coffee down and sniffed. "Smells good. You start the coffee and I'll call him," he suggested, turning.

"Don't go. Call him from in here." Only something really awful would have made him so nice, she was convinced. She hadn't asked about Virginia Mae, but wouldn't her own mother keep her ap-prised of anything bad there? After all, Julia was as much a chatter-box as her sister when it came to family matters.

Gordon stayed where he was and punched in some numbers on the wall phone. "Michael? Hey, how's everything?"

He listened and frowned and then his face softened. "Sure, I re-member. Yes, I'd be glad to do that." From memory he quoted the name of the therapist he had offered a long time ago as well as her phone number.

"I think you are doing the very best thing, Michael. Sometimes it's hard to sort out personal stuff. Yes, I will. Please let me know if I can do anything."

Carol, who had shamelessly hung on every word, suddenly realized she had stopped counting the teaspoons of coffee she was putting in the filter.

"Aw, damn," she muttered, dumping it back into the can and starting over.

When it was safely brewing she looked at Gordon. "Michael is actually asking to see a therapist? I can't believe it. Oh—" Another thought interrupted her words. "Come to think of it, it makes perfect sense. Have you heard about Kellan?" When Gordon shook his head, Carol filled a plate with cookies along with two mugs of coffee. "Just listen," she said.

When she was finished he looked at her thoughtfully. "You're sure Michael knows everything?"

Her nod was emphatic. "Elizabeth told me and said I could share it with you. But you can't tell anyone else. Not even Virginia Mae knows, which I think is wise."

"Definitely. But I don't think that's the reason he wants to see someone. I'm not going to speculate. I'm just glad he's going to talk to a professional and figure out some things. I know he hasn't been very happy with Elizabeth living elsewhere."

Carol drummed her fingers on the kitchen table. "I just hope everyone's going to be all right."

"I guess that's all any of us can hope for," Gordon agreed, reaching for another cookie.

Chapter Thirty-eight

Elizabeth was making notes. So far, she had three long notebook pages filled front and back and knew she was forgetting something. The phone rang just as she jotted down another idea she wanted to suggest to Kellan.

"Hello?"

"I just want to know one thing, Elizabeth." Her mother's voice signaled she was on the warpath and Elizabeth sighed.

"What do you want to know, Mother?"

"Is she pregnant?"

Elizabeth blinked. "Who?"

"Blast it all, Elizabeth. Kellan!"

Elizabeth started laughing. It was too stupid a question to even bother putting into words. "No! Mother, how could you even think such a thing?"

"Well, why are they having to get married so fast? I mean, it is absolutely breaking my heart at how everyone has to rush this way and that, when we could plan such a beautiful, lovely wedding if only we had time. So I asked myself this morning, *Why?* It's the only answer that makes sense."

Elizabeth's smile was gentle as she shook her head. *Only her mother.* She wished she had time for such foolish pondering. No, she was not going to get rattled this morning; she simply had too much to do. Besides, nothing could destroy her peace today. She was helping her daughter put together her wedding, and it would be beautiful.

"Kellan is not pregnant. They are getting married in a month because that's what they want to do." Her voice made their wishes perfectly understandable.

She almost broke into a smile as she heard her mother utter a noise that sounded suspiciously like a snort. "What do they know? I mean, Elizabeth, when I think of how absolutely enchanting your wedding was, how it was the envy of all my friends, and good Lord, it took us the better part of nine months to pull it off."

Elizabeth's memory was a little different. Her wedding had grown from the simplicity she wanted into an ostentatious event that had been mildly embarrassing. From having only a maid of honor, Carol, and Michael's best man, the wedding party had mushroomed to ten attendants each because Virginia Mae insisted extended family had to be included, which meant second cousins on her husband's side. Disagreements arose daily and were always decided based on what Virginia Mae wanted. Elizabeth always felt like her mother would know best and had acquiesced. Ultimately, her mother had the wedding she'd always wanted.

It was one of many memories that weren't really hers, Elizabeth thought.

Virginia Mae was making a suggestion, her voice sweetly cajoling. "I think I have a solution. Why don't I give Kellan her wedding dress and pay for the honeymoon? By doing that, I should be able to leverage a little more time out of them, don't you think? And perhaps we could talk about not having it at the river. I mean, most of our friends and family live near the city; it would be so much more convenient, not to mention more spacious, to have it at our church, don't you think?"

"Mother, we don't need a solution because there isn't a problem."

She waited for her mother to think of a response. She couldn't help but feel a little giddy with the freedom of no longer feeling an obligation to her mother's happiness. How on earth that had happened in the first place, Elizabeth hadn't a clue.

It seemed she had spent most of her adult life letting this woman finagle her way into every crevice and then changing to suit her, always hoping it would make her mother happy.

"Yes, I know, but Elizabeth, don't you think you could talk to them and—"

"No, Mother, but thanks for asking. Now, I have to hang up because I have a lot of things to do to get everything ready for June fourteenth. Good-bye."

Invigorated, she picked up her notes again and added several more ideas, then got the phone book and began looking up numbers. It was good to be busy; it helped her ignore the discomfort in her legs. While the numbness had not gotten worse, it had not got better either, and Elizabeth was undecided over what to do, hoping either she could live with it or it would get better on its own. She had thanked God more than once that it was no worse.

Michael. At odd times Elizabeth would suddenly start thinking of him, wondering what he was doing at that precise moment. She hadn't seen him since the day he brought Kate Wilkins to see her and everyone else had come. The day Carol talked Mehalia and Serenity into going to New York.

That was someone else she really missed. Mehalia would have great ideas for the food next month. Elizabeth sighed, thinking again of how pleasant it had been to have someone to talk with, work with. The new house cleaners she had hired were straight-by-the-book businesspeople. The young girl with two older helpers would screech into the drive precisely at 9:00 a.m. every Tuesday morning, fling open the van, and each worker would come in laden with cleaning tools, buckets, a vacuum cleaner, and no time for idle chatter. Two hours later she would be presented with a bill, the house smelling of cleaners and lemon polish. And silence.

Michael's face edged back into her thoughts, and she did what she had started doing on the same day she saw her first and only sun dog. Without thinking, she started praying for him that afternoon.

It was late in the day, long after she returned from church, brimming with the magic that had been divined just for her. She almost called him, she felt so wonderful, but at the same time she didn't want to chance hearing the habitual coldness in his voice.

Without thinking, her spirit suddenly leaped up and started praying for him. Asking God to protect him, fill him with joy, wanting him to be as happy as she was. It made Elizabeth feel more connected to him, somehow, than seeing him in person.

She had not told anyone of that remarkable day, had not been able to even write about it. It was still too shiny, too immense. Sometime later, when she had lived with this new knowledge, absorbed it more fully, then perhaps she could find the words. Perhaps.

After a brief, quiet moment of holding her husband in her heart, she sat up, looked at the clock, and started making phone calls.

Chapter Thirty-nine

Gregory decided today was going to be the day. Somehow he had let Kellan waffle out of it until there was only a week before the wedding, and he still had not bought her an engagement or wedding ring.

Oh, the excuses had been valid. First schoolwork had to be completed, then the paperwork for transferring, then looking ahead and signing up for next year's courses.

But he was putting his foot down. She was due back at his town house in fifteen minutes. It was Saturday, and he was taking her to the most expensive jeweler in Old Towne Fredericksburg. She would select the ring he would put on her finger on their wedding day, where it would stay forever.

When she got back from dropping off an overdue library book, he kissed her and wouldn't let her take off her jacket. "Time to go," he said firmly, pushing her out the door, and Kellan, who already knew his intentions, could see there was no way out. A firm jaw squarely set told her so. He was determined.

She was touched, she really was, but this was the last thing on earth she wanted. She had no interest in going anywhere and spending lots of money for what in her mind was a shined-up rock. Pretty, yes, but still a rock.

She had to let him make the effort. She smiled back at him, linking her arm through his and was swept away again by his generous smile, his eyes snaring hers in frank admiration. How'd she get so lucky?

Two hours later, Gregory's smile had slipped and the jeweler, Adam Sheffield, was trying to keep his intact.

"We could always custom-make whatever you would like, but that takes a great deal of time," he explained yet again to Kellan, who nodded. "You could get your plain gold band to use for the ceremony, while we make your design for the engagement ring?" he offered, obviously worried over their dilemma, wanting to make sure all the details were tied up nicely for this young couple.

Kellan offered a startling smile and touched Gregory's arm. "Gregory, why don't we go get a cup of coffee and talk it over?" She bestowed an even brighter smile on the older man, who was obviously getting anxious. "Thank you so much, Mr. Sheffield. You've given me a lot of things to think about. I appreciate it."

"If that's what you want . . . ," Gregory said, disappointed she hadn't found anything she liked.

He couldn't help thinking of Melanie. She had known exactly the kind of ring she wanted, and they had been in and out of here within the hour. And she still had it, he thought glumly. When he had broken off the engagement he'd told her she could keep it if she wanted to. Incredibly, she did.

Now he wanted something much better for Kellan. "You're sure?" he asked again.

"I'm sure," she said, giving his hand a squeeze.

"Thanks, Mr. Sheffield." Gregory shook the man's hand, who advised them he'd be open until 5:00 p.m.

Moments later they were seated in a small coffee shop fronting Main Street, not too far from the college. Kellan loved everything about this town. The history, the diverse shops that beckoned with antiques and art and clothing and crafts and cuisine. She took a small sip of excellent coffee and smiled.

"This is so good."

Gregory didn't touch his. "Kellan, we have to do something today. There are other jewelry shops around. Why don't we go visit some; maybe they have what you've got in mind." A thought suddenly alarmed him. "You *do* have something in mind?"

Her smile broadened, her eyes danced as she opened her purse. "Of course. I know exactly what I want." And she pulled a small bag out and handed it to him.

"What's this?" He could feel the shape of a box crinkling through the stiff brown paper.

"Open it."

Puzzled, he pulled out the small box. Nestled inside were two silver rings with writing on the sides. "Kellan"—he picked them up, frowning—"I don't understand."

"The writing is in Latin." She picked up the larger one and took his hand. "It means 'I am my beloved's and my beloved is mine.'" She slipped it on his finger, already knowing it would fit perfectly. "It's from the Song of Solomon. A very sexy description of what marriage should be."

His frown remained, but his eyes were puzzled. "That's nice, but . . . why are you giving me this now? We need to find the rings we'll be using next week."

"These are the ones I want to use next week," she said softly.

He looked at the ring and then at her. "I bet these didn't even cost a hundred dollars together."

"With tax and shipping they did."

"I must be a little slow, because I'm not getting this . . ." He glanced at the ring again. It was nice, but nothing in the class he wanted for her.

He watched her take another long taste of coffee. "It's a bit of a story. I guess I should have told you before, but I was waiting for these rings to come. They finally did today. Besides the library, I also stopped by the post office. You know I rented a box at school the last time I was here."

"So why are we out shopping at all? If you've already made up your mind," he said, a little hurt and irritated. "I meant it when I told you I wanted to buy you a ring you'd be proud of, something really spectacular. I mean, this should represent how I feel about you and this . . ." His voice trailed off. Yes, these rings were nice and he didn't want to hurt her feelings by saying anything bad, but hell, this wasn't at the top of his list.

"I know." Kellan could see he was upset and thought about how best to explain. Honest and direct, that was probably the best. "This is the way I feel about diamonds and emeralds and all these other so-called precious jewels." She stared directly, seeing he was still a little put out.

"They're dressed-up rocks. Shiny, but still . . . just . . . rocks." Impulsively, she reached over and held his hand. "But there's a bigger reason, and it goes back to something that happened when I was a very little girl."

An involuntary smile creased his face as he thought of her as a young child. Then he became attentive to her story about being at her grandmother's house one day when she was about five years old.

"She used to show me her jewelry box and take out all these sparkly rings and bracelets and let me try them on. I loved watching the lights dance and ripple over those stones. She even had a tiara she would let me put on my head, and I'd look at myself in the mirror and pretend I was a princess." Gregory watched the memory shimmer in her eyes and felt his heart melting; he could practically see the thrilled little girl.

"One day Grandmother was in the kitchen with the house-keeper, discussing the menu for lunch, and I wandered into her bedroom looking for something to do. She usually kept her jewelry box locked, but this time it was on her dresser and the lock was half open. I had to stand on a small stool to reach it, and as I tried to pull it off I didn't realize it would be so heavy. So of course it fell, I fell, and all the jewelry tumbled out. They could hear the crash down-stairs and Grandmother came running. She got to the door panting and shrieked when she saw what had happened. She strode in, hands clenched on her hips and started yelling, 'You horrible child, look what you've done! Do you have any idea how much all this is worth? These are the jewels of my lifetime. My husband gave me these, some were from my mother's mother—heirlooms, you bad, bad girl, and now everything's scattered to high heaven. Kellan, how could you be so bad?' She fell on the bed, her hands over her face, crying and muttering. Miss Maude the housekeeper came and chastised me again when she'd seen what I had done. She shooed me out the door as she tried to comfort Grandmother and started carefully picking up the jewelry. Then later my mother fussed with me terribly about touching those jewels. 'Someday, if you behave yourself, some of them might be yours, Kellan. Now, don't ever do that again.'"

Kellan still smarted at the memory and how it had made her feel. Through the years the memory still held the absolute shock; for the first time in her young life, *she* had not come first in her grandmother's affections—the jewelry had.

At that moment she knew she never would want that jewelry or wear it. It was a certain knowledge that would permit no compromise.

"I also decided I didn't want to own anything that would make me that unhappy if I lost it." She paused and looked at him almost shyly before adding softly, "I think I'm taking a big enough risk loving you. If I ever lost you I—" Her voice caught.

Gregory reached over and covered her hand.

"Shhhh, everything will be all right. Everything will be just fine." He kissed her and then grinned. He held up his finger with the ring. "I can't think of anything nicer. I love it." He kissed her again, ignoring the glances of the few other people at nearby tables.

After a moment of thinking, he wondered aloud, "Has your grandmother given you any of her jewelry?"

She grimaced and then laughed. "She's given me several pieces, including my great-grandmother's wedding ring, thinking I might use it next week. They're all in a safe-deposit box at the bank."

He nodded, impressed beyond measure by her integrity. How did he get so lucky, he wondered again. "What are you going to do with them?" It wouldn't surprise him if she planned on selling them and giving the money to charity.

With a widening smile and mischief in her eyes, she looked up at him, loving the feel of his hands caressing hers. "Give them to my daughters one day."

She watched as it took some moments before his smile started wavering as her words slowly were absorbed, and then his face went pale.

"Kellan?!" He jerked back, heart hammering, a swirl of confusing thoughts sweeping in waves as he suddenly realized they had never, ever talked about children. But he thought it was a foregone conclusion they couldn't have any . . .

Then he saw the grin that widened into a smile as she reached up and tweaked his nose. "Just wanted to be sure you were paying attention," she whispered before she kissed him.

Chapter Forty

The morning of the wedding came much too quickly for some and not quickly enough for the couple.

Elizabeth woke early, praying that the weather forecast had changed. Last night at midnight they were predicting rain showers at the time the wedding attendants would be stepping outside. The wedding would take place in the long side yard, the ground even and lush with manicured grass.

She smiled, happy that this day she would see her daughter marrying a good man. Then a slight frown puckered her forehead. She would also see Michael for the first time in . . . a very long while. He hadn't been able to come last night to a simple meal for both families to meet. The wedding party was so small, the service so simple, it had seemed ludicrous to have a traditional rehearsal dinner. Kellan had called it a getting-to-know-you dinner. Elizabeth had enjoyed meeting Gregory's mother, sister, her husband, and their new baby. Alex Jamison had been there with her parents and two of her younger brothers; the two older ones would also be attending the wedding today. Even Virginia Mae and Julia seemed to have a good time, after a slightly rocky start. Well, there was nothing she could do to fix *that*, Elizabeth told herself.

Michael had been out of town until late last night. He had promised to be here at least an hour before the wedding, which would start at 3:00 p.m.

Elizabeth had talked to him only briefly on the phone just once in the last month. She willed herself not to anticipate the worst.

God, let it be all right, let him be all right, and I'll thank You now for fixing this for me, she prayed, trying to ignore the doubts, the feeling that this was going to be an impossible task.

She stopped and mentally shook herself, knowing that with God everything was possible—perhaps not obvious, but definitely possible. She reminded herself that it didn't matter what she felt, because it was all faith—not feelings. She repeated that small phrase over and over again until, hopeful, she began to slowly get out of bed.

✦

Virginia Mae had not slept well. Fretful thoughts kept churning over in her mind, pushing away sleep. These facts nagged throughout the night: that she had no say-so in the wedding planning; the wedding was actually taking place outside and without a doubt it would rain; she was miserable it had to be so far away when there was their own big beautiful church right in the city that could have suited everyone so very much better. Her teeth gritted as she remembered the tiny guest list on which, again, she had not been consulted—none of her friends, only immediate family. When she had been made aware of that decision she had just known they wouldn't let her invite her own sister.

When she had called Elizabeth she was practically in tears. Elizabeth—who still insisted on an appointment before her own mother could visit her—told her right off that Carol and Gordon were coming, and of course Aunt Julia was expected. Would Virginia Mae care to ride with her sister? Arrangements had been made for them to stay at a local bed-and-breakfast nearby.

It didn't completely appease her. Virginia Mae couldn't help but remain sorely aggrieved over not being allowed a whisper of input into the most important day of her granddaughter's life.

This morning it was safer to focus on all her disappointments because she couldn't, wouldn't, think about Elizabeth.

Shudders ran through her. What she had seen last night nearly drove her to collapse in tears, but everyone else seemed so casual, so unconcerned . . . no, she wouldn't go there. Virginia Mae wondered, not for the first time, if there wasn't a conspiracy to drive her stark-raving mad.

She added to the list and her mouth flattened as more angry thoughts unfolded. *Who* was Gregory Jamison? She didn't like it at all that Kellan had known this boy for such a short time and now was going to enter into a legal arrangement. The whole thing was ludicrous and headed for disaster, but again, no one seemed the slightest bit interested in what she thought.

She felt a dull throb at her temples and told herself she had to relax. It didn't help that the mattress she was resting on had as many lumps as bad gravy. She sighed deeply. Her life was as sad as it ever had been. Nonetheless, she tried to relax.

It seemed mere seconds later, though the clock said two hours, when Julia banged at her door. "I want to go to breakfast at that little restaurant down the street," her sister trilled, the steady knocking uncannily matching the pulse hammering in Virginia Mae's temples. Virginia Mae groaned and wondered what she had ever done to deserve this. "Oh, all right, Julia, stop it. I'm getting up. At least let me get dressed, won't you?"

Virginia Mae frowned darkly as Julia gave her a time limit of ten minutes; this day was beginning rotten and probably would get no better.

∽

Gordon woke oddly restless. Was it because he was sleeping in a new place, this bed-and-breakfast Elizabeth had found for him and Carol to use for the weekend?

Or was it because Carol was sleeping right down the hall from him, in this devastatingly romantic place? The house seemed to have been built for lovers, or at least renovated for current ones. He had a Jacuzzi in his bathroom that would easily accommodate another couple of people. Or at least one.

As emotions swept through him he hadn't felt in years, the scientist in him tried to analyze them.

When he and Carol had arrived last night, it was more than a mere social occasion. It was to meet the family Kellan was going to become a part of this day.

As stupid as it sounded, magic was in the air. All you had to do was look at the wedding couple to believe true love was possible. They were young and earnest and caring, and he was impressed with how attentive they were to each other, how gracious they were together and to everyone else. Love. It was as tangible as the shrimp and oysters they ate last night and lingered with a perfume all its own. He couldn't stay in bed after he woke up.

Consequently, after he showered and dressed, he went knocking on Carol's door, because he wanted his best friend to journey out with him.

Surprisingly, the owner was already in the kitchen with coffee brewing and making breakfast to tempt any hungry soul to sin.

By eight, well-fed and content, they were out on the streets of the town, walking until they darted off the main street and began strolling on a deserted beach. It was sandy and private, because the people who owned it were either not up or absent landowners. Public beaches were not unheard of in this county, but extremely rare and hard to find.

Finally, they stood just where Cockrell Creek started joining other creeks and rivers heading toward the Chesapeake Bay; this was where the point of land known as Reedville ended.

Its heyday was the early 1900s. Then it boasted the highest per capita income in the nation, thanks to the booming fishing industry and the ship captains who called this place home. These wealthy men built opulent homes for their women, gingerbread Victorians and one-of-a-kind masterpieces. Over the many seasons of economic downturn, many had fallen into disrepair.

In the last several years, wealthy northern Virginia couples seeking an escape to a slower, more genteel way of life had discovered the place. Many of these old homes had been bought, upgraded, and either made into bed-and-breakfasts or kept as private homes.

As they walked around the town, Carol thought wistfully that this was a romantic place to be. She wondered about all those who had lived, prospered, and died right here by the river. The changes over the last hundred years had been immense. Wealth to genteel poverty to a resurrection for some.

Since last night, when they left the city and came here, her soul had been invaded by a sense of leisure. On one level, she felt like she was on college break, with no responsibilities.

"Gordon, does Michael know?" Carol finally asked, her hands shoved into the pockets of a lightweight summer jacket.

"Considering the fact *we* didn't know until last night, my guess is no." And he wasn't quite sure what to do. He wasn't Elizabeth's doctor, but yesterday she had offered few words of explanation.

"It's just a very small problem," she had assured him with a jaunty smile as she pulled herself up, firmly holding on to a streamlined black shiny walker.

"I can walk, but the balance has gotten . . . a bit problematic over these last weeks. Soooo," she breathed dramatically, "this is helping to keep me straight." She looked demur and winked. "You might say I'm gravity-challenged—temporarily, of course." Her humor and ease had dimmed the awful shock he had felt at first.

Carol had also been wide-eyed. Concern roared through her, as she wondered what had happened to her cousin, all of it making her feel a little faint.

"Elizabeth, are you sure you're up for all this?" She couldn't believe there would actually be a wedding here tomorrow, not when Elizabeth seemed to be having so much trouble. But she looked absolutely stunning. Her face was shining and even if her body seemed in distress, you would never know it by the way she looked.

"I'm fine." Elizabeth's smile declared total conviction. And she stood up and took several firm steps just to show them. She ignored their initial reaction with a deft ease that was intriguing.

For her part, Elizabeth was deeply gratified that by the time Virginia Mae arrived with Aunt Julia, all the other guests showed such a casual acceptance that it seemed to deflate the shock in those two old pairs of eyes. She wished people could just look at *her* and see nothing else. It would make life so much nicer.

"Should we call and tell him?" Carol was startled to realize she was actually nervous for Michael. She had not really thought too much about it, but the fact that he had been part of Elizabeth's life forever made it seem odd he was never around now. And he was seeing that therapist, which seemed a positive thing. How would it affect him to see his Elizabeth using something that usually only old men and women used because—well, because they were old? She felt her eyes begin to mist. Elizabeth was not old, she had done nothing to deserve any of this, and here she was laughing and being charming and making them all feel better. Carol shook her head. Elizabeth looked genuinely and vividly happy.

"Gordon." She waited for him to turn.

"Yes?" He sounded distracted.

"Is it truly possible Elizabeth can really . . . be as happy as she seems, even though this new thing has happened? Or is she putting on a good face?" It seemed too incongruous. Yet her cousin certainly was playing her part like a trouper if that was the case.

"Yes." There it was, that certainty, as if he knew something she didn't.

"How can you be so sure?" She suspected he was just saying this to stem any more conversation about Elizabeth, that he really didn't know anything. He surprised her.

"Because I've seen patients who have had this same kind of . . . I don't know, I think of it as a spiritual leap, going from the stress of illness and uncertainties to a . . . an understanding that provides peace—after they've accepted what they can't change. Truly accepted."

Her nose wrinkled. "Accepted? You mean giving up?"

He shook his head; his eyes were cast toward the river, mesmerized by the sparkling diamonds the light from the sun created on its surface. "No, it's not giving up. Giving up is the last resort, when you have no more choices left. I've known people in unrelenting pain who have no other option and they give up and die. What I mean by accepting is you're choosing to hurdle across to a place where it can't touch or hurt anymore. One of my patients, an older woman who lives with a variety of problems, once described it as being on the other side of a broken heart. I don't know if I can explain, but she said it's where you choose to put what you can't change into the

smallest part of you, so you can get on with the rest of your life—
where you can still have a life."

She, too, was watching the constant shifts of the water, squinting
to see the outlines of a lighthouse in the far distance. The constancy
of the water was almost hypnotic, and Carol could barely hold on to
what Gordon just said.

It didn't make a lot of sense on the surface, but what did she
know? The only really sick person she knew well was Elizabeth, and
she didn't understand her at all anymore.

But she still loved her. She hoped that might count for something. She blinked. "Let's go get some more coffee." She pulled him
toward the road and within minutes they were inside a small café,
ordering homemade bread and coffee.

"How about that lovely card from Serenity and Mehalia?" Carol
asked.

Gordon sipped the steaming liquid. "Big surprise. Especially the
check for fifteen hundred dollars."

"Yeah, I know. I think it was a . . . thoughtful thing for her to do."
Carol sounded distracted. The thought of Michael still jabbed, but
at least there they could do something practical.

"Shouldn't we call Michael and make sure he doesn't walk in and
get knocked for a loop like we were last night?" It was nagging her,
feeling like a scrape that needed attention.

"I don't know," Gordon answered truthfully. Would it be better
to let Michael be as blindsided as they had been, or would it be better for him to have some warning?

Put that way, he knew which choice he'd prefer and he was glad
it made everything simple. "I'll go call him."

Carol drained her cup and looked around for the waitress, wanting a refill. She was going to need to be fortified to get through this
day with all its changes, where everything was different and wonderful and awful all at the same time.

If it hadn't been so early in the day, she might have asked for the
coffee to be laced with something stronger.

She finally caught the waitress's eye and held up her cup.
Maybe things would be better, after all. She watched Gordon walk
back, frowning.

"What's wrong?"

"Nothing. He didn't answer . . . which means he may be on his way here, or still sleeping or at his office. I don't know, but I'm going to hang around in front of their house and try to catch him as soon as he pulls up."

Carol nodded. "I think that's a good plan. I'll help."

⁓

As they pulled up to the house, they discovered they were too late. Michael was already there. They could see him and Elizabeth standing at the patio. It was close to where the wedding would take place hours from now. An archway decorated with flowers and ribbons was where Kellan and Gregory would stand at 3:00 p.m. and promise their lives to each other. They were not too far away to hear everything but too uncertain to move any closer.

⁓

Michael was tired but had been too excited to stay in Richmond that morning. He had left brimming with hope and anticipation. His baby was getting married today, he would see his wife, and he would do his level best to romance her back into his life. He had it all planned. After Kellan and Gregory left, he would suggest Elizabeth leave with him for what would be a romantic dinner on the water.

He would make her feel pretty, desired and adored. The thoughts of what he would do kept a grin on his face as he drove the car over Downings Bridge, anticipating the whole day with relish.

The sessions with the therapist had made him realize how poorly he had handled the whole thing. He had let fear and anger wrap him up so tight, he had forgotten the one indisputable and most important fact when it came to his wife.

He loved her. Even if he couldn't fix her body, she was still the woman he loved. The changes didn't make a difference to his heart.

After he parked the car and got out, he was practically floating as he went through the front door and moved to the back room facing the river. He saw her standing with her back to him out on the patio and then she was walking toward the arch. He immediately headed there.

She was alone. It couldn't be a more perfect setting for their first meeting in months. She would see he was a new man, he had changed, and soon everything would be patched up between them and their lives would be better than ever because they would be together. All these thoughts were racing around in his head; his emotions were on fire for this moment to be memorable.

His long strides carried him quickly to the love of his life. "Elizabeth!" He heard the warmth and gladness in his voice and knew she must hear it, too.

She turned and his eyes dropped.

"My God!" He stopped, immobile, as if someone had decked him. A walker. *A walker?*

She had gotten worse; she was . . . how could this have happened . . . crippled . . . His mouth tightened as an uncontrollable fury washed over him like a fire, angry acerbic words spilling out before he had a chance to think.

Elizabeth had turned, surprised to hear him, a smile just starting but it faded immediately as she saw herself vividly reflected in his outrage.

"My God, what have you done! What have you done to yourself? You let it get worse, my God, my God, why didn't you call me! How did this happen?" His words were disjointed, coming out in gasps. He was angry enough to take on God and the whole might of heaven for doing this to his wife, but all he did was spark a hatred in the woman he loved more than life.

Fury exploded inside her and she despised him at that moment for making her less than she was, for making her see through his eyes just how damaged she really was.

"Michael." Her voice was like ice and then her words slit his heart, stopping everything, all feeling and thought. "When this day is over, I never want to see you again." Her words were dangerously measured and intent blue eyes held his until she saw the flicker of understanding and then, still holding on to the wheeled walker, she moved with surprising grace and left. He heard the door slamming behind her as she went inside; the lock snapped into place.

Immediately, Carol moved to go inside the house from the front, as Gordon moved swiftly, barely making it before Michael started sinking.

It was unfortunate Virginia Mae and Julia arrived at that moment. The old ladies waved to the gentlemen outside and, chatting
noisily, went inside.

"Elizabeth," Carol whispered as she made it to the kitchen and
saw her cousin, trembling and white. Carol's eyes closed briefly as
she heard her aunt and mother come in, thinking it couldn't be a
worse time.

"Are you all right?" Carol whispered, trying to shield her cousin
from the old ladies walking in. Elizabeth seemed not to hear her.
Virginia Mae came in complaining about the accommodations at
the bed-and-breakfast, but faltered as she saw her daughter.

"Elizabeth! Sit down, my child; you look awful. Carol, get
some . . . some, goodness do you have smelling salts around here?
Elizabeth, you look like you're going to faint." Virginia Mae was in
her face, touching her hair, pulling an arm to get her child to sit
down, concern making her babble.

"Mother." Elizabeth's voice was as clear as a bell and daunting in
its clarity. "Leave me alone."

She pulled away abruptly, her eyes cold. Virginia Mae just gaped
at her, at first hurt and then the anger took over.

She was sick and tired of her daughter being downright selfish,
and she for one was fed up, hands on her hips, her face red with
emotion. Next to her Julia stood, confused.

"Well, excuse me, Elizabeth, for caring about you. I am extremely
sorry if my concern makes you angry. But what in the living hell am I
supposed to do? You go your own selfish way, you won't confide in
any of us, you won't let us help— Oh, I know we failed miserably at
first, but instead of telling us how to help, you just shut us out, you
didn't even try. Now we aren't even allowed to care? I swear, if I
could hate you I would. But I can't!"

Mother and daughter stared at each other, separated by a generation of differences, yet bound by the irrevocable ties that made
them forever a part of each other. Virginia Mae stood her ground,
never wavering or tearing up, she was just too livid.

"Aunt Mae, I don't think you understand," Carol started to say,
but Elizabeth put up a hand to stop her.

Elizabeth stood there, stunned that fury would blind her to any
more rage, or even more destructive thoughts.

Flooding her were all her good intentions for this day, Kellan's day. She, Elizabeth Whittaker, didn't matter. What her mother just said was as clear as mountain water and just as honest. She blinked, discovering with wonder that she had indeed been selfish . . . and uncaring . . . and everything she thought she wasn't. And suddenly the peace of God welled up inside her, forcing out the shadows of all that had upset her just moments ago, all that had tried to snatch away her joy.

"Elizabeth?" Carol's concern grayed her face and voice, but that was banished when Elizabeth turned.

The smile was a solid radiance so soft it was intensified by the absence of all the darkness that had been wrapped in this room just seconds before.

"Carol, I'm sorry. Mother." She turned to wrap her arms around Virginia Mae, who now couldn't keep the tears from tumbling out. "You are right. And I'm more sorry than I can say."

Carol watched as even her mother, overcome with emotion, wrapped arms around her sister and niece for a long moment before coming over to her daughter, embracing her for once with a hug as big as her heart.

⌒

"Michael." Gordon helped ease him onto a patio chair, concerned. His friend was bent over, misery making him old. He kept a grip on his shoulder until Michael seemed to be breathing more regularly. Color was slowly coming back and Gordon wished he could do more . . . wished he'd been able to talk to him before he got here this morning. He had heard what Elizabeth said, saw what it had done to Michael.

In Gordon's long experience, emotional cuts to the heart were sometimes irreparable. He hated to think this would be the case here, but it sure didn't look like any healing would take place this day.

"Gordon . . . I just can't bear it." Michael's voice was more than sorry, it was defeated.

Gordon helped him up. "Come on. We're getting out of here."

He helped him to his own car, and then went back to Michael's car to get the hanging clothes bag and smaller suitcase. As they drove off, he figured he'd watch the clock and get them both back here before the wedding, but it sure appeared to him that a little venting had to happen to get bad feelings out of his friend before anything else happened.

Silence remained unbroken until they got to the accommodations. "Up for a walk?" He waited for Michael to shrug. Within moments they were on the cement sidewalk heading toward the tip of town where he and Carol had been earlier. "Carol and I tried to call you this morning. Sorry we didn't catch you."

"Did you know?"

"Not till last night."

They were on the small sandy beach that would within hours be covered when high tide muscled through.

"Ah, Gordon, if she had only taken better care of herself." Michael sighed, his face wrapped in despair.

As gently as he could, Gordon said softly, "It would not have made a difference."

Michael snorted, anger at his friend pumping him with a little energy. "How can you know that? If she'd been on any of those therapies they wanted her on—"

Again, the interruption was soft but the intent clear. "She is. Has been taking them since before she tried the marijuana."

Michael looked blank. "But she said she had stopped it. You were there, you heard her."

Gordon nodded. "I know"—he shrugged—"but last night she told me she was still taking it. And she's been on oral steroids to try to get rid of some numbness in her legs, which may be contributing to the balance problem. And she's getting physical therapy. Just started that about two weeks ago."

Michael shook his head, not getting it. "Why couldn't she tell *me* all this?"

Gordon said nothing, watching his friend closely.

Then it hit Michael, as if a ball had just landed at his feet. "If she's on one of the therapies, then why is she having any trouble at all?"

Gordon sighed, wishing people would absorb all the information he told them instead of just the parts they wanted to hear.

"It doesn't work that way. It has *never* worked that way. It has been proved to slow down the disease process. That's it, which is really so much more than we've had, but it does not, I repeat, does not eliminate exacerbations." He watched as Michael visibly struggled with that, recalling countless other patients to whom he had told the same things over and over until realization finally hit. And it always hit hard.

Michael's mind churned over a sickening array of memories, thinking of all the stupid things he had just said to Elizabeth, had said to her over these last years, incredibly unjust things because he didn't know. Or didn't want to know. God, he felt like such a coward, such a . . . bully. He looked over at Gordon, wondering if he could live through this, already knowing there was no choice. Slowly, the words came out of his mouth reluctantly. "It's all really . . . just a crapshoot, isn't it? I mean, all we can really control is the way we react to the things that happen to us."

His friend's slight amusement had a hard edge of reality to it as Gordon extended his hand and pumped Michael's up and down. "Welcome to the real world, my friend."

Chapter Forty-one

Elizabeth finished dressing in a long soft dress of coral appropriate for the mother of the bride. White earrings and long pearls accented the lovely layers of silk. She wasn't wearing the brace because she had decided to wear sandals, and she couldn't do one with the other. Besides, she would have the walker, which had turned out to be the best security blanket of all.

She heard muffled giggles as she walked toward the kitchen and wondered if the caterers were having a joke about something. When she entered, Kellan, her mother, Julia, and Carol were all standing in a line, dressed for the occasion. Her eyes filled with tears as she looked at her daughter. A slim dress of ivory glistened; her hair was left long with small braids pulled away from her face, a circlet of flowers on her head.

"Kellan, you look . . . so beautiful." She held out her arms as she moved carefully toward her daughter, but stopped as Kellan held up her hands. Elizabeth then noticed Carol trying hard not to laugh and then suddenly everyone stepped aside. Kellan flung open both hands. "Tah-dah!"

Sitting right in front of her was a concoction of ribbons, ivory, and coral, along with a bevy of flowers in the same colors rippling over the handles and twining down black steel with a bow at each of the four wheels.

Elizabeth gaped and then her mouth widened as she dissolved into laughter. "You've got to be kidding; this is wonderful!" Her entire four-wheeled walker was decked out for the wedding.

"We figured your steed needed some color coordinating," Kellan said brightly, hugging her mother hard.

"*We* thought nothing of the kind," Virginia Mae corrected her granddaughter sternly, waiting for startled eyes to turn her way before she grinned. "We don't have that kind of imagination. Kellan thought of the whole thing herself, but she let us help."

"Mother, Julia, Carol," Elizabeth marveled, touching the shiny walker. "And my Kellan. Thank you, thank you so much . . . it's wonderful." Tears started burning her eyes and she sniffed. "I'm going to cry my eyes out at this wedding, I'm already halfway there."

Kellan patted her on the back fondly. "Promise me you'll tell Ian and Adrienne Moore that Gregory and I are taking them out to dinner as soon as we get back. I wish they had been able to come."

"So do I." Elizabeth smiled. "But they really needed to visit their friends in Pennsylvania."

"I understand." Kellan's smile was as bright as her future.

Then they all stilled as the music started playing. The musical trio featuring flute, clarinet, and French horn had started the prelude, which meant it was precisely fifteen minutes before showtime. Giggling like young girls, all of them hurried out, holding the door open for Elizabeth to walk out in style pushing her grandly dressed walker.

They went quickly to the front. Gregory was already there with his brother-in-law, the best man. Father Joseph Wells stood ready for the ceremony to begin.

At the back with the rest of the party, Gordon escorted Julia and Virginia Mae, one on each arm, to the chairs at the very front.

Michael, somber in a dark suit, held out his hand for his wife and then colored as he realized she wouldn't need it. Her eyes were cold for the brief moment she glanced at him and then she started pushing the walker slowly toward the front, keeping in time to the music.

She almost misstepped, though, when Michael's hand covered one of hers and kept it there until they got to their seats at the front next to her mother and aunt.

As soon as Elizabeth sat down Michael left, thrilled and misty that in moments he would be walking his daughter down this grassy aisle.

Elizabeth nodded to Father Joseph, standing tall under the arbor, his face beaming. He loved weddings. Especially when the couple was as in love and as honorable as these two young people were. He had counseled them three times prior to this date; he knew about the situation they might be facing and he had prayed with them and for them. He felt a divine light surrounding them. This was a very holy union, and he was thrilled to be asked to participate.

One of Gregory's cousins escorted his mother and sister, carrying her baby, to the groom's side at the front. There were only about twenty guests made up of the two families and close friends.

And the wedding march began. Michael looked at his daughter, marveling that it seemed like yesterday that he was teaching her to ride a bicycle, that they were hitting her first tennis ball together. His throat closed up as her face lifted and she smiled at him. "Ready?" Her voice was soft but vibrant.

Barely, he thought as they hooked arms and started walking toward her future.

Elizabeth felt a tear slide down her face, her heart swelling with wonderful, marvelous emotions seeing her baby walk toward the man she loved.

But when Michael came to stand next to her and touched her arm she flinched. Her anger from this morning toward him had never dimmed; it had merely been shoved aside to get to this moment.

In her mind she was already demanding a divorce from him, completely justified because of his horrid, despicable behavior. She meant it when she had told him this morning she never wanted to see him again after today. She would not put up with anything more from a man who could slam her to the ground emotionally.

Her face never showed her cold rage. She clung to the piles of righteous indignation even while she made herself listen carefully when Father Joseph began to speak.

"I would like to say before we actually start the marriage service, how thrilled I am to be part of this blessed event." Father Joseph smiled, his face suffused with the rightness of this moment. "It is an honor. I know without a doubt God has brought these two young people, Gregory David Jamison and Kellan Lane Whittaker, to this moment through His love and His desire.

"I know that you have a living example in your midst that can help as you make your own way as a couple, and that is Michael and Elizabeth Whittaker. They have known great changes in their own lives together, but I can see they are still as in love with each other as Kellan and Gregory are at this moment. May God bless you so each of you may enjoy the wonders and the learning moments you may find, always with God's help, as you journey through this uncertain life, secure in the knowledge of your love for each other and always of God's all-abiding love."

Elizabeth dropped her eyes, swallowing hard. *So we won't get divorced, fine, but I am not living with this man who is sitting next to me playing a charlatan, smiling as if he cares when he does not.*

She looked up and devoted all her attention not to only ignoring her husband but to listening and watching every second of her daughter's wedding. A tear even trickled down her cheek as she watched her baby walk hand in hand with her new husband down the aisle, followed by Carol and the best man, and then she, the mother of the bride, followed with Michael.

And that was what she did the rest of the afternoon. She had nothing to say to him and so much to say to other people. She smiled and laughed and often went out of her way to hug her daughter one more time.

❧

The large shrimp and jumbo crab legs had been pretty much devoured, champagne toasts had been lifted to the couple, and Gregory and Kellan had changed and were getting ready to leave.

"Come on, all unmarried women, get up here," she called, laughing as she held up her bouquet in the air, teasing.

Kellan waited until Gregory's cousin Alex and her former roommates were there, and then she made Carol come up. "Come on, no getting out of this," she declared, waiting for them all to get lined up before turning her back and tossing the flowers high into the sky.

When Kellan turned around she saw her godmother looking astonished, holding the bouquet. "Look, you've got to do this over again; I'm never getting married," Carol protested, trying to shove the flowers back into Kellan's hands.

"Now, you never know," Kellan drawled, grabbing her new husband's hand and running toward the car.

Carol, dismayed, looked at the other young girls. "Look, I'll throw them again. One of you younger ones need to catch this."

When they merely laughed and moved away, Carol felt even older. "You ain't over the hill yet," admonished Alex, throwing a friendly arm across Carol's shoulders. "Besides, that's a pretty swell-looking guy you're with," she pointed out, grinning before one of her brothers walked up, telling her their mother needed her.

Carol immediately looked at Gordon, who was talking to Gregory's best man. For a startling moment she saw him through Alex's eyes. Yes, he was a very attractive man, she realized, a little surprised at how very attractive he was. It was odd . . . they had become such good friends, Carol had never seriously thought about him that way.

She shrugged away from a sadness that covered her like a brief cloud, instead glancing at the white bouquet, shifting her thoughts. She wondered if she should dry the flowers and make potpourri for the couple. She turned away to go find Elizabeth.

"Carol." She jumped slightly. Virginia Mae was standing next to her. "Did you see the ring Kellan was wearing?" There was a faint wisp of dejection in those words.

"No, as a matter of fact, I didn't. Why?"

Virginia Mae waved a glass of ginger ale. "Oh, no reason. I just wondered. I thought perhaps you knew something . . ." Her sigh was heavy with some heartfelt disappointment only she could know and then Virginia Mae turned away. "I'm going to go find Julia. I'm a little tired, dear."

"So how are you?" Gordon walked up on her other side, acutely aware of how pretty she looked in the simple soft yellow dress. It was cut square in the front, sleeveless, and came to mid-calf. She was a very elegant lady, he thought.

"Fine. Tired." She smiled at him. "I can't believe my little god-baby is now a married woman!"

"You and me both. Watching the children of friends grow up really sets the benchmarks, doesn't it?"

"Probably for you," she said sweetly, "but I'm not old. Not at all. I'm just beginning."

"Carol? Can you help me just a minute?" Elizabeth called and Carol hastened over. The women talked to the caterers, trying to fig-ure out what to do with the leftovers. Elizabeth wanted Carol to take some home with her. Then there were other things Elizabeth wanted brought into the sunroom.

As the women talked, Gordon looked over at Michael, who was talking with Gregory's mother and holding her grandchild. Pity Kel-lan wouldn't be having any children, he thought. She would make a good mother, but then again, maybe it would all work out some-how. His thoughts were aimless, enjoying the warmth of the day, seeing the brightness of the wedding still reflecting on everyone, in their eyes, their smiles.

Except when Michael got near Elizabeth. And then things seemed to go flat. It was a damn shame they couldn't patch up things be-tween them, he thought. He idly wondered how two people who had loved each other so much could get so unbalanced by things they couldn't control. They needed to just tack into the wind, he suddenly thought, thinking of sailing. Choose a place and then move up to capture the wind—head straight for it, looking nowhere else but that one destination.

Carol came up and asked him to move some large plants and flowers into the house. He was glad to be doing something pro-ductive.

Finally everyone had left except Michael, Carol, and Gordon. It was harder for Elizabeth to ignore her husband, but the anger she felt toward him, her justification undergirding that anger like pil-lars, had not diminished. The clarity she had felt with her mother this morning did not extend to Michael. The two had nothing in common.

Michael knew he had screwed up, but he wasn't leaving here today without trying to set things right.

"Elizabeth?" He could see the ice still in those blue eyes. Michael straightened his shoulders, determined they would talk. At least he would talk and she would listen. "Please. I need to talk to you alone. Will you come outside with me? To the patio?"

She didn't say a word. Regal in her quiet resolve, she gripped the walker handles and walked past him. He followed her out to the patio where they sat facing each other. At first she would barely look at him.

"Elizabeth. I'm sorry about this morning. I should never have said those things. I was in shock and I didn't mean any of it, I swear. The last thing I expected," he said with sincere frankness, "was seeing you needing this. I know, I should have handled it better, but . . . let's face it, I've gotten failing grades all the way around in dealing with this. And I'm more sorry than I can say."

She was at least looking at him, his own eyes never wavering. *God, let me get through to her.* His mind was asking this as well as his heart; he was desperate for her to understand and listen.

She was still encased in rigid self-righteousness, but the way he was looking at her, the humble apology did make her feel slightly more forgiving. He was, after all, the father of her daughter, and they had shared many years that had been wonderful. She nodded slightly, letting go of some of her anger. They were still oceans apart and she knew that would never change, but . . . perhaps they could be friends.

"Elizabeth," he said, his tone suddenly changing, "there's something else I need to tell you."

Her eyes narrowed as she looked at him sharply. What else? How much more apologizing could he do?

He snatched what sounded like a guilty breath. "I have a confession to make."

Maybe it was because her emotions had been stretched to the extremes today and she couldn't be objective or neutral about anything. His words hit like a blow. The knowledge rushed at her like a speeding car, crashing into her. Because she knew, she *knew*!

He had found someone else, he wanted a divorce; that's why he had been able to say those horrible things to her just this morning—because he already had someone to take her place. Her mouth went dry. Gone and completely forgotten were her own hateful thoughts during the wedding; now she had to endure the fact that he had found someone else and he really and truly intended to leave her.

She couldn't stand it, it hurt too much . . . Her gaze started blurring and then she couldn't keep them back, tears started falling in torrents.

Her hands flew to her face, even as he grabbed her and held her, trying to think of something, anything to say, but dammit, also trying to allow her to cry. The memory of what she had written in her journal about crying was vivid enough to keep him from shouting out the first thing that came to his mind. Oh, but he hated to hear her cry. He stayed firmly in control, sweat beading on his face in the effort to keep his mouth shut. He just kept rubbing her back, apologizing over and over again, until the weeping finally, thankfully, started to subside. She took the handkerchief he held out.

"Thank you," she said in a small, watery voice.

"Are you all right?" He still had an arm around her shoulders and watched as she nodded.

"I'm sorry if I made you cry, Elizabeth. I'm so sorry, honey, about everything." She heard the bafflement, but she wasn't going to explain it; she wasn't going to make it easy for him. Instead she took a steadying breath, wishing she could retrieve some of this day's anger for a shield, but she was completely vulnerable now.

"What about this confession?" she said, sitting up rigidly, forcing his arm off her.

There was no easy way to say it. "Well," he began, almost wishing he hadn't brought it up. She was rigid and pale, waiting for the words to come.

"I read your journals."

She looked at him, stunned.

"My . . . journals?" What did that have to do with anything?

His eyes fell away, ashamed to admit he had invaded her privacy. "Please don't be upset. I read them on the Sunday morning after the preliminary hearing, when Kate told me everything had gone exactly right. I was really missing you, and I didn't understand why you were still living here and not with me. I . . . wanted to try to understand."

He glanced up at her, too relieved she wasn't looking angry to notice her shock.

"I read enough to realize what a jackass I've been. My way of handling everything . . . was wrong. I want you to know I've been seeing a therapist, one Gordon recommended. And it's helped. You may not believe that after this morning's debacle, but I'm trying. I want to be with you. I want us to try to work this out together. Please, Elizabeth. Will you give me one more chance? Will you? Please?"

He had read her journals? She shook her head slightly and then looked at him hard.

It didn't matter that he'd read them, what touched her was that he'd done this on the very same day she had seen her one and only sun dog . . . the same day God created a moment exclusively for her.

Suddenly all the surprise and the anger evaporated as she also realized it had been the day she started praying for him. The peace of that day made the nonsense of this one slide away like running water down a drain. The bad feelings were gone, and she felt her soul blossom like the roses on the arbor, its perfume surrounding them.

Her eyes saw his sorrow, felt the simple, humble love he was offering so honestly. In a blinding moment of clarity, she saw how responsible she had been for this morning. What if it had been her seeing him in such a situation? Wouldn't she have been as upset for him? And how selfish she had been not to tell him, warn him. For the very first time she glimpsed their life through his eyes, and she was ashamed. He didn't deserve this.

But he was willing to try again, because he loved her. He was trying to understand and reach out to her in a new way. Could she do the same?

They both had changed, that was true, but maybe it was high time they started changing together.

With God, all things are possible, she thought, looking at her husband, a slow smile of hope dawning until her face dazzled like the sun. He caught hold of it and blinked. His own smile was of enormous relief as he gently put an arm around his wife, slowly pulling her to him, his eyes asking permission, waiting for her decision, waiting for what she wanted and then she was moving slowly, gently, even closer.

⌒

"Gordon, look, there's a sun dog!"

They had been out front, quietly talking, murmuring their worries about Michael and Elizabeth; the conversation suddenly stopped when Carol glanced up at the western sky.

"Sun dog?" He looked over his shoulder where she was looking.

"You remember? That sermon Father Joseph preached about the sundog moment? I don't think Elizabeth has ever seen one, and I promised a long time ago to let her know if I saw one. I've got to go tell her." She turned around toward the river side of the house but got only a few feet before Gordon's hand stopped her. They both could see them, these two people who had seemed so at odds and worlds apart mere moments ago, were in each other's arms, shutting out the rest of the world.

"I don't think she'd be interested in a sun dog," Gordon observed.

Carol nodded stiffly. She was more than a little irritated. "I must say I'm surprised. Elizabeth was so angry with him. And he was so stupid this morning . . ."

Gordon took her by the hand and led her back to the front where they could sit on a bench under one of the maples. "So tell me about the sun dogs. I vaguely remember," he prompted.

Carol scrunched up her face in thought, trying to remember the details.

"Well, it has something to do with faith . . . but an actual sun dog is a weather sign. It's when cirrus clouds form near the sun, and light glints off the ice and makes little rainbows." She pointed to the one in the sky. "That means the weather is going to change, either in twenty-four or forty-eight hours, I'm not sure which."

"So it's about change, huh?" Gordon was still holding her hand and he could see she was a little puzzled. "I've been thinking all day I'm ready for a big change."

"Oh, really?" Skepticism raised an eyebrow. "And what kind of change are you looking to make? No, let me guess."

She pondered this seriously. "Hmm. I know! You'll see patients Monday through Thursday and golf on Friday instead of what you do now, patients Tuesday through Friday and playing golf on Monday, right?"

Her yawn underscored the boredom in her voice, but she couldn't hide the mischief in her eyes.

Unexpectedly, he squeezed her hand hard to get her attention.

"No. What I'm thinking about—" He paused with a lazy grin, waiting until she looked directly at him. "I'm thinking about asking you out for a date."

Instead of mocking him with laughter, instead of acting affronted, which Gordon half expected her to do, Carol surprised him completely.

She squeezed his hand back even harder, her smile as seductive as a promise.

"What took you so long?"

Reading Group Guide

1. What is a sundog? Have you ever seen one before? If so, did you know what it meant?

2. A "sundog moment" is a tangible moment of hope you can wrap your arms around when life suddenly changes and you feel you no longer have control over anything. One real sundog moment in the book is the story of Ian and Adrienne Moore's godchild. That was the story of Gregory Bowen of Lancaster County, Virginia. Can you identify other sundog moments in the story? Have you had any of your own?

3. Discuss Virginia Mae—do you know anyone like her? Can you understand why she sees life the way she does? Why she is so worried about her daughter?

4. Why do you think the Moores reacted so differently to their circumstances than did the Whittlers? Have you encountered situations you have no control over? If so, how did you cope with them?

5. What did you think of the essay from Lynn Sears Howard? Can you relate to any of it?

6. How did you react to Carl Sanders's situation? How did it make you feel? What do you think happened at the last moment of his life?

7. Should people with chronic illnesses be allowed to use medicinal marijuana? How has the government handled this issue? Has your opinion changed after reading this book?

8. Faith is the substance of hope, the evidence of things not seen. Can you relate to this in your life? Is faith important? Why?

9. What is more important—to be physically or spiritually healed? Does it matter?

10. Carol and Gordon become friends because they are both hurting. At the end of the book, their friendship seems to deepen. Were you surprised by this?

11. Gregory's future is uncertain, but Kellan is not afraid of what could happen. How would you feel in such a situation? Do you know someone who has dealt with this kind of issue?